ALSO BY JULIE BAUMGOLD

Creatures of Habit

THE
DIAMOND

A NOVEL

JULIE BAUMGOLD

SIMON & SCHUSTER
NEW YORK LONDON TORONTO
SYDNEY

SIMON & SCHUSTER

Rockefeller Center
1230 Avenue of the Americas
New York, NY 10020

For information about special discounts for bulk purchases,
please contact Simon & Schuster Special Sales at
1-800-456-6798 or business@simonandschuster.com

Book design by Ellen R. Sasahara

Manufactured in the United States of America

1   3   5   7   9   10   8   6   4   2

The author gratefully acknowledges permission from the following sources
to reprint material in their control: Frontispiece on page iv: © Tate, London 2005;
portraiture on pages 1, 89, 185, and 281: Réunion des Musées Nationaux / Art Resource, NY

Library of Congress Cataloging-in-Publication Data
Baumgold, Julie.
The diamond / Julie Baumgold.
p.   cm.
1. Regent diamond—Fiction. 2. Diamond mines and mining—Fiction. 3. Diamonds—Collectors and
collecting—Fiction. 4. Las Cases, Emmanuel-Auguste-Dieudonnâ, comte de, 1766–1842—Fiction.
5. Napoleon I, Emperor of the French, 1769–1821—Fiction. I. Title.
PS3552.A8453D53 2005
813'.54—dc22   2005041265
ISBN-13: 978-1-4516-2397-0

For Pete Hamill
and those closest:
Norma Baumgold, Edward Kosner, Lily J. Kosner

Author's Note

The Diamond is the true story of the Régent diamond from its discovery in India in 1701 until it was sent to the Louvre in 1887. It is told by my re-creation of Emmanuel de Las Cases, a writer who went into exile with Napoleon in 1815, and by "Abraham," a man who never existed. The facts and chronology are true and based on real sources, but this is a novel and there have been departures. The characters speak words that are my own as well as those recorded in other books and accounts.

PART I

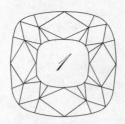

My Mistake and Where It Led

O N OCTOBER 16, 1816, ON THE FOUL ISLAND OF SAINT HELENA, in the middle of precisely nowhere in the South Atlantic Ocean, I watched the emperor's hair being cut. As the hairs floated to the floor, I was waiting my chance. The emperor seemed to be staring at a portrait of the King of Rome riding a sheep. Santini, the barber, had spread a cloth over his green coat and was holding the razor aloft. The window was open on the usual evening smell of something tropical and crushed.

One large tuft finally landed at my feet and I bent quickly to pick it up and slip it into my pocket.

"What are you doing, *mon cher?*" Napoleon asked.

"I dropped something, sire."

"You too, Las Cases?" he said and leaned forward to twist my ear. The pinch was a bit harder than usual, but like his other men here, I had learned not to flinch. He knew and now almost accepted that all of us had begun to collect pieces of him as relics. Still, I had to distract him from my blunder.

In the strange way that a mind in panic will disconnect and leap back to some random moment in time, I remembered a conversation we had at the summerhouse. I had just found a miniature of him dressed as first consul and asked what became of the big diamond in his sword—a famous stone known as the Régent. He had been about to reply when we were interrupted. Now, again, I asked him what had happened to that diamond.

"Are you trying to divert me? Your face has gone red," the emperor said, shifting suddenly and swinging his legs. This evening he was still in his white swanskin pantaloons with feet, streaked black on the pocket where he had wiped his pen.

"Sire, please do not move," said Santini as a damp wind seized snips of the precious hair.

"The empress carried it off and I never saw it again," the emperor said. "That diamond brought its misfortune to all who possessed it. It was my enemy Pitt whose family brought it to light. I should have considered its source."

He was silent then as Santini finished and swept the hairs carefully from the floor. He tied them into a square of linen and withdrew, looking back at me, triumphant in his malice. A rat crossed the floor by the silver washstand.

"The diamond was named for the regent, a libertine cradled in depravity," the emperor said, "but then you, *Monsieur le Comte*, are our historian."

"One might almost believe the stone was cursed," I said.

"Curses are just excuses for the bad behavior of men," he said. "Discord followed the owners of that diamond—madness, too, in all the Pitt family. Once I thought it brought good fortune; it was then my talisman. Man is ever ready to chase the marvelous, to abandon what is close and run after what is fabricated for him."

"What became of the Régent?" I pressed him.

"It has a long history. Open the door and let us walk in the air which God made."

We left the room, where the curtains had already blown to rags. Five portraits of his son, the King of Rome, stood on the gray wood fireplace, next to which hung a watch on a chain of the last empress's hair.

"It is a bad haircut this time, is it not?" he said, rubbing his head as we passed a mirror already pitted and misted by the weather.

In the room where I take his dictation (for what I shall call my *Memorial of Saint Helena*), his large creased maps fluttered to escape their colored pins. He picked up the billiard cue that he uses as a stick and a measure, and we entered the darkening garden. Immediately, the guards raised the yellow flag that meant the emperor was outside, and one of the English "dogs" appeared.

He took my arm.

"You wish to know more. You are always seeking the genealogy of things," he said.

The emperor was right. I now had a mighty curiosity to know all about this diamond from his sword, a jewel of the first water, the size of a small fat plum. The Régent was the first diamond of France, known as our National Diamond. I thought of the kings who had worn it and at once began to see how a chronicle of the ancient diamond could be the story of us all, our lost France and how we came to be here. Could I find this story and tell it?

"I will help you," said the emperor.

We crunched over the whitened bones of the sea that once had covered this part of the island—razor clams, tubes long hollowed of life, mounds of silvery silt that had drifted from far away. In the distance, green clouds had collapsed on Diana's Peak. We walked out into the leftovers of the volcano—the chopped black rocks, charred ravines and gorges, one of the "dogs" still following.

"I can tell you my part in the diamond's history from when I first possessed it to the time Louise fled," said the emperor, gripping my arm so that I felt a bruise begin.

"I took all the papers regarding the imperial jewels so I might prove my case on what they owed me. Some may still be in my trunks, though they were so plundered I scarcely know what I have or lack. I once had records of those who stole the jewels, and even many papers from the Pitt ancestor *in Engleesh*."

I feared we might come to the subject of the English lessons I was trying to give him. The emperor's progress had been slow. He blamed it on his mind being too old to learn a new tongue. I suspected it was rather his ill health, lack of sleep, and the pestilence of the winds here on Deadwood Plain.

The emperor then began to speak of phenomena and ghosts and how long ago Josephine had gotten him to read palms for her friends. He would look at their faces and just make up their fortunes. He said General de Montholon now believed there was a ghost in our house, Longwood.

"I am their only ghost," he said. "We always seek to place blame on things—on a jewel, or the maledictions of spirits, when the fault lies in the natural progressions—youth to age, pleasure to disappointment, fidelity to betrayal."

"Then you do not think your good fortune deserted with the stone?"

He made no response. The wet air clung to our faces as a permanent sweat. Often we would lie motionless on our sofas as pearls of warm dew skittered across the stunted lawns. The crosswinds blasted dry all that should have been lush. All that might have grown had been forced down or askew. We had yellow skies, blue nights, and red dawns, forests of coromandel ebony, and lavender misted mornings streaked with marigold. If they were beautiful, no one noticed. The English here made boundaries for him who once drew his own.

I asked the emperor if I might search the trunk where he suspected the documents lay hidden.

"It was only in getting rid of the diamond that I was victorious at Marengo," he said, "for we rode on horses the diamond bought when it was pawned. If you wish to put together a brief history, I will search out the papers, but it must not outweigh your attentions to me or your son."

I readily agreed. I almost never disagreed.

We walked along a bit in silence. A cloud of fat blue flies rose from the gum trees to nibble at us. Even on the brimstone, heading to nothing, the emperor moves fast, his gait between a stride and waddle, for he has spent much time mounted. I could scarcely keep pace though we are almost the same height.

Actually, the emperor is taller than I am by several inches. When we walk side by side, however, I have caught him rising to the balls of his feet when he pauses and turns to address me. I have scrunched myself even lower so as to obviate this need of his, but he only seems to rise higher. At those times, I must try to remember all he says until I can race to the nearest ink pot. As though he knows this, he seems to say the most interesting things then. When a gentleman is taller than the emperor, he does not look up, and I have seen many men contort themselves to gain his eye.

Suddenly, the emperor's attention was drawn to a captain he particularly disliked, one who always followed too close upon his boots. This guard was too attentive to the emperor's every pause and glance, even when he just bent to inspect some foliage or a snail.

"One escape is never enough," said the emperor, reversing course to Longwood, his prison and mine. From his room I heard the sounds of his metal trunks being moved and opened amidst the most terrible oaths, and the thump of his fire poker on one of the rats. The hair in my pocket was soft as a child's hair.

Eventually, he emerged, disheveled, with a great bundle of papers, some still bearing thick seals with the crests of ancient houses and the governments of the Revolution upon them. Wax splinters from the cracking seals fell onto the floor.

"The Régent was a thing of the kings. I should never have brought it back," he said then, and allowed me to take the papers.

I began to think how I might write this history in the evenings as a diversion from my endeavor to tell the emperor's life for my *Memorial*. At such times he would be absorbed by the *Iliad* or *Odyssey*, Herodotus, Pliny, or Strabo. He read of past thrones and ancient wars, of dead heroes and conquerors almost on a par with himself. He read of families turned upon one another. Sometimes he told stories of his past or read plays aloud, taking all the parts, and we listened together, our jealousies and conflicts forgotten.

"Shall we go to a comedy, or tragedy, tonight?" he would say, then send my son, Emmanuel, for the play. More often than not it was a tragedy.

Unless invited to sit, we stood or leaned against the damp walls, and in this invisible etiquette, he found the last trace of his power. The valets in full livery passed among these generals and marshals of France with bad coffee, their silver lace as tarnished now as the braid of the uniforms. Sugar burned in vermeil bowls to correct the air. We had stopped mixing with our English jailers, for those of any note refused to call him "sire" and he would see no others.

In the times he would not receive, when he was ill, had scratched to blood the itch that always plagued him, or lay with cold cloths on his great aching head (a head that grew still larger every year), I would put together the story of this bright and cursed object. I remembered the diamond the size of my thumb and index finger meeting in a circle. Also it was very deep.

To find it I would have to pull a string through history much as I had done in my *Atlas historique, chronologique et géographique*. I would follow it through my time back to times way previous and places unknown. Even as the emperor and I felt ourselves fading into the dim unworldliness of this island, the diamond stayed in the world, permanent as all things. A porcelain cup, a plate, a sugar bowl with scenes of Egypt from the Sèvres factory, a table with all the imperial palaces depicted in marble—all these things would outlast us.

I began to see how my task could be done with the documents at hand. I could make up the rest as a fiction. Since I had spent ten years on my *Atlas*, I knew many of the facts, but now I might free myself of charts and maps. Because of the unrelenting nature of my work with the emperor, I needed a diversion, a way to go outside the situation that had been imposed on us. I needed to travel from this island as I did in telling the emperor's life. I wanted, in contrast to the emperor, something inert, the very opposite of the man who engaged my best hours—something that was acted upon. In any case I have always had an interest in jewels. The emperor has called me his magpie because I am drawn to small shiny things. As we walk, I am the one to pick up the mica rocks, the lava-crusted pebble, while he taps the small rosebud of his shoe in impatience.

"You never put down anything you have picked up," he said to me once.

The Régent had been found, then lost, hidden, stolen, then retrieved. It was back to glory in the world and I doubted either of us would be. At times, I felt my position keenly as the prisoner's prisoner, and I had forced my son, Emmanuel, who is but fifteen, to this as well. By exposing him to the emperor, by making him part of his daily life, letting him copy down his words and receive his fond taps and hard pinches, I had changed his destiny. I had jeopardized Emmanuel even as I enriched him beyond all measure.

Long ago, desperation became despair, then quickly enough turned to resignation among those of us who followed the emperor to this island. I was not alone in feeling I was living my life inside this larger, uncomfortable life. This feeling had been shared by his soldiers, servants, and wives, for whom the life before and after him was all preface or afterword.

To be always aware of the wounded creature in the house, to hear its rasped breathing and feel its torment, to know that misery, was to live ten years in every one on the island. Thus, we all aged at an unnatural rate, as did the objects around us, for already our collars had been turned and the women's dresses had lost their fresh elegance.

As we worked, I sat to the emperor's right, Emmanuel next to me as he dictated. At the dining table, he sat in the center with Dimanche, the dog, warming his feet; I again to his right; then Emmanuel; Count de Montholon; the ample presence of Montholon's wife, Albine (who always seemed to be wearing red even when she was not); sometimes Grand Marshal Bertrand and Fanny up from Hutt's Gate; Gaspard Gourgaud, the other captive general—all but my son resenting me, for I was the one the emperor preferred. We nudged our way into the room still fighting over precedence and seating. Each meal, none lasting for him more than twenty minutes, was a competition to be first to lift the pall.

There was never complaint from him (though often observations). Soon enough, however, we saw with his eyes. We were all too attentive. We heard his boots—lined with silk, soft as slippers—whispering on the wooden floors. At night, he moved from one iron field bed to its twin in the adjoining room. When he had not slept, his tread was heavy. We waited to be summoned. We waited for the steps. When they did not come for us, we hated those who were called. We kept restless watch on one another as the English kept watch on us.

Disappointment would come upon us suddenly in the night and proceed in familiar stages to horror. Then, in pain, I knew the emperor would wake his valet and begin to read or ask for a bath to be drawn in this large wooden trough he now uses. (Contrasts are the real poison to us here.) I would arise and, tiptoeing round my boy asleep on the floor, tour the silvery rooms until it was calm. In front of his door, the last Mameluke half raised his head like a dog disturbed and, until he could make me out, reached for his saber.

As I walked, I would hear the words he had spoken the previous day and relive his dreadful glory. I turned from his words and vowed to begin the story of the stone, and on the next day, almost as an omen, he spoke again of the diamond.

The emperor had been dictating all that morning. As in the early days, he spoke so rapidly I needed someone to relieve me with the dictation, for I was always a sentence or two behind. Great long paragraphs reeled from him this day, which I wrote in code for Emmanuel or the valets Ali or Marchand to recopy. As usual, he wore his green coat faced with the same green and trimmed with red at the skirts, and the stars of two orders. We were both uncovered and he held his hat under his left arm. His hand raked at his snuffbox long after it was emptied. He scooped absently, placing nothing to his nose and sneezing merely from habit. He took a licorice pellet from the tortoiseshell box that held the image of his runaway wife, the empress Marie-Louise, and their son, Napoleon II, born the King of Rome.

"You wish to know the treasures of Napoleon? They are immense, it is true, but they are not locked away," he told me just as Frederick the Great's clock chimed. He had begun this catalog in response to the English newspapers newly arrived that claimed he had concealed vast wealth. He wished to dictate his response right then.

"They are the noble harbors of Antwerp and Flushing, which are capable of containing the largest fleets," he said; *"the hydraulic works at Dunkirk, Havre, and Nice, the immense harbor of Cherbourg, the maritime works at Venice, the beautiful*

roads from Antwerp to Amsterdam . . ." And on he went through a list of roads and passes, of bridges, canals, and churches rebuilt, the works of the Louvre, the Code Napoleon, and so many treasures and achievements that my hand cramped at the size and scope of the wonders this man had wrought.

"Fifty millions expended in repairing and beautifying the palaces of the crown . . . sixty millions in diamonds of the crown, all bought with Napoleon's money—the RÉGENT itself, the only diamond that remained of the former diamonds of the crown, having been withdrawn by him from the hands of the Jews at Berlin, with whom it had been pledged for three millions . . ." With this he looked significantly at me and then continued.

It was the diamond again, this royal jewel seized by various monarchs as they fled. I felt it was an indication now to begin my labors. And as the emperor observed that the physical powers of men were strengthened by their dangers and their wants—so that the desert Bedouin had the piercing sight of the lynx, and the savage could smell the beasts of prey—so too we, doomed to this island, watched and wanting, living within a camera obscura, perhaps had gained the power of re-creation and remembrance.

The emperor says of himself, "Men of my stamp never change." I, not of that stamp, have changed much. I have changed my identity, danced and hidden behind masks, and taken other names. Born into the *ancien régime,* I became an émigré who fought my native land, a father who left his family to go into exile forever with one who had been my enemy. I was a naval officer, a tutor, an author, the emperor's chamberlain, and councillor of state. A collection of professions, a collection of selves. Dislocation forced and chosen—departures and brief returns, launches pulling to new shores. And yet, have I changed that much more than others? As the emperor has said, no one can know another's character, only his actions. All is complication and contradiction, and everyone is filled with secrets.

In my ten years of exile in London, I had studied the history of the English. William Pitt the Younger was our hero then, and I had traced his family back to Governor Thomas Pitt, never imagining that I might interest myself in the Indian diamond that once bore his name. I now have found among our few thousand books the inventories that the emperor ordered made on the provenance of all the imperial jewels. I also found Pitt's own chronicle and the histories of the French kings, without which I could never begin this diversion to make a fiction out of fact too often remote.

"If I were you, I would begin with Madame," the emperor told me the next week. "Otherwise, how could anyone understand the courts of France— even you, who were presented and lived among them? And to understand the diamond, you must understand the setting, no?

"You must travel with a stranger, this young German princess, into this court. To understand their foreign ways, you must start with her. Madame, my wife's ancestor, was the mother of the regent who bought the diamond. She wrote to every court in Europe, and fed all her royal cousins with gossip. Those who say the diamond brought its mischief and harm into France do not understand how deep the rot went, even in the court of Louis XIV."

"But sire, I believe this takes place before the stone was discovered," I said, for I had begun my researches. "When Madame came to France the great diamond was still buried . . ."

There was no turning the emperor.

"She kept records, as did the duc de Saint-Simon and Louis XIV's mistress Athénaïs de Montespan, and I have their court histories and volumes of their letters here in my library."

No turning him, ever.

And so I will leave the Régent buried. It has already waited through deluge and explosions, through aeons and the earth's turmoil for volcanic pipes to squeeze it to the surface. It will soon be discovered in the Indies, cut in England, and find its way to the crown of France. In this vanished thing I see the fall of the kings and the empire. I suspect the history of the diamond is the history of us all—the Mamelukes drawn far from Egypt, the remaining Corsicans, our English jailers, and misplaced generals. It is the story of the two William Pitts, raised up by the diamond to oppose us, defeat us, and send us here to the rim of no place.

Thus I begin this part of my story with Elizabeth Charlotte von der Pfalz, Liselotte, she who became the duchess d'Orléans, and was known as "Madame" in the court of Louis XIV. Liselotte lived and died in almost the same years as Governor Thomas Pitt, but their course and place in life were very different. She was enslaved by the strictures of high rank and normally would never have been exposed to a man such as Governor Pitt—and yet she was, just once, because of a single fabulous diamond.

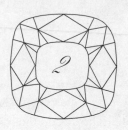

The Remarkable History of the Régent Diamond

by Emmanuel de Las Cases

With Corrections, Emendations, and Observations by the Emperor Napoleon

IN LATE OCTOBER 1672, LISELOTTE, A YOUNG GERMAN PRINCESS, not beautiful at all, was leaving her castle in Heidelberg to come to France to marry Monsieur, the brother of Louis XIV. The red leaves were falling on their carriage, and her father, the elector Karl Ludwig, remembered how she used to play in the leaves. He called her *Rauschenblatt-Knechtchen,* the little knight of the rustling leaves, a name she had brought back from Hanover, where he sent her to live when he was divorcing her mother. He said good-bye to her at the Inn Zum Ochsen in Strasbourg, and she never saw him again.

First the princess had to stop in Rheims to renounce her Lutheran faith and become a Catholic, a gesture that would in time prevent her from becoming the queen of England. Traveling with her was Ann Gonzaga, the Princess Palatine, who had arranged the marriage, and Linor von Ratzenhausen, who had been Liselotte's friend since she was eight and wild. She was now nineteen, and wild only in her heart.

The princess knew her husband had been married before and that his wife, Henrietta, daughter of the king of England, had died. In their bed in the night Linor started whispering to her in that little fluttery way she had that made light of the most dreadful things.

"One says Madame was poisoned by Monsieur's favorites. He has unnatural tastes."

The princess, who was young in the way only a German princess can be (for in France our princesses are corrupted at thirteen), did not understand. She had lived with her aunt, and then in the household of her father and the Raugravine, her mother's servant, who had slept in the room with her parents and had supplanted her mother after their divorce. She had lived outdoors playing with swords and guns and the new children her father had with the Raugravine. She then would come inside to take lessons. She danced and played music and learned needlework and languages. She knew just who she was, but she did not know the world.

"The miracle of enflaming the heart of that prince is not revealed to any woman in the world," said Linor, who then explained.

"*Mein Gott!*" said Liselotte. "But why did they poison her?"

This Linor could not answer, and it was morning, and the bishops waited for her downstairs. Liselotte was afraid they would ask her to renounce her family as heretics. This she would not have done. She cried for two hours, then went down to the bishops, who did not require it after all.

Later, she asked the Princess Palatine about Henrietta, dead at twenty-six, after nine years of marriage to Monsieur.

"It was in the summer and she went to bathe every day, leaving in a carriage because of the heat and returning on horseback. She was followed by her ladies and the king and the youth of the court, all with a thousand plumes waving on their heads. After dinner they would mount the calèches as violins played, or they would walk half the night around the canal." Liselotte later wrote that the Princess Palatine sounded almost dreamy when she said this, as if haunted by the sweetness of the reverie.

"She was very beautiful," the Palatine said. "It was perhaps the habit of bathing that killed her. The king had just sent her to England to help France's alliance with her brother, who was then king of England. Eight hours after she returned, she and Monsieur went to Saint-Cloud. It was the end of June, and though she had a pain in her side, she wished to bathe in the river. Then she walked in the moonlight and had her chicory water."

"It was poisoned!" said Liselotte.

"French gossip," said the Palatine. *"On dit, on dit*—'one says.' The whole court is full of *on dit*. She drank, put the cup back in the saucer, grabbed her side, and said, 'Oh, what a stitch!' Then she did cry out she was poisoned, but only when she was twisting around begging for the antidote, and they brought her the viper powder . . ."

"Who did this?" Liselotte later asked Linor, who then told her of the cabal of male lovers who possessed Monsieur. She even named them—the chevalier de Lorraine and the marquis d'Effiat, and the servants who rubbed poison on the rim of her little cup.

"I am so frightened," Liselotte said, and felt herself captive and reduced.

In Metz, Liselotte was married by proxy, with the *maréchal* de Plessis standing in for Monsieur. In the Palatinate of the Rhine, there were ghouls and cannibals, but nothing of this strangeness. She sobbed from Metz to Chalons. As "Madame" now, aware of her rank, she entered France and its court of spies and whisperers, of galantries and secret entrances, a land of *redites*, things repeated, where the national pastime was to find fault.

Monsieur had gone to Chalons to meet his wife and consummate the marriage. They were a shock to each other.

Madame flung herself into the drawing room. She had been walking outside, and her skin, scandalously bare of paint, was chafed. She was wearing a blue silk court dress that was too fancy and too light for the weather. Her eyes, blue and small as a sow's, passed over him.

Monsieur stood—small, sure, and surrounded, indubitably the face in the miniature she held. To Madame they seemed to be of different races— she fair and Teutonic, he complicated and magnificently dark, with pin-pricks of light flaming from his jewels. Monsieur was laced, bowed, and beribboned, and scented with violet right to the tips of his Spanish gloves. Madame suspected that he painted and powdered. Madame herself drew slightly back. He came to her shoulder. His black eyes were fierce and full of disappointment.

He bowed before her, the perfume from his gloves rising with him as he studied her large face with its thick badger nose tilted to one side, then her long flat lips and sturdy body. He saw she was without graces and had never troubled herself to think about them. She would never have to be poisoned because she carried her poison, as do many ugly women, within. Madame was not without hope, however. And her shock at the sight of Monsieur made her smile. That was the second disaster. Monsieur fell back and stumbled on his very high heels.

Madame had been eating pomegranates and her teeth were flaming red. He too smiled, and his teeth were dark and rotted. From his pocket he took a sweet and handed it to Madame, and turned her heart. She was overcome with pity, for she knew that Monsieur had been corrupted. Once she was able to feel pity she fell slightly in love with Monsieur. Already there was tittering and rustling among the ladies and gentlemen who accompanied Monsieur. She had not spoken a word and she was already out of favor.

At Chalons there was a second wedding, and as the bells rang through the town, Monsieur told Madame that church bells were the only music he could stand. Often he would go to Paris just to hear the bells of the "Vigil of the Dead."

In the bedroom, Monsieur opened his brocade robe. Monsieur wore holy medals on his private parts. No one had prepared Madame for this. He took them off one by one as they sat on one side of the lace-draped bed. His big heavy rings landed with clanks on the table; his dark hands were small as a child's as he reached for her. Though he lingered long in the act, Madame felt almost nothing.

A few days later, Madame met Louis XIV, her husband's brother, at Saint-Germain. His queen, Marie-Thérèse, was not there. Madame's tutors had taught her the French kings—Louis the Debonair, Charles the Bald, Louis the Stammerer, Charles the Simple, Louis the Foreigner, Louis the Indolent, Robert the Strong, and Philip the Fair. She knew Louis the Fat and Louis the Lion, Philip the Hardy and Philip the Tall and Philip the Fortunate, Charles the Beloved, and Charles the Affable. Now she stood before the king who was already Louis the Great and saw the disappointment in his face, too. And yet she was drawn forward as to a light, for he was like her, fair as the sun, of the northern people, taller than Monsieur and straight. Monsieur was standing to the right of and almost behind the king, so that all she could see of him was his ribboned sleeve and the small flash of his diamonds. As she spoke, his sleeve kept fluttering. She could barely see the king for the blaze of diamonds on his buckles and buttons and hat crocket. A large diamond so blue it was almost violet gleamed from his sword. His baldric and insignia were diamonds. She had heard of him, the king who danced in so many ballets with his fine legs, his small feet. By now she knew he had selected her to keep his brother in check.

"Sire, to my mind you are one of the handsomest men in the world, and with few exceptions, your court appears to me perfectly fitted for you," she said. "I have come but scantily equipped to such an assemblage."

"Few exceptions, Madame?" he said, already intrigued.

"Fortunately, I am neither jealous nor a coquette and I shall win pardon for my plainness, I myself being the first to make merry at it."

At this, ten or twelve ladies began to laugh. Madame was struck in her tenderest organ, which was her pride, for she was the daughter of the elector of the Palatinate, as well as the granddaughter of the landgrave of Hesse-Cassel, on one side, and of Elizabeth Stuart, the Winter Queen of Bohemia, on the other. This French court could never understand, for they were all so ignorant, all surface wit, bon mots and chitter-chattering that vanished the next instant from the mind. A gust of careful laughter while looking round to see who else was laughing and if it was acceptable, the well-trained effect, the strained-for cut. And under it all, the fear. The king's mistress Athénaïs de Montespan, beautiful with a dreaded wit, was first among the ladies who laughed, and Madame never forgave her. It became Madame's crusade to mock her.

"You put us completely at our ease," said the king. "I must thank you on behalf of these ladies for your candor and wit." His voice was pleasant, though when he did not speak his mouth hung open in an awkward way, releasing a plume of bad odor. The king saw that Madame was artless in a court where art counted for everything.

The king came to see her at the Château Neuf and brought along the dauphin, who was ten and restless. He led her to meet his queen, Marie-Thérèse.

"Do not be frightened, Madame," he whispered. "She will be more afraid of you than you of her."

Madame bowed and the queen limped forward, the size of a child. There were jewels all over her dress, big pearls shaped like pears, and Madame heard the little clickety-clack of the pearls banging on brocade. She had chocolate on her teeth, her eyes popped out, and Madame began to feel better.

During the series of presentation balls and masquerades at Saint-Germain, the king sat by her side, and whenever a duke or prince entered the room, he would nudge Madame gently and she would rise. The queen sat on his other side, splendid and unimportant, with small diamond chandeliers on each ear. The arrivals approached and made their pauses and reverences, their interrupted bows and curtsies. Madame knew that when she danced at a ball, all were obliged to rise, and she saw too that the king liked her.

The king knew that she had wit and honesty. Alone in his court, she would go her own way, and it amused him. Madame and Monsieur had an apartment in the Palais Royale and Saint-Cloud and Viller-Cotteret, and a household of 120, but their place was with the king at Saint-Germain or Fontainebleau, then Versailles, which was just being built.

Madame was different. She dressed as she wished. She jumped out of bed in the mornings and did not have *ruelles* so that courtiers might come to her bed rails to whisper their poison as she sat in her dressing gown. She never had a dressing gown and never would. She saw the court for what it was, a place of spinning worlds, each tangled with its own interests, smacking into one another, here where the sun was inside.

Her first meal with the king had shocked her. The king, alone without a hat, sat in his armchair in the middle of the table of his family and ate with his knife and fingers—to begin, perhaps a hundred oysters washed down with the red champagne from the Benedictine Dom Pierre Pérignon. Behind him the courtiers' hats popped up and down through the meal. She had never seen anyone eat so much.

A few days after the marriage, when Madame was still caught in the strangeness and alien banter, the king commanded Madame to come to him to discuss the death of Monsieur's first wife. Her torchbearers preceded her and her ladies in waiting followed, and both leaves of the door were thrown open for her. The train of her grand habit dragged on the floor, which squeaked slightly (and does to this day).

"Madame, I have heard of your suspicions. I am too honest to have you marry one who is capable of murder. My brother . . . ah, Madame, I see that you bite your nails," said the king, who was in a fauteuil. Madame was in an armless chair, a chaise.

"Sire, no one could have uglier hands than mine," said Madame.

"If you do not chew at them, I promise you they will improve. I am told that you have refused your physician."

"Sire, I am never sick, and if I should feel ill, I take a walk of five or six leagues and am cured." Madame smelled the amber that did not quite cover the odor from his mouth. "I do not approve of the purges and emetics and bleeding. I have never been bled or taken a physic. I eat my good German food. The sauerkrauts and bacons and good white cabbages."

"I should like to try some of your foods," said the king. "And I will walk with you, for no one here likes to walk, especially my brother, whose heels are too high. I would show you the wonders of Versailles. I have heard, too, Madame that you have begun to learn to ride. You must hunt with me someday."

And with that the murder of Henrietta of England was passed over and the king's mind turned to German bacon salad, Savoy cabbage, and pancakes with smoked herring.

If the king was the sun, and here he was, Monsieur was the moon, white and increasingly chilly. When Madame put her arms around him she thought she might break his bones like little winter twigs.

Monsieur disliked to be touched when he slept, so Madame had to lie on the very edge of the bed. Sometimes she fell out like a sack.

Madame soon became an expert rider and rode from five in the morning till nine at night, pausing only to eat and relieve herself, and burning her skin in the sun. This gave her an excuse to stay in her riding clothes all day. She wore a man's large wig, which was often slightly awry, a tricorne hat, a man's voluminous bowed cravat, and waistcoat, over which was a man's coat with long *basques* and baubles and fringes and bits of lace and knots of ribbon as men wore. She was quite a sight.

Madame looked at the court the way she had looked at nature as a child in the mountains eating cherries and bread at dawn. She saw that the vice against nature, called "the fashionable vice," was all over the court. Men liked little boys, women liked one another and spoke of their passions openly. Men set out on military campaigns with their male lovers and were happy to do so.

In February 1672, a few months after Monsieur's marriage, the king asked his brother what people were talking of in Paris. Monsieur said they were talking of the chevalier de Lorraine, who had been banished for loving Monsieur.

"And do you still think of this chevalier de Lorraine? Should you be obliged to anyone who would restore him to you?"

"It would be the greatest pleasure I ever experienced in my life," said Monsieur.

"Well, then, I will give you this pleasure. I will do still more and appoint him field marshal in the army I am to command."

Monsieur flung himself at the king's feet and embraced his knees, and kissed his hand for a long time.

Madame's marriage was still happy then, for she did almost as she liked and Monsieur was kind to her. He came to her in her apartments, where they spent hours in facing armchairs talking of pedigrees. Each knew genealogies going back many generations, and all the bastards as well. Sometimes Monsieur would catch sight of Madame striding along in her riding clothes and think of a big blond German boy.

He had a red dress made for her of his own design. He carried a little pot of paint for her cheeks. He invented a cream to make her skin white as his own. Monsieur was a great improver and completed the Palais Royale, where they lived when in Paris. Monsieur was a great fusser. He pulled at her curls and glued silk patches of a crescent, star, and comet to her face. Madame twisted and giggled and let him do as he wished. When he was finished, Monsieur agreed with Madame that she might wash the paint from her face.

Madame went hawking and hunted with the king, and the court saw she was in favor. That made her the fashion; it made golden all that she did. She went to Saturday *medianoche* (late supper), praying with him in Athénaïs de Montespan's rooms. She was often a third there, for the king liked to play two women against each other and often the next mistress was servant to the last.

Madame walked with the king all over the Tuileries gardens, since the others were lame or would pant after a few steps and rarely left their sedan chairs. She put on an old sable cape for the cold and all copied her. The king played his guitar for her and the court stopped laughing.

Then Madame was pregnant and carried about in a sedan chair. After five years Monsieur was still attentive and they lived in harmony. They had a son, then another, Philippe II d'Orleans, who would be regent of France and buy the diamond. The king was burning Madame's land, the Palatinate, when Philippe was swaddled and the *grand cordon* put on him. Last, Madame had a daughter, after which Monsieur left her bed forever. Madame who was twenty-four then and tired of lying on the edge of the bed, said she did not mind as long as he was kind to her.

In 1675, when Madame had the smallpox, Monsieur had tended her night and day and wrote to her brother, "I don't believe there was ever a more perfect marriage than ours since the world began."

That was probably because he had his lovers about and was in thrall to them. Her enemies the chevalier de Lorraine and marquis d'Effiat were joined by Elisabeth de Grancey, mistress of both, who had charge of her daughter. They were oozing around Madame's household causing trouble, and she began to suffer. At this time, her son Philippe was just one of the little princes running around the palaces in his dresses. He was delicate and wary. At chapel, when the little prince kneeled, he usually fell over. When he was four, he had some sort of attack of apoplexy that led to his poor eyesight. He began to squint.

The king tolerated the way Madame kept to her own ways, her tongue that now was even sharper than others. The court went to Versailles for fetes that lasted several days, though the king no longer danced in the ballets. He was fifteen when he had first appeared as the sun (born on a Sunday, he would die on one, as is often the way). During one fete he had descended from a sphere, covered in gold embroidery thick with rubies, a crown of rubies and pearls and white plumes and sun rays of diamonds on his gold head. Then had come the Enchanted Isle series, an allegory of the glory of his reign that saw France as the heir of Greece and Rome. His mistress then, Louise de la Vallière, had ridden a Barbary standing upright on its bare back, galloping with only a silk cord passed through the horse's mouth. She had been taught by a Moor who was one of the king's grooms. But of course there would come a day, as it comes to all favorites, when the king would pass through her rooms on his way to Athénaïs. And still she stayed on, as the old ones do, hoping for the return of his favor.

The tableaux, the sound-and-light shows of the fetes dazzled Madame. When she was with the king she almost forgot that he had brought back the chevalier de Lorraine. There were water spectacles and islands and fireworks on the Grand Canal, with an obelisk on fire to symbolize the king's glory. In her time there was Lulli in music, Beauchamp in ballets, Corneille and Racine in tragedy, Molière in comedy. As much as she liked the plays, the real comedy and tragedy for her were the court. She remembered all the dialogue.

"Is the diamond not the most beautiful creation of the hands of God, in the order of inanimate objects?"Athénaïs de Montespan would say to Louis XIV as they sat together trying on jewels. She had collected diamonds since she was a child and had a collection worthy of the princes of Asia.

They were sittting before two huge pedestals veneered in rosewood, and divided inside like a cabinet of coins, into several layers (she described them in her memoirs). The king had brought all the best diamonds of the crown there and many mirrors.

She and the king pulled out the diamonds, examining them, sometimes with a glass, planning new designs, for they both had the fever. It was almost a sport for them when his affairs permitted, and always cheered them both up.

"They are durable as the sun," said the king, whose symbol was the sun and whose bedroom at Versailles was built to face the rising sun as a reminder. "My brother cannot keep his hands off them."

"They shine with the same fire, but unlike your sun, they shine by night. They unite all its rays and colors in a single facet," she would say in her rapid tinkly voice, and pull out another sparkling tray.

The king's ambassadors would come to him with news of all big diamonds found in Asia or Europe and he would do anything possible to outbid all competitors. Often he bid against Monsieur.

The king showed his diamonds to Madame, who had entered his rooms carrying a book. He looked at her book as though it were a stranger at court and then showed her the eighteen large diamonds Cardinal Mazarin had left to the crown and the immense blue diamond bought from Tavernier that glowed violet. He pulled out trays of diamonds colored rose and yellow and brown. He had sets of diamond buckles and buttons, and insignia and pins for the garter and baldrics, giant brooches and crowns. She pretended to be interested because she did not want to seem impolite. He told her the queen did not like jewels either, so he and Athénaïs de Montespan and Monsieur had full use of them.

Madame saw that in this too she was like the queen, who kept to herself and ate her Spanish dishes with chocolate and garlic and Spanish sauces and pretended not to be jealous.

For Madame a pleasure greater than beholding a spill of diamonds was rubbing her face on the wet hairy muzzle of a horse or one of her dogs. Sometimes even one of her children.

The court moved back and forth, to and from Versailles, the palace that the king had been building around his father's old hunting lodge since 1660. Here Madame hunted stag with the king. In the year her oldest son died, she fell from her horse. The king was the first to reach her, his face white as he bent over her. She felt his big fine hands holding her head, feeling it all over, turning it with great care, and then he had led her back to her room and sat with her to see that she was all right. If she was dizzy at all it was from the painful happiness that begins love. (She knew Monsieur came to her from an impossible land.)

Madame saw that the balls and masques and pageants and changes of costume, who sat on a fauteuil, armless chair, or footstool, who passed her the shift at her levee and preceded her through a door distracted everyone as the soldiers fought on. Those at court ate until they would burst and then glided away as their emetics took effect.

Court was a contest without end. One shoved another aside to get the king's dark blue eye turned with beauty or dress, the new equipage or dish or phrase. Flattery, the only way to speak to him, was a lie to Madame, who left the contest early on. She watched them in their heavy court dress melting before him. They were commanded to always be there, sick or well, following from palace to palace as his horses, the Enraged Ones, tore over the roads. Everyone tried so hard. She watched the spies creeping to his cabinet by the back stairs, the doors opening in the tapestry. People secreted themselves in alcoves and closets and nooks. Servants stood behind chairs and carried dishes with averted faces and open ears. "Madame had a new visitor today," they would report. Then she would find her horse and the woods and a stream where she might look for huckleberries, humming a forbidden Protestant hymn.

Within the silk and whispers they were all weak, kept at court like the dangerous beasts of the new menagerie at Versailles. Only one was strong, and he, the king, feared hell. Monsieur had been raised in dresses and kept to female pursuits just so he would not be a threat. He was not permitted to lead an army, because he had been too brave to suit the king. After one battle when Monsieur was cheered at the same time as the king, the king took him away from the wars.

Madame, who lived with the murderers of her predecessor, found she needed her own cabal. Big court women, one in a mask, another silent for years, surrounded her as she rushed through the halls. Madame, who had acquired her own viper powder, had the peculiar strength of the perpetual stranger. Still, one is lonely at Versailles without an enemy. She found this out immediately and was never lonely. Outside her own household, Athénaïs de Montespan was Madame's first enemy.

Madame had no one to speak to, so she wrote. Her letters told as much as she could and she copied them for herself and history and me here on this damp lost isle. She was a writer in the only way a royal could be. She rose at four and wrote till ten-thirty in her otter skin stockings and petticoat as German princes and electors looked down on her from the medallions on her wall.

She wrote with her back to the room, facing a window full of Versailles. A little dog sat on each foot, on her table and lap—seven little dogs around her, staring with their endless dog love. The duchesses swore and called out as they played at an ombre table, and still Madame's quill scratched and she heard all. She wrote all day and the letters often grew to thirty pages or more. She fell asleep and woke and continued writing—*For there is one thing about the French: one can deal with them only if they have great expectations or if they are afraid*—without pause. Madame found if she wrote it she did not have to live it, or at least she could live it in a different way. She wrote her own tragedies and comedies and spread her hatred like a great blanket over the landscape of the court.

She sprinkled sand from her shaker and rang the bell for the servant. Her hands were always stained. It was said if she had written fewer letters her son would not have been as depraved as he was.

She knew the Black Cabinet read her letters. They copied out passages and sometimes whole letters to show to the king. Her letters were sealed but the spies had a form of mercury that took the shape of the seal and hardened when removed so it could be used to reseal the letters. She knew this and still she was crazed with imprudence, daring as only a disappointed aristocrat could be.

On and on she wrote. France is falling apart and starving, the streets are filled with shit. The court was a false family. Its children were defective, lame and paralytic and weak, crooked and hunched. Five of the queen's children died. All the king's bastards had defects, if not of form, then of character. One princess, who died at five, had a mouth that was almost entirely on her left cheek. Then she described shitting at Versailles.

After twelve years, the king left Athénaïs de Montespan for the poor Widow Scarron, whom Athénaïs had hired to nurse her children with the king. While Athénaïs got fat, the Widow had waited and prayed and dressed simply. The king made her Madame de Maintenon. Madame called her "Old Slops" and "Old Ape" in her letters. It could be said that Madame chose her enemies poorly.

"Where is your diamond in all this?" says the emperor, coming upon me just now with but the faintest rustle. "You have gone far from it." That is how I know he has been reading this manuscript, just as he had read my journal on board the *Bellerophon* to see if I was fitted to his great task.

"I am coming to it. I have followed your command."

"Is all this true?"

"As true as I know how to make it. For of course it is a story of things that happened before I lived to those I could not know. And I lack so many documents."

"Do not make it too true," he said. "History is only a set of lies that people have agreed upon. This is not your *Atlas* with its charts and maps, nor is it my story, where you must tell only what I say of my life—though I might appear here too at the end, no?"

"Oh, indeed, sire. It is by placing the diamond in your sword that you gave it grandeur. It is but the story of a rock. It cannot feel or bear witness. Thus, it must be the story of those that coveted it or did not want it, those who needed it for whatever reason. It must be the tale of those who possessed it for a time, and of their times and places; and if I have given face and voice to some of them I did not know, for that I must call it a fiction."

"Good night, then, my little friend. Remember, the night gives advice."

He is always saying things like that. Everyone here is scribbling away.

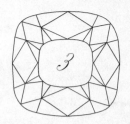

"What Can't Be Cured..."

I N 1688 MADAME ASKED THE KING NOT TO TORMENT HER FATHER with his claims on her land, the Palatinate.

"I will see," said the king. By now Madame knew Louis XIV's "I will see" never happened.

They were in the gardens of Versailles, approaching one of the new fountains. Suddenly waters leapt from Apollo's mouth and the dolphins began to spit, for gardeners crouched below at the taps, unseen, wet and cursing. Twenty violins followed, playing at every step the king took. Then came the procession of sedan chairs from which dangled pale hands cuffed in gold lace, the fingers cocked in a pose. When the king walked on, the waters fell and dripping gardeners raced ahead through the woods to turn on the next fountain.

The king spoke to a man, who immediately swept off his hat. He raised his hat half off for the next man, who was titled, and took it off for any lady or chambermaid or prince of the blood he came upon. None of this interested Madame any longer. After ten years at court, now living at Versailles, she saw them all as victims of grandeur, crowned slaves, prisoners, standers around, and great actors. Sometimes, when she heard the king's music approaching, she hid.

Then her father died and Madame was forced to go to Strasbourg with the king, in his carriage. It took all the skill in deception she had acquired in

France to bounce along and smile as though she had forgotten that he had hounded the elector to his death, to forget that Strasbourg was where she had seen her father last. The cabals noted that Madame was no longer at ease with the king, and thus vulnerable.

"Why are you so sad? What is the cause?" said the marquis d'Effiat one day after the trip, his lips forming something that verged on a smile. His glistening hair was placed as carefully as a guest at dinner, his eyes were pewter and shameless.

Madame made no response. Whenever she turned a corner either he or the chevalier de Lorraine or Elisabeth de Grancey was always there. Every princess needs her dragons, but she had none. One by one they deprived her of the ladies in waiting who were loyal to her.

They invented a romance between Madame and the captain of Monsieur's guard. The king visited them and saw how cold Monsieur was to her, and Madame felt like the elephant she had just seen dissected in the presence of the king—large and spilling disease. She begged the king to let her retire to a convent.

"My friendship for you prevents me from allowing you to leave me forever. I absolutely refuse to permit it. Put the idea from your mind," he said and reminded her of her duty.

"I will be poisoned like the first . . ."

"No, Madame," said the king, who brought in Monsieur, and they reconciled somewhat.

By then poison had come very close to the king himself. The Chambre Ardente, the special tribunal to look into witchcraft, had been stopped when it reached Athénaïs de Montespan. It was said she gave the king love potions and performed nude in a black mass where a baby was sacrificed. Still, poison arrived in milk and wine and enemas. Snuff was poisoned and so were gloves. Monsieur's daughter with Henrietta, who married the hunchback Philip and became queen of Spain when she was twelve, was poisoned by raw oysters given by her maid. Her nails fell off and she died, the poisoned daughter of a poisoned mother.

When she first arrived at court Madame thought she had traveled far from the spirits of the Rhine, where her uncle Rupert was thought to be a sorcerer and his black dog the devil, so that armies had fled before him. But here in France were ghosts and spells, and bags with a toad's foot holding a heart wrapped in a bat's wing in a paper covered with symbols none could read. She had heard too of the queen's black baby spirited to a convent. The queen had been given Osman, a dwarf Moor, only twenty-seven inches high, who followed her like a pet, holding her train, hiding his face within, bouncing on her lap, until all the court ladies adopted tiny Moors and they were even painted into portraits. One day when the queen was with child Osman jumped out and gave her such a fright that the child was said to have been born black (for the child becomes what one looks at in fear when one is pregnant). After the queen's unfortunate experience, young pregnant women were said to be afraid to look at Madame.

Every Monday, Wednesday, and Friday was the *jour d'appartement*. The king was building a great gallery all the way from his apartment to that of the queen. The part that was done was turned into an endless salon, with seven reception rooms. Madame strode past the tables where they were cheating at lasquenet, trictrac, picquet, l'hombre, summa summarum, and chess. Around her the courtiers howled and hit the green velvet tables with their fists, making the gold fringes and the golden louis jump. They pulled at their wigs and wept and never rose even for the king when they were at play. Others watched from the silver benches under the crystal lusters, and some knelt on the chairs called *voyeuses* tittering, whispering, hissing in the orange flicker.

Everyone paused at the mirrors to adjust a curl or ribbon or turn in admiration, and some stationed themselves there by the orange trees in their silver tubs. The scents mingled—orange water and the king's amber, Madame de Maintenon's jasmine. Along came Madame and her remaining ladies in a flood of whispery bon mots. All of them turned to the mirrors except Madame. A thousand mirrors on both ends of the room bounced them back at one another.

"I have just come from Pahi," said the dauphin, who lisped as did all the king's children.

Coming toward Madame was her husband, Monsieur, the master of the revels—the organizer of the fun, the last-minute calèche ride in the moonlight, the masked ball. He paused longest at the mirrors.

Monsieur had the heightened pallor of the Parisian drawing room, the skin of a belle raised in candlelight. Triple ruffles flapped about each braceleted hand as he adjusted his cravat and collar of Hungarian petit point, each finger weighted with rings. He strutted on and the ribbons fluttered from his heels that Lambertin the boot maker had just made two inches higher. His green silk coat, striped with gold embroidery, was gathered in folds at his hips. There were emerald buttons on his rose silk waistcoat embroidered with gold flowers. Across his chest and rising with his large stomach was the blue cordon of the Holy Ghost. He was pierced here and there with diamond crosses and stars, and diamonds circled his sword hilt. He bowed to Madame, brown and rough and beaten, having fallen from her horse twenty-six times by then.

He looked at her with his lynx eyes, checking the placement of her few jewels. She thought Monsieur, who pretended to have gallantries with women just to be in fashion, never once flagged in flamboyance.

The chevalier made a remark and their laughter floated back to her. It still hurt.

Monsieur pretended not to see Athénaïs de Montespan, who was still lingering in a French point dress, her hair in a thousand futile curls tied by black ribbons mixed with pearls.

Monsieur paused to talk to his cousin James, called the "king out of England." Madame, seeing some of herself in the exile, gave him one of her rare smiles. After all, had she not converted, she would have ruled England.

Madame walked in the labyrinth at Versailles and saw it was her life, blocked at every likely turning. The queen died and the king said that was the only time she had ever caused him any trouble.

One day Madame came upon some servants on ladders applying leaves to the private parts of a statue.

"Not big enough," said Madame de Maintenon, who was standing at the foot of the statue with a big cross hanging from her big pearls. The king had married Madame de Maintenon but would not make her queen.

Though she had once been a Protestant like Madame, it now became Madame de Maintenon's crusade to drive all the Protestants from France. Her piety also killed all the fun of the court.

The king made a claim on the Palatinate in Madame's name and laid waste to it when his claim was refused. He burned castles and huts and uprooted trees, and Madame did not sleep, for when she did, the nightmares came of the people in cellars; of Mannheim, which her father had built up, now in rubble; and Heidelberg in flames.

Madame withdrew as much as she could. When she spoke to a servant now, Monsieur would rush to him to ask what she had said. It was the same quizzing with her children.

Monsieur told Madame he wanted to make his old lover the marquis d'Effiat the tutor to their son. If she did not agree, he would make her life as hard as possible.

"There is no greater sodomite than he in the whole of France," said Madame.

"I must admit that d'Effiat has been depraved, and that he has loved young boys, but it is many years now since he corrected himself of this vice," said Monsieur.

Madame then went to the king. The doors were flung open for her. It was winter and the furniture of the Grand Appartement was embroidered velvet (flowered silk in summer); the chandeliers and candelabra were silver. As always she stopped in front of Giorgione's *Musicians* and Leonardo da Vinci's *La Femme d'un Florentin Nommé Giocondo,* for that woman appeared to have secrets as she did, and a restraint that soothed Madame. Eight pointer bitches ran to sniff at her, pushing their muzzles deep into the folds of her court dress.

"It is no honor for my son if he were thought to be d'Effiat's mistress," said Madame.

The king, who was eating a hard-boiled egg, assured Madame he would appoint an honest man as tutor to her son. He was swinging his legs, and his red heels were now even higher than Monsieur's.

Eventually, after the death of the good Saint-Laurent, the obscure but learned Abbé Dubois became her son's preceptor, and he was corrupted anyway.

"M. *Author,*" the emperor says, using the English term, "I am still waiting for the Régent. Surely it was dug up by now?"

"No, the slave would not find it for many years," I said, and wished to tell him to be patient but did not.

He was leaning over me, the tails of the madras kerchief he wears in the mornings dangling on my head. As the comtesse de Remusat once observed, he does resemble an antique medallion.

His eyes began to darken as they do when he is thwarted. The blue orbs, dappled with black, turn completely dark, and the black eye that none can withstand is upon one.

"I will soon tell all."

"Do not forget Madame's farting contest," he said.

Here I might mention that when the emperor comes upon this manuscript, he corrects whatever page is visible, and I have included his corrections. As he does with his own manuscript, there are corrections upon corrections and he never hesitates to write even upon a clean copy. He uses pencil for it takes too long for him to dip his pen. In his other works, whenever he writes for a long time, Emmanuel or someone stands by sharpening his pencils.

When he comes upon me even as I write I insert what he says as he says it. I am surprised by how much he knows of these early courts. He has just read Madame de Maintenon's memoirs and admired her style of writing. He told me that when she was old and the czar came to visit, she hid in her bed. The czar entered, pulled aside her bed curtains, stared at her, and left.

I am hiding some parts of this manuscript from the emperor. I always see evidence of his searches. Also, I am writing parts in code. I cannot let him take over this account.

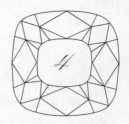

"... Must Be Endured"

MADAME AWOKE IN THE HOUR OF THE WOLF, SOMEWHERE between three or four. The seven dogs sleeping around her, a shroud of odiferous breathing fur, raised their heads as she did. She had all her clothes made with tabs so she could fasten them herself. She wrapped her heavy court dress around her; her legs and feet were bare. She left her apartment, the dogs surrounding her. In the long Galerie des Glaces she passed close to the mirrored walls, so close she stepped on the pebbles of wax at the base of the candelabra. She did not look at herself in the dark mirrors but she knew her long white hair was loosened and awry. The hall was filled with the aroma of oranges.

Madame stepped lightly, her heavy gown with its train a comfortable weight holding her to the place. She looked down into the dark gardens and shepherded the dogs down the stairs and outside. Night was still fighting the dawn for precedence when she reentered the palace and was startled by a sound at the other end of the hall. There was Monsieur behind a statue in the corner. She could see him quite clearly in the last of the moonlight. In his embroidered dressing gown, he was lifting a curl from one of the pages and twining it around his finger. The page was leaning against the wall and Monsieur was leaning into him and she could guess the glitter of his eyes like a cat in a night forest. The page, looking out, saw her pass though she was quick, as the two figures slumped down together.

The squares of Versailles seemed to fuse into one another—smaller squares dissolving into the larger oak squares of the floors, the squares of the mirrors in the Galerie des Glaces all becoming one. And now other things dissolved and merged—the colored *fleur de pêche* marbles, the statues back into their niches, the menagerie of courtiers asleep inside into the menagerie of zoo creatures outside in the night. One blinding shine—the crystal above flickering with the last candles, the swags of gold leaves and rococo scrolls above the solid silver tables, every door and wall and material glistening and dripping. For her it was a thick rich soup, like those the king ate four at a time.

The next day she saw the page wearing a diamond brooch.

Love within marriage was not to be found at court and often existed only in mésalliances. "Mouse droppings always want to mix with the pepper" was the way Madame put it.

Madame's son, Philippe d'Orléans, was seventeen when the king forced him to marry Mademoiselle de Blois, his daughter by Athénaïs de Montespan. It was the supreme mésalliance and polluted the Orléans blood. For Madame, it brought back the maid who slept with her parents and became the Raugravine and broke up her childhood home. The king sent for Madame and told her that Monsieur and her son had already consented. She made a slight reverence and withdrew, betrayed again, this time intolerably.

That night at the *appartement*, Mademoiselle de Blois appeared all dressed up but with no idea of what was going on, and still such a child she sat on Madame de Maintenon's knees. The announcement was made, and everyone, in the usual whispering clusters, was for once surprised.

Madame's tears splashed in her food that night. The king made an especially low reverence to her, during which she swiveled away. All saw the bustle of her dress twitching with her fury.

At mass the next day when her son kissed her hand, as Saint-Simon says, Madame smacked him so hard the slap rang through the gallery. Soon after the wedding, Philippe d'Orleans went off to fight. Like his father, he was too brave to suit the king. He was wounded at the battle in Flanders and right after two bullets were removed, he returned to the fight.

The king, who read Madame's letters, had turned from her and shut the door in her face. He took all the women of the court except Madame to the siege of Namur. When she did get in to the *appartement*, Madame de Maintenon would drift out the doors.

Hypocrisy, in the form of piety under Madame de Maintenon, forbade plays and operas. Men and women were not to converse in public, so the men turned to boys. The girls of Maintenon's convent, Saint-Cyr, were in love with one another.

Monsieur, besotted in his second youth, was giving gifts to his boyfriends. "You are welcome to gobble the peas, for I don't like them," Madame wrote of her rivals. But it had been long since she had tasted the peas . . . Monsieur melted down her silver and sold his jewels so his little pages could buy their linen in Flanders. The chevalier de Lorraine was fifty-three and the other favorites, who had made fortunes from their looks, now were old.

When Madame turned her back, Monsieur, as though he was injured that she didn't fight for him, hissed about her to the king and their children. Another way to punish her was to allow their sons' debaucheries. They both led their sinful lives in Paris, while Madame was in title and rank the first lady of the court.

It was almost the end of the century when Marie-Adelaide, Monsieur's granddaughter through Henrietta, arrived at court to marry the dauphin. At twelve, she won the king's love and outranked Madame. Marie-Adelaide was a wild and fairly beautiful child. She let the footmen play wheelbarrow with her, holding her ankles as she walked on her hands. She scampered around the king, who excused all her impertinences. She was tiny, with red lips that always looked bitten and chestnut hair, and she was thin as the wind.

She caressed the king and Madame de Maintenon, rumpled them, and read their letters. Once, with her back to the hearth, the dauphine had herself given an enema in their presence before they all went off to a play.

"What are you doing, *mignonne?*" de Maintenon asked.

She held it in the whole length of the play. She was quickly brought into the intrigues and gallantries of the court. Her marriage was consummated when she was fourteen, the same year she drove a lover to throw himself from the window to his death.

Madame's son, Philippe d'Orléans, was even more of an outsider than Madame, for he was a deist and skeptic in this court dominated by Madame de Maintenon's intolerance. As a young man he went with Monsieur Mirepoix of the black musketeers to summon the devil. They howled imprecations to him in the tar pits and, when the devil did not answer, d'Orléans denied hell and lived as he liked, reading Rabelais at mass while his mother dozed.

He worked with his physician doing chemistry experiments in a lab for so many hours they were referred to as the sorcerer and his apprentice. He went around court with his stained hands smelling of chemicals and knew what it was to be misunderstood. Such a man needs compensations, and the next thing, the next woman, might prove to be his solution.

"You write yet of Philippe d'Orléans?" the emperor asks. "Saint-Simon said he was born bored. It all went wrong because he had too little to do. He was a good soldier and they would not let him fight." (The comparison with us here in our lost court is too obvious to state.)

I agreed there was much talent wasted in Philippe d'Orléans for he spoke several languages, wrote two operas, and knew history. He had six Rembrandts and collected Raphael, Titian, Veronese, Caravaggio, and Tintoretto. Like Monsieur, he loved beauty, but when a thing was in his hand, he was restless for the next.

"It was a competition to corrupt him," says the emperor. "First his father's favorites, then the roués. He was a tragedy long before he came to buy the diamond."

At this, he caught sight of Emmanuel carrying a large tower of books and papers. I stepped forward to help my son, whose heart was not strong.

"I see your son has brought me what I requested," said the emperor. "Now I must work, though I would rather discuss the man who bought your diamond . . ."

Emmanuel had been busy collecting facts and dates, supplying the emperor with copies of the *Moniteur*, notes and bulletins of the Grande Armée, that he would read over quickly. The room was awash in periodicals and maps—all that he had told him to look for. He would read everything, then the dictation would begin and then the corrections, then more corrections. That was our process—here we had all come to live for paper.

Until I began to research the diamond, the emperor's work was all I had to do here beyond survive. His memoirs consume all of us, however, and I must wait my turn as we divide up his large life. Then I turn to the diamond, for I have no friends among the men or in Albine de Montholon, who thinks of me as a rival, and Fanny Bertrand, who resents my being here. The lies, the small fictions I can tell in this work, have become my escape.

"Write!" says the emperor and I put aside my chronicle and follow him into the room, where he paces and begins his dictation. Outside, the life of the island continues—slaves with baskets on their heads sway along the roads with the British in red coats and the Chinese.

"His Majesty is served," Marchand says several hours later. The emperor gives him the dark eye; he withdraws and we continue. The emperor tries to whack a blue fly with a rolled map and misses. The chef, Pierron, walks by the window trying to catch my eye, but we continue for two more hours.

After dinner the emperor plays chess with Emmanuel and tells him that a piece touched is a piece played.

The roués were with Philippe d'Orléans every night, finding him actresses and opera house dancers and those who would drink with him and take him through the night until the dawn collapse.

"How can any woman run after you when they should fly from you?" Madame said to her son.

"Ah, *Maman,* you do not know the libertine women of the present day; provided they are talked of, they are satisfied," he said. "Besides, in the dark of night all cats are gray." He was the first to say this.

Madame, who tried to restrain herself, gave a small chuckle at his badness.

Finally, fear and piety had crept up on Monsieur. His confessor forbade him his "strange pleasures" and he dismissed the aging favorites. Now that his health was failing, afraid of hell and the impatient devil, he returned to Madame. They reconciled and she was happy again.

One winter evening in 1693 after supper, Monsieur and Madame, their daughter, and their son, Philippe d'Orléans, were together in her drawing room at Versailles when Monsieur let out a gargantuan fart.

"What is that, Madame?" he said, looking round.

Madame turned her back to him and released one of her own.

"That's what it is, Monsieur."

"If that's all it is," said Philippe, "I can do as well as Monsieur and Madame," and he farted too. They all laughed and then quickly left the room.

Monsieur went to the king to plead for his son, who had not been given a command as promised and was condemned to walk the galleries of Versailles. The king said that Monsieur's son was betraying his wife, that mistresses should be kept out of sight, and he threatened to cut Monsieur's allowance.

They began shouting and Monsieur grew dangerously red. Still enflamed, he sat down to eat until his emerald buttons popped open, and then went off to Saint-Cloud. At supper, he started talking gibberish and fell over onto his son, who held his fat little embroidered body in his arms. Monsieur's lower lip hung slack and he dribbled. They stretched him out where all could see as the scullions and household moaned and keened. Louis XIV did not come when first summoned, and when he did, it was too late. Madame, who now did not want to be sent from court, was already howling, "No convent!"

Madame went to Monsieur's boudoir, where the walls were silk and the tiny furniture stood on spindly, gold bowed legs. The air was scented with violet; it was the most delicately beautiful room of the palace. She knew he was one of those men in love with beauty, who in another age or rank might have built and decorated great houses, amused his hostesses, and seduced their pages. Everywhere were bits of Monsieur's ribbons and laces. His drawers were stuffed with heavy rings, sweets, and letters from boys scented and tied with ribbons. Madame saw how many had loved Monsieur and how much they had received from him. All her loneliness was in those drawers, all the missing love. There were hundreds of letters full of mischief and secrets. The boys were appallingly ignorant and childish in their spelling and their needs and Madame stopped reading. A smell of old violets, mingled with the wax of the seals, rose from the letters as she burned them. In Paris they rang the funeral bells, Monsieur's only music.

At Versailles the next day, the king was already singing an aria. Madame de Maintenon pulled one of Madame's old letters from her bosom and showed it to her.

"Am I the 'prune face' you write about?" Madame de Maintenon asked.

Madame looked down at the floor.

"You say that I am not even married to the king, when all know that is false. It is because you have written such poison that the king has turned from you," said Madame de Maintenon.

Madame humbled herself as much as she could, and Madame de Maintenon and the king forgave her as much as they could.

36

It was about this time that a merchant from the East came to Versailles and told Madame of four-footed animals who preyed on the crocodiles of the Nile and bit off the private parts of the men who swam the river. In Egypt he had seen flying animals with human faces and the crowned snake that the Egyptians thought was the devil Asmodeus.

He told of a great diamond the size of an orange pulled from a riverbed mine in the Indies. The slave who found the diamond was murdered by a sailor who later hanged himself. The diamond, a wonder like no other, had been sent to England to be cut. He was, of course, speaking of the Pitt diamond, which would become the Régent.

The merchant was going to put his stories into a book that he promised to dedicate to Madame.

Just in time, the additions to our library have arrived on the *Newcastle*! They include some works on Governor Pitt and how he bought the diamond. I had requested them from Lady Holland* who quickly did the researches herself, along with my friend Lady Clavering. I think of these good women in the London libraries I once knew well standing at the stanchions where the books are chained, dipping their quills, calling upon their great energies and resources to aid me (and always the emperor), and I am overcome.

The emperor fell upon the cases with the utmost joy and retired to his room with a large stack of *Moniteurs*. We did not see him for the rest of the day, one that again rained in brief heavy bouts.

That left me free to read through the information on the great diamond and its origins. I have enlisted Emmanuel's help and will work with him as the emperor works with me. The tar paper lining our low rooms has begun to steam and gag us with its smell.

It was this day that Emmanuel first questioned my work on this chronicle and asked why I occupy myself and him with the story of the diamond.

I reminded him of the one time we were happy on the island, when we lived at the Briars, in the summerhouse pavilion belonging to the Balcombe family. When we first came to Saint Helena, Longwood was still being turned from a cowshed into a dwelling fit for a prisoner emperor. We had ridden up to the house and the emperor told Monsieur Balcombe he wished

---

*Elisabeth, wife of the liberal leader and our friend in England.

to live in his summerhouse. The generals were to stay on in Jamestown. The emperor and I then were almost alone.

Never—even in his campaigns—had the emperor been in quarters that small: one large room in the style of the English Regency, with windows floor to ceiling. It had an attic of seven square feet, where I stayed, with Emmanuel sleeping on the floor. The emperor's two valets, Ali and Marchand, slept wrapped in their coats in front of his door. In the first weeks, Pierron brought our food from the town; the air was clement, the soldiers at a remove, the rituals relaxed. I would say that the emperor's predicament had not yet quite gripped him with its full horror. A half-starved black dog with three white paws had come out of the woods and, knowing the top dog here, went right to the emperor's boots. Though it was Emmanuel who rushed to feed her, she became the emperor's dog, Dimanche.

One day at the summerhouse, the emperor was showing his baubles to Betsey, the Balcombes' pesky fourteen-year-old daughter, who was full of her usual flirtatious noise and clatter. His large green *bijouterie* was open on a vast display of snuffboxes, pictures, and trinkets. On one of the larger boxes, surrounded by rubies, sapphires, and diamonds, was an enamel reproduction of a portrait of the young Napoleon as first consul. He is wearing a red velvet suit embroidered in gold, with his hand in his breast and the diamond in his black sword. All the glory was beginning then. Since the portrait did not look like him at all, my eye was drawn to this great square lump in his sword, for this image—ornate, filigreed, and golden with promise—seemed to collapse inward to the beam of the diamond. He was over by the celestial globe, spinning it as he watched Betsey's reaction to the full splendor of his past.

"The Régent?" I had said, pointing.

"Disappeared," he said in the way he had of closing a conversation. "A story for another time." And as I told Emmanuel, I let it go until that moment when I picked up his hairs and had to distract him.

"That is not a reason, Papa," he said.

"For me it is."

And now I shall work into the night in our unquiet yellow house and in the weeks ahead begin to tell as much as I know of how the diamond was found and where it went thereafter. When I looked in to bid the emperor good night, he was still reading his newspapers in a cacophony of crickets. Ali came in to draw what was left of the curtains.

It must be completely dark when the emperor sleeps.

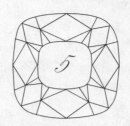

The Remarkable History of the Régent Diamond (continued)

"The Great Concerne," 1701–1717

IN THE SOUTH OF THE KINGDOM OF GOLCONDA, NOW CALLED Hyderabad, in the gorge formed by the Kristna River, a slave found a diamond of prodigious dimension. Exactly how it came into being, a stone so large, this aberration of the earth, I cannot presume to know. I do know that it was found in river gravel at the Parteal mines in 1701. It was the size of a tangerine fruit and bore the greenish crust that marked the finest raw diamonds of the region. The area was called Golconda after the fortress and town where the merchants traded. From here came the Koh-I-Noor and the diamond known as the Tavernier Blue, but after the Régent, no other of that size appeared.

Here the merchant Jean-Baptiste Tavernier, who sold the blue diamond and many others to Louis XIV, saw an army of tens of thousands digging and sifting the river mud and sands. Merchants staked claims to the riverbed mines and paid off the rulers with levies and percentages. Next to where they dug, they marked off an area and built a low wall with holes and gates around it, and here women and children would bring the gravel from the dumpings.

When the slaves had dug to the depth of two men, they brought pitchers of water and tipped them into the walled area. Then, after a day or two of pouring, they opened the gates to drain off the water and mud, and what was left was sand sprinkled with river diamonds, a kind of diamond soup.

Naked slaves walked the sand looking down. Their heads were shaved and only their loins were girded so nothing might be concealed. They picked through the gravel and raked over any lumps. They pounded these lumps with large wooden pestles and when they struck upon something hard, it was almost as often a diamond pebble as it was a stone. They shoveled in the soup or sifted the dry diggings for ten hours as guards cradling scimitars watched them. The guards had no mercy.

The diamond that would come to be called the Régent was found silently. He who found it did not jump about in the riverbed shouting hosannas to summon the overlords. He looked down at the lump and knew what it was. He must have kicked it aside or pushed it into the gravel with his foot as his heart clenched and he tried to figure things out. Otherwise there would have been shouts and people pointing and guards rushing to him. They would have taken the diamond from him and offered it up to the Great Mogul. The Mogul had first right to all extraordinary stones, though a few, through trickery, slipped away. The diamond was from first sight a royal stone, a monster meant for monsters.

Perhaps no one was looking the slave's way. One account says he gashed his leg and hid the diamond in the wound—or in the wrappings round the wound, says another. Our historiographer Duclos says a freeman found the stone, one of those who worked years in the mines. When such men left, they would be purged and given an injection to discharge what they had hidden in their bodies. This freeman hid the diamond and then cut open his thigh as if he had fallen on a sharp stone. He called for help and, covered in blood, shouting with pain in which his joy was well concealed, was carried out without the usual precautions taken. He was allowed to rest after his wound was dressed, then pretended he was unfit to work and left.

As I have learned, history has many versions. Saint-Simon, who was not always accurate, claims the slave hid the diamond up his ass.

Despite the usual purges given to those who leave the mines, somehow the slave was able to escape with his treasure and reach the coast. There he met up with a rogue of a white ship's captain who offered him safe passage.

The slave knew of no other place but paradise. That is what the captain promised him. Then he got him drunk. They went in a small boat to a larger boat over the warm water. The captain's blue eyes watched the slave as the blood leaked from his filthy bandage onto his loose trousers. There were not many places on his poor body where he might have hidden the stone, and the captain considered each one. He thought he saw a bulge behind the man's left knee, a darkness on the thin fabric.

The captain put the slave's head under his arm and crushed his throat. He found the diamond, which had been strapped to an intimate place, but the heinous act so played upon him that he sold the stone for a thousand pounds to a merchant. With this money and his black conscience, he bought drink without end, the arrack wine of the region and Bombay opium. He died of remorse mixed with overindulgence and was found hanging from a beam in his room.

(Deceit and blood already covered the rough diamond, but all this has a most fanciful ring and cannot be proved. The origins of these great hunks of treasure are always disputable and often bloodstained. Perhaps it comes from prying things from the earth or washing the silt of ancient rivers, from disturbing what is best left alone. Diamonds and crime have ever been linked. Of this stone that would come to be called the Régent there is even the rumor that it was stolen from the eye of an Indian idol. It is hard to imagine the rough stone in the idol's eye or to conceive its pair, for it was then of 426-carat [303-mangelin] weight. Historians and gem dealers often bury these jewels in lurid stories to lend them further romance.)

Somehow, the diamond came into the hands of Jamchund, a native gem merchant famous throughout the Indies. Jamchund's greatest pleasure was to roll a fine gem between his thumb and forefinger and make up a lie about it. He knew the stories of the oldest stones, with their histories of risk and crowned heads, blinded sheiks and blood, for he had invented some of them and acted in others.

Jamchund knew the interior world of these stones, how they were full of lakes of liquid, mountains of crystal, mineral flower and fauna, streams of fire. He would chatter on about the finest rubies, whose color was the hue of the first two drops of blood that appear in the nostrils of a freshly shot pigeon. He would point to their inclusions and their needles woven together to give the appearance of silk. He knew the jardin, the pool of yellow-green in emeralds. He knew that all emeralds have flaws, and some a blue flower, and that greasing can improve their color.

He had traveled to China and, in his own country, seen the idols' eyes, and even as he prostrated himself, thought of prying the gems from their lodgings. He knew the Darya-I-Nur and the Nur-Ul-Ain, and diamonds so blue, so green, so pink or black in their fire they astounded the Mogul himself. They were named the Light of the Eye, the Circle of Light, the Sea of Light. He was a large, round man with a pointed black beard, ticklish, loving women, jolly only in times of profit. He was covered with ruby beads and tassels of emerald beads and coral ropes. Small sacks of gems hung all over his body in places too intimate and disgusting to consider. Others he kept in a box in his palanquin.

As he was standing in Fort Saint George, Madras, thinking who might buy his treasure, a commotion of drums and pipes and trumpets shook the dirt beneath his slippers. First came eighty armed native soldiers, then three hundred English guards in red coats carrying the Union Jack and East India flags. In between was a palanquin with six natives holding the poles and perspiring into the red dirt. Inside the palanquin, sunk on pink silk cushions, was Thomas Pitt, governor of Madras, president of the settlements on the Coromandel Coast, official of the mighty East India Company, which ruled nearly a fifth of the world. When Jamchund saw the great governor approaching, he knew just where the diamond would go.

Thomas Pitt was small and solid and his face was red as a ripened pepper. His nose was wide with flaring nostrils; his mouth returned to its small pursed state when he was not shouting. He reminded some in the fort of the disenchanted trolls of fairy stories, the ones who burst from chronic anger and plotting revenge on mortals. To others he was the Great President. In private, men touched their hands to their foreheads and salaamed before Pitt. When they were out of his sight, they shook their heads at the idea of Governor Pitt, the opium dealer and former pirate.

Pitt lived with the company factors and writers in the governor's lodgings in the inner fort, White Town. Maqua Town, to the south, was for the boatmen, and Black Town was where the Indian merchants lived. In this den of self-righteous sin were Armenian merchants and Topasses (mixed black Portugese) and one despairing Capuchin father.

In 1701, the governor was beset with worries and almost ready to quit. The Mogul general Da'ud Khan was threatening siege. The year had brought Pitt restrictions on the export of silver—how was he to buy his diamonds? He wrote to one of his Jews, Alvaro da Fonseca, that unless the company gave permission to import silver, the trade would go farther north to

Masulipatam. China, too, wanted silver. There England traded lead and wool and bought *ch'a*, which was tea, and spices and silk. The company sent opium from India to China to do its harm there.

King William III had terminated the powers of the old company in favor of a new East India Company, to which Pitt would never surrender. There were problems with the Marathas and all the pains of a settlement growing into a city.

Captain Kidd had been hanged for piracy in the Indian Ocean, a fate Pitt had escaped by becoming governor four years ago. In India they called those who did business outside the company "interlopers," and among those rough types, Pitt, the younger son of a rector, was the fiercest.

At forty-four, he was already rich, the owner of factories here and great houses in England bought with his illicit trades, owner too of huge ships. By thirty he had been in Parliament and was used to living in state, negotiating with princes, arriving with chests of treasure unloaded on the docks, and well-bribed officials bowing. In the early days, his company had hunted elk and fished sturgeon in North America. He had already been in jail and bought a rotten borough, but the East Indies was where the money was. Now he lived like a minor Bourbon, a little king of puckah houses, of roads with sand in the middle for the carts, of rivers swollen thick by monsoon and the hot winds. Jackdaws in the trees, turmoil among the right-handed and left-handed castes of Hindu workers, the Shia and Sunni muslims. All of it strange, still strange after all this time in India, and always to be strange. He was king of people he at once did not understand and disdained.

A few Jews lived with the English almost as equals because they knew diamonds and trade. Pitt always had his Jews about, would summon them at any hour. In name they were all in thrall to the East India Company (which owned Saint Helena too until just before we got here); in reality they saluted no flags.

Around him were all these men and a few women who had left their families and country to enrich themselves. Their greed was in the air, along with the jasmine and frangipani, the river smells and fever. Their common sport was scheming to go home as country gentlemen and purchase coronets. They were the first nabobs, drunk every night and very spoiled with their palanquins and hookahs and opium dreams and mistresses in the zenana and boys to procure and valet for them. In the fort were murderers and thieves and men living in sin with concubines. In the starlight they all stood on the wooden balconies and thought of home.

Pitt worked in the mornings in the consultation room he had set up to imitate the armory of the Tower of London. The walls were hung with the emblems and flags of the company. Rifles worked in ivory and silver, pistols and bayonets and swords were arranged to form stars and sunbursts between which pikes formed columns. Pitt went from there to the godowns in the factories and wharves to inspect and sort the cargoes.

One morning at the godown Pitt had found his eldest son, Robert, just back from Canton. Robert was fingering a piece of rich stuff, his long nose twitching with the spices sifting through the air. Robert saw the governor disapproving and kept doing whatever it was his father obviously disliked. His father's brows had their own life, like dancing caterpillars.

"What is it, Robin, are you ill?" the governor asked and cuffed him fondly.

"I am tired of here," Robert said, meaning the entire East. "And this," he said, meaning the world of trade that he had come to after his university in Rotterdam.

The governor suspected the boy had too much of the Orient in him, an overfondness for luxury and indulgence. People in the Indies sank into this, their own imagined importance. As far as the governor was concerned his son and heir might almost have been French. In fact, Robert hated India and wanted to go home to Harriet Villiers, the English girl who wrote him letters that he treasured.

In the time of the hot winds, the season of the heats, the monsoon had cut a path and the river discharged into the sea. Governor Pitt sat panting in the garden house of his new garden. (Disappointed men often turn to their gardens, as I have seen here, where he who once ruled Europe plants geraniums.) The governor retired to this garden in the afternoons, but was always ready to do private business if a deal was to his advantage.

Before him on this afternoon were a silver bowl of fruits, a dish to wash his fingers, with lace cloths to wipe them, and another bowl of wet cambric cloths. Indian boys raced around him like courtiers—swatting and swabbing and bowing. As usual, the governor regretted his tight and heavy English clothes, which made no concession to the climate and made him feel like a fat swaddled baby. All afternoon, for four or five hours, his servants bathed his brow and wrists as heat-struck silkworms dropped from the trees where lemons rotted and grapes shriveled and parched before they could grow to maturity.

The governor had his tea dishes before him and sugar candy and con-
served little lemons, which he dipped and sucked with his small mouth.
From where he sat, he could see the wide walks and bowling green and the
teal pond and curiosities, but none of this gave him any sort of pleasure. He
stuck out his leg with its gouty foot and panted like a dog, and the water
dripped down his red face and streaked it white with salt. His spittoon
bearer backed away on tiptoe.

Jamchund came along the spacious walk and found him in his usual
black humor. All the heat of the day had collected in one flame that shot to
the pagoda tree and shimmered round him and set forth the smell of the
flowers. Once he had made out the apparition, Pitt offered Jamchund re-
freshment and then sent off the *houkahburdah* and his boy. Jamchund often
came to him in this hour, knowing that he was somewhat weakened, his
senses assaulted.

The two rogues had played each other many times in the past and respected each other's duplicity. Jamchund had abnormally bright eyes, like
jet jewels drowned in moonlit waters, surrounded by dark craters of age, debauch, or intelligence misspent. His eyes made him look both sad and pro-
found, a great advantage in business.

This was the time when India supplied Europe with diamonds and rubies, garnets and pearls, and Europe traded them amber and Mediter-
ranean coral from Marseilles and Leghorn. The red coral was the most
precious. Strings of bright red coral swagged across Jamchund's turban and
circled his wrists and ankles and throat. When he died, his coral would all
be burned with him in his cremation ceremony. Coral for silver and then diamonds was the basis of the diamond trade.

Jamchund—who knew the governor had been searching for large spectacular diamonds and that already he had heard (for India has no secrets)
about his new diamond—produced a green silk pouch from under his waist
wrappings. He scattered some of the lesser rubies, called spinels, into his
palm, then some large rubies, and laid each on a small square of white silk.

"What else?" said Pitt, who looked down only briefly, attentive rather to
the man's still face that promised more. "Your Excellency, I have a surprise,"
Jamchund said. His chest was bound with a length of turquoise silk worked
in gold, which he began to unwrap, until he came to a large heavy purse
beaded in coral that must have caused great discomfort against his skin. He
looked about at the Shiraz wine and arrack punch and fruits, the cold colla-
tion before him on the tea table, then unwound the silk cords that circled the

pouch. He began to play with the knots, all the while declaring that what the purse contained was forbidden, was promised to the Great Mogul, was a rarity beyond any price.

"If you took all the expense of the universe for two and a half days—that might be its worth," said Jamchund. "If a strong man took five stones and cast them east, west, north, south, and straight up, and filled all the space within with gold and gems, it would not equal its value. Men have already paid the ultimate price to possess it, for they have died for it."

"Give it forth," said the governor.

"I'll show it to you, but it cannot be yours."

Jamchund, whose motto was "If the snake bites before it is charmed, then the charmer hath no advantage," had prepared the ground. Years before, when he first felt Pitt's diamond fever, he had told him legends. He told how Sinbad the sailor had found the Great Valley of Diamonds with enormous serpents slithering around the diamonds scattered in its soil. Suddenly great slabs of greasy meat fell at Sinbad's feet. Vultures and eagles dove for the meat coated with diamonds, which they then carried back to their nests. Up on the cliffs the diamond merchants, who had tossed the meat, then raided the nests. Jamchund told him how Alexander the Great also found diamonds guarded by serpents whose look alone would kill. With mirrors Alexander made them gaze upon one another. Danger was in all the stories right next to the diamonds.

In Jamchund's hand now was a rock of telltale green almost the size of his fist, with bits of fire piercing the stone. It was a magnificent freak in a land of others, for here were twins joined at the trunk, a two-headed boy, six-legged cows, and bearded women. Right away, this diamond belonged to history, to rulers, to emperors and conquerors and collector queens. It also belonged in the Indies. It was not meant for Thomas Pitt, and that was why he had to possess it. From the moment he saw it, Pitt felt the same hot desire as the slave. He saw the diamond in his future crest. At once, this was the cornerstone of his fortune, his way home in glory, the foundation of his dynasty.

The diamond already had a little window polished in its surface. The interior was white as Pitt's wife.

"I have heard of this diamond," said the governor.

He could not begin to put a value on the stone and thought immediately of the Jews Isaac Abbendana and Marcus Moses, who used to travel from Madras to the Golconda mines, where the stones cost less. They had taken chances equal to his own, for the roads were filled with bandits. Gaming, piracy, trading—risk was the common disease here, and none of the English would ever go back until they were rich or dead. The Jews of the fort knew diamonds and the London markets, for they all had Christian partners in London. How might the deal be struck? From the moment Pitt first saw the diamond, he never thought of it as anything but his. He liked the idea of something that must be transformed to be valuable.

"I am trusting this remarkable diamond to Your Excellency, to keep it while I am at the mines," Jamchund said, and then he left the fort for a week.

When Pitt was first acquiring diamonds, Jamchund had educated him in the trade. But Pitt, who had already been instructed by one of the Jews, pretended ignorance to test Jamchund. Each now knew the other's tricks— how Jamchund could not reject a bad offer but would simply ignore it, how he would perspire when he was emotional or deceiving Pitt, how Pitt became even haughtier than usual when he craved a packet. As anyone who ever gamed must know, the tic always betrays the man, and he who is ready to walk wins the bargaining.

Nine years later, on his way home from India, Pitt's ship stopped at Bergen in Norway, and he wrote this mostly true account of the transaction, which appeared in a magazine in 1710. By then he was in trouble, for the Mogul was asking for the diamond to be returned. Pitt had to justify his purchase, so he wrote:

> ...About two or three years after my arrival at Madras, which was in July 1698, I heard there were large diamonds in the country to be sold, which I encouraged to be brought down, promising to be their chapman, if they would be reasonable therein, upon which Jamchund, one of the most eminent diamond merchants in these parts, came down about December 1701, and brought with him a large rough stone, 305 mangelins, and some small ones, which myself and others bought. But he asking a very extravagant price for the great one, I did not think of meddling with it, when he left it with me for some days, and then came and took it away again, and did so several times, insisting upon not less than 200,000 pagodas (£85,000), and as I best remember, I did not bid him more than 30,000, and had little thought of buying it for that. I considered there were many and great risks to be run, not only in cutting it, but whether it would prove foul or clean, or the water good. Besides, I thought it too great an amount to venture home in one bottom, so that Jamchund

resolved to return speedily to his own country, so that I best remember it was in February following he came again to me (with Vincaty Chittee, who was always with him when I discussed about it) and pressed me to know whether I resolved to buy it, when he came down to 100,000 pagodas and something under before we parted, when we agreed upon a day to meet and make a final end thereof one way or another. When we accordingly met in the consultation room, where after a great deal of talk, I brought him down to 55,000 pagodas, and advanced to 45,000, resolving to give no more, and he likewise resolving not to abate, so I delivered him up the stone, and we took a friendly leave of one another.

Jamchund and his companion were back an hour later.

Mr. Benyon was then writing in my closet, with whom I discoursed on what had passed and told him now I was clear of it; when about an hour after my servant brought me word that Jamchund and Vincaty Chittee were at the door, who being called in, offered it for 50,000. I offered to part the 5,000 pagodas that was between us, which he would not hearken to, and was going out of the room again, when he turned back, and told me I should have it for 49,000. . . . Presently he came to 48,000 and made a solemn vow that he would not part with it a pagoda under; when I went again into the closet with Mr. Benyon and told him what had passed . . . so I closed with him for that sum, when he delivered me the stone, for which I paid very honourably, as by my books appears, and thereby further call God to witness that I never used the least threatening word at any of our meetings to induce him to sell it to me. . . . As this is the truth, so I hope for God's blessing upon this and all my other affairs in this world, and eternal happiness hereafter.

Written and signed by me, in Bergen, July 19, 1710.

THOMAS PITT

Pitt left out many details. They were in the consultation room, where sunbursts of swords on the walls indicated the terrible might of the East India Company. Every time Jamchund dangled the stone he told Pitt he held the queen of diamonds, that it was idolatry to gaze upon such a rarity. Only once in a thousand years is such a thing found. The treasure of treasures, the prize of the court, fairer than any beauty, for one man's eyes, not blue eyes. Jamchund made the stone forbidden before he named a price that made

Pitt, who suffered like most rich men over every pound and pagoda, want it all the more.

Jamchund left him alone with the stone. By then Pitt had sent ships from Balasore and run blockades and traded with China. He had fitted out ships as a privateer in the French wars. Now, as he went among the silks and pepper and Coromandel screens, adding and doing percentages in his head, the stone was with him. It was not on his person, but it was all he thought about. Each time Jamchund carried off the stone, chattering away in his language to Vincaty Chittee, his jaws wobbling with indignation, complaining of the outrageous price the governor had offered, Pitt felt some relief, for how would he ever dispose of this great gem?

Pitt wrote to Sir Stephen Evance, the agent in London to whom he sent diamonds. He said he had been reading Tavernier and realized that there was no stone as large as his would be when cut. In his wild hope, he forgot the Mogul's diamond of 280 carats.

Pitt then summoned Isaac Abendana, a Dutch Jew who was one of his advisers in the diamond trade, to see the diamond. Pitt, given to secrecy and fear, trusted him as much as possible. Pitt felt the Jews had diamonds in their very blood. Abendana caressed the stone as a lover caresses his beloved's neck. Pitt asked him to make a model of it quickly for the stone might be taken away.

"I am going to buy it and I am going to sell it," said Pitt. "A king is waiting."

"What king?" asked Abendana.

"I'm not quite sure," said Pitt. "Maybe a queen."

Another time, Pitt had Jamchund come to him in the morning. The governor's dressing was like the levee of Louis XIV. He stood still as a statue and clothes were applied to his body with great ceremony, the servants bowing very low and touching the forehead with the inside of the fingers, and the floor with the back part. They brought him a clean shirt and breeches and stockings and slippers. The barber shaved him, cut his nails, and cleaned his ears, then poured water on his hands and face and presented the towel. All the while writers and solicitors, their complexions ruddy from the climate, stood attendance, as did Jamchund while the head bearer and consumahs fussed and spied. Often the governor would note a sudden rustling outside a door, an impression of hasty movement retreating behind the putty-colored pillars, the slide of silk, the averted face, and news of his business would be known throughout the fort.

Only one who has lived in a court (as we have) could understand the value of these regimented ceremonies that preserve order and keep kingdoms. Pitt had wanted Jamchund to appreciate how he lived, as though such a thing could frighten him from his price. In fact Jamchund, who lived this way himself, discussed other, smaller diamonds and took away the big stone.

Sir Stephen Evance wrote to Pitt that Louis XIV, who was then fighting for existence in the War of Spanish Succession, would not buy it, nor would any other prince, and advised Pitt not to tie up so much money.

Pitt bought the diamond knowing there might not be a buyer for a time. He bought it in keeping with his nature—to want a rare thing desperately and then, almost immediately, through nervousness, shrewdness, and perversity, to want to be rid of it.

He had his son Robert, who was then twenty-two and increasingly in love with Harriet Villiers, carry it to London. The diamond would free him of India. Also the governor needed Robert at home to take over his affairs.

The *Loyale Cooke* left Madras in October 1702 with Robert Pitt and the diamond. Before the trip, Robert read Tavernier and provided himself with certain books for the journey that he bought from the Jews in the fort. He spoke privately to the Jews, for he expected to be in charge of the cutting of the stone and saw in this process a way to redeem himself with his father. Like the diamond, he too seemed to have to be transformed to be valuable. So he read *Le Parfait Joallier,* a seventeenth-century translation of *Gemmarum et Lapidum Historia,* and got almost halfway through. He learned the legend of the Bruges cutter Lodewijck van Berckem, who may have invented the grinding wheel and the dop to hold the diamond as well as the idea of adding castor oil to diamond dust to make the abrasive paste.

Governor Pitt came upon him as he was reading. Robert caught his expression and thought of the dogs he had once seen thrown to a tied-up bull. The bull gored the dogs two at a time and tossed them in the air, their blood arcing into the sawdust. This was considered a sport at home in London.

"Robin! You are at your books," the governor said.

Why does he hate me? thought Robert.

"Have I told you about the pirates?" said the governor, and told him yet again if an enemy took the ship, he must throw any papers relating to the diamond overboard. He should dispose of the diamond as he could.

"Where, Father?"

"You might attempt to swallow it," said the governor, who then pretended to be jesting. Robert knew if he swallowed it he would die and wondered which loss would affect the governor more, though he knew the answer.

"You must understand this diamond is my exit," said the governor.

A big fear started up in both Pitts then. The governor consigned the stone jointly to his son, his friend Alvaro da Fonseca, and Sir Stephen Evance. Of the three he trusted the Portuguese Jew, da Fonseca, the most. He told da Fonseca that the king of France or Spain was the likeliest buyer unless Parliament would buy it for the British crown. He cautioned not to part with it without receiving its full value. He wrote that princes covet jewels that can't be equaled.

The diamond went off the ship in London—still crude, unshaped, but intrinsically valuable. Pulled from its native soil, the diamond was already full of blood—with two deaths and suspicions surrounding it. Soon enough, this rarity was no secret. Lady This wrote about the Pitt diamond to Lady That.

Robert borrowed from the stone's fame and got to marry Harriet Villiers, the long, dark daughter of Lady Grandison, who had two dukes of Buckingham and many big houses in her family. In doing this, he defied the governor, who had wanted him to go to Oxford, read civil law, and enter himself in the Inns of Court. The diamond had freed him from his father's wishes.

Too quick and secretive, said the governor, who knew this marriage would also be expensive.

The governor wrote to London about the diamond every month and began using code, calling it "the great Concerne," "the elder brother," and the "Philosopher's Stone." Meanwhile, everyone in a certain London called it the Pitt, or that Pitt diamond, or that great gob of stone about to be cut over at Cheapside.

The governor wrote that if Sir Stephen and da Fonseca were in treaty to sell it to some foreign prince, they should never let it out of their hands but send Robert with a model. Pitt had ordered a crystal model—a very optimistic one—made to indicate how it would look cut. This was to show about while suggesting that such a diamond might possibly be for sale. They should take the model to the Jews of Amsterdam to determine its value. Someone suggested that the king of Prussia was the likeliest buyer, or again the king of France, if there was peace with Britain. By September 1704 the cutting had begun and Pitt wrote, " 'Tis my whole dependance."

The stone was making Pitt sick. His letters were full of worry and fear, for he was a man who could not surrender control and would have cut the diamond himself were it in his power.

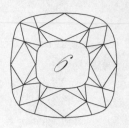

Diamond Cuts Diamond

I N ALL ENGLAND THERE WAS ONLY ONE MAN ABLE TO CUT THE Pitt diamond, and that was Joseph Cope, who did not especially want the job. It was Alvaro da Fonseca who persuaded Cope to examine Thomas Pitt's stone.

"They have shown me the cutting model," Cope said, "and I have never seen one this bad."

Da Fonseca agreed and was pleased because he disliked Isaac Abendana, who had made this model back in India at the governor's request. He said they would have another model made for the cutting and added he would have young Pitt bring Joseph Cope the stone itself. Already, da Fonseca had excused himself from handling the diamond, though he was to sell the pieces cut off. And yet he lingered.

When Robert Pitt and Sir Stephen Evance appeared at the London jeweler Harris with the diamond, Joseph Cope was standing in his workroom with da Fonseca. It was a laboratory of dops and wheels and mortars and pestles, scaifes in lignum vitae and sieves, filled with gray light, through which streamed filaments of the white and powdery diamond dust that had escaped. Cope's sleeves were rolled up on particularly long arms thick with blond hair. He was wearing a leather apron and thin leather gloves that he did not bother to remove. He looked to be about forty and very strong.

Da Fonseca had explained to young Pitt that Cope's hands could feel vibrations in a stone, that he saw crystallographic axes and cleavage planes, and all geometry was his. Cope had a skill as rare as the diamond that would encounter it.

When they put the diamond down on his worktable, Cope made as if to sit on his bench and had to put out his hand first to steady himself.

"Good Lord!" he said, though he was a Jew who did not believe. He had known the weight was 426 carats but still he was unprepared. He could not help smiling.

Through the window in the crown of the stone Cope saw the blue-white of Golconda. The body seemed very clear, with only two small flaws perceptible at one end. He knew at once this was the largest diamond he would ever see and his chance to do the best work of his life.

"There is a new cut," he said. "The diamond would lose weight to achieve brilliance and play, but it will dance."

"You mean the 'brilliant'? It is a risk," said da Fonseca, who already had approved this way to go. "But better pure and smaller than bigger and foul."

"I don't know," said Sir Stephen Evance.

Da Fonseca, who did not trust Sir Stephen and thought his business was as shaky as his character, held himself still.

"You have come here to be extraordinary, not safe," said Cope, who had the habitual arrogance, assurance, and nerve of the best cutters.

Robert then asked how much would be lost.

"Perhaps as much as two-thirds," said Cope. "There is one other like this, the Wittelsbach Blue, cut long ago—a pavilion with many facets in the shape of a star. It is magnificent but irregular. This would be three times its size and perfect."

"Perfect?" they all said and almost forgot their differences.

Cope, who practiced cleaving in his sleep, told them that if the stone was cut this way, he could make white light into rainbow fire. What he was proposing was a most daring experiment.

"I am the only one," said Cope. "You can forget those in Amsterdam."

Then Robert Pitt made a decision bold enough to redeem the rest of his life. For once, he stepped outside himself and became the man who had gone to India at eighteen and traded in China for two years, the son Thomas Pitt would never quite know. He agreed with Cope's plan, and changed his sons' and grandsons' lives for the risk. Until he did this one extraordinary thing, Robert had been of the generation that follows greatness and exists only to breed another great man.

"Seven thousand pounds," said Joseph Cope, and they went back and forth until he agreed to five thousand.

"How long will it take?"

"Perhaps two years," said Cope, and that is what it did take because it was cut by hand.

"I will be coming around every day," said Robert, who now saw this as his job in life.

The great diamond spent 1704–1706 on the wheel. It took Joseph Cope one year just to cut the 410-carat stone in half, using its own diamond dust as paste on a grinding wheel. First he cut the octahedron to a pyramid, then sawed the top off, forming a table stone.

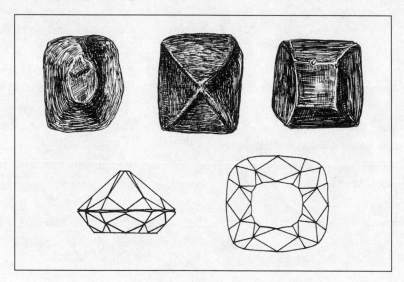

Illustration by Emmanuel Las Cases, age fifteen

Then, in the second year of the cutting, he began to turn the big stone into a brilliant cushion cut of fifty-eight facets. He made lead molds during the cutting process and Emmanuel has copied from drawings of them here above. The Great Pitt, as the principal stone now was known, was probably the first great diamond to use this cut.

Cope wrote to the governor. At first he thought it would be 280 carats, and then he knew it would be half that, 140. The flaws kept appearing. Unexpected flaws, for if the central part was perfect, the outer was unexpectedly foul. The diamond was deceptive, and nine big pieces had to come off. He dreaded the answers he got back from the governor.

Every day Robert came to observe and wrote to his father that when a piece was sawed off, he matched it to the place it was taken from to see if it fit exactly and nothing was stolen. Whenever he did this, Joseph Cope, sitting on his three-legged stool by the window, thought of taking the young Robert and slicing off parts of his face. He thought of his head in a dop and the scaife wheel smeared with oil and diamond dust approaching. Robert thought Cope was very calm for a Jew.

Robert was intrigued by the transformation, the slow metamorphosis from dark to light, cloudy to clear, the grinding and slicing, taking—no, slowly wearing—the bad away. And using the great stone's own dust to change it. It was at once destruction and creation. He began to see Cope as Vulcan. He called him Joseph.

At times—for there were problems with his mother and sisters—the diamond and Harriet were the only light things in Robert's dark, bad-smelling city. He knew the diamond would change them all even as it changed itself.

The diamond had other visitors though the governor had forbidden this. The famous men, the great lords and dukes of the day and those from the royal court, wanted to see it. Robert let them in until Cope finally forbade this circus except for an hour a week.

All along they had the nervous governor to contend with. Robert blessed his distance and the fact their letters took so long. Pitt had written he wished the diamond had kept some of its magnitude. Robert explained that Cope said the flaws went so deep that he had to saw off pieces.

Cope well knew the diamond could shatter or split if dropped at the point of cleavage. He felt the vibrations of the months of sawing. His work was cleaving, bruting, and polishing. The day he was about to cleave it, when the diamond was in the tang, he had a headache.

"Not this day, sir," he told Robert. The headache lasted almost a week. Then Robert appeared with his wife, Harriet, who had never seen a Jew before and clutched at Robert's arm as though Cope were the very devil at his forge. She clung like a sea anemone struck to its rock in the hardest surf. Harriet had something of the insect about her beauty—a too tiny head on a long thick neck, a long form, her hands like fluttering feelers sensing danger ahead in the Jew.

This lady won't wear the diamond, Cope thought; not ever—and said as much to da Fonseca.

As Cope cut, he knew what the diamond would be. He knew the proportions and the angles were perfect. Its main angles were forty-five degrees on both crown and pavilion. The shape was balanced, the facets perfectly symmetrical, and the polish flawless. Its fourfold symmetry was reflected on its culet facets as well as the split-star facets. But it was not without flaws. There was still a small flaw, a crack or inclusion, in the girdle, and another in a corner on the underside. They were almost invisible and did not bother Cope.

He was almost ready.

"Look at it," Cope said. He pulled the shades down over the bad London light, covered the skylight, and lit all the candles. "It is beginning to dance. It will dance a long time."

"Forever," said Robert Pitt.

"By the application of a deliberately wavy girdle I have produced almost identical angles of inclination of the main facets all around the gem. The result is uniform brilliance—unheard of in a cushion-shaped diamond."

Robert nodded as though he understood what Cope had said. He found that he could not stay away for he fancied he could see it change from day to day. He stayed at the jeweler's later into the evenings though he now had an infant daughter.

The size of the culet let the small facets produce a fire. The sparkle spread over the surface, dove into its depths, and then hurtled out. The diamond split light, swallowed light, and sent it leaping forth. The fire it gave off was made to shoot forth in the flicker of candlelight. The whiteness of its water could only be Golconda, but Cope had given it this power of dispersion and cleanness.

Cope never again thought of who would buy the diamond or wear it, but he began to be jealous of Robert and whoever might take it away, and told da Fonseca this, too. His creation was a private pleasure for him and the workroom as he locked it away for the night.

Robert had been there almost every day, never bored, watching through the seasons as it lost 289 carats on the wheel and exercising Cope's mastery of tension. Cope's predictions were right, for the resulting yield was 32 percent of the original stone—$136^{14}/_{16}$ carats. What Cope had before him was a cut that would come to be known as the baroque brilliant. He knew this was the best work he would ever do.

The shape was a slightly rectangular cushion measuring 31.58 millimeters in length, 29.89 millimeters in width, and 21.05 thick. He was sure the cut, the clarity, the lack of color, and the intensity all made it the most beautiful and the biggest diamond in the world. He showed Robert how the hearts and arrows cut inside the diamond were perfectly aligned. The especially large open culet on the bottom of the stone was a portal for the owner to go into the diamond and see whatever he wanted; this was part of its magic.

They finished the polishing in March 1706. Cope laid it on a velvet pillow in a beechwood box.

"I do not know what the governor will say, but I believe you have done the job well," said Robert.

"I am sorry to lose it," said Cope, much relieved that Robert with his disastrous sneezes, his long nose over the wheel, and his calipers would be gone as well. Robert had amused him each time he put his glass down to the stone instead of bringing it up to his eye, yet he never had corrected him.

Robert put the small box in his waistcoat pocket and buttoned it over. He had two strong servants accompany him to the back of Sir Stephen's jewelry and banking establishment, where they locked it away in an iron chest with three keys. Sir Stephen had one key and Robert had two. Robert had ordered a new crystal model made of the diamond in its final shape to show to the Jews of Amsterdam.

Da Fonseca arranged to have Abraham Nathan, who was connected to the German court Jews, buy the parts that were sawed off the Pitt diamond. Pitt wrote to Sir Stephen and Robert, when they told him the sawed-off pieces would fetch £1,500, that he thought they must have left off a zero.

In the year the diamond was finished, Madame, now grown fatter in her misery, saw the eclipse of the sun in the presence of the court at Marly. The shadow swallowed the beds of narcissus and tulips, crawled down the statues and along the marble horseshoe. It crept down each of the twelve fairy palaces, consuming them one by one, and it was like a dark fear had taken them all.

Later that year Madame's son, Philippe d'Orléans, was wounded in the battle of Turin in the War of Spanish Succession. A musket ball hit him in the hip and his left arm was shattered below the elbow. It mended and he was able to play tennis when he came home, but it never hung quite right again.

The governor had wanted the diamond kept a secret even from his wife, Jane Pitt. In India, the Mogul was already demanding it back. By then, Jamchund was dead of a cancer, and an inquiry was going on about how the diamond came to Pitt.

No ostentation, the governor kept saying to Robert. But again, he was much too late.

When Robert had returned to England four years earlier, he carried a letter removing his mother from overseeing the affairs of his father. Eight years before, Thomas Pitt had left Jane in England with two large houses at Stratford and Blanford. Two friends from the company were to help her sell the diamonds and goods he sent back. However, she had bought land and did not tell him, she did not keep sufficient records, and she was indiscreet in handling his affairs. She was alone in England with her four children and had never gotten over the India of her girlhood, where Pitt met her twenty years before. Things had been done for Jane Innes there before she even could voice her desires.

After filing Pitt's letter with the courts, Robert fought with his mother, who resented his taking over her affairs. He fought with his sisters, who took her side, and turned them from his house. Robert had the Pitt temper, gout, and enjoyment of trouble. In his quarrels as in his face, the son was the father, only spongy at the core.

Robert, too grand to go into trade, still asked the governor for money. The governor, running his fort and trading diamonds so as not to sell the big diamond until he got his price, resented the way his son was living. As he feared, the Indies had left Robert with a high taste for gorgeousness. Along with the diamond he had brought home an urge to lie back on dark woods and be tended. He was infected with this "Orientalism." The English are devoted to having things done for them, and in India this need had been cultivated to an unimagined degree. Once, during the visit of Da'ud Khan, Robert sat down to a dinner of six hundred courses, after which nautch girls danced. In London, Robert lived in Golden Square with a cook and five in livery, his coach and six matched horses—exhausting his and his wife's fortunes while keeping the governor's in his sights. He had the Pitt desire not to be overlooked or crossed.

The dark winds were blowing upon the governor's family. Pitt had been away from them for too many years, and now they acted up. In 1706, Jane Pitt went to Bath and got into a scandal with some rascal, or perhaps she did not. There was only a whiff of impropriety, but that was enough. Pitt stopped all letters, cut her allowance, and vowed never to see his wife again.

Then his youngest son, William, died of smallpox in 1708. Out in Madras, Pitt got more and more difficult. A curse seemed to have come upon him. The year before, Robert had sent a long account of cutting the diamond and told him of the flaws they had found—unforeseen flaws like those in his family.

"What hellish place is it that influences you all?" Pitt wrote. "Have all of you shook hands with shame?" He was in a frenzy and at a helpless distance. "Did ever mother, brother, and sisters study one another's ruin and destruction more than my unfortunate and cursed family have done?" (I note the word "cursed" here.) His family hated each other in a way that only those who know each other's secrets can hate.

The diamond had poisoned his life and still was not sold. Those who think they have made this kind of a mistake either take it inward and become sick as with a cancer or take it outward by yelling and banging and quarreling. Pitt fought with his council and mishandled a quarrel between the left-handed and the right-handed castes and was finally recalled from his mighty position.

Before Pitt left India, there was a scandal about the origins of the stone that never quite went away. In August 1709, a Lieutenant Seaton was brought to the council room of Fort Saint George, where he accused the governor of taking bribes and buying the diamond to the company's prejudice. The judgment went with Pitt, and Seaton was sent back to England a prisoner on the next ship. Still, the Indians were all churned up over this stone that had left their shores eight years before.

Outrunning disgrace, Pitt left India in September 1709 on the *Heathcote*. He had lasted twelve years in the valuable post through changing governments. France was then entering the hard winter of 1709, a time of mass starvation when the Rhône was covered with ice and olive trees froze in the ground. Whole families starved and died in their hovels while the king and his nobles sent their plate to the mint, melted down the silver furniture, and ate oat bread at Versailles.

Despite all Pitt's cautions to keep the stone quiet, talk of a diamond big as an egg was all over London and Europe. This was no surprise for it had been peddled all over and models sent about. The real Pitt diamond had spent the last three years at Strathfieldsaye* in Hampshire, the home of a cousin, George Pitt, taken—not without difficulty—from the back-office safe of Sir Stephen Evance, who had gone bankrupt.

---

*This house that sheltered the Régent became the country home of the duke of Wellington, who defeated the emperor at Waterloo. It amuses the emperor that he now keeps there, as we have heard, Houdon's bust of the emperor as first consul, as well as one of him as a Roman emperor.

"Take a seat, Sylla," the emperor says now, misquoting Corneille as he always does when we begin our dictation, "and tell me where you are in your other history."

So I did, and he asked if I was still making things up.

"Oh indeed, sire, I confess to having imagined much and many of their words, for I fail to find so many documents."

"Chi cerca, trova" (he who searches, finds), he said in Italian, "but not always here. Tell me more of the diamond," he said, stirring through the pocked limestone rocks with the toe of his boot, for we were in the arbor this afternoon. He had made a small hillock and was invading its perimeter with a wedge of stones stirred by his other scuffed toe.

"The volcano's pressure makes such big diamonds deep inside the earth and then they are forced to the surface, no?" I nodded. "Well then, volcanoes have a role here, for a volcano created this diamond and we are trapped on a volcano island as you write about it. Is that not curious?"

A *V* formation of firebirds was heading to the ocean, calling to one another as they flew over the lava rocks, and we both turned to watch them as though they were the last birds on earth.

"Shall we begin?" (It was not a question.)

"Semper paratus," I said, using the motto of our family crest, which means "Always prepared," as we went inside. The walls of his study now were mapped with spores of black mold, the islands of no known world.

After five hours of fast writing with almost no pause but to stretch my cramped limbs and eat the food Ali brought to us, he stopped. I groaned with relief and asked if he were not tired. At this he bid me apply my hand to his chest. I felt no heartbeat and drew back like one burned.

"Don't you see I am fine? I am formed to work like this. Do not be alarmed. My pulse is always slow. Let us continue, for the work is good today."

And so we did until I dropped my quill. I saw only black before my eyes.

"I cannot repeat. You made me lose my thought," the emperor said. And then he took mercy. "Open the window." Our windows were all *à la guillotine,* the upper half fixed with a bolt holding it.

I drew what was left of the green taffeta curtains, and streaks of the blue evening came in through the holes and lay like little diamonds on the floor, reminding me of yet another task.

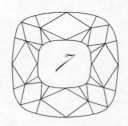

"Diamond Pitt" Goes Home

As Thomas Pitt sailed north, he felt all the heat leave his body. There was still the memory of pink flowers and fans waved in rosy rooms, tea fields laid in green squares, elephants and palms, Moors in their thin loose clothes putting down silver-covered dishes and wine in the year of its vintage, crocodiles, silk, perfumed oils, and stench. He knew he would never return.

The diamond was not only unsold, it was causing him problems. It had caused trouble before he left and the trouble had followed him round the Cape of Good Hope, onto the Danish ship, and into Bergen, Norway, where on July 10, 1710, he felt he had to write his letter explaining how he bought the stone.

In Copenhagen Pitt asked Robert to send him the model of the Great Pitt and a letter of credit for £1,000. He was going to do business. He took the model to Amsterdam to the same Jews who had seen the model with Robert. He did not trust Robert's reports. They shook their heads and many of them shrugged as they consulted one another, for who had ever seen such a wonder? All calculations seemed useless.

In London, Robert met his father at the dock with the new campaign periwig the governor had requested. On deck Pitt stepped out into a new kind of noise and British birds in the gray air. He saw his new valet and two footmen wearing alarmingly fancy blue-and-silver livery, standing by a big carriage. He did some calculations.

"Robin, you have not told anyone!" he said. "Already they call me Diamond Pitt. I heard it all over Amsterdam."

"Whenever anyone asks about the diamond, I say I wish it were true," said Robert, who might also have said that all London knew, that the diamond was already a famous curiosity of the coffeehouses.

The governor eyed his son's new plumpness, his rich clothes, and the smudge of food on his mouth. They went back to his stateroom and Robert took the diamond out from his boot heel and passed it to his father. The governor sat on his ivory-and-silver chair and held the stone. It was somewhat smaller than he had expected and much brighter, blazing forth to thrill him.

The diamond was now about an inch and a quarter and weighed about an ounce and an eighth on the scale he produced. It was heavier than the model, and so different. To Pitt it looked and felt very important. He put it to his lips and felt a small cold cushion.

He wrapped it in a chamois cloth and placed it in cotton wool in the extra high, hollowed-out heel of the shoe he had prepared. He limped about a bit to show off to his son, who had never before seen the governor's antic side.

Then the governor grabbed Robert and waltzed him about the cabin in a hopping jig. He imagined that he felt the stone rattling and looked down frequently to check. The new wig from France was curly and full and bounced from his shoulders; the drop locks in front did their own happy dance.

Then he took the Great Pitt out again.

The governor had spent twelve years in the Indies this time. There was no wife, a dead son, and the family to reassemble. While he was in the Indies, King William had fallen from his horse and died, and now Queen Anne, the second daughter of James II, ruled.

Those reprieved from exile know what it is to be again a stranger, returning to the unfamiliar, starting over with people who do not know one's history or accomplishments. Fame clears all that to some extent, and now he was famous. He was the Great President or Diamond Pitt, and would have no other titles, though contemporaries wrote his biography and called him, like the diamond, "the Great Pitt."

As they rode through the city, Pitt saw a new, thick London, denser, higher, and blacker than ever. Robert told him he now needed a candle to write his morning letters. Squares filled with houses and palaces and churches filled the old cornfields. He felt old in all that was new and, to him, worse.

Robert showed him Saint Paul's Cathedral, too new to be touched by smoke. People walked through Saint James's Park in black masks, and Pitt assumed some were harlots. His carriage could barely move, so clogged were the streets with hackney coaches and chariots, phaetons, curricles, and sedan chairs. There were blacks about, and lascars who had sailed the company's ships, and Pitt felt himself lost in the spread-out darkness. He kept looking back to see if they were followed.

In the jostling and clatter, the sense of dark rush, he felt as all do who return—the potential for being and even staying lost. (I felt it a century later—when I landed in London—lost, poor, with all unfamiliar.) He wondered whether his India life had been his true life or was but the preface for this life he was about to resume.

He could almost feel the infection in the city and kept swatting the air in front of his face. He heard cries for herbs and news, for roots and mongers. "Oranges!" "Twelve pence for a peck of oysters!" "Maids, buy a mapp!" (mop).

"One large diamond here!" he whispered to Robert, who now thought his father light-headed.

He had been away from the diamond for eight years, during which it had been cleaved and ground and rubbed into the finest diamond in the world. Pitt had to be sure. He was old now, almost fifty, and exhausted from the journey; his gouty foot hurt him, but still he insisted on being driven to the Tower to see the crown jewels.

"Now, Father?" said Robert, for the governor had not seen his other children or those of Robert.

As the footmen waited out of sight, he and Robert reported to the Yeomen of the Guard and checked their swords with them. He indicated to his son that he wished to be incognito. One of the yeomen went with them as a guide.

They passed the narrow gate where the nobles were taken out by boat up the Thames to be condemned. Not to seem too hasty, they peered into the old house where four lions were confined in the same space with a dog, and dutifully marveled at the sight.

"If these natural enemies can be confined together, why must you fight with your sisters and brothers?" said Pitt.

They saw wolves and a tiger, two ancient eagles, and two large Indian cats of a species Pitt knew well. There was the armor of all the old English kings—the huge armor of Henry VIII lined in red velvet and stuck all over with pins as a jest. Any person who wished was presented with a pin as a charm against impotency or infertility. They saw the axe a swordsman brought from France that beheaded Anne Boleyn and cut the throat of the earl of Essex.

Walking about under the trees was the ancient Lord Griffin of Dingley Hall, a colonel in King James's guards who had been convicted of treason. Every month Queen Anne saved him from execution.

"Vile Jacobite. I hope they hang him soon," Pitt said. The old Whig was very disturbed by Robert's Tory sympathies, yet another cause of the bad blood between them.

Pitt was still turning around to see if they were followed when they came at last to a bolted door with two sentries in front. Inside was a partition and an iron trellis through which they could view the English crown jewels as they sat on their benches. Pitt yearned for the yeoman to disappear and leave him to the sights before him.

He saw many diamonds, pearls, and sapphires, a model of a castle in gold, two huge amethysts—one in the Parliament crown and another in the great orb—a fine large emerald, and three giant pearls, one large as a hazelnut. To Pitt they were mere nuts when he had a plum.

"That one is known as the Black Prince's Ruby," said their guide, "for Prince Edward, who was buried in black armor. The ruby belonged to Abu Said, one of the Arabic rulers of Granada. Pedro the Cruel, king of Castille, murdered him and gave the ruby to the prince . . ." And now he was telling how Henry V wore it in his helmet at Agincourt and how Captain Blood, dressed as a parson, once had stolen the jewels . . .

"Why, it be large as an egg," said Robert, much given to the obvious.

The governor was not listening. He was making a circle of his thumb and forefinger trying to measure the ruby against the stone in his boot and paying no heed to its red fire sparks climbing the dungeon walls. He liked the idea of great jewels meeting, even though this one came with such a past and his, he knew, was just beginning.

By then Pitt had his stone's color and fire so marked in his mind he could see that none here matched it. They left and gave the guide a gratuity. Outside Pitt remounted his carriage, crossed his leg, and looked down at his boot.

"I feared our diamond might prove a dog among the lions," Pitt said. "But it is a lion."

"*The* lion, sir," said Robert, who realized his father had never thanked him.

A few weeks later, on what the English call All Hallows Eve, a group of German scholars were drinking together in the Paris Coffee House in London. Among them was Zacharias Conrad von Uffenbach, who was on the grand tour with his brother Johann, stopping in each city to buy thousands of books and rare manuscripts and to inspect the famous collections of others. (Fortunately he published a journal, which the Balcombes have lent me.)

He and some Silesians were discussing how peculiar the English were and how expensive they found London when Baron Nimptsch, a Silesian chemist, interrupted.

"I have seen Herr Pitt's diamond. I have held this phenomenon in my hands."

He said someone had offered £80,000 sterling for it and kept talking about it, until the von Uffenbachs said they would like to see such a wonder.

"*Nein, nein,* you must not even inquire after it," said the Baron. "Herr Pitt is constantly changing his name and lodgings when he is in London for fear of being attacked and murdered for it. The Great Pitt is said to be much larger than the diamond belonging to the duke of Florence. I have written out a small description, which I will allow Zacharias to copy for his journals."

Chance had in fact brought the von Uffenbach brothers in collision with Pitt himself two weeks previous, at Tothill Fields, where people were electing a new member of Parliament to the lower house. The old governor had ridden out in support of his fellow Whig General James Stanhope, hero of the Spanish wars.

"Pulpitshisser!" some men called out, for they believed Stanhope and his friends had once relieved themselves in a pulpit. They began to throw stones and filth and shout insults. Those who were mounted beat at one another with the large clubs hanging from their saddles.

As Pitt's horse was led forward, the mob attacked a smith's apprentice who supported Stanhope. He rolled under the von Uffenbachs' coach. Since the mob could not get at him, they threw cudgels at him.

Then the old governor rode forward to extend the scared apprentice his hand. Pulling him forth and swinging him onto his saddle, he came eye to eye with the von Uffenbachs before riding off, the young boy's leather apron flapping in the breeze.

Later Pitt would tell this story to Stanhope, who lost the election and three years later would marry Pitt's favorite daughter Lucy, the pretty one.

Soon after his arrival the governor, who had two daughters to marry off, took a lavish house in Pall Mall. Around the corner were six dukes and many barons and such. His cook was trained in France and his cellar filled with remarkable wines, some a year or two old. He opened his doors to the great men of his day and felt without doubt he was one with them. He was back in Parliament, elected from his own rotten borough of New Sarum. He sat on the green-cloth-covered benches of the House of Commons and was pointed out to every new member as the owner of a choice curiosity.

But—and there is always a but—the Silesian was right. The diamond had made a gypsy of Pitt. The Great Pitt was the end of all sleep, the moon shining in Pitt's eyes, a glittering torment. The governor took up disguises and hats and, like our Bourbon kings in their royal progresses, tore up and down the roads between his big estates. When he limped into his club, slumped old men were nudged awake to peek at him from behind their journals. Most had heard the stories of this thing from the Indies, this diamond bigger than all others, and believed the worst of Pitt. No servant was allowed to stay long in Pitt's big houses. In the way Thomas Pitt slunk around looking backward there was little difference between him and the worst branded criminal.

The wars had been very inconvenient for the sale of the Great Pitt. Pitt wanted England to buy the diamond for Queen Anne. The queen, who was well into her forties, had women favorites who told her what to do and who were her lovers, or so it was said. She had already fallen out with Sarah Churchill, wife of the duke of Marlborough, and now Abigail Masham, who was once her maid, had taken Churchill's place.

Pitt conceived a scheme whereby he would display the diamond to the queen. Hearing that she was going to receive the sacrament, he went to Saint James's Chapel with the diamond sewn and pinned onto the front of his tricorn hat.

After the sermon, the queen's retinue walked up the center aisle. First the sword and four long scepters with crowns were carried up the aisle, followed by the limping queen, then her ladies-in-waiting, including the duchess known as Carrots and Lady Masham, who had a red nose. The queen was stout in a masculine way, her complexion blotched and enflamed to copper though she no longer drank much but tea. She wore a gold brocade dress with a big brooch, and a second chin wobbled down from her square face.

Usually, Queen Anne was carried about in a sedan chair. This day she walked, stiff from gout and sad with the familiar disappointment that, with her husband and seventeen children dead before her, she would be the last of the reigning Stuarts. As Queen Anne took her seat by the altar and the music began, those who were not of the court had to leave. The little governor stood, all the while flourishing and swinging his great hat back and forth as a censer, the diamond flashing away to catch her cold eye. The queen did not notice and, anyway, was in no mood for wonders or big diamonds.

The Great Mogul still wanted *his* diamond back. In the end of May 1711, a Brahmin with six horsemen rode into Fort Saint George to present a letter to the governor of Madras. Duan Sadullah Khan claimed the diamond for the Mogul and said it had been stolen out of his land. They read the letter in the court of the East India Company in England in July and read Pitt's letter from Bergen in response. In December, they questioned Pitt. The company told the fort not to let the Moors embarrass them over the diamond but to find out how it was acquired and if the company lost in the process.

Queen Anne died of apoplexy in 1714 and Pitt supported the succession of George of Hanover, the grandson of Madame's aunt the electress Sophie.

James Stanhope, Pitt's son-in-law, was nominated a secretary of state, and now three of Pitt's sons—Robert, Thomas, and John—were all in the House of Commons and, like his daughters, married into the aristocracy.

No one was more bourgeois than this well-fed old pirate. He who had once negotiated with the nawab of Bengal to build a trading station on the banks of the Hoogly and traded horses and sugar in Persia and on the Malay archipelago; he who lost cargoes and gambled on trades now was building fifty Anglican churches. Yews cut like urns, firs cut to spikes and cones, topiary globes and pyramids and green Adams and Eves filled his gardens.

Only one thing remained: Pitt must have his portrait painted. He chose the German Godfrey Kneller, who painted all the kings as well as Robert and Harriet Pitt. Kneller was of the Van Dyck school without quite the talent.

Kneller's German was good enough when he went to paint King George and his English was good enough for Pitt when he went to paint him. He had to approach the subject of the diamond delicately: would it be in the portrait or not? Kneller was used to the delusions of his sitters. He had accustomed himself to painting his subjects as Roman emperors and with all sorts of odd accoutrements of grandeur.

Pitt did not want the diamond to be his one great defining thing, and yet how could he escape it? So he stuck out his foot, with the high hollow heel of the famous shoes. He had one hand on his hip, a limp glove dripped from the other, and his expression said: This is just who I am. He had a full wig of shiny curls and two chins. A curtain was draped behind him on one side, and the other showed a universal green England through the window. On the window ledge was a bicorn hat, in the center of which was the diamond. No one could see this portrait without asking, "And what is that in his hat? Could it be *a diamond*?"

"Have you painted a king who might wish to buy this?" Pitt asked Kneller.

"Ha!" said the artist. "Ha! Ha!"

Kneller painted the gout from his leg and the diamond big as a beacon in his hat. After every sitting, Pitt limped from the room and hid the diamond away in yet another spot.

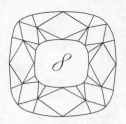

Enter the Seventh Fairy

I WARNED THE EMPEROR THAT ALL—MADAME, THE GOVERNOR, Louis XIV, the diamond—are about to collide. But first came the *annus horribilis*, the year of the deaths.

When Monseigneur, the first dauphin, died of smallpox in the heart of night, howls and cries and sobs and yells rang through Versailles. It was midnight, and the court came rushing forth in their dressing gowns, hair awry, and began, as Saint-Simon says in his memoirs, to compete in their grief. Along came Madame, in full court dress, for she still did not have a dressing gown, and began to howl with the others. Her son, Philippe d'Orléans, also forced a few tears because it was the thing to do. This went on for six hours.

Now again all she did was wrong.

The king left for Fontainebleau and when he returned, measles had come to court. Marie-Adelaide, the new dauphine, was sick, and Madame tried to keep the doctors from killing her.

"Today dauphine, tomorrow nothing," Marie-Adelaide said and died.

A week later, her hunchbacked and lame husband, the dauphin, had the measles.

"I die with joy," he said, for he loved his wife very much. And everyone began to think poison.

And then their two little boys were sick. Their eldest son, age five, who was the third dauphin, died. That left only the pretty baby duc d'Anjou,

69

who was kept away from the doctors with their bloodlettings and emetics so he would live to be Louis XV. The same hearse carried mother, father, and son to Saint-Denis. Four royals, three generations of heirs—son, grandson, and great-grandson—were dead in eleven months, with their hearts in jars. Though measles was all over, everyone began to look to Philippe d'Orléans, so good with his chemistry, so ostentatiously impious.

The duc du Maine, the king's bastard son, and Madame de Maintenon spread the rumor that d'Orléans had poisoned all of them to put his daughter, the duchess de Berri (married to the king's grandson), on the throne. Now Madame's son was shunned. When he entered the king's apartments or salon, others drew back as he passed, and when he approached a group, it broke apart and reformed, like the fragments in a kaleidoscope, leaving him in a void. They ducked around columns to avoid him.

This was the year that Madame, who accused the French of being hard-hearted and who had seen the king and court turn their backs on death and ride to the next château, described her own thirty-eight-year-old-son to her aunt.

She said he was like the child in the tale of the fairies. Each fairy comes to the child's christening with gifts—ordering that he will be handsome and eloquent, learn all the arts and sports, and have courage in war. But the seventh fairy, who was not invited, comes in to spoil it all. She ruins all the gifts the child has been given so a heavy black beard covers his face and he looks like a hunchback. The seventh fairy fills him with such boredom that he abandons all his arts, shuns honorable people, has bad luck in war, takes to drink and debauch and so forth. When Madame looked at her son, she realized it is impossible to understand anyone truly, even one's own child.

The year of the deaths in the king's family, 1712, was also the year that Marcus Moses first brought the model of *le Grand Pitt* to Paris. The diamond then had its own life apart with the touring Jews.

It is hard to think that anyone at the court would have approached Louis XIV at that time. The king, who was then seventy-four, no longer went to his Boulle diamond chests and slid out the trays of stones, no longer consoled himself with his sets of ninety-six diamond buttons and buttonholes, for he was in mourning.

With the death of the dauphine Marie-Adelaide and the others, even the remnants of pleasure had gone from the court.

The king was sad and bored. Versailles, now only for the old, was no longer much of a court. Some courtiers, no longer afraid, even dared flee to

Paris. Once the most dreadful condemnation had been when the king said of someone, "He is never seen"—like *les disgrâces* forced to slink away. Now there was an awful quiet. The card tables were removed. The king had done nothing but build Versailles and make war, and the wars had all been fought, the territory gained now lost in the Treaty of Utrecht.

And now again the doors were opened to Madame, who spoke to the king of the old days and tried to distract him with trifles. It was almost as it had been thirty years before, when she was new and he was young and filled with glory.

One day they stood up together and she realized with a shock that the king had shrunk. He was a head smaller than he had been when she first arrived, when he and Athénaïs used to sit in the window at Versailles mocking all who passed. It was an old court now, weeping in the alcoves, nervous in the gardens.

Madame wrote that it made her flesh creep to see the king. She remembered a day years ago when she was in the gallery and heard his music and the applause rippling as he walked by, louder and louder until it was upon her. She saw the count de L———, who was waiting behind a pillar, slide forward, for he told Madame he prayed for the favor of carrying the king's cane. From a distance she had seen the king strutting, his elbows out as though to push aside a throng, his eyes rolling side to side to see who awaited him, his toes turned out like the ballet dancer he had been. And for one moment she had seen him as a duck. She saw his fine legs and dainty feet on the high red heels and those favored to go on the walk, the train of nobles—toes out, cinched at the waist, elbows out, carrying tricorns under their arms—all strutting ducks, each so wide a figure in velvet coat with giant skirt, brocaded waistcoat halfway to the knee, diamonds on the sword hilt. The others clapped so hard at every step that puffs of powder from their huge periwigs lingered in the air.

The king had not cared to notice the count de L———, who just once had been permitted to hold a taper during the king's toilette. The candle was wrongly placed and wax had fallen on the count drop after drop, and though he grimaced and almost fainted from the pain, he had made not a sound.

Madame, who understood the barnyard, then thought it was better than Molière and was never again—or almost never again—afraid or bored.

In the middle of October 1714, soon after King George I of Hanover arrived in England and even before he was crowned, Governor Pitt went to see him at the palace. The king's thirty-one-year-old son was with him and did not stop smiling a bitter smile.

Pitt stayed with them over an hour and showed them the great diamond. They admired it and seemed to want it, and Pitt hoped the nation would buy it for them.

George, though great-grandson of James I and Madame's cousin, was a minor German noble of fifty-four who spoke almost no English. The interpreter told Pitt the king liked his diamond as the king put out his long fingers for the jewel.

His son was watching full of the usual hatred. (All the English Georges would hate their sons, and vice versa.) Once the young prince had tried to swim a castle moat to see his mother, whom George had imprisoned for thirty-two years for her supposed affair with the Swede Philip von Konigsmark. The Swede had disappeared and many thought pieces of his body lay under the floor of the palace in Hanover.

The king and Thomas Pitt were both men who believed themselves betrayed by their wives and had difficulties with their sons. Pitt knew it right away by the way the king and his son occupied the room. He saw the same blend of challenge, anger, jealousy, disappointment, fear, and helpless love that he knew well.

Both Pitt and the king were strangers possessed by the places they lived in when they were young—Pitt with India in him and George with Göhrde, his hunting lodge near Luneberg.

Pitt handed the king the diamond while saying to the interpreter that it was just to show, not a gift. He heard a lot of German and had an awful moment then when he feared the king might not give the stone back.

The king had never taken his pouchy blue eyes from the diamond. He put it in the center of his scalp, where his wig parted into two powdered peaks. He walked to a large gilt mirror. Then he put it on his lace stock and lowered his long pointed nose.

Behind his back the governor knotted his hands and smiled so hard that tears were forced to his eyes.

The king handed back the diamond as slowly as possible.

It was later in October 1714 that Thomas Pitt came to Fontainebleau to show *le Grand Pitt* to Louis XIV.

Madame, who grieved over the recent death of her aunt the electress Sophie, was in the throne room with the king. She saw that the king's feet now dangled above the floor as he sat on his throne. On Wednesday they had hunted, with the leaves crunchy under the wheels of Madame's calash, for she was too heavy for any horse and had been so for some time. She had always liked Fontainebleau because the Swiss Hall looked just like an old German hall with its bay windows, the wainscotting, and heavy carved benches.

The king had a bad stomach that day. At lunch, the roasted larks and spun sugar sailing ships were carried away untouched. Into the heavy pall limped Governor Thomas Pitt, his stick announcing his progress across the parquet of the throne room.

He was scared and saw in a blur the immensity of the vaulted arches, the frescoes above—flesh, wings, ribbons of gold wood, swirling draperies, the old courtiers in the window recesses.

On one leg he wore a heavy high boot inside which sloshed a bit of fresh blood. But an hour before, the French doctor had yanked the beating hearts from two parrots to apply to his throbbing foot. The governor was all done up in his uniform and decorations, slowly bowing and deeply flourishing before the king.

Louis XIV sat on his throne on a dais flanked and mocked by two bronze satyrs attached to the chimney. Behind his head a younger version of himself rode to hunt on the Gobelin tapestry. The king looked glum.

Every jeweler knows a man must be in a certain mood to buy a great jewel, and that mood is neither heartbreak nor repentance. One must be exuberant, in celebration, unable to feel the futility of existence.

It had been long since the king had gone to his diamond cabinet to examine the earthly reflection of his glory. He no longer opened his *livres des pierres du roi*, to run his finger over their dimpled vellum. Therein each stone was listed by color and form—boat, heart, table, helmet—and he might read of the diamonds bought from Tavernier's sixth voyage. Tavernier, the first European to see the treasures of the Grand Mogul, had told him he, Louis XIV, had the biggest rubies. Tavernier then had laid out the immense diamonds, some in their brut state. And the king had taken them all, including the blue diamond. That had been forty-five years before, when he was young and in love with Athénaïs de Montespan, who loved the jewels as he did. That same year, he had bought many other diamonds and pearls and two immense topazes from Bazu. He had bought the great violet rhomboid sapphire from Perret that he wore as a tie pin. All this was before his intense building at Versailles, which had become his ultimate and final jewel. Already he had Richelieu's rose diamond and three rubies, including the Côte de Bretagne spinel, and the five-sided pink diamond, Hortensia. He had all the diamonds Cardinal Mazarin willed the crown, including the Mirror of Portugal and the Great Sancy, in the shape of a pear, the most beautiful diamond of all.

He was cranky that day and had nothing to celebrate. The devil was creeping closer. Now when he went to pray, he meant it. All the distractions—Monsieur and Marie-Adelaide—were gone. He had been punished on earth with five dead infants, the malformed children forced to walk strapped onto an iron cross, three dead dauphins, and a court that had drifted away one by one now that he was no longer amusing. He loved Madame de Maintenon as one can only love one's salvation (or damnation); as Madame said, he loved her "terribly."

The king knew that both Queen Anne and King George I of England had refused to buy *le Grand Pitt,* and for a moment, he wanted to possess what his great enemies could not. He wanted to buy what they had been unable to afford, though the Peace of Utrecht left France weakened, with an empty treasury, poor from his wars.

"*Sire, la diamant,*" said Thomas Pitt.

"*LE diamant,*" said Louis XIV.

Pitt handed it forth in its fitted case lined with blue velvet. Immediately, the king saw that it was even more beautiful than the Great Sancy and three times its size. He thought of Athénaïs, dead like the others, and how she would have laughed and gasped and held it in her plump pink hand and said something clever.

He had a surge of wanting it as though its light could wipe out age and death and restore his chic and power. Yet he had no one left to impress as once he had awed the minister of Siam and all the others. Who would wear this diamond after him? He considered his pretty heir, who was five, and his nephew, who was forty and debauched. He had the moment that comes to each collector when he knows this is the one he cannot possess. He had almost six thousand diamonds then but would not have this last beauty.

Madame, who still had no interest in diamonds, nonetheless leaned close, for she knew this must be the same diamond the merchant had told her about many years ago.

"I have one as large," the king said, thinking of Tavernier's immense blue. "I do not need this pretty pebble."

"*Mein Gott!*" said Madame at the sight of the stone. "*Mon Dieu!* What a fine egg! Perhaps it is good for the state."

"The state is me," said the king.

The stone had bred copies and models and replicas that could travel. Existing alongside the diamond was its myth—that it was illegal, that it belonged elsewhere and there were claims upon it, that it was beyond price. The third grand duke of Tuscany, Cosimo de' Medici, had made an offer.

The grand duke, who roamed Europe incognito because his wife did not love him and lived with another man, had seen the diamond. He thought he might win her back with it. Then the duke had second thoughts, for he was already old and possessed many treasures and none of them had kept his wife from her lover, and so he became the next one to turn from the stone out of general heartbreak. And soon the line of the Medici would be no more.

Governor Pitt needed the fame of the diamond to sell it to a king, and yet the more it was known and connected to him, the more he suffered. His neck ached daily from looking over his shoulder. Strangers bumped up against him on the street and he jumped. He avoided the roads at night. Even though he did not carry the Pitt about with him, they might kidnap him to possess it. His coachmen were aware of all this. He lived with terror.

The diamond had its own bad reputation. Queen Anne, her enemy Louis XIV, and King George did not want the Pitt diamond. It had been around England too long. It was like a beautiful woman left unpossessed who fades like old ink into parchment. It depended for its value on shock—the first sight, the initial dazzle.

One day King George dispatched his minister James Stanhope, Pitt's son-in-law, to Caroline, the Princess of Wales, to convince the king's son to return to the cabinet and Parliament. Stanhope lost his temper and reminded her he had helped settle £100,000 a year on the prince.

"We could make an act in Parliament making this money dependent on the king's favor," Stanhope said as a threat.

"Would you add your father-in-law's great diamond to the new act to tempt the prince?" said the princess. Stanhope was not amused; any reference to the Great Pitt made the perspiration come to his brow.

Nonetheless Princess Caroline did her best with the prince, who eventually returned to the cabinet and Parliament.

The governor had called Robert's son, his grandson William Pitt, to him. The governor was in a special chair made to cradle his gouty foot, which now was big as a melon and wrapped in stained poultices.

William Pitt, then seven, was afraid of his grandfather, who never allowed a joy to be untouched by sorrow or any sorrow to be relieved by small hope. He tried to temper the universe for William Pitt, who, being young, believed in absolutes.

"Look, boy." He took the Pitt diamond from his pocket, and the sun coming over his shoulder did its work.

"Is this why they call you Diamond Pitt? May I hold it, Grandfather?"

The old man handed him the diamond and said he wished he could let him keep it because even then he had hopes for him alone among all the family.

"I shall sell it and put the money to work for you so you might serve your country and be a great man."

"How will the diamond do that?"

"You will do that yourself, with the help of the Lord."

"May I keep it or give it to Mama?"

"Definitely not," said the governor.

During the worst days of the War of Spanish Succession, Madame's son, Philippe d'Orléans, was out every night. Often he was with the roués, those he had so named because they deserved to be broken on the wheel (though they claimed the name came from their being so devoted that they would be broken on the wheel *for* him). Sometimes they went incognito, and one such night found them at the house of the tragedian Duclos, where all the most famous players went to game. The house was sumptuous, with great feasts displayed in every room. Its music was the clickety-clack of ivory and nacre plaques. Painted faces spotted with beauty patches moved in and out of the candle flicker. The shouts and laughter and wine spilled over into the great clatter of the games.

D'Orléans, taken all too easily by fruity wines, dry wit, and the kind of beauties who did not have to be forced, was not given much to play—he preferred other amusements—but he went from table to table until he saw a crowd gathered around one. There the play was faro, a dangerous game.

A handsome pocked man was acting banker. He had appeared rather suddenly with two enormous sacks of gold. He played with such lordly unconcern that Philippe d'Orléans inquired who he might be, for he was obviously both foreigner and stranger. The man was tall, fair, and richly dressed, and had a habit of tapping the deep cleft in his chin. He played without limits.

"Las, Las," everyone was whispering.

"Hélas?" (Alas?), d'Orléans said, and he felt an immediate attraction and sympathy for the banker.

D'Orléans had been taught by his old tutor Abbé Dubois that there was no such thing as a good man, and he saw in this one a fellow rogue. D'Orléans knew mathematics and he perceived this fellow *"Las"* was doing some computation in his head that allowed him to win. He had a system, but then all faro players think they have a system, and those who play regularly are reduced to poverty while the dealer and bankers, who do not play against the game, win hugely. (This, unfortunately, I know too well.) Reckless extravagance was the soul of the game but not the soul of the one he watched.

No man who did not cheat was that lucky, and he saw the foreigner did not cheat. He seemed to have mastered the very laws of probability. He counted the cards that had passed and knew the odds of what was to come. The duc d'Orléans was fond of unusual methods and of those who did not seem to care.

When the play grew hot, the stranger kept his sangfroid. D'Orléans saw another like himself drugged on risk, without fear or faith, and asked again who he might be.

Most around him knew the man's story in part—born in Scotland; the duel over a gallantry in London, where he killed a man and was to be hanged; the exile; the years of wandering Europe at the tables, always winning until he had amassed a fortune. They told the duc this man was learned in banking and commercial matters, had studied monies and finance, the lotteries of other countries, and the movement of precious metal. For his skill at the tables, at understanding chance and recurrences, he had been thrown from all the capital cities, somehow escaping disgrace and taking on legend. The romance of his life, its freedom especially, attracted d'Orléans, this bored, captive man. He had almost guessed much of this, for often two men of bad reputation know each other on sight.

Law was only a few years older than the duc, and they had more in common than either suspected, for both their wives had physical defects. Madame Law—who was not quite a wife—had a strawberry stain on her left cheek, and Madame la Duchesse d'Orléans had one shoulder higher than the other, plus a palsy that made her head shake. She usually lay supine, dropping tiny cooked birds into her painted mouth, crunching the bones while her head shook in perpetual denial.

"Every faro player has some peculiar system," said the duc to one of his roués, "but in the end all systems fail."

Upon the death of Louis XIV, Philippe d'Orléans became regent of France, ruling for Louis XV, who was only five years old. He had become friends with this *"Las,"* whose name was John Law.

Governor Pitt had a growing list of grievances against his heir. Robert was a spendthrift; he was not kind enough to his brothers and sisters. James Stanhope had gotten Robert appointed clerk of the green cloth to the prince and he had not bothered to take up the position.

In 1715, a rebellion for the Stuart pretender began in Scotland. Pitt would do anything to keep what he called the "French kickshaw" away. Robert's Tory friends could have led to his fall. The governor was sixty then and raising a regiment with his own money to fight alongside his younger son Thomas. The diamond was still unsold.

The rebellion was crushed, and for his loyalty, King George made Pitt the governor of Jamaica. On June 19, 1716, Pitt went to kiss the hands of the king and prince and princess to accept. He was supposed to leave before the summer's end and began studying the tropic island. In December, he was still arguing over what his powers might be when, a month later, France told him it was interested in *le Grand Pitt*. Negotiations began, and at the other end was John Law.

1717: *The Year of the Stone*

AS THE REGENT HAD REQUESTED, JOHN LAW WENT TO VISIT the duc de Saint-Simon every Tuesday morning at ten. He usually stayed for an hour and a half, sometimes two hours. Law's great coach bore him through the streets of Paris, crowded and feverish because of him, and filled with the usual din. He had never gotten used to the constant bells, which were still Catholic and strange to him. Sometimes he put his fingers to his ears, but not on this summer day in 1717, for he held a small square parcel and he held it tight.

He passed a prison where captives were clustered, waiting to be led to the docks. In America the foundations had just been laid for the city of New Orléans, named, of course, for the regent. Men were needed to settle there and in the vast Mississippi territories that La Salle had claimed for the Grand Monarch (which the emperor would sell back to the Americans in 1803). The prisoners were to be shipped there along with the Mississippi brides, and this too was because of John Law.

The skirts of Law's coat, woven with gold vines and tendrils, spread out on the seat as he rocked from side to side; his long fingers held the parcel to his lap. In his head, numbers cascaded into calculations; on his shoes were diamond buckles. He had his coachman stop so he might buy a baked potato. He placed the parcel hard under his arm. The vendor was in awe of the fair foreign prince, and the potato cost the same as it had the week before. Law threw it in the street.

The ancient houses tilted toward him from both sides of the narrow streets, ready to topple inward, spilling their singing birds and flowerpots and all the secrets within. On both sides of the bridges the houses seemed to be kissing as he crossed to the left bank. The highways were so crowded that every day trampled citizens were brought still gasping to the morgue, to be left with those who had drowned in the Seine.

Law's coach entered the gates and drive of the duc de Saint-Simon's mansion, Firmness.

The footman announced *Monsieur Las*. Saint-Simon, who came up to John Law's shoulder, noticed the parcel Law was carrying, as he saw all things, but would never have inquired about it.

John Law was clearly in distress. He scarcely raised his hat, which offended Saint-Simon, and he almost forgot to give him precedence as they went through the doors. The duc was shocked and his head quivered at Law's shoulder. As the late king had told him, he was too quick to take offense, especially regarding rank. As a new noble, he was an intent one. No one made a greater fuss over distinctions or had so treasured holding Louis XIV's napkin at communion or his candlestick as the king got into bed. In this he was the opposite of the regent, of whom the historiographer Duclos wrote: "Personal superiority made it unecessary for him to glory in his rank."

To Saint-Simon, these meetings with Law were a chore. Law always seemed to be looking about as though the house had lessons to impart. He was never quite sure of the egg Law had hatched from and suspected that Law's talents, like those of the regent, were matched by his errors.

To Law these mornings were a way to put his system through Parliament, improve his spoken French, and learn the gossip of the nation he was then enriching. It was a most useful intimacy.

"Ready for my lesson, Monsieur le Duc," he said with his horrible Scottish accent. "What have I done wrong this week?"

The little duc ruffled up, for he felt he was not being taken seriously.

As every Tuesday, Law tried to interest Saint-Simon in making his fortune with shares in his bank and the Mississippi Company.

"Louis . . . ," Law began, as Saint-Simon shuddered at his name used without ceremony. "I have set aside some shares for you and Madame la Duchesse . . ."

Law lifted a wig curl and started to twirl it round his finger, a habit that repulsed Saint-Simon with its slight suggestion of sensuality.

"A bait most fatal," said Saint-Simon, and explained yet again how he detested the idea of enriching himself at the expense of others.

Law assured him that anyone could buy shares and make even a thousand percent on his money, and he could face all bearers of the paper notes.

"What works in a republic can never work in our monarchy, where a variety of causes can undermine such a system," said Saint-Simon. No one was more monarchist than the little duc, nor was there a greater defender of those who needed it least.

"Systems are like rats that pass through twenty holes, only to find the two that will not let them through," he continued. "Of course, I cannot quite understand, I know no maths." And indeed the brilliant little duc was ignorant of the most basic arithmetic.

As usual he warned Law not to make more notes than he could back up with gold and silver. He suspected Law of being a radical and was, of course, correct, for Law would upset the classes long before our Revolution did. Then they began the real purpose of the visit, which was gossip.

"They have let that fellow Arouet out of the Bastille," said Saint-Simon, who, like all courtiers, was a snob by profession. "He is our notary's son, after all, and now he calls himself 'Voltaire.' "

Saint-Simon, who thought all Paris a sewer of depravity and collected tales of the low morals of his times, was about to part with an anecdote when he looked up to see Law's face in such obvious misery that he said nothing.

They sat in two armchairs, leaning forward. Law studied the furniture—sinous and twisty as its owner—and the shiny floor, and did not seem to be listening. He held the parcel on one knee and as he spoke played with the cords. Saint-Simon kept looking, and to annoy him, Law now bounced the parcel from hand to hand.

Saint-Simon was describing the latest escapades of the regent's daughter, for his wife was her lady-in-waiting. The young duchess de Berri had taken on royal pretensions and now went through Paris preceded by cymbals, kettle drums, and trumpets.

"Barring avarice, she is a model of every vice," Saint-Simon said, pausing to make it sound spontaneous. "But what is that in your hand?"

"It is of no consequence now that the regent has refused it." Law lowered his large blue eyes as a woman might, and Saint-Simon understood why, despite his pocked face, the ladies were so taken with him. Suddenly Law rose and unshielded his sword, the very one that had killed a man long ago in London, and cut the cords binding the parcel.

"*Un diamant*? It cannot be!" said the duc.

"No, it is but a model of the exact size. The real diamond is in England now. King George has refused to buy it, as have other monarchs. We could step up and get this treasure, for it is surely . . ." He was about to say "the finest diamond in Europe" when he saw there was no need.

Saint-Simon had placed the model on his shoulder, and was prancing to his mirror, its frame newly painted white and gold. Now he was holding it above his head as though in a crown.

"This is the actual size? It is a plum!" He went to a silver bowl and held it next to a plump Reine Claude plum. "What is the price?"

Law gave a price—4 million livres—that shocked the duc, who knew Law had many grandiose and amusing schemes regarding credit, the Mississippi territories, paper money, tax farming, and such, for the regent had given Law all France with which to gamble.

"I told the agent that was quite impossible. I think we can get it for half," said Law, who knew this to be true.

"Then the regent must buy it for the king"—the king was then seven—"and for all the kings to come! What is its story?"

Law, who also had a gift for stories and romances, told his tale of the stone. Years later, when Saint-Simon wrote his memoirs, he said a worker from the mines had hidden the diamond up his ass and made his way to Europe, where its price was too high for many princes. Then he had a crystal copy made and went to Law, who offered it to the regent. When the regent found it too expensive, Law enlisted Saint-Simon. Of course, this is quite wrong, but it shows what tricks time and invention can play with any tale. Or perhaps Law told it wrong. Law could sell any man anything, and after all had sold the regent an entire system for the finances of France.

"The king of France cannot balk at the price; it does not suit with his greatness," said Saint-Simon, who by now considered the purchase his idea. "The more potentates who refuse it, the more reason for it to remain in France. We must send for the diamond."

"Together we must convince the regent, my friend," said Law, who, in his delight, forgot himself further with this familiarity. "We must go to him."

As he had studied the combination of cards, Law studied the combination of men. He knew Saint-Simon, who had grown up with the regent and was almost his age, could prod the regent to action, if not virtue. All the work he had done on Saint-Simon paid off.

"Yes, *Las*," said Saint-Simon. None of them could ever say his name.

The duc saw him to the head of the stairs. Though the doors were opened wide enough to accommodate both, John Law held back.

Philippe d'Orléans, the regent of France, had a routine that he followed as closely as he could, for one who was immediately bored. He never dined, but took a cup of chocolate at three, when people were permitted to enter. His days were for work and his nights, which began after he visited his mother, were for his only sport, debauch.

First he would go to see Madame at five or six. Madame, chronically discontented, scribbling maniacally, and now a hefty sixty-four, had passed into a stage of almost complete withdrawal. He would kiss her hand and remain standing unless she invited him to sit. Often she forgot. She saw little of herself in any of her children; all her joys were distant in time, in the black forests and little courts of another land.

Then the regent went off into the night to his twelve roués (from whom he kindly excluded Saint-Simon). His unmarked coach could be seen clattering through Paris so fast it shook the lamps on chains stretched above the streets.

The roués always waited for him to begin. The vilest rumors were true— the chorus girls, the actresses from the Comédie Française, the occasional twelve-year-old, preseduced by his valet (for the regent would never force a woman), the clothes removed, the rhymes and lampoons, the bodies heaving in some corner. Masked men, women riding their laps, spankings. Sometimes a laden table rose from the floor filled with his obscene china, its silver surtout reflecting shards of unspeakable scenes as the roués vied to provoke the regent from apathy and shock him with their impiety. The servants set down the food and scurried away before the perilous revels.

The regent enjoyed confusion; he needed things stirred up. Thus the nights when he confused rank and passed his mistresses along to others in these rooms where there was neither rank nor memory.

"Begin the *con-fu-sion!*" he would command in English, giving an impish twist to the last syllable and letting his voice rise as he banged his stick on the floor. His wild wounded eyes would then squint and scout the room for further entertainment.

In the first eighteen months of his reign, the regent had attempted to bring a new order to France. He recalled many sent away for religious reasons and freed those seized for unknown offenses from the Bastille. He joined with England, Holland, and the Holy Roman Empire to check Philip of Spain's attempt to succeed to the French throne if the boy king died. But the Chamber of Justice had not lived up to its name. Servant testified against master, the Bastille was newly restocked, and in weakening Catholic Spain, he had weakened our most natural ally. He had failed already. Industry was stagnant, agriculture poor, and the kingdom in debt for years to come. It was no wonder that Philippe d'Orléans waited for the night.

Law had seen that credit was needed and brought in his scheme of a bank—a private bank now but soon to be a royal bank with paper money. Law then conceived of the great trading companies. That he was a foreigner, a Protestant, a gambler of ill repute, and opposed by Parliament made his success even more remarkable.

The regent allowed Law to issue banknotes and had deposited a million livres with him in the most public way possible. He believed in Law as he believed in few things, with a fervor that only one scoundrel can summon for his like.

They sat together and their eyes would rise for the same passing woman; they played tennis and would laugh at the same time. Thus Law was allowed to invent credit for France while the regent drank and whored till dawn.

In the morning the regent's memories returned one by one. He was like someone touring a large room with his candle. In each corner was a sight best left darkened, a furtive scurrying of trapped squeaking creatures. He recalled random words, clothing fallen, misplaced drunken endearments. Sometimes on this unfortunate prowl through his memory he saw the light eyes of his daughter, the duchess de Berri—he saw her even in undress, for on many nights she joined his impious revels, as all Paris knew.

Every morning he descended into valleys of chagrin. Every night he had to shut things out. It was a blessing that there was no longer any court. When the regent dissolved his court, closing Versailles and Marly and moving to the Palais Royale in Paris, the old ones were without a center. There were no longer the *appartements,* no one dined together anymore. The new ones were in Paris at salons and masked balls, where they could do anything under cover of their black velvet masks.

The regent rushed to sequester himself in the Luxembourg Palace with his daughter and the roués, or in Saint-Cloud as the season allowed, and was lost.

Etiquette now became internalized, a sort of verbal structure. Wit—the quip, the *bon mot*, the cruel thrust and practiced parry—replaced manners. The regent had grown up among all the inbreeding, the sapping and countersapping at the court—thrust, riposte, crack, crack, crack. It had had a hardening effect. Bred for intrigue, forced to marry at seventeen, he had never found his devil, but still looked hard. Louis XIV, suspecting that he was not as bad as he pretended, had called his nephew "a braggart of crimes."

The regent tried to be as bad as he could and see who would still love him.

The duc de Saint-Simon would never lower himself to scheme with John Law, and yet, without stating it, both knew morning was the best time to persuade the regent. When his eyes were weak and the fumes still upon him, the regent would sign anything.

Thus, they duly appeared one morning at the Palais Royale with the model of *le Grand Pitt*. The walls had been painted by the sly Watteau in scenes of *fêtes galantes*. In the Pierrots and Columbines, the cavorting nymphs and satyrs, in the bulging mounds of flesh with draperies clinging in ways that defied the natural properties of cloth, Watteau had commented on the revels of the regent and his daughter, the duchess de Berri. Languid shepherds with hands planted on their hips lounged on the greensward around him. In fact, the regent could not see them very clearly unless he approached closely.

This day the regent had a champagne headache, in which the red bubbles of the previous night had become a thousand needles. Law and Saint-Simon saw the fierceness of his customary squint and his desire to agree to be more quickly rid of anyone in the room.

"That rock again," said the regent, squinting through crimson eyes.

"Sire, Saint-Simon agrees you should buy the diamond for the honor of the crown," said Law.

"You know how I respect my ancestor who promised each man a fowl for his Sunday pot. I won't permit such an extravagance. They would blame me for this."

"You are as frugal as Madame," said Saint-Simon. "Your father, who loved diamonds as no man ever did, would not let this treasure escape."

"Why are you so interested in this English purchase? What is in it for you?"

"Sire, nothing at all," said Saint-Simon. Law did not respond, for he stood to gain £5,000. Nervous of his commission, he was delighted that, with Saint-Simon there, he did not have to speak.

"You are correct to think of your subjects," said Saint-Simon, "but think of the glory they will feel at the sight of such an object stolen out of England. It is reprehensible for a private gentleman to spend money for mere adornment when he owes debts he cannot pay, but for the greatest king of Europe, it is an obligation."

Saint-Simon was almost bouncing on his tiny shoes as he saw the regent stare down at the crystal model. Since the regent was no longer able to distinguish colors, it had a mesmeric effect on him.

"But is it worth the four million?"

"Sire, value depends on rarity, not use. Water is of great use, yet little value . . . diamonds are of little use, yet of great value because the demand for diamonds is much greater than the quantity of them and none is as this," said Law.

It was Governor Pitt who introduced the notion, later to be taken up by John Law, that any object is worth what someone else will pay for it. It was Pitt who induced India to exchange diamonds (that which was almost common to them) for red coral (that which was rare to them). If the value of a thing or currency lies in its perceived value, then paper could be money and coral could be diamonds.

"I will see," said the regent, borrowing his uncle's favorite expression. (His own favorite was *"Divide et impera"*—Divide and conquer—the game he played with the Regency Council, his roués, and his women.)

"No, you cannot let it slip," said Saint-Simon. "Such a chance may not come again, for surely then it will be in Spain with your cousin, or back with King George or the Austrian emperor . . ."

"You might pay some part and pledge some jewels until the debt is paid," said the great financier. "I fancy you might get it for two million . . ."

Rivalry, the spirit of the age, came over the regent and combined with his perpetual inability to say no—he often said "maybe," which was the same thing. He knew all the other monarchs would hear of it. Thus it was almost political to buy the rock.

Czar Peter of Russia, who was coming to the end of his six-week visit to Paris, had only glanced at the crown diamonds displayed before him at the duc de Villeroi's apartments in the Tuileries. He had twitched—a habitual grimace due to a poison given him when he was a boy—and turned aside from all the magnificence. He had refused the gift of a diamond-studded sword and offended the regent. He had turned down the apartments of the queen, finally residing close to the arsenal, where he slept in a field bed in a closet. The czar, who hated luxury, later said decline was inevitable for a people so given to opulence.

Like the regent and many rulers (including the one I know best), the great czar was impatient. If his equipage was not ready, he entered the first carriage he found. Also he was a barbarian, his clothes torn and filthy, without gloves or powder on his hair, reeking with the diseased sweetness of too many nights of revelry.

"It is a symbol of all that France can be again, as in the first days of the Grand Monarch," said Saint-Simon. "It would be a glory for which the regency will long be remembered. Besides how far would two million livres go to relieving the finances? Monsieur *Las* can tell you the expense would hardly be noticed."

Law nodded so hard his wig loosened. The duc de Saint-Simon was like one of those overbred dogs that filled the court. Having latched on to a bone or a silken stocking, it would shake its head and pull, growling happily at whoever was on the other end.

"It is then a fixed idea with you?" said the regent. Saint-Simon could see the regent was becoming bored. Ennui was at once his enemy and his essence.

"The diamond would be called 'the Régent,'" said Law, thinking how he had also named New Orléans for the regent. The regent had seen his schemes for France come to naught; his eight children, even the bastards, were all defective and dissolute. Always before him was the grandeur that preceded him and might follow (though he had some doubts about the boy king). Few of the great diamonds of the crown had names; the Mazarins were known collectively as such. Here was a way to be remembered.

While Saint-Simon was working on the regent—it took several weeks— Law was persuading Pitt by letter that he would never find a buyer at his price and he would lose by having it cut up. Pitt lowered the price from 4 million to 2 million livres, equaling £140,000. He was to be paid £135,000, with £5,000 going to Law.

Thus the old governor, who threatened to disinherit any of his children who gambled, had his diamond sold by the slyest gambler in Europe. On June 6, the regent made his council agree to the purchase as a way of showing their confidence in his finances.

Saint-Simon was proud of himself for forcing this purchase on the regent. The Régent would be the symbol of the regency, one grotesquely big diamond to astonish, shock, and distract the populace. Saint-Simon had said the diamond would be popular with the people of France, and perhaps it was.

Anyway it was a beautiful distraction.

As I wrote this last, I felt the emperor's hand heavy on my shoulder and smelled the eau de cologne with which they rub him every morning as he calls out, "Harder! Harder!" The smell was like mint torn in a summer sun, crushed with bay and something ferrous like gun oil.

"Las Cases, you are so naïve. You cannot ignore the politics of that purchase. James Stanhope, Pitt's son-in-law, was then negotiating with Minister Dubois, and this had been going on for a while. The alliance with England was most important to keep France out of war and confirm the regent's power.

"The first George wanted France to expel the Stuart pretender and dismantle the fortress of Mardyck. The English were afraid that we would ally with Czar Peter and invade the king's homeland, Hanover. Dubois tried to bribe Stanhope with six hundred thousand livres, which he refused. Then he found a better way."

"You mean buying the diamond?" I was truly astonished.

"But of course. It was one of the costs of the Treaty of the Triple Alliance. There is a political reason for everything.

"Also you are wrong respecting Saint-Simon," he continued. "His own account shows him mistaken, for he claims the regent bought the stone uncut, when we know it was cut. Still, I like your fantasy and his much better. You may keep it thus. The little duc was most entertaining. He increased his role in all the events of the court. Yet he was loyal when it counted to Law and the regent. He was steadfast in the most corrupt of times and he was right not to invest with John Law."

PART II

Pitt Parts with His Diamond

FINALLY, GOVERNOR PITT HAD A BUYER FOR THE DIAMOND. Forty thousand pounds was deposited in London as part payment, and Pitt set out for Calais. He traveled with his youngest son, John, who was a captain in the guards and otherwise, as far as his father was concerned, good for nothing, and also Charles Cholmondeley, who had married Essex, his uglier daughter. Robert stayed home.

The governor wore a deep blue velvet coat and fortified himself for the journey with several cases of his best wines. They all rode together in his coach, bouncing over the cold ancient highways, wrapped in furs, the diamond bundled in cotton wool in the heel of his boot, four swords at the ready for the highwaymen they might meet on the slopes. They had a basket of cold meats and wheels of cheeses—Stilton and Colchester cheddar and Portland stone—and breads, which they cut with their pocket knives, and flasks of hard cider.

" 'Tis said the regent has bedded his own daughter," one said.

"They are disgusting in their morals," said the governor. "It is low time and a danger for their little king." They began making jokes about the French.

That first night they stopped at the Crown Inn at Canterbury, where Pitt's second son, Thomas, now Lord Londonderry and a colonel of the dragoons, was quartered with his men. Lacy, the proprietor, was a convivial fellow who had been consul at Lisbon. He was a puffy man much given to strut and wide gestures as though clearing the air around him. He gave the gentlemen a fine dinner—a barrel of plump Deal oysters, roasted meats, and fowls and soups and savories. The governor apologized for not buying the wines of the house, but his own were so much better. To prove it, he invited Lacy to taste of his burgundy. Lacy demurred, Pitt prevailed.

"I wish I could have offered you as good," said Lacy, wiping his hands and bowing a bit, for he knew exactly who was before him.

They drank, and the candles burned down and the fire grew low and broken, and Pitt told Lacy what a fine man he was, and might he do some small service to thank him?

"Ah sir, you own a pebble which might do me the utmost service indeed," Lacy said in all innocence.

"'Tis the end! I'll be waylaid!" the governor shouted.

"Father, it was but a joke," said both his sons, who nonetheless could not help themselves and looked right at the shoe where the diamond was hidden.

"This whore's son will murder me! 'Tis what I feared all along."

He stood, overturning the table, and was about to draw his sword. Here, finally, was the ghost who had followed him from the Coromandel Coast through the black streets of London and onto the roads at dusk, when he was far from his big houses. The governor still turned from those who would not remove their gloves, knowing they had been branded with the thief's *T* on their right thumb. He had given this fear a form—it was the Moor who sprung from the crowd and flung himself in his path so the outriders and soldiers, the drummers and bugle blowers and stanchion bearers all were halted. His cohort burst forth with his scimitar and Pitt's head rolled in the red dust. Now an English innkeeper had come for him. . . .

Lacy was backing away, then running toward the kitchen, and the dragoons were charging forward. There was great bedlam and rushing about all over the inn, and barking dogs. Then came red faces and apologies and excuses for attacks of nerves. The sons assured the old man that if he told no one, no one would know he had the diamond on him then.

That night, Pitt's gout flared up so he could barely mount the carriage the next day. After an ample breakfast of cold turkey pie, red herring, wine, and anchovies, from which Lacy absented himself, Pitt insisted on an escort for the rest of the journey.

Thomas's officers and their servants trotted alongside the dragoons, splendid with their red costumes frogged and braided, so that a small army headed for Calais. The governor had insisted Lacy come along so he would not spread any news of the diamond.

They stopped at Dover and the governor paid for a great meal—the sole of the region and new potatoes with cream and bottles of fine white burgundy—after which they were so mellow that all agreed to go along to Calais.

Pitt has written it that on the boat to Calais he almost decided to keep the diamond. Though it had worried him for fifteen years, it also defined him. It was the accidental thing that made him extraordinary. He had made a city out of Fort Saint George and could have ruled Jamaica, but he had come to like being Diamond Pitt. How could he be that without his diamond?

In those days oddities and curiosities were kept in the curio cabinets of castles and great houses all over Scotland and England. There was no end to the peculiar things men kept under glass to stare at: bird nests, idols, mosses, freak creatures, tusks and shrunken heads, ancient instruments and coins, wax puppets in nuns' habits, mummies, stuffed birds, and unidentifiable rodents. There were wax Cleopatras, earth and celestial globes, locks, watches, hard plaid boxes carefully and obsessively accumulated. None could dispute Pitt's oddity—its fame and peculiar infamy. He had adopted this freak, shaped and lived in agony with it. He had grown to love this fabulous mistake of the earth. Pitt knew it was a source of money, and it was beautiful. At the same time, if it were a cursed thing, to get rid of it and redeem the expenses it had caused him might bring about a healing in his family. Somewhere on the channel crossing the fear suddenly left him, for the stone was no longer his and he need not care. He surrendered it then in his mind. He had little doubt that Laurent Rondé, the French crown jeweler, would approve the diamond, though he hated the idea of selling it to the French, the enemy of his country for so long.

The governor held the Great Pitt in his hand at the rail of the tossing boat, and the sun danced within it. He began to see the chalk cliffs and the red roofs of the port of Calais. No matter how long he held the diamond, it never grew warm.

Often there are two stories from the same event; sometimes I have found three and even more. I have come to think of them as assorted versions of one truth, or many possibles, of which one is most probable. Some say Laurent Rondé went to London and met up with the diamond there. No, he waited at Calais for Pitt and his group to walk over the dunes.

The governor and Rondé met in a stone house. The windows were open and the gulls were shrieking. Pitt took a last look at his diamond in the pale yellow light with a smell of apples and port in the air.

Laurent Rondé was everything Pitt hated in a Frenchman, and Pitt hated everything French. Rondé was an artiste and a courtier, now released from his usual twisty habits of flattery and obeisance, free to make trouble if he chose. He was flounced and curled and puffed with incipient nastiness. A pleasant manner covered him like a crust. He fluttered and his tiers of laces caught up.

"It is too much small-air than I expected," he said, bending over the stone and trying to control himself at its beauty. "And I zee a speck. *Une petite glace dans le filetis et une autre à un coin dans le dessous.*"

"What is the damned frog saying?" said the governor.

"A speck!"

"*Non,*" said Lord Londonderry, who had been educated in and spoke a tolerable French, but with the usually atrocious and cavalier English accent and many mistakes. "*De toutes les pierres princières il a un blancheur éclat et une beauté de forme unique . . .*"

"There are two little flaws—one hidden in the mounting and from the *filetis,*" said Rondé. His lips, painted a deep rose, curtsied in disapproval as his jowls danced with emotion.

"*Filetis? Quoi?*" said Captain John Pitt, a terrible rogue and libertine who welched on his debts and once stole all the rents from one of the governor's estates by sweeping them into his hat with his sword.

"*La ligne exterieure de la table qui forme la centre de la partie supérieure du diamant . . .*"

"Bullshit! Enough of that!" said the governor.

Lord Londonderry circled round behind Rondé and pressed his palm with a large packet of banknotes. Pitt had spent his Indian years shaking a full hand with other men; now he saw his son doing it. That made two bribes to get rid of the diamond.

Rondé went to the window for the natural light all gem dealers want, and the stone shone hard. Then Rondé gave over four packets of crown jewels as security for the rest of the money, and the Great Pitt became the Régent.

Governor Pitt received one-third of the money, and the remaining sum was to be paid in four payments every six months, with five percent interest. For security he would have the four parcels of crown jewels—one to be surrendered at each payment. Rondé gave Pitt a bracelet with diamonds worth 8,819 livres as a bonus for the expenses of his journey. Pitt had no one to give it to.

The regent could not let Czar Peter return to Russia without giving him one of his little suppers. The giant czar went incognito as Bombardier Peter Mikhailov, the name he had assumed years before when he traveled through Europe. Then he had collected engineering and naval information and learned Western ways. When he returned to Russia he cut off his boyars' beards and their long sleeves, which were always dipping in the soup. He also cut off about eight hundred heads.

The regent and his roués and the czar and his retinue had this in common—they all knew how to get paralytically drunk and had the rusty faces to prove it. The czar, like the regent, could not get rid of people to whom he was accustomed; both needed their teams to get them through the night. They knew how surprisingly small were royal worlds and the number within them whom they could trust. This is why the regent's boyhood tutor, Abbé Dubois, was the first minister and ran the kingdom.

In public, at their audience, the czar and the regent had both sat in armchairs. The regent made a deep bow, which the czar returned with a nod. Czar Peter had picked up and embraced the little king, hugging him so hard that both the smelly czar and the little boy had tears come to their eyes. (A year later the czar would have to put his own son Alexis to death.)

This night the "bombardier" was wearing his new French wig that had come out too curly and long and had been trimmed and recoiffed into the short bowl style he favored. His suit was barracan; he wore a wide belt with a sword and no cuffs on his shirt. He had washed for the occasion since he was to be presented to the courtesan known as La Fillon, whose fame had traveled even to the court of Saint Petersburg, the city that he built.

In a caravan of unmarked coaches they went to La Fillon's *hôtel particulier*, which was done up in the modern taste—rococo, mirrors, pastel colors, much white and gold, with rounded commodes by Charles Cressent, encrusted with gilt bronze. Everything flowed with the swollen curved lines borrowed from nature. Obliging beauties met them at the entrance. The czar had never seen anyone so blond as La Fillon. At over six feet, she stood almost as tall as he, with the oddly incongruous proportions of ancient statues and skin that shone like a sea pearl. A haze of beauty surrounded her so that it was hard to see whether she generated it or just lived contained within it. Pale thick hair fell in loose curls over her magnificent bosom, then continued to her knees, covering her like a mantle. She had a small straight nose and eyes of clear emerald that were slanted up and set wide apart. The czar immediately forgot that during the six weeks of his visit he had pretended to know little French and gone about with an interpreter. He suddenly found fluency as La Fillon led the rulers through her establishment.

La Fillon, who projected a strange young purity, was the regent's trusted spy, with a key to his apartments in the Palais Royale. Whenever she liked she might enter to whisper to him her information, facts she also shared with Abbé Dubois and the policeman d'Argenson.

The regent, who collected paintings and was an artist of some talent, had set aside a room in the house of La Fillon that he turned into a grotto. It was lit only by some small rays of sun, which fell upon a bed of rush matting. Here La Fillon would stretch herself out on the rush mats, covered only with her magnificent hair, and the regent might contemplate her for hours. Sometimes the hair was known to slip a bit. At night candelabra would do the work of the sun. Now the regent, whose face had grown even darker, prevailed on La Fillon to accompany him to the secret chamber. The czar protested, but the regent urged him to be patient. Czar Peter of Russia waited at the door to the chamber. The regent himself lit all the tapers in the room as La Fillon disrobed completely. The regent arranged her in a classical pose and lifted the two ropes of hair, baring her breasts. His heart beat painfully and he puffed a bit.

"One more thing, mademoiselle," said the regent, drawing closer still. Into the blond curls of La Fillon's small pink sex he placed the Régent diamond, and there it rested in its thick warm bed. The regent could scarcely breathe. La Fillon, looking down, marveled and laughed gently.

"Do not move," said the regent. He went to fetch the "bombardier," who was waiting most impatiently in the corridor. It is not known but must be imagined what the reaction was when the czar of all Russia first saw the stone in its moist furry bed.

It is known that Czar Peter the Great of Russia bought the secondary stones that had been cut from the Régent for £10,000 sterling. Some said the rose-cut diamonds from the cleaved material were sold to him by the Jew Abraham Nathan. It was not a hard sale to make.

It was the regent's habit to laugh at scandal. In his time trifles became important, and important matters like war and starvation and marital fidelity became trifles. Since he was impious himself, and timed his orgies for the holiest days of the year, he respected impiety in others. This did not prevent him from sending Voltaire to the Bastille for some impious verses. Voltaire claimed he did not write them; others said he certainly did.

When Voltaire was released, his play *Oedipe*, written when he was nineteen, was presented, with Voltaire as one of the actors. To show he was above it all, the regent, accused of incest in the pamphlets of the time, attended.

"Soon shall thy conscious soul with horror feel / The weight of guilt," said Voltaire playing the high Priest and looking right at the regent sitting with his daughter.

The duchess de Berri had been the regent's favorite child since she was seven and sick with the pox, and he had saved her. With a mistrust of doctors inherited from Madame, he had sent them all away and cared for his daughter himself. When she recovered, it was as if he had created her himself. He permitted her everything, so she appeared under a canopy at the theater and received the Venetian ambassador seated on a platform and went about without stays. As Duclos wrote, the regency was a time when one could regulate one's rights on one's pretensions.

Louis XIV had forced the young duchess to travel when she was with child. Though she had gone by boat to avoid the rough roads, the boat had capsized and she lost the child a few days after it was born. Then she had lost another child, and, like the regent, she came to live for compensations.

Six nights a week the duchess would eat from eight in the evening until three in the morning and gamble and carouse at the little suppers. She was his Venus the night they played "The Judgment of Paris," when one mistress was Juno and another was Minerva and they were all undressed and the Duchess placed the Régent diamond in her hair. She lived with 800 servants and was known to have given a ball with 31 soups and 130 desserts, with 200 valets to serve and 132 to pour the wines. The regent saw her almost every day and never condemned her, for she was part of the ungovernable luxury cultivated in his times.

When the performance of *Oedipe* was finished, the regent had Voltaire come to the royal box. The regent congratulated him and, always liberal with writers and artists, gave him a pension. He liked the way the young man looked. He had one of those strong French noses more than once inter-rupted by bumps and the big swollen brow of genius (I have seen it in the emperor), nobby and vast as though the brains were battering the brow bone with their vigor. All descended to a valley of a deeply dimpled chin.

The comte de Nocé, chief of the roués, had first brought Voltaire, fresh from the Bastille, to the Palais Royale to present him to the regent. While he was in the antechamber a ferocious thunderstorm had begun.

"Things could scarcely be worse up there if they had a regent to govern them," said Voltaire.

Nocé repeated this to the regent, who forgave all for wit, and probably would have done so even if this were not the age of wit. The regent had a good laugh and paid Voltaire a sum.

"I owe Your Royal Highness my warm thanks for your board," Voltaire said, "but no more of your lodging, if you please!"

The regent had seen some of Voltaire's *Henriade*, which dealt with the loves and conquests of the Protestant Henry IV, the regent's only hero, who said, "Paris is well worth a mass," issued the Edict of Nantes, and loved so many women. The regent admired the play's daring, too.

The little king fell out of bed in August 1717. A valet saw him falling and threw himself on the ground so the king might fall on him. Instead, the seven-year-old Louis XV crawled under the bed and would not speak. He did this to frighten his attendants. He felt he was too closely watched, with his governor, the duc de Villeroi, always there locking up his food and his clothes and never letting him be alone, even with his great-uncle the regent.

Shortly after this incident, the regent decided to show the diamond to the boy king. The regent walked through the long hall where servants were cleaning up carnage. The famous mirrors where the court had preened were smeared with blood and feathers to which clung broken beaks and claws in a kind of vile paste. Little birds, dead and fatally wounded, were underfoot so that the regent had to step carefully to avoid crunching the bodies on the Savoneries. The hawks and falcons, hooded again, had been removed. The pages were carrying out trays and sacks of sparrows, their broken necks dripping over the trays, their torn bodies stiff, claws frozen up in the air in the death salute. Some were still faintly heaving.

The regent's soft shoes trod on a bird. He drew back and wiped his sole with a fine cambric cloth bordered in Spanish lace, then threw it on the floor.

The duchesse de la Ferté, the boy's godmother, had devised this sport to harden the boy and teach him a king's cruelty. The king would be led in to stand at the very end of the hall of mirrors filled with a thousand panicked sparrows when the hawks were released among them.

"They have no escape," said the little king, who rarely spoke at all, the first time he saw this spectacle.

On either side of the king stood the ancient duc de Villeroi and the duchess de la Ferté, their hands on his shoulders as the hawks tore the sparrows to pieces. The duchess's soft hearted sister, Madame de Ventadour, excused herself. The boy wanted to follow her from the room but the duc pressed down and held his shoulder fast.

The next time, the boy made no response.

The boy king liked to milk a dwarf cow and make soup and chocolate and marzipan at La Muette. In a few years, he would have brief enthusiasms for cards and then shooting. He had a tame white doe that he fed from his hand. One day for no reason he shot the doe and wounded it. Still it crawled to him and tried to lick his hand. The little king—soon to be called Louis the Beloved—had the doe taken back and shot it again.

The regent might have recognized himself in the boy. Being bored or pretending to be bored was a defense to avert disappointment. The king was silent because he preferred not to speak. He had been conceived in a year of famine, 1709. His mother had been the antic Marie-Adelaide, legs in the air, grooms holding her ankles while she shrieked with laughter in the moonlight. His father too had loved games, playing battledore and shuttlecock even as Lille had fallen. He was more than an orphan—father, mother, older brother all dead of the measles when he was two. The court at Versailles and the king's household were gone, Marly closed, the card tables abandoned, the nobles dispersed or in Paris. The little king had only just moved back to Versailles.

A month before the boy had revoked his great-grandfather's edict that had made Louis XIV's bastards princes of the blood and gave them power alongside the regent. He had arrested the duc and duchess du Maine, who had plotted against the regent. He was learning.

On the afternoon of the dead birds the regent had placed the diamond in his pocket. He brought it forth.

"For your crown, my master, *Ludovicus Quintus Decimus, rex Franciae et Navarrae*," said the regent, in that mocking way of his.

The boy took it from his palm and turned it round.

"*Oncle*, will you tell me the secret of the man in the mask?" He said this every time he saw the regent.*

"Not until your majority." This was the game they played. It alone seemed to animate the boy, who otherwise was so taciturn as to seem mostly absent.

"We will give the diamond to Sieur Rondé for the crown when the time comes."

The boy yawned. His eyes were dull again. His abnormally long lashes made his eyes look like a drawing of stars. The birds had fatigued him. A small brown feather was lodged in his fine blond curls. The regent did not point this out.

"It is not a toy," the regent said and put the stone in his pocket.

His governor, the duc de Villeroi, rushed in, very upset that the boy had spent thirty seconds alone with the regent, still infamous as a poisoner. With him was a band of boys, among them Villeroi's grandsons, who were all wearing a blue-and-white ribbon round their necks. An enameled oval hung from the ribbons showing a star and a tent representing the pavilion on the terrace where the boys played their games. When the king played toy soldiers, he played with these young costumed and sashed noblemen.

The little king had a trick of lopping off the top of his soft-boiled egg with a knife. He was remarkably quick and deft.

"Long live the king!" his little friends shouted every time he did this magic. This caused Louis XV to continue this performance long after he was grown.

The emperor has said of the Bourbons, "Talleyrand was right when he said they have learned nothing and forgotten nothing."

---

*The French court was, as always, full of secrets, alliances and mésalliances, calumny, those in favor, those in disgrace, but all, always, observed by the universal eye. Only one secret had been kept—that of the man in the mask held in the Bastille, guarded by two musketeers, who had orders to kill him if he removed his velvet mask. He was beautifully formed, with a charming voice and very devout. Madame said he was an English lord who had been involved with the natural son of King James in intrigues against King William and he wore the mask so the king would never know what had become of him.

The regent, true to his word, did not tell Louis XV the secret of the man in the velvet mask until the day before his majority. He would not tell him even one day before. Louis XVI did not tell Marie-Antoinette despite her wiles. The regent did tell the duchess de Berri, who told her lover, the duc de Richelieu, the beau of his age, who, as an old man, told the world that the man in the mask was the twin brother of Louis XIV, younger by eight hours. (The emperor and I do not believe this.)

The Seventh Fairy Reappears

I REMEMBER WHAT THE EMPEROR HAS SAID ABOUT NATURAL progression, how beings and things must eventually come to ruin, and so when I imagine John Law's carriage, now trimmed with velvet and heavy gold fringe, leaving Place Louis-le-Grand with troops clattering ahead, I know what lurks around the corner like the gargoyle crouched on the parapet. I fear for the Scot, who, denying probability, allowed himself to bask in happiness, even to stick his head outside the coach and let the gold fringe drip summer rain on his handsome scarred face.

Paris was full and rushed in 1719, two years after the diamond entered France. Strangers from England, the Low Countries, and the German states fought for seats on coaches into the city and slept in kitchens and attics, for they thought Paris would make them rich.

Law saw young boys carrying travelers on their backs across the mud. People crossed on small wooden bridges that the bridge men wheeled out. They crept along, arms out, hugging the buildings, or they slipped and fell, were run over, and carried to the morgue. Law's carriage went so fast he could not hear what the scissors grinders and water carriers were asking that week. And everyone watched him, always. If he smiled, they bought shares in the Mississippi Company, and if he seemed distracted, they sold. When he walked into a drawing room, something he rarely did anymore, lorgnettes were raised and bodies began to slide toward him as though the whole room had been upended.

The silver-trimmed tricorns of the archers rose above the crowd, prodding along the usual dregs—vagrants and criminals, the refuse of the hospitals and prisons, women who had only themselves to sell. To Law's displeasure even they, the most abject citizens, did not want to go to his new world. It did not matter to them that he had created duchies and earldoms and marquisates out of air in Louisiana and made himself the duke of Arkansas.

He passed the Bois de Boulogne, where a tribe of Indians imported from Missouri hunted stag. At night they danced at the Italian theater and the regent went to see them. Paris was in love with the exotics, with their beads and skins and hard black hair. Their princess had married a French soldier and been baptized at Notre Dame (that did not prevent her tribe from murdering all the French when the Indians returned home).

Law held these Mississippi lands that were many times the size of the kingdom of France. He funded the national debt of the kingdom and lent money to the crown, and even to the king of England, that country which had condemned him to death. He controlled the mint and the right of coinage, all public finances, the sea trade, tobacco and salt revenues. He was the first foreigner we let in that way before the emperor.

His bank was a royal bank now; he had profited mightily, but lost some control. His paper money was everywhere, not always backed by gold and silver.

At eight every morning guards beat drums and lowered the barricades at Rue Quincampoix. Then the princes and ducs, the comtes and marquises charged from one end of the street to meet their valets, the friars and shopkeepers, and doctors in wide hats rushing from the other end. Women hoisted light silk dresses and stained their little slippers rushing through dirt to their ankles in the foul narrow street. Elbows flying, full of the new drink, coffee, they traded shares right out in the street, with no rules to govern them. Such a din! And the smell of the geese being cooked from Rue des Ours!

This was where the Revolution began, for the ducs stepped down from their carriages, and the regent himself, a son of France, traded and profited. Common people bought our disguises—the clothes heavy with gold and silver thread, the carriages, jewels, opera seats, and footmen in livery with crests never seen before. They hired genealogists and bought titles. They stroked new satinwood surfaces of chests by Boulle and Cressent, hung fresh Gobelins on the wall, walked over bright Aubussons and Savoneries on newly laid floors. Years of gaming had trained everyone's avarice until nothing was enough. Eighty horses, ninety servants, an instant château. Any mystery we had perished, for it was only money and a carapace of behavior. Do not think they got it right, however. They fooled only themselves and others like them. Meanwhile the princes behaved badly, for they rode off with wagons of gold. For now, why revolt when everyone could make a joke?

There was a new word for this new class, "millionaire." Law was one, and the regent many times over. The diamond itself had even been called "the Millionaire": it *was* the regency—an exaggeration of an exaggeration, a big show hiding its flaws. At just this point, on June 14, 1719, it was officially added to the crown jewels. The regent, already bored with the diamond, had tossed it to Villeroi to keep with the other crown jewels.

At last, the regent had his *"con-fu-sion,"* for these sudden fortunes upset our order; rich and poor nudged closer too quickly in the nervous city. In the cafés, the traders and foreigners played quadrille and talked and talked, for conversation, rococo and rehearsed, was the art of that time. They talked in languages, they talked in teams. One fed the other the line that led to the quip. Would it survive to be repeated? Outside a humpback bent over and rented himself as a desk on which to write Mississippi shares. Then at five, the drums again; the rails were raised. Some couldn't leave even then and took apartments in the street. Interest rates were one and a half percent. Everyone borrowed to invest, and shares rose ten points every day. Some made a thousand percent on their money, and everywhere there was hectic laughter. As Duclos wrote, "It would be hard today to make people understand the frenzy which possessed all minds. There are follies that are proper only when they are epidemic."

"It was the same during the Revolution," the emperor says. "And I suppose they had that frenzy for me . . . My soldiers did, and some still do."

"Surely so. You were their great long love affair," I said.

"With the required ending."

"And never the forgetting," I wanted to say, but did not.

On one particular Tuesday, John Law, who was not quite so handsome now, rushed in to the duc de Saint-Simon, who was sipping a cup of chocolate. Their Tuesday visits had continued, and now they spoke to each other with a confidence ensured by the fact that Saint-Simon had saved Law's life the previous year when Parliament was about to hang him as a foreign meddler. Saint-Simon had advised Law to hide in the Palais Royale. He had seen the great man break. Law had cried from fear in this very house.

Law had come back, for, like every outsider, he longed to belong to the greatest kingdom in Europe now that England was bankrupt. He wanted his son to dance in a ballet with the little king. He wanted duchesses to court Katharine, the Englishwoman who posed as his wife. He bought the Duchy of Mercoure and would buy twenty estates, more land and jewels, and a library of forty-five thousand books.

This was the summer of long lines and blind faith. The shares were 1,000 livres in July, 5,000 in September, 10,000 in November, even 20,000 in December and January—fifty times what they had been. Such was Law's glorious *système*—a revolt without blood, made out of paper.

Architects widened doors for the panniers the women wore, beauty spots covered the face and the next day were banished. Gilt bronze crawled up the legs of the furniture and almost completely took it over, invading, encrusting the shiny woods and laquers. The ladies flew along in loose dresses without bodices, noses dirty from snuff, with their hair high as their upstretched arms, then short and curled and lightly powdered. Madame, heavy as an old dog, did not understand what she was seeing.

Every week, Law told the little duc stories Saint-Simon had already heard many times—of the duchess who kissed his hand for Mississippi shares and the lady who had her carriage overturned in front of Law just so she might meet him. Crawling from the wreckage, her wig awry, she had given him her arm, the torn silk hanging from it, and begged him for shares. Another lady who passed in front of the house where Law was dining had her coachman call "Fire!" so he might come rushing out. They forced his door, climbed through the windows of the Hôtel de Soisson from the garden. They fell down his chimney into his study.

Princes and officers and clergy lined his antechamber, studying allegories of Judgment and Wealth in the alcoves, waiting as though it were the old court, for he was now a kind of king. They waited and would not leave even as the day turned to frantic evening. When Law opened the door even ever so slightly, he felt the push of bodies against it, and the rustle of heavy new Lyons silks and the rush of scents and rare perfumes and desperation came in at him.

It irked Law that the whole nation wanted shares and still the little duc, the man who saw him every Tuesday (though now for only an hour), alone held out. Sitting on the railing of the orangerie leading to the Bois des Goulottes at Saint-Cloud, swinging his red heels, the regent himself had urged Saint-Simon to accept shares from Law.

"You are a fool," Law said.

"Since King Midas, I haven't heard of anyone who was able to touch what he turned into gold," said Saint-Simon. Still the regent increased his allowance.

Before the regent had bought the diamond, he had vanquished his enemies, disciplined Parliament, thwarted Spain, and found his way to Law and his system. We know of his triumphs. How long can pleasure last?

The regent's daughter, the duchess de Berri, who had lost her two babies, was busy eating herself to death every night. She stuffed herself with pâté, melons, figs, hams, sausages, iced beer, cakes, and pastries. She ate until dawn, walked a bit in her loose dresses, devoured a huge breakfast, then went to bed and screamed when the bedclothes touched her swollen feet. Her household wore white livery, and white horses pulled her coaches as though they were bearing an angel. She was bled in her feet, then defied the doctors and shut herself in her apartments, where she ate more melons and figs and milk and all that was forbidden her. Her feet filled with water, then she seemed to burst and was wasting. The regent sat by her side during her fevers, and this time could not bring her back from death. She was in the Luxembourg Palace, the walls of which Watteau had painted, and she died among his *fêtes champêtres* and *fêtes galantes* and all the wood nymphs pursued by cupids into forests she would never see again. She was twenty-three years old, and her life had been so wicked no one would say a funeral oration for her.

In 1719 Law was still in his glory. The regent could not sleep from grief. The wits filled the cafés. The kingdom bought shares and spent. Across the seas was the wild land where no one wanted to go.

Then in September, eighty newlywed couples, chained to each other behind their backs, were paraded through the streets of Paris and held at La Rochelle for transport. The girls of fifteen had been forced to marry criminals. Law, who knew probability, did not know our native temperament, our dislike of strange wild lands, our needs for the pleasures of home, the crusty breads, the *saucissons,* the deep wines, the ripe cheese running fat rivers across the faience plate in the late afternoon sun. (How I, too, in my exile, miss all this!) And our need not to be meddled with.

In January, Law was made controller general of the finances of France, and shares were at their highest, but the calendar had flipped into 1720, a year of disaster. The air was filled with the winds of infection. Those dead from measles, smallpox, and purple fever were carried through the streets, and the children who were to have danced in the king's ballet were sick as well. Among them was Law's son. The little king was bored with the ballet anyway.

Another one hundred girls scratched and bit the archers who held them at La Rochelle for transport. The archers fired on them, killing twelve. As the news spread many people turned on Law.

In November of that year, the investors began taking profits, and large amounts of stock were on the market. Prices for land and houses, meat and butter rose. The people could not buy their bread. Since their money changed in value week to week, they had to repay debts in currency worth half, and families were ruined.

Law became morose and anxious. The marks of the pox had eaten deeper into his face, which seemed to be slipping off its bones. Now, like the regent, he could not sleep. He had outbursts of temper and took the wrong measures. Duclos later wrote that never was a more frantic tyranny exercised by a hand less firm. Law, who had sold the biggest diamond in France, outlawed the wearing of diamonds and precious stones without written permission. Everyone had to use paper money, and many hid their coins. In came the soldiers tearing up floors and ripping out walls. The archers grabbed people from the streets. The crowd shook their fists as Law rode by protected by a regiment of Swiss guards.

A mood of lawlessness spread through Paris. Torch boys lit the fearful through the streets as bodies were tossed into the Seine. There were kidnappings and robberies and even princes committed crimes. Now Rue Quincampoix was loathsome to Law. After years of secret police, knocks at the door, mockery shielding misery, willy-nilly laws, it was our nature to resist.

The regent's contempt was an infection that spread. Banter entered the Council of the Regency, where the little king sat stroking his cat. The old etiquette, based on the most refined civility, was replaced by coarsened manners, lampoons of the sacred, cruelty. Out of all this arose a group of young men, the *Méchants*. They staged kisses with women who wore the painted faces of famous women under their masks. And then the mask would slip, compromising their victims.

Finally the Bourse was ruined. Parliament called Law corrupt and said he deserved death. Shares fell, and there was a run on the bank. Shopkeepers did not want paper, only coin.

The tortured regent refused to admit Law publicly to the Palais Royale, but snuck him in a side door. That was the essence of the regent's character, a fatal confusion—for, three days later, Law sat in his opera box.

One night in July, fifteen thousand desperate souls were lined up waiting for Law's bank to open, and sixteen were pressed to death in the crush. Men fired shots to advance in line. They mounted the garden wall. The mob went to the Louvre to show the little king the body of a woman who had been killed, while others went to the Palais Royale to show the regent. The mob tore apart Law's carriage, broke his coachman's leg, stoned his daughter.

"I want to know who is wearing the diamond all this time," said the emperor. He was cutting a sliver off a pear, for he never ate a whole fruit.

"I do not think anyone was wearing it," I replied.

"Then how can this disaster be blamed on the diamond? Or was it merely contact with the stone that cursed them both?"

By then I had begun to wonder if an object can change its owner as the owner can change an object. Surely, there is some transference between the two. Does the fetish partake of the deity it adorns? Would the diamond, while itself transformed, have the power to alter its owner, to cast its spell for generations?

My son, Emmanuel, was outside the window playing ball with one of the servants. I heard the seabirds shriek as Grand Marshal Bertrand rode up the path and applied the smile he would need to enter Longwood.

In October 1720 an edict closed the *système*. The regent had stuck with Law as long as a weak ruler could. Now there were poems and impromptus for them both; for no people are so fierce as ours when our betrayed love becomes hate. Law went out incognito, in unmarked or royal carriages with guards. The regent rose later and signed anything. The Mississippi million-aires were all persecuted and taxed with huge fines.

Then plague came off the ships from the east—first to Marseilles, then Aix-les-Bains, then Toulon. The fourteenth-century Black Death was reborn. Doctors walked the streets covered with oiled silk, wearing high wooden shoes as the miasmata, "the pestilence which walketh by noonday," seeped around them. Galley slaves, called "crows," threw bodies into the tumbrils and buried the dead. And as they had danced at the opera balls in Paris, now there was an "outburst" of sensuality. The plague was in Avignon and then, despite the cor-don, in Paris, and a hundred thousand poor souls died.

John Law went away in the night and his old companion, luck, did not go with him. Nor could his wife and children. He took with him only one small diamond. The regent broke his promises to Law, who never got his money out of France. When Law fled to Brussels in December, bread was 4 or 5 sous, and the next year a single gold louis bought a share of stock that had sold for 20,000 livres. He had the particular hell of knowing that it was not the *système,* but the abuses of it—printing too much paper, the greed of the nobles—that ruined him.

Law had stayed too long at the tables. He lost £600,000 to Thomas Pitt's son Lord Londonderry. Law could not pay, and his banker had to go out of business when Law left Paris. Then Law was back in England, seen at court, wandering the drawing rooms wherever the stakes were high. Wher-ever he wandered, he wandered alone.

Five million people lost money in the *système* and the attempts to correct it that followed. Still the masked balls and the demented gaiety continued, for the kingdom was possessed. At this time, the regent said of himself and of his minister Dubois, "Rotten kingdom! Well governed by a drunkard and a pander!"

As bodies burned in the autos-da-fé in Spain, John Law played his last games in Venice, his lace cuffs a bit stained and yellowed now. In his palazzo crowded with hundreds of Titians and Raphaels, paintings by Leonardo da Vinci and Michelangelo, Tintoretto, Poussin, Veronese, and Holbein, John Law died of distemper in 1729. He had been obliged to pawn the one dia-mond he had taken with him when he fled France. The regent and Saint-Simon had abandoned him. He had sold the Régent and lost his reputation, his family, and his fortune.

He had never seen the great diamond worn for a state occasion.

"Really, Las Cases, how could you know that about his lace cuffs? Too much about cuffs anyway," says the emperor, returning with Grand Marshal Bertrand. "You must stay with the facts to serve your history."

Bertrand was enjoying this scolding.

I dared not answer the emperor or remind him he had instructed me to invent. If I had descended below the dignity of history, it was in service of a tale, just as he had urged me.

Later, I came upon Bertrand, Gourgaud, and Montholon. They were standing in a cluster, fanning themselves with their hats, and they fell silent as I passed by.

"To what history was the emperor referring?" Bertrand asked.

"A little diversion I am attempting on the Régent diamond."

"That thing in his sword?" Gourgaud asked.

"It has seen much of our past," I said.

"You are better served writing about the emperor. Is he not enough for you?" said Bertrand.

Soon after, I heard laughing, and one of them, I think Montholon, said, "How typical of the Jesuit!"

"Monsieur Rapture, you mean," said Gourgaud. (I believe they call me this because it is my nature to admire things with effusion.)

It became clear on the *Bellerophon* that the generals will always think of me as an intruder. If the emperor was the good Other, all that was above us, I was the bad Other, stepped out of another court, one in which a thing like the ancient diamond might matter. To them I was forever a traitor to the Revolution, tainted by the king who had honored me long before the emperor.

Though, at forty-nine, I am the oldest here (the emperor is forty-six, Bertrand forty-two, Montholon and Gourgaud only thirty-two), they cannot respect me, for my battles were not their battles. They will never forgive the fact I was born as I was. Nor will they forgive the two months I spent alone with the emperor in the summerhouse at the Briars.

Both General Montholon and Gourgaud, who hate each other, have turned on me. Their hatred of me is all that unites them, for after three months at Longwood, Gourgaud wanted to duel Montholon.

"Be brothers," the emperor had said then. "You are here to soothe me, not provoke further excitements." That day he was so sick he lay flat on the floor with Dimanche's head on his heaving stomach.

We are all on top of one another here except Bertrand, who lives down at Hutt's Gate with the sullen Fanny, a cousin of Josephine's, who keeps her distance from the emperor.

The emperor wanted us to be like his family, and that we are, with all the jealousies, the petty nastiness, and discord of the Bonapartes.

I heard a small moan from one of the rooms just now. It could have been almost anyone, or else the ceaseless wind.

The Distraction

LOUIS XV LIKED TO SEE THE DIAMOND'S EFFECT, FOR IT DREW some of the attention from him and he had always been scrutinized. When he was seven, he had been made to walk naked in front of the entire court—women and men, princes and princesses, doctors and apothecaries, any of whom might touch and examine him to see that he was whole and well formed and male. No one did touch him, however, and all sank down before him.

I have seen portraits of him as a boy—the overly large eyes outlined by heavy long lashes, the square face with its bud mouth (in which lurked the promise of a sensuality that was more than fulfilled), the dimpled chin, long full shiny curls. Over all a solemn regard. Madame says he changed color too frequently, perhaps meaning he had not yet adapted the mask of kings. He was then given to striking those who opposed him. Sometimes he bit.

Louis XV was not heartless so much as without a whole heart. As a child he had been spoiled and deprived, and the effects of both were upon him. He was raised in the central paradox of kings: told he was the emanation of God, but smart enough to know he was not.

All was known, even that he was but eleven when he had his first nocturnal emission and became in theory a man. He was watched without mercy or respite, as all the kings had been. Later, he hoarded his secrets like jewels.

In that year of 1721, when he was eleven, Mehemet Effendi, an ambassador from Sultan Ahmed of Turkey, came to France to visit the regent.

When *The Arabian Nights* first became known in our country, people began to read about the Great Mogul, Asia, and the Indies, the lands where diamonds were found. They read of harems and seraglios and high-voiced eunuchs, the courts of the East, and the prophet Mohammed. They had themselves painted as lounging sultanas in *Turqueries,* for it was an accepted way to show bare flesh. It was then that Montesquieu, hiding under anonymity, wrote *The Persian Letters,* the story of a Persian noble traveling in regency France.

The book appeared just when Mehemet Effendi, an object of great wonder, arrived. Such crowds had lined the riverbanks to see the ambassador as he sailed to Toulouse that some fell in the water and drowned, and others suffocated in the throngs. The courtyards of the hotels were filled at three in the morning as they awaited sight of him in his loose, billowy pants, the high wrapped turban, and slippers that flipped up at the toes as if he was rocking backward. In the winter, as Mehemet Effendi and his entourage rattled over the roads from Toulon to Paris, their wagons breaking down so that they had to abandon their luggage, they were met by a splendid delegation in feathered hats and embroidered coats. This band seemed to have materialized from the forests.

"I ride from the regent to welcome you, great lord," said their leader, who was the size of the young king and most eleven-year-old boys. "We are here to guard you from the robbers on these roads."

The leader presented his companions, all of whom seemed to be young nobles. Of course, there was a feast in the woods with truffles and boars and the best ports of Portugal. Then the Turks staggered to their silken tents to sleep under their fur robes.

Cartouche, the bandit who was the leader of these men, then robbed the Turks of all their gifts, including two immense diamonds they were bringing to the king.

All France was in love with the idea of Cartouche and his men even as they had to pay his protection to travel the highways. He had been a soldier and now rode at the head of hundreds of men and women who would do all he asked. Ruined nobles rode with them and those who would spread his legend as he cut C's with his sword and threw handfuls of coins to the poor. He stripped houses and wagons until he had chests of jewels. Since danger was his pleasure, he lived at just the right time.

At night, as he rehearsed his disguises, he planned his most daring crime, for he had decided to steal the Régent.

Mehemet Effendi and the envoys of the Sublime Porte at last made a grand entry into Paris and met the young king, who delighted in examining their robes and daggers. On March 21, 1721, the king received Effendi at Versailles. Cartouche, in disguise, was sitting in the stands, for anyone might purchase a place to watch the kings at their ceremonies.

Louis XV appeared in a coat of red velvet with his great-grandfather's matched set of diamond buttons and diamond buttonhole surrounds. He wore the pear-shaped 53-carat Great Sancy, the most beautiful of his great-grandfather's diamonds, on his hat (this insouciant use of the most spectacular stones characterized all the Bourbons).

Mehemet Effendi did not know where to look first. Accustomed as he was to splendor, the magnificence of Versailles and the court seduced him—the angel women with their silver cheeks, the shining boy king.

As he salaamed, then rose, he saw the king's shoulder. A knot of diamonds and pearls held the Régent, a diamond greater than any of Sultan Ahmet's treasures. In the stands, Cartouche did not take his eyes from the king's shoulder.

Mehemet Effendi described the audience:

> *"What think you of my king's beauty?" asked the maréchal [Villeroi] ... "Isn't his figure beautifully proportioned? And, mark you, this is his own hair."*
>
> *So saying, he made the king turn round, and I contemplated his hyacinthine locks, and gently stroked them. They were like meshes of golden thread, perfectly even, and they reached right down to his waist.*
>
> *"His carriage," his guardian went on, "is also very fine." Then, turning to the king, he added, "Come walk about a little and let us see how you move."*
>
> *The king, strutting with the majesty of a partridge, walked to the middle of the room and back again.*
>
> *"Walk a little faster," said the Guardian. "Just let us see how light you are on your feet."*
>
> *Whereupon the king began to run as fast as he could.*

On this very day, Madame wrote in a letter, "Whoever does not make himself dreaded in France soon has cause for fear." She told of three great ladies who ran after the Turkish ambassador and made his son drunk and held the son three days as they seduced him repeatedly.

"Las Cases, I fear you neglect me for that diamond," said the emperor just now. "And where have you come upon the notations of the ambassador here on this rock? To read this is to see that Villeroi loved the king, but what a little puppet he tried to make of him."

"Sire, Villeroi was ruined by his own grandchildren, for it is they who tried to pollute the king. First, his granddaughter grabbed the king in the most intimate place, and then his grandsons committed sodomy in the woods of Versailles. Villeroi banished them and said they had torn down palings in the park."

"They said anything about anyone then and now," said the emperor. "What is history but revisions contemporaneous with the times?"

"Soon enough they took Villeroi away."

I told the emperor that after the scandal with the young lords, the regent had the roués force Villeroi into a sedan chair and he was banished to his château. The little king cried and refused to eat for the old man who had told him, "Rule: Don't be ruled," and, "Never allow yourself to become fond of anyone." Villeroi had always been there to teach him demeanor and lock up his handkerchiefs and bread and butter lest they be poisoned. When Villeroi was finally allowed to return to court, the boy, who then lived inside himself, would not speak to him. He became a king with a hard crystal shell, almost as if the diamond had covered him.

Later that month at Notre Dame, at a Te Deum to celebrate his alliance with Spain, Louis XV wore the Régent in its shoulder knot with a costume of lavender velvet. It was now part of him.

Cartouche, the robber, was the street counterpart to the regent, and the people loved him far better. He was the subject of many plays in Paris. Finally he went to see one of the plays about himself and was caught before he could get his little hands on the Régent. He and hundreds of his followers were tried and broken on the wheel.

In July, the young king was sick for five days and the nation, now hating the regent, mourned that he might continue to rule if the king died. At the same time, they were fascinated, and when the regent gave a fête at Saint-

Cloud for his new mistress, carriages lined the Seine for miles to see the fire-works, and Voltaire rushed to celebrate her. This was our duality, hatred twined round fascination, like a snake on a curving Chinese tree.

Madame, then seventy-one, was not well but forced herself to the corona-tion of the thirteen-year-old king in October 1722, in Rheims cathedral. Be-fore the coronation her barber bled her twice. He fainted the second time, so the wound was never properly closed. Madame was weak and faint when she went to Rheims.

Laurent Rondé and his son Claude had made Louis XV's crown, setting rubies, sapphires, emeralds, topazes, and all the diamonds into a light ver-meil ring. Eight fleurs-de-lis rose from the base, with the Great Sancy on top of one. Before this, red stones had been in the front of the crown to sym-bolize the blood and sacrifice of Christ, for the king was his representative on earth. But the Rondés put the Régent in the front of this crown.

The *Mercure* announced that the richest crown in the world could be seen in the Rondés' atelier at the Louvre. This was the first time the people of Paris could see the Régent up close. To look down at the top of the crown was to see the sun with its rays flaming in a garden of jeweled lilies.

The lawyer Barbier, whose memoirs we have here, went to the Louvre to see the crown. ". . . the most brilliant thing and the most perfect work any-one has ever seen," he wrote. The Régent "is surprising for its bigness; one calls it the MILLIONAIRE. . . . One says there is not another as large in the court of the Mogul emperor. One says also, I do not know if it is true, that the one who brought it, so as not to be surprised, had his thigh opened, and that one shut it in some lead, and that when he was here, he had his thigh opened. It is certainly larger than a pigeon's egg."

At the coronation, the king took off the crown and laid it on the altar. Madame again saw the diamond she had heard about so many years ago when the merchant from the East came to court. She saw the diamond Louis XIV had not been able to buy but her son had gotten for the king. All big diamonds made her remember Monsieur, whom she had loved after all. He had a diamond a quarter the size of the Régent named the Grande Mademoiselle for the princess whose fortune he had inherited.

On Louis XV's return from Rheims they burned incense and the people shouted for the beautiful young king. The guests dined at three thousand tables and drank eighty thousand bottles of champagne with fifty thousand plates of fruit and cakes as fireworks burst overhead. Madame was ill and suffering.

Madame knew her hour was fixed and she would not live a minute beyond it; nor did she want to, for, as she said, "The pitcher goes so often to the well that it is broken at last." They bled her when she was too weak to resist, as doctors always do what they like when the patient is feeble.

One of her ladies came to kiss her as she lay dying of the dropsy. The lady bent to kiss Madame's hand.

"You may kiss me properly now. I am going to a land where all are equal," Madame said. All her life, she who insisted on her privileges had been the victim of her rank and the foreign land and situation into which it had led her.

She died at four in the morning and the regent wept hard all the next day, sitting amidst giant haystacks of parchment as her letters covered the floor. He saw then just how unhappy she had been, how she felt she had failed, how his mother's whole life was a navigation through troubled waters.

Then minister Dubois died, exploded really, and the regent said, "Dead is the beast, and dead the venom," and took his place as minister.

The regent died four months later in the arms of his mistress, the duchesse de Phalaris, in the early evening at Versailles. At forty-nine, Philippe d'Orléans had a beard of red flesh hanging under his chin and a large hard belly. He had decided to disobey his doctors, keep to his bad habits, and like his daughter, kill himself with the ghosts of pleasure.

"Do you really believe God exists, and that there is a heaven and a hell after this life?" he had asked the duchess, who said she believed.

"If so, you are very unfortunate to be living the life you are," he said, then collapsed. The duchess ran all over Versailles looking for help.

When they opened the regent's body before embalming, they removed his heart to take it to Val-de-Grâce, as was the custom.

His Great Dane flung himself on the organ and ate most of it. The last of the roués, who were standing by the table for this final moment, tried to restrain the dog. The animal shook his head, the bloody heart in his mouth, and snarled and glared at the roués. One of them began to laugh for the dog's red eyes resembled those of his master after one of his many hard nights.

People considered this a curse because the dog was certainly not starving.

The regent's contempt had seeped into the land. His regency was a time of greed, pretension, and too sudden wealth. Outward all was puff and pom-poms, inward corruption and the secret police at the door. France was a woman with beauty spots glued on her face to hide defects and the marks of the pox.

Madame had written of the seventh fairy at her son's birth, the one who renders all his gifts useless. Was it the fairy, or the diamond? Or perhaps it was Minister Dubois, in league with England and in its pay, who sabotaged him. Or the regent's addiction to dissipation or his inability to complete things, or to refuse people. Every human carries the seeds of his ruin along with those of his progeny.

Were both he and Law cursed by their touch of the stone? I cannot say. For each man came to the diamond with his own defects of pride. They were both horribly arrogant.

"Learn to suffer," Governor Pitt wrote to himself. Across the channel, the young Louis XV also suffered from melancholia. To touch the stone was to know sadness, and feel the grip of mortality at any age.

After Governor Pitt sold the Régent, he spent half the money on Bocon-noc, said to be the finest house in Cornwall, then added Swallowfield in Berkshire, where he lived, and a house in Pall Mall on forty-five acres—all this is recorded. He bought land and great houses in London, Wiltshire, Dorset, Devonshire, and Hampshire.

The houses were big enough for his rages. He went into furies and yelled as he had in the Indies. His gout plagued him and things turned sour, though he had wealth, alliances with noble families, and political connec-tions. He soothed his spirit with his gardens, creating vistas, carving yews into fountains and cones, planting temples and grottoes, all of which pro-claimed his dominion over helpless nature.

He had taken in his dead daughter Lucy's children. When he was in one of his moods, they would hide, turning the other way when they saw him limping at the far end of one of the great halls. All his wildness and his lost power had made him a tyrant of country-house kingdoms.

He dwelt with the dark residue of the diamond—the fear that it might be taken had become the universal suspicion that he had come by it through deceit. And still he missed his diamond.

He had lost money in the South Sea Bubble, a copy of Law's scheme. This was his life's mistake and it ate him up. He was too ill to fight to get money back and had to live out his last years with the feeling he had been duped.

At seventy-three, in 1726, Thomas Pitt died of palsy and apoplexy. Even at his funeral, the Reverend Eyre spoke of "The tongue of the Slanderer, which this PERSON, whose property was so wonderful, could not escape."

The reverend mentioned his enemies and the "abusive story" of how he got the diamond. He even said he had seen an account of the sale and was satisfied with it. He said of the slanderer: "And, if, when such a Viper fasten'd on an innocent person . . . when you see it shaken off, it . . . may well raise your thoughts of him, who bore so horrid an abuse with so much patience."

Be that as it may, his sons and heirs began a long battle over his will. There was a surprise for them all. They had lingered around him and supported his foul humor when there were hopes, but the estate of £100,000 was much smaller than expected.

The regent had died three years before the governor and his debt for the diamond was never fully paid. Pitt's children made a claim to our government for the rest of the money owed on the diamond. France reminded them of the usufructuary laws whereby the debts and past transactions of one French king were not honored by the next. Though I assume they got to keep some of the jewels, the Pitts felt themselves cheated of at least £20,000. This left a residue of bitterness against France that may have changed history. It perhaps explains why William Pitt the Elder and the Younger, neither a rich man, hated us beyond all reason. They were enemies of the very Bourbons and the emperor who wore their diamond in their crowns and hats, on their shoulders and sword. In their times their particular antagonism to France became the policy of their country.

The emperor has told me for my *Memorial* that if England was so opposed to our revolution it was due to Monsieur Pitt the Younger, who inherited his hatred for France from his father. The Pitts led their country up, while our last kings led France down. The Pitts had a certain purity and a moral quality; not so Louis XV, who had to contend with Thomas Pitt's grandson.

The Black Humor Follows the Diamond

D O YOU DOUBT THIS IS THE FACE OF A HAWK, WITH THAT Bourbon beak?" the emperor said as he studied the portrait of William Pitt the Elder* in the book I had open. I had been researching the Pitts for I did not want to leave them too far behind in my quest for the Régent.

"And see how he bears in his physiognomy all the typical signs of intelligence," the emperor continued, pointing to a high swelling brow like his own. "The face is a long slide downward, which gives a mournful cast; the lips are thin with constant judgment and have an imperious curve. Surely his intellect placed him apart as a boy at school and he became aloof. When he was angered, one would have to look away."

"Louis the Fifteenth thought he should be executed," I said. "The Pitts were much feared in the court of the Bourbons. He said Monsieur Pitt was a crazy man and very dangerous, that he deserved to be hanged."

"And that is the man my diamond raised up!"

"The diamond left all the Pitts a legacy of madness and melancholia," I said.

---

*Robert Pitt's second son, Governor Pitt's grandson.

"Or maybe it was just the progenitor, Las Cases, not your diamond at all. But continue on with your theories."

So I explained how I thought the melancholia of the Pitts alternated with a fevered activity and thrust to greatness. It went beyond the normal eccentricity, the cherished peculiarity of the English. Pitt the Elder, who became earl of Chatham and led his country to an empire, was often sunk in misery. From the governor on, all the family's greatness was plagued with pain. Furies chased them through the ages—raised them and led them into extinction.

At the end of his life, the Elder Pitt spent a year in a locked room, banging on the floor with a stick when he wanted food. His great face was wet with tears, his head was down on the desk in the halo of his arms. The voice that had thundered was now mute. His body shook and he had fits of tears; he could not stand loud noises, then any noise at all, and quivered with nervous distress. Meals came through a hatch in the wall; no one was admitted. And then he revived in a burst of nervous excitement.

His sister Ann had to be placed in restraints and died in a home for the unbalanced. Another sister was thought to be mentally ill, as was his cousin Baron Camelford and an older brother. At the very least, they went their own peculiar way, like his daughter Hester Pitt, who went to live with the Druzes on Mount Lebanon.

"Mad, perhaps, *mon cher,* but he could *speak*. The Pitts talked their kingdom into greatness," said the emperor. "They hypnotized with their language. The Elder was Cicero, Demosthenes—the best actor of his times. He had all the tricks of oratory and such ardor. They said his voice carried down the stairs and into the lobbies of Parliament, where strangers stopped to attend."

"It was a power I surely never had," I said, laughing, remembering how I had frozen and disgraced myself in the emperor's council.

We then spoke of how, full of gout, William Pitt would literally crawl into Parliament, and how after hours of debate he would speak at one in the morning and none would leave. He was a champion of scorn and smirking wit, could raise an eyebrow and demolish anyone. Georges I and II both detested Pitt the Elder and could not bear to have him around. George II did not speak to him for years until his abilities made that impossible. When Pitt finally took office and had to kneel to the king and kiss his hand to receive his seals, George II cried from fury.

"Still he became in effect their prime minister, and head of Commons," I said. "He was ever a monarchist hoping for the right monarch. If he had only served you . . ."

"I had enough trouble with the son and that lunatic who tried to kill me."[*]

The emperor said Pitt understood war, had led England through the Seven Years War to her triumph. Pitt had said, "I know that I can save England and no one else can."

"Men like us know those things," said the emperor. "We are sure and must be."

We were in the garden then and the emperor stopped to put his nose into some pink geraniums he had just replanted after Dimanche disturbed them. I felt my foot slip and leaned on a shrub for balance. The emperor looked strangely at me. I did not tell him that that very morning I had woken into a floating gray blur. I saw Emmanuel edged in black and all the objects in my room furred in outline. My vision cleared after a moment, but I dreaded it as a foretaste of what might happen.

"War became Pitt as it did me," the emperor was saying. "He knew how to build England's navy and hire soldiers to fight in Europe. He won England an empire without fighting a single battle himself. Nobles who didn't even know him left him legacies, and once the crowd unhitched his horses and pulled his carriage. England then led the world in the way the Romans had and as I did."

I said I found it strange that the old pirate Thomas Pitt had produced such honesty in the two William Pitts, men without fortunes who lived high, but still refused all gifts most scrupulously throughout their public service.

The first William Pitt, like the governor, was a second son with something to prove—an outsider without rank or fortune, whom the aristocracy hated.

"You see we were not so different," the emperor said.

The people loved Pitt's ways for he was kind to his inferiors and often unpleasant to his equals. He behaved, in fact, just like a Bourbon.

In his last years, they carried Pitt, who was by then Lord Chatham, around in a sedan chair with an enlarged boot. His arm was in a sling, his legs were wrapped in red flannel.

"What would the Pitts have been without their pain and lowness, if they had not been held in check by disease?" said the emperor. We discussed how

---

*Their relative Baron Camelford tried to assassinate the emperor.

the gout made them pop in and out of history, taking their opiates and living in spas like Bath for months at a time.

The emperor then went off to stand outside the kitchen and command more of the white food—the chickens, pale breads, and cheeses—that he will eat, as always, much too quickly. Since his boyhood, through all the campaigns, he has never entered the place where food was being cooked. This may be because of his acute sense of smell.

I might add that since the emperor is the focus of all here, we have all developed a perhaps unhealthy fascination with his habits. Every fit of coughing, every face slap, ear tweak, or whether his soup is hot enough becomes a topic of all-day conversations because it is about him.

This is still a court, make no mistake, with the same emphasis on the sovereign and those who move closest to him. Until I took up my study of the diamond, the emperor was all I had to do beyond survival. The others still have not found outside interests and thus are thrown too much upon one another's pettiness.

I have no friends but the emperor and Emmanuel, so this work delivers me from the pitiless intensity of our days and from thoughts of my wife, Henriette, and Lady Clavering (another subject altogether). I live like a stranger among these men, who get up and put on their uniforms each day as they have done for years. Somehow in this place where the climate is at war with itself and the men at war with one another it seems almost right to dress for the daily fight.

When the emperor returned, we spoke further of Pitt the Elder, who became known as the Great Commoner. The emperor began to pace. His right shoulder kept rising in the half shrug that is his habit, a gesture that often offends strangers, who think he is dismissing them.

"He did everything late in life," I said. "He was thirty-eight when he took his first office, forty-six when he married, and forty-eight when he entered the cabinet."

"I was two years younger when I ended my career," said the emperor with a small laugh that discomforted me. I began to protest and he looked away to the sea.

"When he became the earl of Chatham, the people did not like it," I said. "He had betrayed the middle class that backed him. And then came the caprice, a sudden need for fanciness. He had trees carried from London to a barren hill and bought, then sold, and bought back the same house. He was silent for four years, then made a glorious return. Even the American Benjamin Franklin feared him a bit. Pitt knew there should be no taxation with-out representation and that his country would not win in a war against the colonists."

"Had he been heeded, America might still be part of their empire," said the emperor.

"At the end, he hobbled into the House of Lords supported by his son, our William Pitt. The peers were all in their crimson robes and he wore the black velvet suit he had worn in Commons and black velvet boots and the crutches muffled in velvet. Can you imagine!"

"He had the appeal of the cripple, the powerful cripple—even better!"

"He made a long speech about us, the 'ancient inveterate enemy'—a bit incoherent," I said. "A duke responded and, as he rose to answer, he clutched his chest and they carried him out in a swoon. A month later he had his son read the death of Hector to him and on that very day he died."

"That is just how a man becomes a myth," said the emperor.

That night as the emperor was playing checkers with Grand Marshal Bertrand, Ali brought me a letter written in English.

Sir Count Las Cases,

I write you this letter for say to you that you had done a very good book [my Atlas*]. It is not that it is not some fautes [mistakes], but you shall may correct them in the next edition: then shall you may sell your work five pound every exemplaire [copy]. Upon that I pray god that He have you in his holy and worthy guard.*

I looked at the checker player, who, pretending he had not written this, was biting his lip and trying not to laugh. I said in English: "Thank you. I hope to write another book with an even bigger subject."

He tried and failed to look innocent.

The Diamond, the Deer Park

LOUIS XV LIKED THE DIAMOND NAMED FOR HIS GREAT-uncle. He remembered the afternoon that the regent brought it to him and how it had removed the idea of the dead birds. That day his uncle had again refused to tell him about the man in the mask. Now he knew the secret.

His reign was the first time the diamond was brought into the light of kings. He wore it whenever he felt like wearing the first jewel of the kingdom. When he had it on he felt that his body disappeared around it; he felt almost invisible, a great relief.

Whatever its origins, the Régent was now legitimated by the king of France, who often wore it just to annoy foreign dignitaries with his magnificence. The diamond was made for nights at a court such as his. Under immense breasts of crystal lit by tapers, he went among them wearing it. It was a mystery how fire could come from a stone so white, devoid of color and yet containing all colors. Those who were new to court peered about to find and marvel at the source of the light that splintered to red, yellow, and blue, fusing to green and purple. The king was quite a sight in his two sets of decorations—one day all white diamonds, the next the same orders repeated in colored stones—the Order of Saint-Esprit (Holy Ghost) with its upside-down dove, the Toison d'Or (Golden Fleece) with its limp dangling ram. Those who bowed and flourished before Louis XV would raise their eyes first to the handsome vacant face and then, as if compelled, to its rival, the blazing Régent. Only one seemed alive. Sometimes paralyzed by the magnificence of both, they would lose their wits and speech for an instant, by which time he would have moved on.

It was the only life he knew. He lived in a time of prettiness carried to perversion and was as pretty and perverted as his age. Beauty everywhere was the main distraction. It was on the ormolu base, the curved ornamented ebony commode, the *bois satine* and parquetry, Savonerie screen panels, the brass and red tortoiseshell inlaid Boulle marquetry.

Inside this heavy beauty, he struggled to be king. He might have said along with Beaumarchais, "My life is one long fight." Missing a childhood, he tried to find what he had never had but felt he had lost. Of course, there were compensations. He and his young courtiers would stroll from their summer dining room out onto the roof garden. Sometimes they ran over the rooftops all the way to the Wing of Princes, and the smell of all the flowers of Versailles wafted up to them.

The women with their floating back panels were like ships under full sail. They caressed one another with their hoops as they passed through rooms of light woods painted bright colors, above which Cupid whispered secrets in Sappho's ear, putti lounged on clouds, and the gentler gods trysted and betrayed each other. When they were in haste, the ladies lifted their skirts and hopped along like little seabirds that flap about on beaches gathering momentum to lift off. They wore flat slippers so light they could come upon anyone with only the slightest rustle as their long trains dragged on the floor.

They scarcely could get into or out of their carriages. This was the time of women whose split skirts stretched wider than their outstretched arms with their veins painted blue to suggest the blood within. At theater sometimes, a seat on either side was left vacant for their padded panniers.

As a young man, I used to see the last of these mesdames of the ancient regime propped against a wall, resting their arms on their panniers or inserting an ivory scratcher inside giant bonnets of hair pierced by diamonds, to scratch the lice. Almost as wide as they were high, they were iced cakes on the move, gliding around with bits and chunks of the earth's minerals on them. They wore their old-fashioned court dresses, immense brocades woven of gold and silver with Spanish point that cost 40,000 livres, to which they added diamond flowers, diamond bows and knots, pompoms, ribbons. Diamond aigrettes trembled in their hair towers and jeweled stems shook with every nod of the head. From their ears giant girandoles hung like miniature chandeliers and their bosoms popped out in powdered white hillocks. When they sank into a powdering chair, they whooshed like collapsing silk balloons. They were horribly snobbish toward me.

Ducs and counts and marquis foamed with lace and were held together with diamonds from their coat buttons to their knee garters and shoe buckles. They skimmed the parquet of Versailles in their peculiar glide, copied from the Chinese court, talking fast in their own court language. Their hair was powdered white so all would look the same and old age might steal upon some unnoticed. A mist of escaped powder made dense the air, obscuring all. Each day, they adopted new phrases or songs that vanished by the next evening when all had learned them. They were their own country, as though they all had a lisp or a common defect.

Peasants were better in bucolic scenes by Boucher or Sèvres fantasies painted on porcelain. They were more attractive, their sacks and aprons bursting with grain, on Gobelins tapestries than pointing to their open mouths and banging on gold carriage doors with their knuckles. At this time, when porcelain shepherds with music sheets tended porcelain lambs among porcelain flowers, our peasants could not weed their land lest it disturb our young game and ruin its flavor. Our serfs then were sold with the land and had to grind their flour and press their grapes at our châteaux, to buy salt four times a year, and work on the roads without pay. The court scarcely knew wars were going on in distant lands. Compared to the court, all lands were distant lands.

Sometimes one has to wind up on a rock where the trade winds pit the skin with grains of little rocks, to see the court for what it was, though there were those who saw it then.

A few said that Louis XV was a good enough king, but weak and ruined by his fear and pride. Others said he was lazy and cruel and hunted too much. He may have been shy, anxious to escape into the woods to shout himself hoarse at death. Perhaps the old stories about the doe and the little birds were lies. There were so many lies when the histories were written in justification during the time of the Revolution.

Louis XV began his long reign beloved and ended it detested, having lost an empire in the fifty-nine years he ruled. When he was sick as a boy, the nation sobbed; twenty years after that, when he was again sick, they erected statues and hung from the trees to see the handsome king return in triumph from war. Then, finally, near the end, they hung mocking verses from the statues in the night.

A wit has said our government was despotism tempered by epigram. Every mistress, every battle, every minister then was the subject of songs and poems that told the truest story of our kingdom. There was a quip on the instant for every scandal and defeat, and France went down laughing with contempt.

Under Louis XV, we reversed our ancient alliances and joined with Austria. France lost the Seven Years War so that, at the close of his reign, the kingdom was less important than England or Austria. Half a million of my countrymen were dead, the ministers came and went. Louis XV smiled at them and then they would receive little notes—go home to your castle, we have no need of your services, never show your face again, and do not try to answer this letter. His minister Silhouette, who lasted a year, gave his name to the idea of a shadow.

Louis XV, the grandfather of three kings, unmounted the diamonds of his great-grandfather. The Régent and the Great Sancy were left as solitary jewels, worn, always casually, for great circumstances. Whenever the king wore the Régent at the outset of an enterprise, it came to naught. His reign came to naught and his marriage died as well.

Louis XV was fifteen when he married Marie Leczinska, the twenty-one-year-old daughter of the ousted king of Poland. He wore a hat with white plumes, the brim of which was caught up with the Régent. Every inch of his suit was embroidered in gold; each button was a diamond. A court robe of gold *crépines* covered the suit.

Queen Marie Leczinska's violet velvet gown was edged with ermine and embroidered with gold lilies; the front was strewn with diamonds and gems. That night the wind blew so hard the lamps went out and the illuminations were ruined.

He was a father at seventeen. The queen had wide hips, good for bearing children and playing the cello, which she did a lot. She sat with the cello between her legs and her head bent and let the music take her away from Versailles. They had ten children (six daughters and one son survived) and seven good years. Then came his mistresses, among them all four sisters of one family. Child marriages followed by infidelity were the way of the times. Among the great whys of the times was "Why fidelity?"—especially in the face of Bourbon sensuality.

The king had chambers for trysts in all his palaces. It was the regent all over again—the nocturnal festivities, the drinking bouts, the flying tables disappearing into the floors to rise reloaded, the servants mopping up after the orgies, carrying the revelers off to their pretty beds. Every time he was deathly sick, the current mistress vanished so he might apologize to God. Then he could not take her back, but sometimes he did anyway.

In 1745 the king celebrated the dauphin's marriage to the daughter of the king of Spain with a masked ball. Versailles glowed like a burning castle all along the Avenue de Paris as carriages galloped by those who walked and rented swords from the footmen. The usual "Turks" were dancing with fleshy sultanas, and satin peasants were stalled by fountains of wine when twelve giant yew trees, cut like pillars with urns, entered.

In came the queen, who, by then, had lost both her allure and her enthusiasm, in a dress covered with pearls. She was unmasked and would have been known anyway because in her hair were the Great Sancy and the Régent—about to cast its light on another drama. She watched the tall yew, dropping leaves and rustling, walk across the ballroom to the huntress Diana.

Diana stood with one bosom bared, holding a bow, with a quiver slung from her shoulders. Jewels pierced her blond curls and circled her black mask.

"Madame d'Étoiles," said someone in the stands outside the windows. She had already appeared at the king's hunts and had become his mistress. The giant yew with black eyes was shedding a trail of leaves.

Now the huntress dropped her handkerchief, the tall yew picked it up, and they left together in the unblinking eye of the court. The queen's head swiveled, the two diamonds finding this public scene painful, but not the first of its sort. With this, Louis XV acknowledged Jeanne-Antoinette de Poisson, wife of Le Normand d'Étoiles. He soon ennobled her as the marquise de Pompadour.

The marquise de Pompadour rehearsed for a summer, hid her baby daughter away, and came to court. She had been prepared since childhood, when her mother called her *"Reinette,"* little queen, and provided masters for lessons in all that could be taught. The rest she learned from her mother, who had been kept. And there is always a fortune-teller in these stories.

Madame Lebon had predicted that Jeanne-Antoinette, age nine, would be the mistress of the king someday (though sometimes people remember these prophecies only once they have come true). She had been born with the surname Poisson, fish, into a class lower than that of any previous official mistress.

"I cannot make out your eyes, Madame. Are they blue, or gray?" the king would say to the marquise de Pompadour. She was at her dressing table as ambassadors and bishops and ministers seated themselves on silk poufs and tradesmen stood watching her prolonged toilette. Little yellow birds were singing to one another as though their lives depended on their songs.

Her lady took a taffeta crescent and velvet star from the box of black taffeta patches and glued them on her face. The marquise moved the star slightly as the woman dusted the wig powder from her smooth shoulders. Now installed, it was as if Pompadour had always been at Versailles, for no one can rise like a determined bourgeoise.

Her collections were already all over the pretty tables—the snuffboxes, the intaglio gems that Guay had taught her to carve, the books she read so she might know more about everything than the king and surprise him constantly. In these exquisite rooms, with her own paintings and drawings propped on easels, she had shown the court how to cut and group together oleanders, yellow jasmine, myrtle, and tuberoses and how to tickle each sense with the other. Others began to copy her and soon her taste was in Paris.

Five perfect pink silk bows lined up the front of her bodice. When she moved, cascades of lace followed her wrists just as she had planned, for she had designed them that way. It was very hard work creating this perfection of self. She was put together of all these bits of lace and flowers and serious thoughts. She had to court the queen and the daughters and fight the cliques. She had to correct the king's scarred childhood and distract him, for he could be shy and nasty at the same time. She had to commission the furniture and porcelain and silver and fabrics and food, and maintain her studied calm. Her eye, her hand were on all. Under her paint, from the strain of maintaining her position, she bit her lips until they were puckered and drained of blood.

A small royal child peered into the room.

"Papa Roi"—Father King—"is with *Mama Putain*"—Mother Whore—
he announced in a loud voice as a hand snatched him back.

Nothing showed on the face of the marquise de Pompadour, but a small
drop of blood appeared on her lips, whose perfect shape would inspire the
marquise diamond.

Voltaire, who flapped around her like a cape, was in the room. The king
was eyeing him, for he did not trust him or his ideas.

Through the marquise de Pompadour, who had been in the salons since
she was fifteen, the ideas of the enlightened might have leaked into the king.
They did not. Though he memorized court gossip as though it were divine
text, he was deaf to the ideas of his age. He was king of a nation that, despite
him, was being awakened by Diderot and d'Alembert's *Encyclopedia* and,
midcentury, by Rousseau—*La Nouvelle Héloïse, Émile,* the *Social Contract,
The Letter from the Mountains*—Montesquieu, Helvetius and the material-
ists, and the influence of England, where all seemed free. These books were
on her tables, all this was in the air.

The people could not read, but they knew. They could not read, but they
could feel, and they felt unsettled. The questions were being asked: Why the
church? Why the monarchy? What use is an empire? The court sneer traveled outward. A great doubt filled the land, the salons, the lodges and literary societies. Now came the ideas that lechers wore priests' robes, that
outside the carriages the people were crying, "Misery!" With doubt came
the possibility that the glass in the Hall of Mirrors might crack and the rush
of the wind might blow out the candles and sweep all away.

Writers filled with the new light walked among those in society, contagious, forming national opinion. Skepticism and ridicule spread from the
court over the land like a miasma. The mood and impiety of the regent's
suppers infected the bourgeois and those in the night cellars. The people
saw the church abuses. The Jansenists were persecuted, then the Jesuits
were expelled and the people became unbelievers.

Still, even Voltaire, who had started all this, wanted to be a chamberlain,
wear an order, and hand the king his goblet of orange water.

"Your people will destroy the monarchy," the king said to Voltaire, speaking of those now called the "enlightened."

"Enough of that!" Pompadour said and went to the clavichord and began to sing. The birds sang hard with her. Or she would tell him a little
story or teach him about gardens or birds or decorating the next palace he
would build for her. Sometimes she acted in plays for those who hated her.

She would receive letters threatening her with poison and assassination; they dropped the little *libelles* by her door then rushed in to pay court.

The king picked up Pompadour's box of beauty patches and carried them off to mark his war maps. He did not like the way Voltaire always looked as though the world existed to amuse him.

Often when he was not killing or moving from palace to palace like a restless shade, Louis XV sat slumped in a melancholy as bad as William Pitt's.

All his life, trailed by remorse for his childhood tragedies, he talked of sickness and death. He talked of medicines and operations and funerals and dissecting bodies, as though by naming his fears, he might scare them off.

Then the marquise would distract him. She brought fun to the once silent man with terrible black eyes. She built houses near Fontainebleau and Compiègne and brought in Boucher and the *ébénistes* (cabinetmakers), installed lacquer walls and tapestries. And she would smile with her bitten lips, for charm was the poison of this court. Louis XV built the Trianon at Versailles for her. She made him a new family, bringing in Marigny, her talented architect brother, and together they created Place Louis XV, with the twin palaces by Gabriel, and the École Militaire (where the emperor and I were at school, he entering as I left).

Still the king could not restrain his morbid thoughts. He would stop at cemeteries and ask with enthusiasm about fresh graves. The marquise told her lady Madame du Hausset it hurt him to laugh.

"When I come to die . . . ," he would say.

"No, sire!" said all the court, denying even that certainty.

"I have the solution," said the comte de Saint-Germain one day.

"No, you will not experiment on the king," said Madame de Pompadour. "I forbid it." She was having her hair dressed; the pomade made from apples and goat's fat was on and waiting for the scented starch powder. She held a powdering cone before her face and sat at a table draped with lace before a Beauvais tapestry showing the king at one of his hunts.

The comte de Saint-Germain, one of the court strays, had been introduced by Marshal Belle-Isle as the son of his old age. One day in 1748, he had just appeared. His horses were all gray; he wore only black and white. His skin looked like white kid gloves stretched on a glove mold. He was covered with the finest diamonds and his perfume was that abiding musk of mystery. He appealed to the king, who was so often sunk and morose.

"Who is he?" said the king, and in this court where all was pedigree, no one knew, but from his jewels, he was vastly rich. Some said Saint-Germain was a Jew or a bastard of the king of Portugal. Or he had married a Mexican and run off to Constantinople with her. Or that he was a Pole or an Italian.

"I cannot say, sire, but I believe him to be immortal," said Marshal Belle-Isle. "He gave me an elixir that makes me feel four and twenty . . . I believe he has defied death itself."

"Oh ha!" said the king.

Though the king knew physics and chemistry, botany and astronomy, and was himself an expert in medicine, he was captivated by the comte de Saint-Germain—this man who called up shades and phantasmagoria, who spoke twelve languages, played every instrument, painted with skill, and knew chemistry, the science of optics, and medicine.

He looked about fifty and yet pretended to be two thousand years old.

"Was the court of Francois I as brilliant as we've been told?" the marquise would ask the comte of him who reigned in 1515.

"Of course there was da Vinci, always drawing and talking about the moon and water," said Saint-Germain, "but in the time of Mary Stuart and Margaret of Valois the court was a land of enchantment—a temple, sacred to pleasures of every kind."

"People are right in saying a liar ought to have a very good memory," said Louis XV.

They said Saint-Germain could transmute metals, that he had the elixir of life, that he could make pearls grow and remove spots from diamonds. He had eyes that captured one. He had creams to preserve and restore youth. He did not eat or drink when he was among others.

"Have an egg, have some wine. I command you," the king would say. Then Saint-Germain would have to moisten his lips while he fixed the king with his terrible eyes.

Saint-Germain was taken up, for no court was at once so susceptible and yet so snobbish as our own. Then abruptly one day he left and was seen with Horace Walpole and the Prince of Wales in England and then with Clive in India. Wherever he stopped, the comte was always brewing potions and medicines and finding new dyes and colors and dangling the prospect of eternal life.

"He is back," said Pompadour in 1757, "and he looks even younger! Did you note his ruby sleeve buttons?" They gave him an apartment at the vast Château de Chambord.

It was as if the king and Madame de Pompadour, who both knew better, were mesmerized. That was the year Damiens, a servant filled by republican thinking and madness, stabbed the king. Even though the wound was slight, Pompadour was sent away briefly so the king might repent, only this time he allowed her back. Damiens was wrenched apart by red-hot pincers and had molten lead poured in his wounds. Six horses were harnessed to his limbs to pull him apart, and when they failed to do so, they chopped him up with an axe, then burned him.

In such a climate the morbid king needed Saint-Germain, for he was amusing and magnificent, the two most vital court attributes. They lived in a time when superstition was never too distant. Spirits could be called from their realm. The Illuminati, Rosicrucians, Knights Templar, and Freemasons were said to be everywhere. Saint-Germain, who roamed from European court to court, was a natural spy. Later, he became one of the King's Secret, which is what they called his spies in those days. (The king also had his Cabinet Noir, or Black Office, to open other people's letters and send him copies every Sunday.)

The king, some lords, and Pompadour talked with Saint-Germain about his secret for making the spots in diamonds disappear. In the room was the other court mystery, the chevalier d'Éon, who was, as usual, wearing a dress. No one was certain if the chevalier was man or woman, but all knew he was the king's spy.

"I should like to have a chance with that very large diamond you sometimes wear upon your hat, sire," Saint-Germain said of the Régent.

"I cannot let you play with it," said the king. "It is a royal jewel of which I am only the trustee. Beyond that, it is without flaw, or so the Rondés have represented to me."

"I should like to see it close."

"*Non,*" said the king. "I would, however, have you try your arts upon another stone," and he went to his marquetry desk full of Sèvres Wedgwood plaques and all encrusted with gilt bronze. He turned a single key and at once every drawer in the desk popped open. From one drawer he took out a flawed diamond of middling size worth 6,000 francs and had it weighed. "Will you try to put some money in my pocket?"

"It may be done; and I will bring it to you again in a month."

Three weeks later Saint-Germain arrived with the stone wrapped in a cloth of amianthus. It was but very little smaller and now without flaw, and increased in value when the king sent it to a jeweler. He sent for it back again to keep it as a curiosity. All this is told by Pompadour's lady Madame du Hausset.

At Tournai, Casanova saw the comte de Saint-Germain surrounded by retorts of boiling liquids. Saint-Germain offered the great lover a white liquid that he claimed was the universal spirit of nature. It disappeared on the instant when its stopper was pricked, so what was its use? Then Saint-Germain burned Casanova's silver coin in a flame that turned it to gold —that was more useful.

The marquise de Pompadour's heart was wearing out even as her taste spread all over Europe. In other countries little Pompadours in the *robe à la française* posed by swollen furniture filled with porcelain plaques under lesser versions of Boucher's putti and Bacchantes.

The marquise was constantly sitting for portraits surrounded by symbols of those she patronized. When the artists took away their easels, she remained in her pose as though preparing for the next portrait. Like a jewel, like the Régent itself, she was something that had been worked on till it glowed. She was the diamond become flesh. And like the diamond, cold at the core.

Off and on she ran France. She had been, in effect, the first minister, appointing her favorites as ministers and generals until our empire slipped away as quickly as her smile. For what were our ministers Bernis or Soubise to William Pitt? She had lasted twenty years in power by understanding the fog of misinformation and intrigue that surrounds a king.

When the king tired of Madame de Pompadour, sometime around 1750, they remained friends and she lived in the palaces as his adviser. She had not given up without a struggle, according to Soulavie, who tells of her sad attempts to entice the king by costuming herself as a nun or dairy maid, jumping out to surprise him, as a shepherdess or cowherd, and terrifying him in the process. Still, he no longer desired her.

The king had asked that old roué Armand, the duc de Richelieu, the source of his sexual vigor, and he had told the king that he frequently changed partners. Fatal advice, for now the king became a corrupter of innocence. Two or three teenage nymphets at a time were brought to live in the small house in the Parc aux Cerfs that was his private brothel.

"It is his heart I wish to secure," Pompadour told Madame du Hausset, "and all those young girls who have no education will not run away with it from me."

The abbess who ran the house told the little girls that their randy visitor was a Polish nobleman. Sometimes he forgot to change his coat and appeared in the *cordon bleu*. Then the abbess would say he was a relative of the queen. That the king was handsome did him no harm, and the dumb little girls did not know enough to wonder that he spoke no Polish. Like the favorites of Henri III, they served his pleasure and occasionally had his children, and then were sent away and married off. They were thirteen, fourteen, sometimes fifteen, and Lebel, his valet, found them and first tried them out.

Then the king was in love with another young girl, and this time Pompadour was afraid.

"Princes are, above all, the slaves of habit," Madame du Hausset told her. "You have formed yourself to the king's manners and habits; you know how to listen and reply to his stories . . . he has no fear of *boring* you."

Still the marquise de Pompadour wanted to see this rival who carried the king's son in a basket to nurse him every morning in the Bois de Boulogne. The marquise had the carriage stop and entered the wood with her bonnet sheltering her face. She pretended to have a toothache so she could cover her famous features (aging a bit) with a handkerchief. There on the grass sat a beauty with black hair covered in the finest laces nursing her child. The marquise de Pompadour was trembling.

"What a lovely child!" said Madame du Hausset.

"I must confess that he is, though I am his mother," said the woman.

"The infant has *his* eyes," the marquise said to Madame du Hausset. She then had palpitations of the heart as well as the beginning of one of her migraines.

After the marquise de Pompadour died, at forty-two, in 1764, the dauphin died, then the dauphine, and finally the queen. Louis XV's daughters had never married but became the bitter and peculiar Mesdames. They were busy raising the king's grandson, who would become Louis XVI.

One summer when the king was sixty, Madame du Barry arrived on the arm of the duc de Richelieu, who knew and loved women as did Casanova. He could discern and would pursue sensuality hidden in even the plain and pious, and du Barry was neither.

The king walked to Madame du Barry, who had dropped into her curtsy. He raised her up and wiped the rouge from her cheeks, for he could not abide paint on such a face. Madame du Barry, with eyes like dirty ice on a blue pool, did not blink. She never seemed to blink as she assessed her effect on others.

The king heard a sound come out of her almost like a purr. He felt a heat from her flesh. Her mouth was too red and too small. She was soon enough in a little apartment on the second floor of Versailles.

Well trained, she glided through the palace, her bodice covered in hard diamond blooms and bows. Zamora, a little black boy who was her godson, padded after her dressed in white and silver with silk boots. Jeanne du Barry, the bastard daughter of a monk and a seamstress, was an official mistress lower in class than any before. As the lowest, she lived the highest and quickly found there was no excess so easy to accustom oneself to as an excess of money.

She had been well educated at Sacred Heart and sent off as companion to a noblewoman. When the woman's son became Jeanne's lover, she was thrown from the house. The comte de Barry became her procurer until she caught the attention of the king. Then the comte quickly married her to his brother to make her acceptable. Her father, the monk, performed the ceremony.

She was quite a different creature from Pompadour, having little interest in politics, though factions bloomed around and against her, and the minister Choiseul was dismissed at her instigation.

The fourteen-year-old Austrian archduchess Marie-Antoinette had come to marry the new dauphin in the Hall of Mirrors. Marie-Antoinette, born on the day of the Lisbon earthquake, had arrived at court much like her great-grandmother Madame (the regent was her great-uncle). She was trained but unprepared, given a flattering false miniature of her husband. And then there he was before her, fifteen and thick. The three fat spinster aunts—known as Rag, Sow, and Grub—were with him like a wall of fat. She noticed du Barry but would not speak to her until her mother forced her to.

"The court is crowded this day," Marie-Antoinette said to Madame du Barry, and never said much else. Du Barry was offended because no one heeds etiquette like a former whore.

When Marie-Antoinette married the dauphin, Louis XV had appeared at the ceremony with the Régent in his crown and stared at Marie-Antoinette's flat chest. Marie-Antoinette, still a child, stared at his huge diamond.

There were nineteen days of festivities, with 160,000 Chinese lanterns and the effigies of the dauphin and Marie-Antoinette illuminated over the Grand Canal. Then, in Place Louis XV, the fireworks exploded and the scaffolds caught fire. Over a hundred people fell in the dry moat surrounding the square and were crushed and trampled. Among the dead were gangs of pickpockets who had robbed them, for there was already desperation in the land.

Marie-Antoinette fled in tears, followed by the cries of the dying and the resentment of the living. Later, she and the dauphin gave their year's allowance to the families, but hatred for her started then, with the wedding.

The marriage bed stayed white and barren for many years because the dauphin's sex was malformed. A small operation, suggested by Marie-Antoinette's brother seven years later, fixed him.

The court hated Marie-Antoinette as much as they had hated Madame, but in a different way, for they had hated Madame for her ugliness and Marie-Antoinette for her reckless beauty. The people hated her because she was Austrian, the Other, the old enemy, the one to blame; they hated her because in her quest for simplicity, she was profligate. She overdid all she did. The beauty that inspires love can provoke disappointment when not accompanied by worthiness. She raised false hopes.

Marie-Antoinette had come to France in a time that was beginning to recognize merit before birth. Dangerous ideas blew in from across the seas: *if* all men are created equal, *then* what is a king? And why should the clergy and nobles have privileges and not pay taxes?

She had arrived when the political party that brought her—Minister Choiseul's—was about to be overthrown, and she made mistakes.

Like Madame, her ancestor, Marie-Antoinette had the impossible desire to be free, and cultivated the idea of escape. She, however, did not have the mental reserves of Madame. Having more to show, she was fonder of show than Madame and surrendered herself to the balls and masquerades and acting in the theatricals. She had fun while she was young and indulged her friends in every absurd whim. Marie-Antoinette learned the court repartee and quickly gave herself over to it. She was young in an old court, and the new ideas infected her, but not quite enough.

Minister Choiseul, who conquered the emperor's native Corsica for France, wrote that Louis XV was "a man without heart or brains, loving mischief as children love to hurt animals. . . . He would have liked above all to witness the executions . . . but he lacked the courage to attend. . . . What he most en-joyed in the hunt, I feel, he most enjoyed the destruction of life. . . . His spoiling as child and heir made him feel that he belonged to a different species." And is that not the point of kings? Like all kings, he was defined by what he had to give up.

At the end, in 1774, he rid himself of Parliament, which he came to think of as an assembly of republicans.

"Things will last as they are, as long as I shall," Louis XV said to Madame du Barry as he had said before to Pompadour. As always, du Barry agreed.

By then, Bouchardon had sculpted a great statue of him mounted with four maidens as the virtues Justice, Prudence, Peace, and Strength worship-ing at his spurs. And soon enough there was a sign "Grotesque monument, infamous, pedestal / Virtues go on foot, and vice on horseback."

Then, in 1774, a little girl at the Deer Park gave Louis XV the black pox, or perhaps he caught it elsewhere. For a long time, since he had suf-fered the pox as a child, he had thought himself immune. Then his face was dark and swelled with postules. The dauphin and Marie-Antoinette were kept away from his apartments at Versailles. Madame du Barry was sent off to a convent so he might confess his sins. An hour later, he wanted her back, but she had gone and could not return. (Madame du Barry lived into an-other age, a feat that is not always a good idea.)

In glided Louis XV's daughters, the Mesdames, in their black taffeta coats, to nurse him.

"When I come to die . . . ," he had always said, and his court had dis-agreed. But now they put out the candle in his window.

Louis XVI and Marie-Antoinette then heard the clickety-clack of hun-dreds of red heels rushing through the halls to them. The pounding grew, would wane as the courtiers turned a corner, then resume louder and louder still. That relentless sound was always the herald of a new king and the be-ginning of his dread.

They burst through the doors of the dauphine's apartment—first the man with the black feather in his hat.

"What a burden! At my age! And I have been taught nothing," Louis XVI said when he saw him. The others found him and Marie-Antoinette kneeling and weeping.

He was crowned Louis XVI, with the Régent in his crown. His grandfather's crown had been made for a twelve-year-old boy and was too small. Aubert the jeweler now made Louis XVI a new crown with the Régent in the center topping a fleur-de-lis with the Great Sancy and the Gros Mazarin.

In the middle of the ceremony at Rheims, as was the custom, the bishops and nobles set out to get the king to bring him to the cathedral. They struck at the door with a baton.

"What is it that you require?" said the chamberlain.

"We ask for the king."

"The king sleeps."

They struck again, same answer. And again, same answer.

"We demand Louis the Sixteenth, whom God has given us for king."

The chamber door opened quickly then, and there was Louis XVI, already fat, pretending to be asleep on a state bed, in a long crimson waistcoat trimmed with gold galloons, his shirt open where he was to be anointed with the holy ampula.* He was twenty then and not a beauty like his grandfather.

"It hurts me,"† Louis XVI whispered when the peers placed the heavy crown on his head. The peers looked at each other.

"May the king have the strength of the rhinoceros," they chanted. Louis XVI, who was physically very strong, was not strong enough for what awaited him. He touched his sore head.

The crown was eleven inches high and heavy enough to make him dizzy. Marie-Antoinette was left out of the coronation.

---

*Alexandre de Beauharnais, the first husband of the empress Josephine, was said to have broken this phial of holy oil to establish his credit during the Revolution, a ploy that ultimately did not work since he was beheaded.

†"It pricks me," Henri III said when he was crowned in 1574. Henri III had liked his jewels, for he once went to a ball dressed as a woman with necklaces on his bare neck. Later a fanatical monk entered his tent and knifed him, ending the house of Valois.

All That Is Taken Away

NOW I ENTER THE TIME OF THE DIAMOND IN WHICH I LIVED, the monarch I served before Napoleon.

The emperor, who watches my work on the diamond with one eye, wanted to know if I had come to Louis XVI in my chronicle. (He knew I had.) He said the king had been an exemplary private man, but a very poor king.

"Prime ministers were invented for those last kings," the emperor said, not for the first time. "I hunted with his gun and the queen lisped, you know." I knew but I let him lead me on.

"Whenever I mentioned Marie-Antoinette's name in Vienna," he continued, "her relatives would lower their eyes. In that court that meant the topic was unmentionable."

He told me how Marie-Antoinette brought a fatal informality to the court and disrupted its ancient gravity. The court mocked everything, but never its own sacred little forms, for they were the way to keep order. Marie-Antoinette quickly tired of the obligations of being a quasi deity, of those kneeling on a footstool to present her a towel or filing past to watch her eat a bite; and whereas Madame had insisted on rank and etiquette, she disdained it; she was considered a *moqueuse*.

"Were they not the same forms that you adopted under the empire, sire?" I asked so that I might write down the emperor's answer.

"Not at all. My *levées* and *couchées* were just a way to meet with my court and give them directions. After all, since I came from the multitude, I had to form a state of external importance. I should, otherwise, have been liable to be slapped on the shoulder every day."

I could not imagine this.

"A king does not exist in nature. He is a king only when dressed," the emperor reminded me, but looking at him in his raveled coat, I had to disagree.

Of course, I remembered all too well how no court was as splendid as the emperor's court, how princes came from all over Europe and lined up to see him. Someone once said that one could tell the rate of his progress through the room by the flush on the ladies' necks and arms as he approached. Never was there such luxury, and yet this luxury—the circus part of his "bread and circuses"—had function. His marriage to Marie-Louise and the King of Rome's baptism were a gift to our jewelers and silk makers and such. The emperor made new nobles and gave them decorations, crosses, and sashes. He created the Legion of Honor and gave out thousands, for the more he gave, the more were sought. As he knew, men were children more than once in their lives.

"We condemn Louis the Sixteenth," the emperor said, "but apart from his weakness, he was the first prince attacked. It was on him the new principles were first tried. His education, his ideas made him believe all belonged to him and always would."

I told him that in the opinion of Bertrand de Molleville, Louis XVI's naval minister, whom I knew well, Louis XVI had an uncommon learning and good judgment and intentions. He asked advice of too many, however, and could not ever decide. He had the Bourbons' memory as well as their need for remedial hunting—as much galloping and pursuit as possible. He had their melancholy and fatal shyness, and he, too, had the orphaned childhood, with his father dead when he was eleven and his mother when he was thirteen.

Louis XVI was the first king I had seen. No one looked away too long when he was in the room. I told the emperor he had a weight and was very polite. He had one of those gargling voices in which "garden" is sighed and exhaled into "guh arrrrr den." In telling the emperor about the king, our positions were suddenly reversed, for I, as a noble, had been presented to the king at a time when the emperor was but a young and obscure soldier. I was embarrassed at this thought of mine, however brief. It gave me no pleasure, for we were both men who, in losing our freedom, had lost all. There could be no contest between us in that regard and should there have been, he, alas, would have won, for I still had my son. He lost all Europe, its crowns and thrones, a wife and child, and all his family. He lost a world and kept only his personal glory. So I let him tell me. . . .

"According to her lady Madame Campan, Marie-Antoinette was not prodigal but stingy," the emperor said, "and the king too, for he would divide a single sheet of paper into eighths and write all over it, his writing becoming very small and cramped at the end so as not to begin a new sheet."

"I believe there are degrees of extravagance," I said, remembering . . .

My friend the princess de Lamballe had told me many stories when we were in exile, never imagining where or why I might recall them. She told me how Leonard, the queen's hairdresser, had climbed a ladder to re-create the old king's inoculation or his funeral or the bread riots of 1775 in her hair. All had large heads then with small chalk white faces smirking underneath. Mouse hair on their eyebrows, red lead and carmine on their cheeks, the ideas of Mesmer and the fraud Caglistro (the comte de Saint-Germain reborn) in their heads. With her dressmaker Mademoiselle Bertin, Marie-Antoinette had changed fashions every day. In the court of frivolity all was fashion—the day's way of speaking, the day's repartee or song, the day's games of *pan-pan*.

There was no learning tolerated except for the ponderous king, who went to bed at eleven while the queen gambled on into the moonlight. This was only a more extreme version of what had always been in the courts, the ripening at the end of the century, but with starvation in the land, it became intolerable.

The princess told me of the visit of the Russian grand duchess Maria Feodorovna in 1782. The grand duchess had just been given a reading of Beaumarchais' forbidden play *Le Mariage de Figaro*. This work mocked the court as did the book *Les Liasons Dangereuses*, by de Laclos. Both books swept Versailles and sent things into an ether full of dangerous murmurings.

There had been a ball for the grand duchess at Gabriel's theater at Versailles. All the ladies had been commanded to wear white satin dominoes with hoops and trains. As they pranced and turned under five thousand candles, Marie-Antoinette entered, her white plumed hat pinned with the Régent tilted over eyes the color of winter Paris skies.

She wore the Régent to astonish, and astonish she did. The Régent found its first beauty with her. Its function then was to enhance what was there—power or beauty—and make it more.

The princess de Lamballe also told me of all those nights in the rose gardens at Bagatelle. She described one fête at the Trianon when ballet dancers costumed as nymphs and fauns raced among the trees as musicians played from a raft on the lake, when the queen was in white gauze with flowers in her hair and Cardinal de Rohan had trespassed. This was the beginning of the affair of the diamond necklace.

Finally all the years of cultivated intrigue had bloomed into this supreme intrigue ten years after Louis XVI became king. The necklace, at 1,600,000 livres, was the most expensive ever made, consisting of long ropes and swags of the most perfectly matched giant diamonds ever assembled. The obscure and crooked Madame de la Motte had gotten Cardinal Rohan to buy the necklace to regain Marie-Antoinette's favor.

The necklace disappeared, the jeweler was never paid. There was a trial in Parliament, and though Marie-Antoinette won, she lost. The emperor always said that this affair of the necklace was one of the three causes of the Revolution.

By that time Marie-Antoinette had given up the heavy jewels and had her own diamonds reset as leaves and botanicals. Then she lost interest, began to shudder at ceremony, put aside her crimson jewel casket, and fell in love with the Rousseauian ideal. Such jewels were old; they were Madame du Barry, who had needed them to define her.

The Régent in that incarnation was no more than a fat drop of water on a jeweled flower—a noble savage of a jewel.

Marie-Antoinette was still led by her favorites and her personal tyrant, fashion. After the trade agreement with England at the peace of 1783, the fashion was for English gardens and goods, ribbons and equipages. The court was intrigued by little-understood foreign ideas like the constitution, the upper house, the lower house, habeas corpus, the balance of power.

I knew those who had been around Marie-Antoinette when she took up country life at the Petit Trianon. They told me how no one would stop what he was doing or stand when the queen of France entered the room in her muslin dresses with her flat straw hat like a crepe. There she leaned on walls painted with fake cracks. She went without her hoop and train for months at a time and let all be seated in her presence. She went out for night walks in her hamlet, where artifice met artifice and pretense prevailed. The crucial distinctions fell away when she abandoned luxury for deadly simplicity.

The king gave his support to the Americans rebelling against the English monarch. Then came the Americans and Monsieur Benjamin Franklin, the American ambassador, with his brown wool suits, unpowdered hair, and fur caps, going through Paris without a retinue. The fashion shifted to his country in revolt. In his image, the men of the court gave up their feathers and ribbons, took up heavy shoes and cudgels, mixed with the mob, who could not distinguish them sufficiently, and got into fights. It was all fashion, and what is fashion but a disguise?

Benjamin Franklin saw Dr. Montgolfier's first hot air balloon rise over Versailles in September 1783. It was blue and yellow and sailed over a crowd containing William Pitt the Younger.

By then Marie-Antoinette was said to be debauched, a Messalina given to sexual abominations with many lovers of both sexes. Now she was supposed to have a diamond chamber at Petit Trianon. *Libelles* against her were dropped in the rooms of Versailles; obscene puppet parodies played in the squares. Anyone could buy the two volumes of *The Private Life of the Queen* with its pornographic prints; soon there were many books of this sort. They wrote that she slept with both the king's brother Count d'Artois and her own, and that she was expensive.

In those days she teased the young English visitor William Pitt, never knowing his connection with the diamond she wore. Monsieur Pitt had told her the story of the man who invited him to France. The man who promised to introduce Pitt in society had turned out to be a grocer. Marie-Antoinette mentioned the grocer and giggled whenever she saw young William Pitt.

At twenty-five, the Queen had stopped dancing and asked Madame Campan to tell her when it was time for her to stop wearing flowers in her hair, when she had lost her bloom. By the time her baby daughter Sophie died, on June 19, 1787, it was indeed gone. Two years later, their son the dauphin Louis-Joseph lay dying at Meudon all twisted with tuberculosis of the spine, weak and full of fever. He was a precocious child who read history, was kind to those who served him, and noble in his soul and manner.

The *libelles* had never stopped. The queen knew that the people outside the court hated her; they hissed or were silent when she passed.

On May 5, 1789, the king wore the Régent and the crown jewels for the last time. That occasion was the opening of the Estates General and the closing of the absolute monarchy, divine rights, and all that. The stone, itself born from disruption, now shone on another upheaval.

The king and queen had to march from Notre Dame to the Church of Saint-Louis as their seven-year-old dying son was propped in the windows. The king waddled along in a gold suit, the embroidery of which was strewn with old rose diamonds newly recut into brilliants for his new diamond sword and diamond buttons. Thierry de la Ville d'Avray, chief *valet de chambre*, who ran the king's household, had the diamonds recut in Anvers. Someone had whispered this to me a year later when I was at court, just as though it still mattered. The king's shoe buckles and garters were diamonds too. He was a mass of diamonds and trouble.

The queen wore silver with the Great Sancy pinned in her hair. They were wearing bits of all the ancestors. New jewels and ancient jewels and the futility of those who wore them came together in one last burst of splendor. Whatever happened after that, it was never to be again. It was the last show until, of course, that of the emperor.

"Orléans forever!" said the crowd, cheering the king's cousin and rival as Marie-Antoinette passed, so shaken that the princess de Lamballe had to support her. Some of the court wanted to halt the procession; she waved them on, but, back in her apartments, she broke down. Her convulsions were such that she ripped at her jewelry before her women could take the jewels off. Her necklace snapped and pearls scattered all over the floor. Her bracelets burst apart and her women were crawling on the Aubussons to pick up her gems. They had to cut the clothes from her body.

The Estates General began the next day, May 6, in the Salle des Menus-Plaisirs at Versailles, the usual vast room with conflicting marbles above, swags of gilt leaves and florets, full of beauty and self-importance, full of what had been. Since the time of Louis XIV, this had been the place for balls and concerts.

The day of the Estates General, the king wore the decoration of the Golden Fleece, his new diamond sword, his orders, the epaulettes of Louis XV, new diamond buttons. In his hat besides a hat ribbon and a loop of diamonds was the Régent, set right in front so all the *Tiers*, the Third Estate, were sure to see. The Régent was like a third eye, the one that could see, for his other two were blind.

For this event they had opened the doors for the first time since 1614. In came the clergy in their cassocks and large red mantles and square caps, the bishops in their violet robes, the nobles with their lace cravats and black cloaks embroidered in gold, their white plumed hats upturned. Then in came six hundred men with muslin cravats, plain black cloaks, and slouched hats: the defiant *Tiers*, the next France. No one let them carry swords.

The king and queen were on thrones, the queen's slightly lower. She wore white satin with a purple velvet cloak and fanned herself with a huge white feather fan sprinkled with diamonds. She fanned hard as though to drive away the strangers, the unpresented, those who hated her and believed the worst, all the demons of trouble.

"Throw open the windows!" someone said.

By then, Louis XVI had studied his history and was trying not to act like Charles I, who lost his head. He spoke slowly and his voice squeaked like one of his locks without grease. He spoke of the financial crisis and the debt due to the American war and said he was the "first friend of his people," which he truly believed he was.

Marie-Antoinette fanned herself. Though it was only May, she wobbled that fan as the diamond aigrette in her hair jiggled and trembled.

That spring of 1789, I visited my mother at Sorreze, then in the autumn went to Coëtilliou, the château of the marquis de Vaudreuil.

Through all my wars and voyages, Coëtilliou had waited for me in the middle of a forest, down a long alley of old chestnut trees, across a moat filmed with limey iridescent green. That château had remained in my mind as the France that once had been, more home to me than my home. Whenever I returned, it was like falling into an enchanted past. By then I had been to sea and the hot spice islands, where I would dream of Coëtillou and find the dream mist lingering all day like a small determined cloud.

Everyone has this one bewitched place that recedes even as he chases it, and those that live in that place become dear by association. There I found again the young Countess Henriette de Kergariou.

I had first seen Henriette when I was sixteen and just out of military school. I was then with my cousin in Toulouse in the household of the duc de Penthièvre, the father-in-law of the princess de Lamballe. Henriette was twelve then, and I paid little attention to the tiny girl with the long black hair who was always hiding or rushing past, looking back over her shoulder with her big night eyes.

I had entered the navy, and then embarked on the *Actif* and took part in the last battle of the American war and the siege of Gibraltar. Two years later, I again stayed at the castle with my intimate friend Jean-Henri de Volude, then sailed for Saint Domingue, where the stomach problems that still plague me began and I had time to read and cry over *La Nouvelle Héloïse*.

When I returned to France and saw her again I was nineteen; her mischief had become liveliness and wit; she was still tiny and had become very attractive to me. I left again, to sail to Martinique, and there had long suppers with the baroness Tascher and her niece the enticing vicomtesse de Beauharnais, who had been abandoned by her husband and as "Josephine" would marry Napoleon and become empress of France.

After much time at sea, I was twenty-one and back in France for the cruel winter of the famine of 1788–1789, when I sat before the fire in Brittany and read of the madness of George III and the popularity of William Pitt.

Now that spring, I came back to Coëtilliou. Henriette had the measles and I sat by her bed, held her dry hand, and brought her new lilacs and violets from her gardens. I helped her father level his land and fell in love with this country girl from my own gentle world. Louis XVI finally made me a naval lieutenant and Henriette was well enough to pin on my epaulettes. It was as if I had made a circle, walked the moat of this castle, and she was the beginning and the end. We were far in place from this thing called the Revolution that was growing in the inns and cafés and squares. Inside the walls, we still gamed and laughed and wore mother-of-pearl buttons that said in Latin that it was better to die than be dishonored.

Louis XVI was blind and closed, but all those I knew believed in him fervently. With the fleur-de-lis had come the debts and the contentious Parlement, the wars and the wheat crises and the changing ministers—Maurepas, Malherbes, Turgot, Necker, Calonne, then the popular Necker again until he was dismissed. The king recalled Necker, but it was too late. Too late, and maybe that is the history of the Bourbons, for now the people rose up in fury.

While we laughed and danced in the country, the Revolution had begun. In the gardens of the Palais Royale on July 14 that summer of 1789, Camille Desmoulins had said, "Citizens, if we would save our lives, we must fly to arms." He tore off a leaf and put it in his hat. The crowd stripped the alleys of trees and, wearing the color of hope, became the National Guard and attacked the Bastille. The Revolution had its own jewel, for General La Fayette had added the Bourbon white to blue and red, the colors of Paris, and formed a ribbon cockade.

"Do they wish to imitate the English Revolution of 1648?" Marie-Antoinette asked the princess de Lamballe. "To make France a commonwealth! Before I advise the king to take such a step, they shall bury me under the ruins of the monarchy."

Many of us fled then and became émigrés ready to fight for our king and queen. The roads to the Rhine were clogged with our carriages and equipages. The Assembly abolished all titles and rank in their wake. All the princes were gone, the ducs and counts with their coats of arms, their nobility rings on their pinkies, their liveries. I lost my title and still I stayed. The courts were reformed; the vote was given to all. The estates of the clergy were confiscated and became promissory notes called *assignats,* the new money. My family and others gave up our ancient privileges and abolished serfs, the tolls, our manorial rights and dues.

Soon enough this ruined all those who fed and clothed us and made our hats and carriages and furniture. The clergy gave up its tithes. The citizens burned castles and convents, tore up deeds and feudal charters, and hacked up tax collectors. We in the country were amazed at not being burned down as we watched the horror advance.

Hail had ruined the crops; the American war had done the rest. France copied Americans for its Declaration of the Rights of Man and became a limited monarchy based on a constitution. It was still not enough; we had not bled enough of the old blood.

On October 5–6, the market women marched to Versailles howling for bread, blood, and change. All the beautiful days now ended with these voices in the night and women holding out their white aprons for the queen's head and entrails. They were in the palace, then in the Oeil de Boeuf, the shabbiest people ever in that room.

"Save the queen!" her women said.

The queen, who had fussed over the placement of a ribbon, now snatched up a bedspread to wrap around herself; her women dressed her and she ran to the king's room. The mob killed the guards at her door and stabbed at her empty bed.

Louis-Joseph, the hunchback dauphin, had died on June 4 covered with sores and coughing blood. Their second son, the new dauphin, was five and in peril. The king was paralyzed and in a stupor.

The mob marched back to Paris with the king and queen, who would never return to Versailles again. Incensed and afraid, they could look out their carriage and see whores riding the cannons, wagons of their corn and flour, the crowd with their pikes and poplar branches like a moving forest of terror. The heads of two of their bodyguards were on pikes. The mob stopped to have the hair on the severed heads powdered and dressed so they would be recognized as aristocrats. In caskets were the Régent and the other crown jewels that had been kept at Versailles since Louis XIV. Along with the jewels went all the treasured toys of the kings—their vases and objects of sardonyx, agate, lapis lazuli, jade and jasper, rock crystal, amethyst, quartz, and amber, many mounted in vermeil or gold. There was a baby rattle from Catherine the Great, the vessels of Louis XIV, gifts Tippoo Saib had given in August, the year before the bad harvest and the pillaging of the granaries.

The jewels had belonged to the state since the time of François I, who started the collection two centuries ago; the kings only had use of them. The commissioners of the Assembly placed them in the Garde Meuble, one of the two new buildings constructed by Gabriel in Place Louis XV.

The National Assembly left Versailles for Paris and moved into the riding academy of the Tuileries, where they gave the king use of the jewels. I do not think he wore them again—at least not the Régent.

At the ruins of the Bastille was a maypole with a sign, HERE WE DANCE. A year after the Bastille fell, I was there on the Champs de Mars on July 14, 1790, when the king vowed to support the constitution and the crowd cheered him. Already I could see some of the bent red caps, like those the Roman slaves wore when they were freed, in the crowd. Red, white, and blue plumes rose from the queen's hat, becoming wet, then limp in the rain and finally drooping. The damp ruined the illuminations, too.

As the queen held her son, the second dauphin, up to the crowd, his legs kicked against her dress in terror.

16

"Bonjour"

I T WAS AFTER ALL THIS THAT I MET THEM. I, WHO WAS BORN OF the nobility of Andalusia in the "Château" de Las Cases in Haute-Garonne (Languedoc), was presented to King Louis XVI and Queen Marie-Antoinette in the spring of 1790, when I was twenty-three. My cousin the marquis de ——— had called me to Paris from my nest of monarchists at Vaudreuil, where, as a game, we chose the jobs we would have as émigrés.

As it turned out, I was the last person to be presented under the laws wherein one had to show oneself descended from the old nobility. Since the fifteenth century my family had fought in the armies of France. When my ancestor went to fight the Moors in Spain and showed great bravery, the king of Portugal gave him *"todas las cases"* (all the houses) near the battlefield. In my family, I had generations of soldiers and knights. After me, no such proofs were required. I was introduced as "Las Casas," for people then took their oldest names.

I had crossed Mantauban and was staying at Hôtel de Toulouse. I approached the Tuileries through gardens where whores sauntered and weeds had grown brown in the fountains. In the palace workmen stood by ladders fixing the decay with no particular urgency.

By then, the king and queen were prisoners. Though no one knew quite how things would end, these last days had the particular sweetness of a fruit the morning before the afternoon it rots. The king and queen were just holding on, and yet nothing dimmed their magnificence for me.

They had just come from washing the (already cleaned up) feet of twelve poor people as they did on Maundy Thursday before every Easter. The king poured on a ladle of water and Marie-Antoinette dried. My cousin brought me to the billiard room of the Galerie de Diane, where the duc de Villequier presented me—"son of the marquis de Las Casas, lord of La Caussade de Puylaurens, Lamothe, and Dourne"—to the king. The princesse de Chimay presented me to the queen and the king's sister Madame Elisabeth and brother Monsieur (the comte de Provence, who would become Louis XVIII's and our enemy). Monsieur was very fat and soft.

The queen was stouter than I expected and her lips twitched as though she were trying to stifle a yawn. Then she managed a faint smile, into which escaped her disdain for my youth and obscurity. She did not resemble this being whom others had seen skimming the floors like a rushed aerial sprite, this queen whose most cherished presumption was privacy. She had the bulging lower lip of the Austrian emperors, and a long neck supported her fine head with the pale powdered hair. I saw her two dead children on her face.

The king, who was only thirty-five then, looked above my head into a distance and said, *"Bonjour,"* in a small cracked voice. His diamond buttons were fastened wrong on his coat, leaving a gap and a puff of silk.

He squinted and looked down as though it were hard to make me out. None of the Bourbons could see well. And then he turned away, even though I was to be his last new noble.

His step was heavy, as were his pleasures, which were for killing stag, lock making, and masonry. I told the emperor that once, in those court days, I came upon him bent over the brass lock of a door. He seemed to be fixing it.

"What did you do?" the emperor asked me.

"I backed away—quickly."

"Tell me more about them," he ordered.

"They were . . . diminished."

"Something of the *citoyen* about them already?"

"No, sire, never. Not even then. They were another species, yet less than they might have been." I told the emperor that sometimes you see a person and sense that even though he has already lived the most interesting time of his life, he still retains traces of what had been, and that is his glamour. He is the repository of generations of kings and courts, bows and ceremonies, fêtes and wars.

I was allowed to be in the king's rooms at the king's *levée* and the *couchée*, for the ceremonies of dressing continued even then. I was way in the background, hugging the silk of the walls, looking past a sea of fancy shoulders against the gray-green boiserie. An old man pulled apart a *duchesse brisée* and Baroness L'Arbredor arose, her movements a slow dance, defying real difficulty with fake ease.

At the king's games, I pulled up the *voyeuse*, and straddled the chair to look over the backs of those playing cards, secrets folded into their pockets. Even in the late court I saw how those last courtiers lived in a kind of war, defending themselves day and night. There was an enemy for every compliment. Their faces were divided with nervous eyes above and flashing smiles below. Even in the brief hollow time I was there, I never could keep up.

Because of his poor eyes, the king could not judge distance and would charge forward into whomever he addressed, backing him into a wall of courtiers, trapping him in uncomfortable momentary glory as he discharged a harmless royal banality.

I went to the Château Meudon near Versailles, where I was astonished to see the king ride his horse right into the salon. This was the first time I saw women who had to crouch and turn sideways to get through a door. I had learned to talk their language, but I was young, remote, and shy. I said very little, and that, I fear, very poorly. I found them all so quick.

I told the marquis who had brought me to court that the monarchs were splendid, but I felt trouble floating about them. Within layers of ceremony, they seemed actually frightened. It was the same discomfort and the special sadness of being out of place that I have found here with the emperor. The Bourbon kings always had a habit of shifting from one foot to the other and I saw the king do this, as though his own weight were more than he could bear. He and the queen were gentle and vague in the creeping brutality of the land; all the old ways and ceremonies were no longer any protection.

For a marriage begun with such horror and disappointment, at the end, the king and queen seemed to have grown into the kind of fierce hopeless love that comes when compromise is accepted. They looked to each other frequently. With their small beaked noses, they were like a pair of proud rare birds hovering on the winds of extinction.

The emperor has said if Louis XVI had openly resisted, if he had had the courage and ardor of Charles I, the king he studied, he would have triumphed. The nobles, the clergy, the army all supported him, as did foreign governments. (Of course, Charles I lost his head, I neglected to remind him.)

"In England, the death of the king gave birth to the republic; in France, the birth of the republic caused the death of the king," the emperor has told me for my *Memorial*.

Where did the monarchy come from? Who was the first king of France? The first king was the best soldier. Then the best soldier's son was king. France, always a military country, crowned her soldiers. Louis XVI was no soldier; his blood was a pale slow stream filled with fat and doubt and manners. The bravery and resistance that had made the first soldier-kings had become noble resignation and the calm that comes with helplessness.

Their life in the Tuileries then was rich only in misery. The king walked in his garden, his crouching courtiers replaced by six grenadiers of the bourgeois militia with an officer of his household and a page. When he returned to the palace, the doors were opened for everyone, though the queen was still walking with a lady and the guards close at her heels. A crowd of unknowns followed. They were prisoners, even though people still took off their hats to them.

And so I too left and joined the émigrés at Worms in Germany. I enrolled in the army of the prince of Condé to fight to save those I had just met. But first we danced.

The king and queen decided to flee to the army of the marquis de Bouille at Metz, and everything went wrong. Count Fersen, who had once been the queen's lover, arranged for the flight on June 20, 1791. He or his former mistress paid for the large green and yellow *berline* to carry them. Marie-Antoinette began the flight for her life by ordering a complete trousseau made for herself and her children. She also ordered the most elaborate *nécessaire de voyage,* containing a Sèvres tea set and a vermeil manicure set. She carefully chose the white taffeta and white velvet to line her escape coach, for even her desperation had style. She had never known another way; fashion was all that was left her.

In the middle of May, a month before the flight to Varennes, the queen and Madame Campan had laid out her personal jewels, the diamonds separated by cotton, on a sofa in her closet. They were ready to be packed away in red morocco leather cases marked with a cipher and the arms of France. It had taken a whole evening and then the queen went off to play cards, leaving her closet locked and the jewels out. (The Régent and the crown diamonds had already been delivered up to the Assembly.) A woman of the wardrobe, a spy with a duplicate key, entered and saw the preparations. The spy prepared a report for La Fayette and others telling of her suspicion that the queen was about to flee.

A month later, the escape took place. They said Marie-Antoinette got lost leaving the Tuileries and wandered the streets of Paris for an hour disguised as a lady's maid. Finally, off they went in the big fancy coach, with the *nécessaire* and the tea set and the king's sister and Count Ferson, the ex-lover, driving for a while. The king, disguised as a valet, stuck his improbable head out. Unfortunately, since his profile was on the paper *assignats*, he was recognized. Also, few people looked quite like that man. All went wrong. They missed the connections with the hussars and troops, they could not get fresh horses, they were pursued, detained in a little town, put upstairs in a little house.

"What audacity! What cruelty! Subjects having the temerity to give orders to their king and a daughter of the Caesars!" said the queen to her captors. That night Marie-Antoinette's hair turned white and dry under her gypsy cap.

She sent the princess de Lamballe a ring holding this new hair with "Bleached by Sorrow" engraved upon it. The princess had shown it to me when we both were émigrés at Koblenz. The princess had put the ring in my hand and a tear trickled down through the chalk on her face. The ring made me shiver.

The queen had given the box of her personal diamonds to Leonard, her hairdresser, who got through to Brussels with the jewels on the same night they did not. Thus when they were in jail, the king and queen of France were forced to borrow money.

The day after the failed flight to Varennes, the Assembly met and voted to make an inventory of the jewels in the Garde Meuble. They were then called "the endowment of the crown," or Civil List. Thierry de la Ville d'Avray, who by then had democratized his name to Marc-Antoine Thierri, supervised the inventory. The Great Sancy, the Hortensia (the Diamond of Five Sides), the huge holy decorations lay on their pale blue silk cushions in drawers in the long red leather coffin of jewels.

When Thierri came to the Régent, sparkling lone and unequaled, he looked at the diamond he had pinned on the king as an old friend and wondered what was to become of it.

William Pitt the Younger, the second son of Lord Chatham, was then prime minister in England. He was already for almost ten years the master of his country while Napoleon was but a captain, chased from Corsica, arriving anew in France. Pitt had become chancellor of the Exchequer at twenty-three, and prime minister when he was only twenty-four.

Marie-Antoinette tried desperately to reach Pitt, to know his mind on the Revolution, to know if he might save them. She remembered the young Pitt who had come to her court and how she had teased him about the grocer who would present him to society. At the same time, she feared Pitt and told Madame Campan, "I never pronounce the name of Pitt but I feel death at my shoulder." She then felt Pitt was the enemy of France, that he was seeking revenge for the support France gave to the Americans in 1781. She even thought Pitt served the Revolution in France. Still she wanted to know his mind.

The queen had asked the princess de Lamballe to try to get to Pitt through the duchess of Gordon, who had great political influence. The princess failed. When she was half inviting and half discouraging the princess to come back to her after Varennes, the queen wrote, "Many about us profess to see the future as clear as the sun at noonday. But, I confess, my vision is still dim. . . . If we do not see you, send me the result of your interview at the precipice." The "precipice" was her code word for William Pitt. Marie-Antoinette was fond of code and cipher and wrote to foreign powers in a cipher based on a certain edition of Bernadin de Saint-Pierre's *Paul et Virginie* (a love story that the emperor likes and that I read to him some nights before he sleeps).

The fatal diamond, now taken from the king of France and locked at the Committee of Public Safety, connected Pitt and the queen of France. What a round this was! Louis XVI, descendant of one who refused to buy Pitt's diamond, now looked to Pitt's great-grandson to help him keep the throne, and Marie-Antoinette, descendant of Madame, whose son had bought the Régent, was petitioning this mighty Pitt.

By then I had not yet begun to fight. I was with the princess de Lamballe in the émigré salons and at the masked balls in Aix-la-Chapelle. The queen wrote to the princess that she and the king were in the clutches of a "race of tigers." She said don't come back to me, but the princess knew just what that meant and returned to her friend by mid-November.

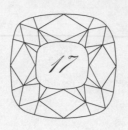

The Emperor's Handkerchief, Bitter Milk, and Blood

THIS AFTERNOON THE EMPEROR HELPED ME FIND A THICK
packet of documents on the famous robbery of the crown jewels
in 1792. As I bent over his trunks, my vision dimmed and I felt
the dark veil fall upon my eyes. I sat back and rubbed, and the emperor
summoned Emmanuel, who made me rest on the bed. Then he himself
fetched me one of his handkerchiefs wetted with cool water.

Because of my eyes we have a new way of working now. When it gets to
be about four o'clock and my turn to read or write with the emperor, Emmanuel uses my "hieroglyphics" to take the emperor's dictation, while I sit
listening hard in a corner. If Emmanuel cannot read what he has written, I
can tell him almost word for word what the emperor said.

Later, I was able to look over the documents from a Monsieur Bapst as
well as some sealed with the commune's red seals and a stack of *Moniteurs*
tied in a great daunting bundle. With these, I hope to give my narrative of
how the Régent was stolen. I knew little of the events of Paris then and have
had to rely on the emperor and others who were there at that time. Of
course, I cannot be certain of anything because I was far away. Nor can I ask
the generals here, for some were too young, others were fighting, and none

wish to relive those days or any days but those with the emperor. Besides, they would not tell me anyway, out of spite.

That September of 1792 I was considered the enemy—part of the force marching to threaten Paris. In fact we—this army of émigré princes supposedly lolling about—were slaves to the Prussians who surrounded us. The Prussians rode by to jeer as we dragged our cannons through the mud, our uniforms in shreds, our gold epaulettes hanging. After we were defeated at Valmy by the army of the Revolution, the duke of Brunswick, who led us, dealt with General Dumouriez and suddenly we all turned around and retreated. No one understood why then or now.

I lagged behind due to the weight of my gear and my fever, and I still managed to cross the frontier while those who were behind me were captured and executed in Paris. All of us then saw how we had been trapped— how the republic had pushed us out to rid itself of us, how we fought for a king no one wanted enough.

I became a fugitive, outcast all over Europe. I could not go to Belgium or Germany and so went to Amsterdam, where I found a ship to England. Five days later, with seven louis in my pocket, I saw the Tower of London, and there Jean-Henri de Volude and I lived a whole other life.

The emperor's handkerchief is of the finest lawn, embroidered with his *N* and a very small crown. I intend to keep it unless he asks for its return.

Every Monday of 1791–1792 the commune opened the big blue doors of the Garde Meuble, the king's warehouse, a kind of Louvre of leftover armor, royal beds, and crown jewels.

"It was there I saw the Régent for the first time," the emperor told me. "I even held it in my hand. Bourrienne* and I went on one of the Mondays when they let everyone in to wander the detritus of the kings. It was a dangerous time. Travelers felt the trouble coming and shunned Paris."

He told me of the crowds in their rags and hobnail boots with their baskets and staves, the women in their *negligées à la patriote*. All wore the national ribbon and many the impudent jewels of the Revolution—stones from the Bastille set into necklaces and bracelets. They had come from towns where even the trees in the squares and the saints wore the red cap and Jesus often had a cockade tied to his left arm.

---

*Antoine de Bourrienne, his school friend from Brienne and later his secretary.

"Some of them were barefoot in this warehouse of the kings," he said. "As we walked the rooms of tapestries and state beds everyone was whispering and groaning in anger. We all wanted to see the jewels. They were heaped out on shelves in an armoire on the second floor. All the big diamonds were stuck on wax in glass vitrines but the Régent had a little low room of its own."

He was smiling now at my interest as he told how he and Bourrienne had lined up and taken tickets and waited until the guard passed the diamond through a sort of ticket window. It was in a solid steel claw with an iron chain padlocked inside the window.

"Both the king and his diamond were in cages then," he said and told how the gendarmes studied everyone but, since all said the same thing, were quickly bored.

"Bourrienne was making vulgar jokes but I kept staring. I felt no desire, for the diamond was impossible to me and desire must include the possible, no? I remembered it, though."

I imagined him so young then, obscure, full of wonder whether he admitted it or not. Perhaps not furious as the others, who, having burned and pillaged our estates, saw the mass of jewels displayed in this time of "nation" as a taunt. The people could not quite touch the treasure, yet it was said to be theirs for they were freed Romans, new Americans, they were the *patrie*, the native land.

A member of the commune had said, "[One] sucks in this house the milk of the aristocracy which has dominated there so long." It was bitter milk. The Garde Meuble was a place where resentment was cultivated and bloomed every Monday. I knew the building well for ten years later I came to live just around the corner, at 6 Rue Saint-Florentin, when I returned to Paris with some money from my *Atlas*. It was even then a bodiless tomb, its cold and lordly rooms echoing with the loneliness of all museums.

Among the people who went to see the crown jewels every Monday of the first months of 1792 was the Parisian Paul Miette. Miette hung out in the Champs Élysées, where the ground steamed with infection and criminals lurked behind every tree ready to rob and fell all who passed except their own. Every fence in Paris was glad to see Miette, "the silver merchant"; as he emptied his sack, every "treasure" had its own lie.

Sometimes Miette was in disguise as he asked, in the name of the people, to see the tyrant's big diamond. The two detectives outside the little room noticed him at once for, like all major criminals, he had something both ordinary and alarming about him. He also had the thief's *V* on one shoulder and four and a half fingers on the hand reaching for the Régent.

Miette saw how the stones might be pried from their settings and sold to the Jews around Mont de Piété. He saw how the door to the Rue Saint-Florentin side of the Garde Meuble sometimes had half-drunken teenage guards and sometimes no guards at all, how close the lampposts were to the first-floor balconies. He did not care that the Garde Meuble was one of twin buildings designed by Gabriel (the other is the Hôtel Crillon) at the bequest of the marquise de Pompadour—only that they were easy to climb. In the center of the square then was the statue of Louis XV by Bouchardon, and often he would pause by the bronze foot of the handsome lecherous king who had worn the Régent as he looked back to study the site.

Miette was thirty-five then, the same age as the king. He had been sent to jail for burglary when he was thirteen and then at fifteen and banished from Paris. Then he was back, caught, and freed until March, when he was caught again. By June he had been sent back to prison for four months. He had made his plans, now he would have to wait.

On June 20, 1792, while Miette was in La Force prison recruiting thieves to rob the Garde Meuble, a crowd of thirty thousand marched on the Tuileries. Napoleon, who had arrived from Corsica the month before and seen the Régent, was having lunch with Bourrienne near the Palais Royale when he heard the hollow clop of clogs running on cobblestones and saw ragged men passing by with a calf's heart labeled "Aristocrat's Heart" stuck on a pike.

He went out for a closer look and was heaved along by the rabble heading for the Assembly. One man held black silk breeches on a cross staff that said "Tremble, tyrants! The sansculottes are coming."

They were in the gardens, Napoleon in the crowd, engulfed by its rage, its smells, as they smashed the doors to the Tuileries and asked for the "idiot," meaning Louis XVI.

The king, backed into a window under the Oeil de Boeuf, had to take the red cap from a pike some ruffian held out. It was too small and everyone began to laugh. They shoved a "Tremble, tyrant!" placard at him and a doll of his wife hanging from a lamppost. They made him drink a toast to the nation.

"What have I ever done to you that you should hate me so?" Marie-Antoinette said to them, and Napoleon, pushed up against centuries of exquisite shiny furniture, noticed her accent and the fabulously huge and exaggerated cockade she wore. The king's torment lasted two hours; Napoleon thought he behaved well, and studied him as much as he could, while pretending to be as angry as the rest.

That morning as he heard the shouts and running feet, Marc-Antoine Thierri, who then lived in the Garde Meuble and was in charge of the crown jewels, took the Régent and the big loose diamonds into his apartment. He had always been afraid for the jewels and had complained many times about the teenage guards, who didn't show up or fell asleep over their Chinese lanterns.

As he held the Régent, Thierri considered each piece of his gilded beechwood furniture, then hid the diamonds in an armoire at the end of an alcove, piling parcels on top of them. He sat down on his fauteuil in front of his blue silk fire screen and held his powdered, imperiled head in his hands.

A month later, the revolutionary government ordered everyone to wear the linen tricolor cockade; previously my family had worn silk cockades of paler red and blue. Now those few of the nobility who had remained in Paris painted clouds over the coats of arms on their carriages and took them off the gates of their great houses.

In August, Thierri was ordered to put the diamonds back into the jewel room. Then the Paris commune stopped the Monday visits, closed the Garde Meuble, and sealed its cabinets with their seals.

On August 10, 1792, even as the mob again invaded the Tuileries, this time to seize the king, the Assembly officially declared the Régent the national diamond of France.

The emperor, a captain by then, told me he was still in Paris that day. At the sound of the tocsin, running to a furniture shop on Place du Carrousel that belonged to Bourrienne's brother, he saw some hideous men now with a human head at the end of a pike who made him cry out, "Long live the nation!"

"I would rather be nailed to the walls of the palace than leave it," Marie-Antoinette said.

"What a lot of leaves. They have fallen early this year," said the king as he and his family crunched through leaves to their ankles as they retreated to the Assembly. He had told his Swiss guards not to fire on the mob.

Later, Napoleon went into the carnage in the garden of the Tuileries and saw the red twisted legs of eight hundred fallen Swiss guards—never in his battles so far had he seen so much death. Many were pleading and still dying even as women with gloves of blood to their elbows ravaged the corpses and committed the worst indecencies. Carrying the queen's dresses and silver, they ran past Napoleon. Thus, he who was made for war met this mess and disorder that was the Revolution and disliked the power of the mob forever more. As he watched the taking of the Tuileries, he never imagined that within twelve years this palace and all the jewels he had seen in the Garde Meuble would be his.

The next day, another mob tore down Bouchardon's statue of Louis XV and hacked it to pieces, even its pedestal and balustrade. Once, I came upon a huge bronze foot at an antique dealer's, who swore it was the foot of this statue. I wished I had had enough money and the courage to buy it.

At the Assembly, they shouted at the king and Marie-Antoinette, who sat like imitations of themselves, for fifteen hours. Then they took them to the Temple and put them in the tower prison. Now the queen's quest for the simple was fulfilled, for what is simpler than a prison? The stone walls and cracks were real, the jailers' peasant faces, the deprivations. The daily indignities made the former dignities that she had suffered seem sweet. The scrutiny she was used to at court was parodied here.

Her bookcase with its leather-bound books, the scraps of her wardrobe all were preserved for later times when every shoe and fabric bit, every shagreen manicure kit and lace fan, every chair where she sat and whispered with her ladies would become suddenly precious. Precious in retrospect as it always is with us. (All here have seen that the rhythm of our history is destruction followed by remorse, then absurd veneration.)

Soon enough, those I had known who did not flee would follow their monarchs into the prisons. And even there, where the rats ran over silk slippers, they kept up a court with all its distinctions. It was still Monsieur le Comte deferring to Monsieur le Duc, still the games, even acting out the guillotine. Some tried to kill themselves with a nail in the heart or by dashing their heads against the bars as their laces shredded, their satin tore, and their hair flattened to greasy strands.

On August 16, after the fall of the monarchy, Joseph Cambon, the former minister of the interior, proposed selling all the crown jewels to back the currency. He wanted Jean-Marie Roland, the new minister of the interior, to guard them. As the first guillotine was hammered into the Tuileries gardens to deliver death with a minimum of spectacle, the Régent was about to be sold.

In La Force prison in the fourth month of his sentence, Paul Miette refined his plan to rob the Garde Meuble and recruited some of those who would participate. Internally then, our kingdom was struggling into a republic. Externally, it was being attacked, for our coalition armies had invaded France, threatening to destroy Paris if the king were harmed. By the beginning of September, we had taken Verdun and were marching to Paris, where thousands of men got drunk enough to enlist to fight against us.

All Paris, incited by Dr. Marat's treacherous newspaper, was enflamed; the government fractured into clubs. Weeks before, the Girondin club had summoned three hundred men from Marseilles—Greeks and Corsicans, and foreign lowlifes from the prisons, who marched to Paris singing, *"Allons, enfants de la patrie / Le jour de gloire est arrivé. . . . Aux armes, citoyens! / Formez vos bataillons!"* The emperor has called this song by Rouget de Lisle the greatest general of the Revolution.

The Girondins had called for them, but soon enough they worked for the commune, for the pockfaced lawyer Danton and Dr. Marat, who saw traitors and foreign plots everywhere. The new recruits arrested priests who would not support the constitution, some nobles and ordinary citizens who looked rich, had a nice watch, or were suspected of believing in kings.

"All yearn, all quiver, all burn for combat," said Danton on Sunday, September 2, and suddenly he was right.

Some priests, including Abbé Sicard, who ran the school for the deaf, were in a carriage on their way to jail at the Abbaye de Saint-Germain. Assassins stabbed them through the open carriage windows as the people applauded, and when the carriages stopped, eight dead priests fell out. The crowds hacked apart the others and ran through the priests at the Carmelite convent, in the chapel facing the bleeding Jesus, where the blood still remains in the stone floors. Two hundred priests were torn from the garden walls they were trying to climb at Carmes.

In the prisons at this time, one day there was a knife with the silverware, the next day the guards took it away. Assassins with axes and pikes, hatchets, and even shovels stabbed and whacked apart hundreds of the helpless at

Châtelet, and hundreds more at the Conciergerie. At the beginning of the massacres, they released the violent criminals to join in the killing and rape of the invalid poor and insane, the boys of twelve, the prostitutes. Women brought them picnic lunches and they sat down to their baskets amidst the carnage.

The planners had put their victims into the thick-walled prisons so the killings would be as silent as possible and Paris could go about its business. Then the commune changed its mind, put seats at the prison doors, and lit lamps in the evenings. For five days screams were followed by *"Vive la nation!"* In their aprons and red caps, with human ears pinned to them as trophies, they put candles on the naked corpses and ate. They drank human blood and stroked it on their faces. Along the way the tribunal held some mock trials. Everywhere there was running, except for those who had no place to run.

Carts of bodies were dumped into quicklime in mass graves while bonfires sent clouds of human ashes to the skies. Children danced around the carcasses as ordinary citizens watched or turned away. The emperor has told me how the air smelled of the vinegar used to scrub the killing sites and how Place de Grève was such a swamp of blood that the guillotine could not be anchored there. Blood was in the people's boots, tracked through theater lobbies, for still Parisians filled the theaters and restaurants, since that is their character.

The dust of insanity blew over the city as citizens ducked behind trees in the moonlight and emerged as cannibals and vampires and diseased beasts. Others closed their shutters so as not to see or hear. A pretty woman I then knew as Rose de Beauharnais hid in her house in Rue Saint-Dominique and played her harp. The emperor has said he too did not join in.

The sansculottes ran into La Force prison, killed four hundred there, and tossed the heads about for sport. In different parts of La Force then were two who had touched the Régent—the princess de Lamballe, who had pinned it on the queen, and Paul Miette, who had held it in its cage—another of those strange linkages, like the joining of Napoleon and Pitt, in the history of the diamond.

During the September massacres, Miette escaped from La Force, though later he swore in court he had been freed at the end of August. He still had his jailhouse face, the pallor of an oubliette, as he ran out into the anarchy, slipping on the blood.

They had taken the princess de Lamballe from the Temple, where she had gone with the king and queen, and put her alone in La Force. The princess had been safe in exile at Aix-la-Chapelle when the queen summoned her back to the "tigers." I was with her then before I went off to fight, and heard one of the voices of Versailles say that since she had once enjoyed the prosperity of the queen, she should be faithful to her now. Such was her tender heart, long ago captured by the lies of novels, that she returned to Paris.

I knew her well for my cousin was her *dame d'honneur*. When I arrived at Aix at the beginning of my emigration, the young princess, who had been widowed at nineteen, received me with the greatest kindness. Around her then was all the debris of Versailles cringing and mincing in their decorative uselessness. At the slightest excuse, the princess had a habit of falling slowly to the ground, rivulets of her famous blond hair somehow always loosening in her faint.

I was going to follow her when she went to Paris to join the king and queen in their final captivity. My parents had given me to her, considering that my young age and the little time I had spent in Paris made me unknown and, therefore, safe and useful to her. At the last minute, the princess forbade me to accompany her from Koblenz and saved my life.

The princess's father-in-law, the duc de Penthièvre, had offered half his fortune to Manuel the Procurer to get her free. Someone warned her never to leave her cell, and when Manuel came for her, she refused to go. She was ever an obedient princess, meant only to coast through palace gardens in a thin dress, trailing a lone dethorned rose. She was meant to dance, plan amusements with the young queen, and collapse when her pretty world became too much. She staggered at the sights on her way to her final questioning and, after thirteen hours, refused to swear to hate the king and queen she had loved so well.

"To hate them is against my nature," she said and fell into the arms of her attendant.

"Free!" the tribunal said as they always did. Then the clerks threw open the doors and the victim was dragged outside and hacked apart.

Crossing the bloody courtyard, the princess fell insensible. A mulatto man she had educated and baptized then struck her head with his halberd. Her cap tumbled off, her hair was loosed and completely covered her. The man struck again. Others cut off the head of my gentle friend. Her headless body was raped and brutalized beyond all comprehension. They disemboweled her, ripped out her beating heart, and ate it—or so I was told. They dragged her naked torso through the streets, shot her arms and one of her legs from cannons. (I can scarcely write this . . .)

They paraded her head with its last lost grimace (and some said her intimate parts) on a pike over to the Temple prison and climbed on each other to hold the head up to the bars.

"There she is in triumph!" they shouted to lure the queen to the window, but the king held her back and, mercifully, she fainted.

As the mob paraded the head through Paris, the long streaming hair of the princess caught on the buttons of a servant who had known her. The young girl with him died of fright six hours later. They carried the head to the Palais Royale.

"Oh, it is Lamballe's head—I know it by the long hair," said Madame's descendant the duc d'Orléans, who by then had become Philippe Égalité.

Far away as I then was, I was not immune. In the night, I would imagine the beat of their drums, the fever of their gabble, their stained aprons and hard sour breaths. I saw axes rising above the white bonnets and bare arms tattooed with emblems of their trades reaching for me and those I loved and lived with and could not save . . .

After six days and nights and thousands dead, the city was not only drunk on blood; it was fatally distracted. The emperor has called the massacres a stain on us. He knew, however, that terror must be part of any revolution, that those who held the offices had to be scared into flight. He felt the rage and, even as he was repelled, began to imagine the new world it might bring forth.

After the massacres, the political clubs had evening sittings. Often there weren't enough candles and in the yellowy gloom one might speak safely from the depths of a crowd. Once, Danton was praising himself, his voice booming, when someone shouted out, *"Septembre!"* Then Danton was silent. They were all *"Septembriseurs"* and no one could turn back to before.

Paris was then a vile garden, its soil rich in worms, the perfect medium for a daring crime. It was a fortunate time for the thieves and murderers and pickpockets who were set free, a handful of them bound for the Garde Meuble and the Régent.

The thieves from Marseilles met in cabarets. They went skimming over the rooftops like cats and broke into every skylight and attic that was not fastened. Every night they climbed into the Tuileries from the attics and stole royal treasures. If the precious objects did not fit through the openings, they broke them up to carry them out. They were practiced in desecration for they had rushed through the large rooms of our estates with sacks and torches.

The police were useless and corrupt. Thieves disguised as municipal police or national guards stopped citizens to ask for their watch chains or shoe buckles for the cause. In the days right after the massacres, pickpockets, the receivers of stolen goods, habitual criminals of all sorts were busy looting and attacking. No one quite knew what was going on, and the confusion was the perfect excuse for crime. Paris, unsafe and giddy at the same time, was autointoxicated.

The Régent waited in the Garde Meuble, inciting another crime by its existence. Paul Miette was gathering his men one by one, looking at each new face for spies and informers. Up on the night rooftops, he was beyond the anger of any cause. He wanted the jewels, he wanted them all, especially the big white pebble of his prison dreams.

"The Diamonds Have Disappeared"

O N THE NIGHT OF SEPTEMBER 11 AT ABOUT ELEVEN, WHEN the big buildings were dark behind the flickering lamplight and the side streets still sticky with blood, Paul Miette and his band met up with a team of thieves from Rouen at the Garde Meuble. Miette directed some of the men to patrol Place Louis XV, while he and five others began to climb the lampposts to the exterior gallery of the first floor. They put their fingers and feet into the grooves cut between the large limestone blocks, stepped over the guardrail, and jumped to the shadowy gallery formed by the colonnade.

They waited, flattened against the stone, and saw no guards. No one had bothered to close the iron shutters; they broke through the wooden inner shutters and, with a glazier's diamond tool, cut the windowpane and reached in to open the latch. Miette knew the doors to the landing and interior stairs were sealed with strips of cloth covered with seals of the commune of Paris that no one dared break. Once in the jewel room, they put strong iron hooks on the inside of the doors to prevent the guards from entering and disturbing them. Miette feared only that their noise might attract the guard on the stair landing of the Saint-Florentin side.

While some held candles Miette broke the vitrines and they stuffed their pockets with Louis XV's decorations and orders, his heavy jewel-encrusted epaulettes. From a porphyry casket they took his diamond buttons and all the jewels sewn on his clothes. They threw the Order of the Golden Fleece—a dead ram hanging limp, its ruby legs dangling—into a sack. This one fabulous jewel, planned by the marquise de Pompadour and Louis XV, united the Côte de Bretagne ruby, Tavernier's huge triangular diamond of brilliant blue, the Egg of Naples, Bazu's diamond, and an immense yellow sapphire. I had seen it last glinting on the considerable stomach of the king.

Miette, who was looking for the Régent, did not know it was put in with the other loose diamonds. He did not find it that night for they did not force the armoires or get the diamonds on wax in their little boxes locked in the marquetry commode.

Three hours later they climbed down and shared with those outside while sitting on the rubble that had been the statue of Louis XV. Finally, they went off to one of their cabarets, where the stone walls were so black they streaked at a touch, the ceilings so low they seemed to hover, and all the odors met and defeated one another in one swinish ragout. In cellars like this they laughed and drank themselves insensible and entertained themselves with the whores.

The thieves rested the next night, and women joined them with others the night of September 13, when they broke open the commode and the doors to the armoire and got to the little boxes with the big diamonds resting on wax. That night they got the Great Sancy, the Pink Diamond of Five Sides (Hortensia), and maybe the Régent.

Again they rested the next night and resumed on the fifteenth, for it had become a leisurely, insouciant, almost continuous robbery with a swig of wine, a crown jewel in the pocket, stones dropped and scattered with their burglar's tools in the big dim rooms. They would hoist a rock crystal vessel, and if the handles—of thin, twisted, jasper, ruby-eyed snakes—broke off, so it went. They were so arrogant by then that they did not even bother to patrol, and all entered the building. The robbery, like the Revolution and the infection in their cabarets, grew each night. Now it was a big anonymous shifting group of men and women, disobedient and unplanned like the Revolution itself—their names unimportant, their betrayals predictable.

They had time for a candlelight picnic, tearing into their bread and sausages, their sacks and pockets bursting, as they speared another square of Pont l'Évêque on their knives. (How I long for such native tastes right now as I write! Though we have Pierron, the emperor's chef and his assistant here, we lack all ingredients. Sometimes I dream the menus of whole meals past, of soups and dainties, of tables with bowls of spun sugar fruits, the candle flames dancing on their hard glazed surfaces like colored jewels. I think of daubs and *frittes,* shrimp jellies, minced pigeons in cream, *rissoles,* white asparagus, and truffles. I dream of bacon and young onions, goose liver, chickens from the farms of Bresse. I could go on but my stomach growls so . . .) How to explain this antic mood of theirs? I must try to see things their way—that they were performing a patriotic act, relieving the tyrant and the "Austrian whore" of their goods. The things of the bad king were bad, profane tokens of a despised past, so they had to be torn down, burnt up, eliminated, pried apart. They were liberating the jewels from this museum of dead and doomed kings, taking back what they had come to think of as their own.

Two passersby bought jewels outside the Bourbon Palace as the robbers were trying to divide the goods. They led police to the banks of the Seine where two rubies glowed like little red eyes in the dirt. The police went along to the Garde Meuble but the seals were of course intact, so they decided the jewels had come from the robberies of the Tuileries on August 10 and thereafter. And that very day—even after a notice was posted instructing jewelers to retain any big suspicious stones—the robbery continued!

Now the robbers wore national guard costumes and sang the carmagnole, so the sentinel took them for patriots and went inside. There were more than fifty from all over France, all young and overwrought. There was a valet, a haberdasher, a shoemaker, a boy whore, all with their *noms de crime*—Little Hunter, Fat Ass of the Good Virgin, Round Hat, Great Stupid Bastard, Little Cardinal, Sailor, and such. That night they fought so loudly over the split that a troop of real national guards on the Rue Saint-Honoré heard and chased after them.

The guard of the archives saw a street lamp swaying on the corner of Rue Royale and ordered the man down. Another fell from the colonnade into a ring of real national guards. Both men had their pockets stuffed with jewels and were drunk. They told a tale of being abducted.

"What! Armed men used force to stuff your pockets with jewels?" said the public accuser at their trial. And here we see the type of young wretch who robbed the Garde Meuble from September 11 to 17 and took all the crown jewels of France!

When the guards and police entered the jewel rooms at five in the morning the floors were strewn with diamonds and pearls and burglar's tools.

On Monday, September 17, the secretary of Minister Roland read this message to the Assembly: "The minister of the interior informs the Assembly that the Garde Meuble has just been forced and robbed; two thieves have been arrested . . . but . . . the diamonds have disappeared."

"It is the remainder of the aristocracy that dies," said Santerre the brewer. "Don't fear anything, it can never revive."

A forger who had escaped prison in the September massacres offered to help round up the others in exchange for a pardon. He met up with the Little Hunter and they searched the streets for fellow robbers. Minister Roland gave one of the fences money so he might trap them.

Soon enough the police found crown diamonds in a pot of cheap pomade, lace stolen from the Tuileries in a box of powder. They found Louis XIV's garter buckles in a butcher shop and Henri IV's jeweled tie. This was indeed the Revolution! They found shoe buckles with the diamonds removed and Louis XVI's garters at the Little Hunter's house. When the police arrived he threw the diamonds in a glass of *eau-forte* out the window.

The Régent was now truly the people's stone, for it was hidden somewhere among them. No one dared bring the Great Sancy or the Régent to any of the dealers. Instead these diamonds were hidden away like any mistake, or perhaps they were savored in lunatic privacy.

Just days after the crime, Paul Miette bought himself Red House in the suburb of Belleville and moved in with his wife, who was a seamstress. When he learned of the arrests, he sold all his furniture and ran.

A month later, Minister Roland said that out of a treasure of 30 million francs only five hundred thousand remained. More than anything he wanted to recover the Régent.

Tonight was too poor for the emperor to walk out. I was happy when he told me we would resume our work on the *Memorial* that had been suspended by our difficulties with Governor Hudson Lowe. The English chose the wrong man to have power over the emperor, for Lowe is one of those picky souls who live only for rules and the trifles of power. The emperor no longer receives him.

The emperor retired early, asked me to join him in his room, and said a kind word on my work on the robbery. (He now reads chapter by chapter.)

"Sitting here on this rock with your bundle of papers you have made order out of chaos," he said. "Until now, I had always believed the jewels were used to buy off the duke of Brunswick. The robbery was not political at all, just a bunch of crooks."

"Right away the crime was linked with the events of the times," I said. "That was the first mistake, for the robbery and Revolution went together only in that the disruption and bitter mood of one made possible the other."

The emperor then recalled the *Mémoires* that Madame Roland had written in prison and went to find her book in our library. Again I heard the poking metallic sound that would seem strange to any but those who lived here and knew he had taken up the fire poker and done for another rat.

Madame Roland, the queen of the Girondists, was the Circe of the Revolution—large and black-haired with full lips.

"No, chestnut hair," the emperor corrects me, "and not so very beautiful. Her feet were too large." (I add here in my code that the emperor could tolerate wiliness but not brilliance in a woman, and the dread Madame Roland, who taught herself by reading all the great ones, was horrible but brilliant.)

She was in Paris at the time of the trials of the robbers of the Garde Meuble and had her own ideas on the crime.

The maids were sweeping emeralds off Rue Saint-Florentin when the trials started on September 21. That was the very day the republic officially began and the palace of the kings became the palace of the nation. That day Fabre d'Englantine, Danton's secretary, went to see Madame Roland at her home at L'Hôtel de l'Intérieure. In her butter yellow drawing room with its velvet bergères and taffeta curtains (this heroine of revolt was attached to her pretty things) she accused him and Danton of having organized the theft.

"The only ones who were arrested and punished were little boy thieves," she wrote, "used as the pawns in the affair of the Garde Meuble, without being initiated into the secret of their enterprise."

("What are those scratches you have written here above?" the emperor says, jabbing his finger at my bit of code. He has torn at the flesh of his fingers, one of his habits, like the way he jabs his penknife, scoring the left arm of all our chairs.

"Just notes to myself to add on Madame Roland," I say.

"Ha! I see these scratches all over your manuscript. I know they are your code. Madame Roland was the result of Versailles, for, despite her learning, or perhaps because of it in that tunnel of ignorance, they snubbed her as a tradesman's daughter. A very proud woman, not one to take to bed.")

The criminal tribunal of the Revolution tried the robbers of the Garde Meuble every week from the end of September through November 1792. These were the times of the greatest struggle among the Girondists and Danton, Marat, and Robespierre. All the leaders of the Revolution, its aristocrats as it were, by then had accused one another of the robbery. Meanwhile, the real trials went on in the Palace of Justice.

The tribunal charged all the robbers of the Garde Meuble with crimes against the state, the punishment for which was death. They tried to get these wretches to admit they were the tools of the princes. Where would such men come to know princes? Of course they denied this. They charged the two drunk boys who had fallen from the lamppost and balustrade with provoking a civil war.

A medium suddenly appeared to tell the tribunal that he felt vibrations from a certain oak tree in the Alley of Widows. He held his quivering hands over a certain spot and said, "Dig here!" and uncovered a jeweled chalice and some of the treasure.

They accused Francisque, a naval officer, of stealing the Régent and Great Sancy.

"Confess and tell us where they are," said the president of the tribunal and showed him the testimony of one of the Jews who had already been guillotined for receiving stolen goods. The young officer, who sat in an iron chair, turned his head aside so he would not have to see the testimony.

On the scaffold at what was by then the Place de la Révolution (once Place Louis XV), in sight of the blood-marked straps and board, the blade and large red basket waiting for his head, Francisque gave in.

He brought the court to his house, in a cul-de-sac, and from the roof of a toilet on the sixth floor brought down two sooty packets containing the Grand Mazarin, the Hortensia, the Fleur de Pêcher, and other giant diamonds.

At his trial a week later, the Little Cardinal said he was a jockey. He was only fourteen and already infected with disease from his life as a boy whore.

"They have corrupted his soul, the cruel ones! They have corrupted his blood!" said his defender, and the Little Cardinal was acquitted.

When a seventeen-year-old dealer in used goods was arrested, his father went into a frenzy. He blamed his wife for being too lenient with the boy, threw a hatchet at her, cut her throat, and swallowed a bottle of sulfuric acid. That boy too was acquitted.

Paul Miette returned to Belleville, where the police found him crawling out the window of Red House. Implicated by all the others, Miette was condemned to death. Of the fifty or so who robbed the Garde Meuble, seventeen were judged, five acquitted, and five executed for trying to overthrow the state. The tribunal did not want to believe in the ingenuity of the people, but in fact these young bumblers had stolen all the crown jewels of France.

In the trials of the Girondins in 1793, Fabre d'Englantine, Danton's secretary, accused Minister Roland and the Girondists. He said there were two robberies—a large one, in which the most valuable jewels were taken, and a smaller one to cover the first. In the second they caught the thieves in the act and blamed them for both. Others accused the mayor of Paris, Manuel the Procurer, and Danton of giving the jewels to the king of Prussia so he would leave Champagne. Marat accused the aristocrats and Marie-Antoinette, who was still in the Temple.

Eight months after the first trials, when many of the thieves appealed at Beauvais, our armies had withdrawn. By then, all knew the robbery was not political, and five of the condemned were freed while others escaped. Miette, who knew how to use the times in which he lived, prepared a long brief filled with the contradictions in the testimony against him. Pages of his dossier had miraculously disappeared and he was freed. Others who were tried got fifteen years, some went to the galleys and rowed themselves to freedom or death.

Most of the jewels were recovered thanks to the finds in the Alley of Widows and on Francisque's roof, but not the Régent.

Sitting here on Deadwood Plain, on this wind-whipped rock with warships in the harbor and guard boats circling night and day, I cannot solve the theft of the Régent. I cannot know anything beyond what is in the documents. In all these names, I cannot unravel the one who reached for it, or even the night he did so. Sometimes in the press of daily life, in my concern for the emperor and his health, for my son, Emmanuel, my failing eyes, and my work, I confess I cease to care. Writing this has exhausted me. What started out as a distraction for me has, in its way, become a further torment, like one of the gruesome blue flies who swell themselves on our blood. I feel consumed by all—by *him*, the men's scowls and moods, this foreign air pounded by winds, even the sea that reminds us we are tossed about. At this point, I wish to fling aside the documents and go back to the emperor—and yet I owe a duty to my labors. Then, too, the emperor may ask, "So, Las Cases, just who did remove the Régent from its little waxen box and what was its journey from that moment until it was found?"

I cannot answer, sire—for this, the greatest mystery in the life of the diamond, is, alas, still a mystery to me. Hidden objects sometimes stay hidden for eternity. Some things (though few of mine) return from the land of lost objects; others stay buried in coat pockets and places long forgotten, lost by those long dead. Sometimes a living hand reaches out for them and the pull of want or accident makes them tumble out to gleam on a floor. Some transfer themselves to other families and start their own stories there so that any city street with stores of old jewels is full of lost stories.

From the end of 1792 until April 1793, there was no trace of the Régent or the Great Sancy. Then the fearsome Jacobins interested themselves in getting the two diamonds back.

When Minister Roland was accused of helping the duke of Brunswick, he demanded that the Convention hear Madame Roland defend him. When she appeared, all began to applaud at her famous beauty. Even Robespierre, the only one in Paris secure enough to powder his hair, clapped, and those nearby saw the twinkle of the little guillotines on his cuffs.

Three days later, on December 10, 1793, the Convention heard this announcement: "Your Committee of Public Safety has not stopped looking for the authors and their accomplices in the robbery of the Garde Meuble. Yesterday, it discovered the most precious of the stolen effects; that is the diamond known under the name Pitt or Régent"—there were gasps—"which in the last inventory of 1791 was appraised at 12 millions. . . . To hide [the Régent] they had made a hole of an inch and a half in a piece of framework in an attic. The thief and the receiver are arrested; the diamond carried to the Committee of Public Safety and must serve as a piece of evidence against the thieves."

So here was the Régent, set in wood, hidden under a beam in the Île de la Cité, now a "piece of evidence," a new role for new times. It was carried to the General Treasury, in a little packet sealed with five seals inscribed *Ne Varietur* (Do Not Disturb), where the commissioners received it.

They had found the Régent in the house of Madame Lelièvre and her sister Madame Morée on December 9, 1793. Lelièvre was the mistress of one Bernard Salles, who had gone out with the robbers on the first night and then immediately returned with his haul to Rouen. Since no one had broken into the chest with the Régent on the first night, I don't know how this could be. No one could ask Bernard Salles, for he had been beheaded.

The two women were sent to Sainte-Pélagie prison. Two years later, they and twenty-five others accused in the robbery were tried. The women alone were accused of stealing and receiving the Régent.

Perhaps Madame Lelièvre did steal the Régent. Young and agile, she may have hitched up her skirts to climb the lamppost and take what the others dared not steal. She could have seen the Régent on one of the open Mondays at the Garde Meuble and gone looking for it. Or someone brought it to Bernard Salles, or another robber tossed it to Madame Lelièvre as he was fleeing. All this is beyond my capacities to unravel.

By then Madame Roland had gone to the guillotine, found guilty of the usual treason. On the scaffold, she had said, "Oh liberty, what crimes one commits in your name"—words she had been rehearsing to make herself even more famous.

Three months after they found the Régent, the committee recovered the Great Sancy, as well as the Maison de Guise, the Mirror of Portugal, and most of the Mazarin diamonds, at the house of a cutthroat and his sister. The murderer fled, but his sister spent eighteen years in chains.

In those times of injustice, over half the robbers escaped capture and over seven millions of smaller jewels were never seen again. The Régent and the Great Sancy were finally reunited with the other royal jewels in a dark jail of their own at the treasury.

"Of course, here, too, there is another version," the emperor told me later. "In the year I became emperor, another thief who called himself Baba confessed to the robbery of the Garde Meuble."

"Sire, I think his real name was Fleury-Dumoutier," I said. "After the robbery he was in Bicêtre prison for passing counterfeit money. He was from Rouen and had been partners with some of the Rouennais."

Then I read the emperor what this Baba said when he confessed to forgery: "It is not the first time that my revelations have been useful to society, and if I am condemned I will implore the emperor's pardon. But for me,

Napoleon would never have mounted the throne; to me alone is due the success for the Marengo campaign."

"My soldiers would be glad to hear that! What cheek!" the emperor said.

"That rascal said he buried the Régent in the Alley of Widows. It behooves a liar to get his story straight."

"It says here"—I showed him a document I had just discovered—"he buried the most recognizable objects, like Abbe Suger's chalice and the Régent, there—things that could never be sold. And then, upon promise of a pardon, he disclosed where they were. What if he did bury the Régent there and then some person who had watched him came along, dug the Régent up, and left the chalice and the other things that they found? It could have been Madame Lelièvre."

"My son, with you there is always a big conspiracy. You would have made a good detective for the police."

"All went to the galleys *except* this Baba. In Bicêtre, they always called him the man who stole the Régent."

"Perhaps he was. What does it matter?"

Seeing how I took offense at this, the emperor became very kind and thumped my back with such affection that I stumbled forward onto Dimanche, who looked up with grave reproof. Still, it plagued me that my work might be in vain.

Émigré

A MONTH AFTER THE RÉGENT WAS RETRIEVED, THE THIRTY-
five-year-old king was no more. As the carriage carrying him
arrived at what, to him, was still his grandfather's Place Louis
XV and the scaffold there, he turned and whispered to the priest who accompanied him, "We are arrived, if I mistake not." Such is ever the politesse
of kings, however in extremis.* It is bred into the royal body and many such
as the emperor who have risen to exalted heights have intuited or acquired
this elegance.

"If I mistake not," the king had added. And then, when he saw the
guards approach his person, ready to loosen his shirt, he repulsed them and
undressed himself. As Louis XVI untied his neckcloth, opened his shirt,
and arranged his neck for the blade, they regained themselves. They surrounded him and made as if to seize his hands.

"What are you attempting?" said the king.

"To bind you," they answered.

"To bind *me*?" exclaimed the king. This says all that ever has to be known
about the Bourbons, who were once and now are again the kings of France.

Santerre the brewer then directed the drummers to beat drums as the
king tried to speak his last words, claiming his innocence, pardoning those

---

*Marie-Antoinette apologized to her executioner for stepping on his foot.

who caused his death, hoping that his blood might never be visited on France. A man in the crowd cut his own throat in sympathy, an act I understand, for I can hardly bear to tell these facts that I learned from the report of one of his priests, Henry Essex Edgeworth de Firmont.

At this time, when I was starving in my sordid room in London, I read in the London newspaper covering my bed that William Pitt called this execution "the foulest and most atrocious act the world has ever seen."

When, in 1798, during the Directory, it came time to celebrate this gruesome event of January 21, the directors debated whether the emperor, who was then the general who had just conquered Italy, should go to the ceremony. They sent Prince Talleyrand, our foreign minister, who in his character defined duplicity, to convince him.

"Why should we celebrate that calamity?" Napoleon said.

"It is just because it is political," said Talleyrand, ever servant of the moment and the stronger. "All regimes hail the fall of a tyrant."

In the end Napoleon attended the ceremony as a member of the mathematical section of the Institut de France and eclipsed the whole Directory that day, for no one looked anywhere but at him, and the crowd cheered him lustily. His soldiers in Italy had ridden on ten thousand horses procured by pawning the Régent, but I shall come to that later in my story.

For now, in 1793, came the Terror, a time when the lunacy of September became the policy of the state and lasted months instead of days, when no blood was enough and mercy died. I went to Holland at the end of the winter of that year. That spring, when Paoli hunted him, Napoleon left Corsica with his family, landing in Toulon in June, when the Girondin chiefs were being arrested. He rejoined his regiment at Nice. That summer I returned to England, where my intimate friend Jean-Henri de Volude and I published *The Voyage of an Unknown in France* under my first pseudonym, de Curville.

"And where had you been during the robbery and the days of blood?" the emperor had asked me late one Sunday. He seemed so low in spirit he could scarcely bring himself to speak, and this show of interest was most unusual. What had come seeping into us like the white winds of the night was the knowledge there would be no escape, no rescue from afar, no boat of loyalists pulling in to Jamestown harbor, no brave charge up to Longwood. No deliverance. To divert him I began to speak of London and the years I spent there as an émigré.

"We might be there now incognito in the London countryside," the emperor said. "You would be calling me 'Baron Duroc' or 'Colonel Muiron.' Or we could be in *Bostan* or *Wash-eeng-tone*—do I say them right?"

He thought that when I was in London I must have seen King George III, the Prince of Wales, Monsieur Pitt and Monsieur Fox, and other great lords of the court. He wanted to know what I thought of them, to set alongside his own opinions.

I told him he could not know the position of the émigrés in London. We were not received at court, and even if we had been invited, I had not the clothes or means to make an appearance. Ashamed of my position, it was then I took the name of "Felix." There was much I did not say, such as how I was so poor I stayed in bed all the winter of 1794 with my empty trunk (I had sold all within) over my feet to keep warm. Nor, for fear it might diminish me and seem a bid for sympathy, did I tell how I sold rings of human hair and walked the leather off my shoes to earn a shilling giving French lessons. (It was then a London bookseller suggested I write romances, never suspecting my life would become a romance far stranger than any I might invent.)

In the great houses I would see those who wore their hair dressed *à la victime*, carefully cut and messed to imitate my friends who had been shorn before being beheaded. Then I would turn away or hide in some alcove until I could collect myself and tamp down my fury.

Supported by my lessons, I researched the geographical and historical *Atlas* that I wrote in ten years under the name Le Sage, which would make my small fortune. It suited my taste for historical research, synoptical maps, the geography of history, the genealogy of princes. I did tables on the epoques of history, the migrations of the barbarians, the French kings, the history of England, and such. I, who was always displaced, liked facts and maps and things that were sure and charted and certain. I like spaces marked, direction, and order. (Around the emperor all is always in order.)

Those among us in London who could sing or play gave concerts or lessons. Some sold hats or ran coffeehouses or furnished hotels. The young duc d'Orleans* was a tutor at a Swiss school, and his brother Montpensier was a painter. Other émigrés worked embroidery, the de la Rochefoucaulds became linen drapers in order to eat. Some remembered, but others had no trouble forgetting these menial jobs when they returned to France and the new world it had become.

---

*Abraham's note: He became Louis-Philippe, King of the French.

George III was interested in us as individuals, but could not receive us as a political group. I told the emperor, who knew this, that it was the first attack of King George's delirium, in the winter of 1788–1789, that had made Pitt the idol of his nation; only the king's love of country made him keep with Pitt, for the minister was repugnant to him.

All the émigrés were isolated then and Pitt and Burke were our lights; Fox to us was nothing but a detested Jacobin. I knew the emperor had put a bust of Charles Fox at Malmaison even before he knew him personally. Thus, in those days we were so far apart that even our heroes were enemies.

I had seen Pitt in Commons, that Grenville nose uptilted so the nostrils became caverns, the body rigid with pride, the fluty voice quivering through the marble halls with erudition or impatience, scorn or sweet persuasion. His cheeks stained by drink, he walked lightly and much too fast, and people pulled back from him or rushed alongside.

Long ago he had refused to marry the woman who became Madame de Staël. He had no wife or child and was always about with his "boys." Along with his niece he lived in a house with powerful men coming and leaving at all hours, staying into the morning after long drunken dinners wiped out the day.

Later, the emperor asked me to make the tale of my ten years as an émigré into a coherent history, for he could not retain what I said because of the disordered way I had told it (much like this story, alas). So I tried to make it into a story, like Dido telling Aeneas of a time she would rather forget. I told him of the days at Worms with the prince de Condé, then at Koblenz with the brothers of the king, and how the princes and country nobles gathered in all their magnificence and resumed the same strutting pretensions as at Versailles. The emperor laughed.

"Truly, my dear Las Cases," he said, "vapouring, credulity, inconsistency, stupidity might be said, in spite of all their wit, to be their special lot."

We were always at the call of the princes to invade our native land to save our monarch. At the battle of Quiberon in 1795, de Volude, the best friend of my life, was taken and shot, as was Henriette's father. After Quiberon, during which I was sick, and after Napoleon's conquest of Italy, I finally gave up all hope that the Bourbons would be restored.

I told him too of my new English family, my cousin who had been lady in waiting to the princess de Lamballe and how she had led me to this rich young couple, Lord Thomas Clavering and Lady Clavering, born Claire de Gallais. For two shillings a week I was hired to teach astronomy to Lady Clavering. What I read in the morning, I taught her in the evening, and then went home to my cutlet, salad, and the good coffee I now could afford. Such coffee had been the one luxury I shared with Jean-Henri at our Sunday lunches and I mourned my companion, for as I have learned, sometimes you feel an absence more than a presence.

Lady Clavering had a salon of the best of the émigrés. She and her husband had cared for me, and when I returned to France with them after the peace of Amiens, their sponsorship allowed me to bypass the formalities of the border.

"You sound as if you love her well, my son," the emperor said. "Where was your wife, the little Henriette?" To this I could not reply, for I had left my wife for years to be with that lady.

Of course, much of my life, like the emperor's, has been exile, marked by the halting drift of the past across my days, the events replaying unbidden at unexpected hours in unsuspected places. This endless play of Saint Helena, where costumes are required and memories wait backstage, is our final exile.

Here, the emperor's life in legend has begun. With each day of invented action, he creates a purpose for us all and makes a last kingdom of this rock. We are his last troops. As he tells us his life, he recalls the desertions of those he made great, the dust of his few defeats, and the more painful victories. All is forced back—puffs of gun smoke over trampled green fields, the horses falling, battle squares that bent forward as men fell with blood scribbling from their mouths and torn uniforms, the days when the enemies threw down their banners before him, the Mamelukes in their robes and turbans gliding through the palaces, surrounding him like an ancient idol.

"Sometimes I think it takes a whole lifetime to prepare for the next one," he says. "We are just rehearsing—yet everyone's play ends the same."

Even as we continue our dialogue of the dead, sometimes he pauses, lost in another country with those absent and now impossible to him. He speaks of yesterday as of ancient times in which the character he calls "Napoleon" did his deeds. At those times I begin to think what to tell in this chronicle, what to exclude, what to contour of that which I receive from him, all of it precious. Sometimes I know he lies, and wonder if he believes the lies.

Then, too, with the monthly ship arrivals, we are invaded by new and monstrous published works about him filled with false versions of stories he knows well. Earlier this very day we received one such work by Goldsmith. I quickly cast it aside for it was abominable on every page, and decided to suppress it from the emperor. I cannot imagine how he came upon it, but this morning I had found him stretched out on his sofa reading it.

"Jesus!" he kept saying, crossing himself as he read each lie. Then he shrugged and threw down the book, but its impression had lingered and he tumbled into this low mood.

Often in telling some story, the emperor says, "I thought the world was at an end." It is only an expression of his. Now he feels it true; his world is at an end and so is mine, here, at the end of the world.

The Régent went from the vaults of the revolutionary tribune, from its box with three locks, to the coffers of the national treasury, where one key was also not enough.

Under the Convention, it stayed locked up with lesser jewels (and all jewels were lesser jewels) confiscated from the émigrés and enemies of the republic. The aigrette that quivered on the hair tower of a duchess kept company with the girandoles of a countess whose head fell in a basket and diamond shoe buckles that sauntered Versailles. Strings of ancient pearls, earrings, jeweled epaulettes, massive tarnished parures, crowns, necklaces, pins, bracelets, diamond hat jewels, and crosses, clips, and yokes glittered dispossessed, the lost baubles of headless ghosts. With them were the seized treasures of the churches and abbeys, jewels stolen in ordinary robberies or taken from conquered countries—all were mixed together in the last days of the Revolution. This collection of stolen objects, plus the art Napoleon took from Italy and elsewhere, would one day form the Musée du Louvre that he created.

The jewels were useless and dangerous in this new climate. At night police banged on doors, pulled citizens out, and if their names weren't on the lists of those within, they were beheaded. A million were executed, whole families erased.

When France conquered the Batavian Republic and made it the kingdom of Holland in 1795, she seized the jewels of the king of Sardinia and added them to the rest. The Convention called in savants to choose which jewels and objects should be saved as models for industry or preserved for the Natural History Museum. The savants chose Louis XIV's rhomboid sapphire, a large yellow diamond and topaz, but not the Régent. They sold some jewels in the Sublime Porte.

Over three thousand lots were auctioned in the deserted ballrooms of Versailles during 1795. They were things so old and beautiful it is hard to imagine—furniture of ormolu and precious island woods, marquetry bureau plats inlaid with ebonized tortoiseshell, walnut fauteuils *à la reine,* gilt bronze prancing horses, portraits of ancestors known only to families who fled or perished in a single day. These portraits became the instant relatives of households less noble, and with them were lost the stories of the past.

Paris was auctioning off the boots and shawls and laces of its murdered citizens. All around the countryside, seized pictures and objects were for sale to those who bid highest. My family's furniture, our silver and tapestries—the armor of our knights, dark stained chests carved with fantastical beasts splayed for a precarious eternity clawing wooden balls, dour countesses, their chins on ruffs caught forever disapproving in heavy gold frames—all our ghosts were gone.

As the nation went, so went the Régent, the national diamond. During the Convention, this time of death and desecration when all was valued at nothing, the diamond was stolen. Now when the Convention was auctioning off so much, the Régent was about to be pawned.

Five directors took power in 1795 and the state jewels were revalued— the Régent at 6 million, all the rest at 11 million. The Directory stopped the sale of the jewels to foreign countries, but still the finance minister burned some tapestries just to extract the gold from their threads. He let army contractors in to browse the bronzes, ormolu-mounted Sèvres vases, and giltwood mirrors that once reflected carnivals of artifice, vanity, and debauch. It was then that I lost, forever, my Andalusian past.

PART III

Josephine and the Diamond Horses

I N THE FOURTH YEAR OF THE REPUBLIC, THE DIAMOND WAS
pawned and the emperor fell in love. I shall mention the latter circumstance first, since in a strange way it led to the former.

The emperor had been enchanted by the very same Creole beauty I had
known in Martinique in 1787, when I was twenty-one. Then a naval officer,
I had come to her island from a winter in Boston, where I learned English
well enough to translate for my captain and the governor of Boston. It had
been a happy time at the end of their War of Independence, when little children kissed our hands in gratitude.

In Martinique, Baroness Tascher had adopted me, and at her house I
first met her niece the vicomtesse Rose de Beauharnais. Rose had been
abandoned by her husband and spent a year in an abbey before returning to
Martinique, her native land. In those days she lived in a haze of slow charm.
Under the banyan trees, fanned by a slave, she spoke well on all subjects,
had elegant manners, an even temper, and the grace that comes from kindness.

She had a magnificent figure, the loveliest arms, and combined many fas-
cinations in her person, though the sugar of her native land had rotted her
teeth to stumps. Not the least of these lures were her thrilling voice and
drooping gaze. She had spoken then of the strange destiny that an old slave
woman had seen for her before she was married to de Beauharnais. The

slave, who crossed herself at the sight of her, predicted her unhappy union, widowhood, and her position as the queen of France.

"Isn't that *drôle!*" she would say, and all the young officers lounging on her porch would agree. Perhaps this was true; she was ever the artificer of her own fortune, as all were in those times. Certainly I had little reason then to believe her or envision her as queen.

Our lunches lasted almost to evening; our dinners were under powdery tropical moons. At their end, pyramids of tiny crunchy pink *crevettes* that we popped whole into our mouths had vanished, along with the plates of thin-sliced sweet fruits, and the barefoot slaves had drifted off into bushes alive with chittering creatures. Rose read cards and told fortunes even then. That one slid her eyes around a door and saw all; she always said no before she said yes, to make the yes more precious.

We all knew her story—she had been sent off to an arranged marriage in Paris at sixteen, and had two children before her husband, Alexandre de Beauharnais, went to live with his mistress. She had been back on Martinique for two years when I met her. After I left the island, she went back to France, where de Beauharnais was in the Constituent Assembly. On the ship, her young daughter, Hortense,* sang Negro songs and danced Creole dances for the sailors until she wore out her one pair of shoes and her feet bled.

Rose de Beauharnais had been imprisoned at Carmes during the Terror when her husband was guillotined. In Carmes, where the walls were brown with the September blood, she had lived her hell—humid, full of vermin, the windows coated. She was imprisoned in the stench with dukes and princes, dentists and tobacco merchants, hairdressers and architects, painters and lemonade sellers, all expecting the visit of Monsieur Death every day. On visits her children brought her Fortuné, her horrid little dog who smuggled in letters under his collar and barked at the rats.

Rose de Beauharnais was one of the few who cried in front of the others in prison. Had she gone to the guillotine, she would have gone just like Madame du Barry, who, unlike many brave duchesses, had sobbed and screamed and twisted and pulled away so none forgot what her death meant.

Perhaps she bore with her the desires that anyone in prison holds—the desire for ever more. She had left prison with her pretty head, a woman made to please and thereafter intent on her own pleasures, looking to recap-

---

*Later this girl would be queen of Holland and mother of Napoleon III—I, "Abraham," add this to the manuscript.

ture the *drôle.* In the courtyard of Carmes, she had seen an old crone holding up her dress *(robe)* and a rock *(pierre)* and making the sign of a throat
being slit. Thus she had known the crisis of the Ninth Thermidor had
ended, *Robespierre* was dead, and she was spared.

Paris saw her then as "the American," gentle and languorous in the island way. This did not mean she was without ambition, for she had provided
for herself as the mistress of three of the five directors, including General
Barras, who ran the government. As the American, she knew hot climates of
thick-leaved trees and spices and fruits where they grew, and something of
the ways of the native people. (Her plantation of 150 slaves was one of the
kinder ones on the island.) She had lived where red-eyed lizards skittered
through hard gray tree roots that arched above the ground, and she carried
all this with her as well as the prophecy.

When the vicomtesse drifted across a drawing room she still swayed in
the island way that was all grace and sensuality. She was neither too tall nor
too short. She had long brown hair of greatest luster and navy blue nocturnal eyes, the long lids of which were habitually half closed and thickly laden
with remarkable lashes. The curls around her face made small impudent
sixes on her fine skin. She had the small hands and feet that the emperor has
always prized, and a strangely small mouth. She would smile without opening her mouth like the woman in the painting by Leonardo da Vinci in their
bedroom in the Tuileries. In the mornings over her head she wore a red
madras kerchief tied in the Creole style, a habit the emperor has taken from
her, for he covers his head with a madras kerchief in the mornings even now.

As the mistress of Barras she was at the center of this demimonde that
grew from the dust of the Revolution. I knew those who had been to her
house on Rue Saint-Dominique—with its blue nankin porcelain, the furniture in yellow wood from Guadeloupe, and in the little room used to dine, a
round table and the mahogany chairs covered in black horsehair. Mirrors
were everywhere, and flowers that always defied the season and climate. A
little bust of Socrates was meant to make her seem serious. Sometimes she
played the harp in the corner and sang a bit. Here she created her little
world of survivors of the aristocracy, the debris of the old world, women
who knew how to make compromises, those who were agreeable and good
mannered, reserved and decorative as the little house. In the midst of
famine she set a luxurious table with hampers of provisions arriving from
Barras. He ran the country from Ninth Thermidor, An II, to Eighteenth
Brumaire, An VIII, and helped pay the rent.

Late at night after the others left, Monsieur de Montesquiou and the duc de Nivernais would stay behind to tell forbidden stories of the old court at Versailles. A shabby young general stayed to listen and stare at her with his unbearable regard, this woman he described as "all lace." That was Napoleon in his worn uniform, in the summer of 1795.

Napoleon by then had taken back Toulon from the English, firing on their fleet from the high ground. In that battle he had been wounded in his left inner thigh above the knee and afterward was promoted to brigadier general at twenty-four. He had been briefly suspected for his friendship with Robespierre's brother, imprisoned at home, and released. General Barras had called on him to defend the Convention against a royalist uprising then heading for the Tuileries. Remembering the madness he had seen on August 10, Napoleon ordered his cannons to fire into the crowd by the Church of Saint-Roch. Hundreds fell and he was made a full general at twenty-six.

How did he meet Rose de Beauharnais? I do not know and have never asked, for he is always sad when he talks about her now. Some said her son, Eugène, had come to General Bonaparte to claim his father's sword and Rose had come to thank him for returning it. Another version said they met at the house of Thérésia Tallien, a black-haired beauty who had been imprisoned under the Terror. From her cell Thérésia threw a note in a cabbage asking her lover, Tallien, to save her and France. He attacked Robespierre in the Convention, hastening his demise. Now Thérésia Tallien lived to further amuse the *jeunesse dorée* surrounding her.

As one of the leaders of this wild lost society of the Directory, Rose de Beauharnais tore around with Thérésia Tallien and was often found in her little imitation thatched cottage. Inside, Madame Tallien had completely re-created the interiors of Pompeii. The oiled bodies of Directoire goddesses like Madame Recamier were always there—hair *à la guillotine,* throats circled in red ribbon, halted in languor on satin chaises longues. The digs at Pompeii and Herculaneum had inspired these *merveilleuses* to imitate the ancient goddesses in transparent muslin tubes over bare skin, tied at the neck and under the bosom, with gold sandals on their feet and gold bands up their bare legs. They plastered curls to their cheeks that never moved when they laughed the harsh laughs of those who had seen too much.

Giddy and antic with relief at being spared, Rose lived with the recklessness of one who had thought of dying every day for months and now spent her days planning what to wear. Around her all Paris was infected. There were dinners with a coffin behind every chair. At the Victims' Balls, they wore red belts and red ribbons around their necks to show they were related to victims of the guillotine and had been in prison. Executioner and victim both danced to the idea of death with steps mimicking the death twitch. A special combination of the macabre and nonchalant existed then in my country, and still does. My nation is cursed indeed by this need for *rigolade* and mockery. Sardonicus became their god; the old vicious court ridicule had again taken the nation.

Rose de Beauharnais' reputation and beauty were a little damaged perhaps, not quite of the first rank, but in the twilit luxe of the demimonde it did not matter. It certainly did not matter to one who then did not know the Parisian distinctions. Napoleon knew she was useful and thought she was rich. When he investigated her fortune just before they married, he found she had lied to him, yet he was enmeshed beyond all escape. The previous April, Napoleon had been the fiancé of Désirée Clary, but now he belonged to this older woman.

She lied, she cheated, she spent, and she owed—even when he was long divorced and on Elba, her bills still came to him—and yet there was always the lightness, the charm, the sugar wind blown over all. She was Rose de Beauharnais then, to all who knew her. It was the emperor who renamed her as he remade her in his mind. He invented a new creature named Josephine.

The emperor has told me of those times when Paris was divided between Jacobins and royalists, with the Directory between the two. It was a most peculiar city then, as I have since heard. Dead poplars of liberty stood in the squares. The mob had pulled down the marble and brass statues of kings, and now wood and plaster idealized heroes of the Revolution stood in their place. The great houses of the Faubourg Saint-Germain that belonged to my friends then were marked "National Property." The street names had all been changed, all emblems of royalty removed. Paris had been purged, stripped of much of its ancient beauty, the tombs of Saint-Denis rifled, marriages void at will, worship forbidden. Riesener, the great cabinetmaker to the king, was then engaged in removing royal emblems from all the furniture. The days of the week, the names of the month, the whole Christian calendar had been changed. Notre Dame became the Temple of Reason, where the goddess wore the red wool cap. Though the tumbrils had stopped and the knitters were gone, I was glad to be far away in Lady Clavering's circle, writing my *Atlas*.

The Bastille was a timber yard and there were fifty-seven new prisons. For 36 francs anyone could go to weekly balls where "nymphs" in flesh-colored clothing danced, or choose the Comédie Française, where all were badly dressed. Paris was still full of robbers and murderers. The government was so poor it seized the receipts of the opera. Madame Campan, who had been Marie-Antoinette's secretary, was running a boarding school for the daughters of soldiers dead in war. Among them were one of Napoleon's sisters and Josephine's daughter, Hortense.

As though from the guilt of the Terror, the million dead, the worthless *assignats,* the ruined châteaux, fantastic creatures had arisen who lived only to dress. These *incroyables*—the *merveilleuses* and *extravagants*—used to stroll past Napoleon in the gardens of the Palais Royale, intent on commanding a second glance and defeated if they did not provoke one. Women in huge bushy wigs were wrapped in immense shawls the color of mud, under which were dainty white muslin chemises tied high under the transparent bosom and all spangled and fringed with gold. Sometimes they wore mannish jackets and carried little sticks or riding crops that they switched against their bare legs as they stared through their lorgnettes. They did not stare at the young general, who made no effort with his dress and forgot to curl or cut his limp hair.

With them posed lisping men with "dogs' ears," curls hanging down to their waistcoats, done in chignons behind or cut in ragged points. They wore oversized bicornes or beaver hats, absurdly high collars, and carried sticks weighted with lead. Copying the studied nonchalance of the English dandies, they pretended to be careless, though numerous fittings had gone into these costumes to make them so dramatically tight or loose.

For a while Napoleon, not wanting to offend Barras, stayed away from Josephine. She had called him back, and after he went to her bed in January, the general was captured. He stood behind the yellow wood chair in her home and wrapped her in one of her hundreds of cashmere shawls, for she was always cold now in this land. Then his hands stayed on her shoulders.

When they married, she was thirty-three and he twenty-seven; and he lied to make himself older as she lied to make herself younger. He was six inches taller than she. They were both island people, always cold in France, with their fires burning. He knew her need for luxury, her gaiety and extravagance were in her Creole blood with all the haunted dreams, the future in the cards. They were both from small lands in pale green seas and he gave her a necklace with a pendant that said, "To destiny."

All this time the diamond was sitting in storage. (I am going to hide the above pages and rewrite most in code.)

In this same year, 1796, with a war budget of more than a billion against the Austro-Sardinian coalition, the Directory needed money and horses. Now it was time for the national diamond to go to work. They took the Régent out of its box and traded it for ten thousand horses—not once, but twice.

Now began what I consider the diamond's dark days, days in which it was but a toy for two men from the middle classes, hostage to show-off bankers who could not resist flaunting this symbol of their success. And yet by pawning it, the Directory won Italy, the emperor's soldiers rode on "diamond" horses, and his glorious career began. This was the paradox of the diamond.

At Josephine's suggestion, Barras had made Napoleon the commander in chief of the Army of Italy. The Directory could raise only 2,000 louis for the whole campaign. Napoleon carried the money with him in his carriage. When he arrived in Italy, the troops were shoeless, hungry, their uniforms in shreds, and they had no horses.

The adjutant general de Parceval, who was in charge of getting horses for the minister of war, pawned the state diamonds. He pawned the Régent to Treskow, a Berlin banker and liquor merchant, for 4 million livres. He pawned the Great Sancy and other diamonds to the marquis d'Iranda of Madrid for a million. Both men previously had supplied the army with horses. Now they demanded guarantees.

Parceval was to carry the Régent to Treskow in Basel, that Swiss city where, the year before, France signed treaties with Prussia and Spain and acquired the left bank of the Rhine. It must have been a nervous journey, for he was carrying a thing more precious than he was. Not a quiet moment, for de Parceval was already an excitable type, an escaped aristocrat working for the Directory, a horseman. As he rode through unfamiliar territories, he traveled with the fear of all those who carry things that can never be replaced.

When the roads were rutted and he had to get out and walk, Parceval worried that the stone might be dislodged. Much too frequently he patted the place where it was concealed as he walked through muck and saw the wheels sinking and the horses' fetlocks turning to thick ropes of mud. If he were injured or killed and the giant diamond undiscovered, it would be buried with him. Then in France the name de Parceval would be ever infamous as that of the man who lost the Régent.

At the inns and stops along the route, I imagine de Parceval suspected any who looked his way. Every creak on the stairs tormented him. He carried the stone like guilt. Could they see on his face what he bore? And then, at night, alone in his room, on the floor, with but one candle, he would pull out the Régent, and its fractured light, released, bounced through the room like a beserk child.

In Basel, this bourgeois city, in this safe country on the banks of the Rhine, de Parceval delivered the diamonds, including the Régent, to the French ambassador, who would hold it for Treskow. And then: a shock! Treskow's representatives rejected it, saying it was worth less than 4 million. Parceval, who knew this was a trick, had to return to Paris, leaving the Régent behind.

The Directory gave him all the rest of the diamonds in the treasury, for what were diamonds in a war for the life and ideals of republican France, a war to make republics out of kingdoms? (Republics that the emperor would make back into kingdoms again, to be ruled by his family.) Parceval returned again to Basel with this huge amount of diamonds—16 million worth of goods in total—which were, of course, accepted. Now the Régent was an émigré too, passing from the peculiar country that was the court and into the hands of merchants. By May 1796 there were tales of Treskow showing it around. We have a letter here from Noël, our ambassador to Holland, who was at the casino that year when in came Treskow, a "usurer from Berlin," right through the potted palms, carrying the Régent with him. The air was smoky and full of that clickety-clack, the tinkling, the many languages that all understood—*"Faites vos jeux."*

Treskow went right through it all—over the carpet, past the women with dresses dusting the marble floor and high hats with feathers drooping and soiled. He strode past the roulette wheel, past bankrupt counts and dispossessed marquises with only their old mine-cut diamonds in their pockets. He had the biggest diamond of all. He unwrapped his handkerchief, laid it on the green baize, and told a story of French kings. Then he would ask to borrow money, using it as collateral.

"He goes from house to house showing the famous jewel, on which he asks to borrow 30,000 dalers. He says the Directory pawned it to him . . . to guarantee a contract made to deliver 10,000 horses to the republic," Ambassador Noël wrote. *"This story much amuses* [the enemy ministers at war with France] *. . . It helps the digestion of . . . a legion of émigré marquis by the drops of bile that it makes fall in their stomachs."*

Ambassador Noël said if the Directory gave him 30,000 dalers and he could have perhaps 10,000 for it, he would bring the Régent back to them; then they could deal with the eau-de-vie merchant Treskow (or "Tresco"). He said Treskow was unlikely to furnish fifty passable horses, and if the government already had advanced him large sums, it would be Treskow's dupe.

In my chronicle of the Italian campaign, I described how the emperor's troops rode to their victories on these diamond horses. Napoleon has said it was at Lodi he first knew his destiny and felt the earth fleeing beneath him as if he were being carried into the sky. He owed Rivoli and the charge of Lasalle's hussars to the diamond. Beginning with the defeat of the Piedmontese and ending with the Campoformio treaty of October 1797, Napoleon left Italy with his army paid and clothed and permanently enthralled by him. Soon enough, too, the troops were crating statues and vases, Giorgione's *Concert Champêtre,* da Vinci's science treatises, and Galileo's manuscripts for their journey north to Paris.

Now Napoleon began to commission a painting for each victory. He managed his image throughout Europe like no one but Pitt. Without pausing to pose, he would be painted on horses and standing by treaties he had signed or pointing—the gesture of authority and larger vision—to his destiny in the distance. Sometimes, because they were beautiful in a feminine way, he hid his small hands, with their long square-tipped fingers, in his coat. He held his bad stomach, a gesture of the times that others copied. All portraits missed the depth of his glance, the force of his face. Artists might show soldiers clinging to his stirrups or eyes looking after him with emotion and later locate him within the flat spectacles or the panoply of ceremonies. Whether he was alone or one of a crowd in a throne room, it was a different man they painted each time, and yet somehow the eye always went to this man and the slight telling distance around him. Those with him realized even then that they must remember his every gesture and word for their children.

At this time, Napoleon wrote intimately to his new wife, Josephine, who was already betraying him, "A kiss on your heart and then another . . . much much lower," in her "little black forest." (The emperor struck out the previous sentence so hard he tore my pages and had words with me, so I have written this chapter in code to add later. Josephine had once shown the letter to my wife, Henriette.) Josephine's lover was the soldier Hippolyte Charles, and later Napoleon knew this. When she went to join Napoleon in Milan, Charles rode with her and Napoleon's brother Joseph in the carriage. At night on the journey, she was bold enough to retire with Charles into his room.

The emperor has described all these Italian battles for my *Memorial*. And I thought often, as he told of his wars, of Desdemona listening when Othello described his battles to her father, she being wooed by the battles he had passed and he by her "world of sighs" that she did pity them. I knew that Napoleon brought luster and worth to military achievement as in the days of the first kings, and thought France's king might again be its best warrior. That, of course, is what happened. It was during the Italian campaign, when I was still in England, that I began to come over to him just a bit.

I told him recently that I had seen Baron Gros' portrait of him on a white horse, flag in hand, crossing the bridge at Arcole.

"Did you take note of just how I sat that horse, my friend?" he asked. I was perplexed.

"The only way Josephine could get me to pose was sitting on her lap," the emperor said. "Baron Gros came in and sketched away, and she did naughty things to keep me sitting there. This was after lunch and soon enough we retired . . . I miss that woman every day.

"The campaign of Italy shall bear your name, Las Cases," he continued then. "It shall be your property. And the campaign of Egypt that of General Bertrand. I intend that it shall add at once to your fortune and to your fame. There will be at least a hundred thousand francs in your pocket, and your name will last as long as the remembrance of my battles."

Thus I too am indebted to the stone, and the merchant of eau-de-vie, for the horses that helped win Italy, that launched the emperor, and may someday save me.

In Fructidor, An VI (August 1798), the emperor was conquering Egypt and defeating the ruling caste, the Mamelukes, who believed they would go to heaven if they died in battle. He went there with the army that won Italy and thirty-five thousand troops. He brought along 175 savants to collect great stores of knowledge.* Denon was drawing the monuments and the Valley of Kings, the great Sphinx. This was after Napoleon conquered the Turks and English at the Pyramids, in the same month when the English fleet under Nelson destroyed the French fleet at Aboukir.

---

*I, "Abraham," add that they also found a stone tablet, the Rosetta, that in my time unlocked all the mysteries of the pharaohs and their tombs.

Napoleon, whose name means "Lion of the Desert," cleared sand from the buried Sphinx. He had told the muftis that his job was to exterminate the Mamelukes and he praised Allah and embraced their faith. (Does it not say much that the Mamelukes he destroyed follow him then and still, one even to this island to sleep at his door and die for and with him?)

"I was left alone in the king's chamber of the Great Pyramid," he told me. "No one dared disturb me and I lay down on my coat and took a little nap with the pharaoh."

While Napoleon was in Egypt, William Pitt was expanding the English navy. In 1798, Sidney Smith stopped Napoleon's march to Acre in Syria. Napoleon's failure there helped Pitt revive the coalition of powers against France. Pitt often funded our enemies, trying to break up the continent so England might trade freely.

In August, Napoleon abandoned Egypt and returned to Paris. He was determined to leave Josephine for her infidelities, but she rushed to him.

"I heard her approach, her dress swishing on the floor," he says. "She had brought her children, Hortense and Eugène. She scratched at my door all night like a wild cat, the little savage she was. What a drama! I took her back. With Josephine, I usually gave in."

I had been with Claire, Lady Clavering, at Bath, taking a rest from my *Atlas* and my lessons when I learned that Henriette was all alone at the Château de Coëtilliou. In August, I slipped out of Britain to go to her. I made the carriage let me off at her gates and saw the flaking rust and paler iron where the crests had been removed. With each step along the alley of chestnut trees, I drew closer to the end of my old recurrent dream. It was the ancient path, thick with brambles and bracken, always just lost—with a surprise at the end. And the sounds—that summer whir as though the haze, humming with insects and small creatures, was speaking, telling me to hurry on or all would be too late.

Inside, the house was torn apart, all I remember gone, holes in the walls and scratching from inside, gauged chairs, paintings hanging askew in the long hall with missing and defaced ancestors. I found Henriette in a thin poor dress, her hair tied back with a string of wildflowers, and fell at her small red slippers. Within days we traveled to a farm she owned in Brittany, where we were wed with two farm families as our hosts and guests. After three weeks, I left her to return to exile in England. I did not know she was already pregnant with Emmanuel.

In a coup d'état Napoleon overthrew the Directory on 18 Brumaire (November 9, 1799) and became first consul. When, a month later, he offered peace to England in a Christmas letter to George III, William Pitt rejected it. Pitt said France was not stable enough and he would negotiate a treaty only if it included the allies.

The next months, Napoleon was back in Italy crossing the Great Saint Bernard Pass in Hannibal's footsteps to enter Milan and fight at Marengo in the second Italian campaign. There General Desaix's troops charged on horses the Régent had paid for, while the cavalry of Kellerman erased the column of General Ott.

After the victory at Marengo in June, Austria signed a treaty with France, and England did the same the following year. That meant the end of Pitt's coalition. (That June also saw the birth of my son, Emmanuel-Pons-Dieudonné. Few knew Henriette and I had wed, and the lewd whispers were painful for her.) I was still in England.

France paid Treskow back in 1798 and the Directory reclaimed the Régent, only to pawn it again in 1799. They had thought to get 3 million in cash, and de Parceval went to get the stone, but the deal fell through before he returned to Paris. Later, in August, the Directory gave the Régent to a Dutch banker, Vanlenberghem, as a guarantee for a series of loans. Napoleon had nothing to do with these transactions.

During the time he had the diamond, Vanlenberghem and his wife entertained in a series of white-and-silver reception rooms in their Amsterdam house. The usual "treasures" and mistakes of nature filled the *Wunderkammer*—stuffed birds and nests, rock crystal, ivory and amber, barometers, biscuit figure groups, shriveled heads too, but it was the diamond all came to see. All the burghers of Amsterdam gathered before one glass vitrine in the center of the most visible room. There the Régent continued its history off the royal bodies, now as a thing of the cabinets of wonder.

"Grote diamant! Grote steen!" said Mijnheer Ton Luyk, who noted how the diamond belonged with both the *naturalia* and the *artificialia* for it was both a work of nature and the work of man.

The Régent was like a masterwork or the child Mozart playing in the middle of a room. (A friend had seen seven-year-old Mozart at Versailles standing by Marie-Antoinette, who was at table translating his words for the court.) The visitors circled it and sidled round the glass-eyed birds, the bits of rare fur, multicolored feathers, and freak embryos in green liquids for another look. Their host enjoyed it all, telling his guests how this diamond had been worn by the French kings, then stolen and miraculously retrieved. All the while, as he listened to his guests, he thought how easy it was to fool people even in this city where all the best diamonds were cut—for the diamond on display was but a crystal facsimile.

An old friend had asked Vanlenberghem if he were not afraid it would be stolen. He nodded at his wife, Mevrouw Vanlenberghem, across the room. "It is in her bodice day and night," he said, trusting this man with his secret.

Mevrouw Vanlenberghem, who sunk it in her stays, was the next woman to wear the diamond after Marie-Antoinette, the queen of France. Feeling the hidden lump, she must have enjoyed all the grandees who marveled at the fake. At night in bed the banker would cradle his head where the diamond had lain and together they laughed that special laughter one laughs only at fools.

Once, when they fought, she stood in front of their immense tiled fireplace, stuck her hand down her bodice, and threatened to throw the diamond in the fire. She never imagined that a diamond would burn (it would) and held it out just to provoke her husband.

"Ah, now you dance!" she said.

Then she thought of their children and handed the stone back to him.

In November 1799, when Napoleon formed the *consulat*, thanks to war plunder and his compensations, finances were in better shape and he decided to get the crown diamonds back. He examined the accounting with the minister of finance, ordered him to settle with Vanlenberghem, and the Régent was returned in July 1801. He also tried to get back the Great Sancy from the heirs of the late marquis of Iranda, but the Great Sancy had disappeared!

"Your diamond must have had a shock," the emperor told me, "plucked from the Dutch lady's bodice still hot, to go into my cold sword. I would have liked it even better had I but known.

"Josephine was after that diamond right away and told me she had seen it in the king's hat. When I told her I intended it for my sword, she took to her bed for two days. From then on she called the Régent vulgar and much too big. Ha! Can a diamond ever be too big? In fact I retrieved it from a vulgar world where it did not belong. It was pawned to men without power, men in casinos," he said with scorn.

"We had one of her dramas over that stone for she wanted it for a diadem and I would not let her have it. I said was it not enough for my little Creole to have the queen's bed?"

When the emperor listed his riches for me in response to attacks from the English, he said he had gotten the diamond back from the Jews in Berlin. Was Treskow a Jew? Or even Vanlenberghem? I was bewildered; perhaps they were both Jews. I did not dare point out the emperor's possible error. His memory, I know, is excellent. As I have written, he thinks of that memory as a great chest from which he has only to pull out the correct drawer to remember all. At night he shuts all the drawers, but even so, some pop open.

As I have said, Napoleon understood the use of creating an image as no man I ever knew. At his first reception for the diplomats in February of 1800, when he was first consul, he entered unannounced in the simplest uniform, devoid of all cordons or braid, decorations or orders, and let himself be noticed by the room. Josephine, who had entered before him on Talleyrand's arm, wore a white muslin dress with but a single strand of pearls, her hair dressed in well-planned disarray with braids held by a tortoiseshell comb. Both of them, young and handsome, sliced through the others in their diamonds and plumes and embroideries like a clean knife.

This simplicity when he was full of glory was deliberate, and since it was an effective trick, he continued it. The gray overcoat, the black hat without trim would come to define him. He also set aside time for his circuses—and for this, he now had the Régent, returned from its exile to join the patched-together collection then known as the state gems. It included the king of Sardinia's jewels and those stolen from the émigrés and our noble families. The diamonds were part of a past Napoleon wanted to restore, a past that had beauty and order, a past he did not revile for he had seen France in full brutality. He had gone from hating France as a schoolboy to a ruler who included all its history even as he created its future.

Quickly enough he moved from the Luxembourg Palace into the king's old apartments in the Tuileries and slept in Marie-Antoinette's bed. He claimed Leonardo da Vinci's portrait *La Gioconda, Ma Donna Lisa* for his bedroom. He has told me that in her ancient face he found answers to questions ever in his mind, and in the land behind her, he and his brothers saw Corsica. He heaped Josephine with jewels (this was not hard), insisted on reviving and exceeding the splendor and the court etiquette. How could a man of such birth know these things? One can only call it the instinct for nobility combined with good coaching.

In the midst of a republic, he was stepping into a monarchy with its palaces and court. The Régent and all diamonds were slightly dangerous then for they, too, were a signal of inequality and kings. Napoleon was already unequal, born superior and apart like a king.

A hundred years after it had been discovered, the diamond had found one with the dimension to match it. Remembering the first victories, the emperor has said he then considered the Régent his lucky charm.

"Be economical and even parsimonious at home; be magnificent in public," he has said. It is true that he ate potatoes with onions on his campaigns and watered his Chambertin, but he also enjoyed and still enjoys his bit of gold embroidery, leaving his clothes where they fall for his valets. He became accustomed to the magnificent rooms, the standing generals and waiting kings, the food ready at the instant he was (once his cooks roasted twenty-three chickens so that he might have a fresh one when he called for it), the tents all prepared for him on his campaigns. He had the women waiting too—wearing white when he came home from the blood. He still enjoys the hush and flush, the quickening of fear that he inspires when we ride out even today, how we live to anticipate his every want before he need speak it, how our eyes follow his so we may leap to fetch whatever he seeks.

He is, in short, necessarily dual. He is the man and the office and he understood they cannot be the same. As an actor does, he disconnected himself from one to become the other whenever it was necessary, until eventually the two began to merge. He showed his skills as an actor when the royalists tried to kill him with a bomb. After the infernal machine blew up in his path on Christmas Eve, he left behind the screams and blood in the street and went on to the opera and sat through it. He returned to the Tuileries with a calm smile then shut the door and was heard shouting at the police.

At this time I, too, was dual, living among the émigrés in London as "Felix" and going out at night as Count Las Cases in my one shirt. I had the same face and manners, but as Felix, I was invisible to those who happily bowed before the count. Then, too, I had taken on yet a third identity for writing my *Atlas*. There I had used the nom de plume "Le Sage." The *Atlas* was finished then and I had the strangely wonderful experience of going out and hearing it and "Le Sage" discussed in my presence in the drawing rooms. I saw my *Atlas* on London tables, even watched those I knew consult it, never suspecting the author in my dingy presence.

Days I scarcely knew who or what I was, for beyond all this I was a foreigner, an exile from those I loved, perfecting the language I had learned in Boston.

"You can always be another self," said the emperor. "I do not believe in disguise, yet I had to hide my face on the way to Elba or they would have killed me. I am one thing here on this island that I never was before. Here our diamonds, like all our lights, are hidden and every day is pretend."

"More than in a court? Or a war?" I asked.

"More than you can ever imagine," he said.

Two Swords

I WANTED TO WEAR THE DIAMOND RIGHT AWAY," THE EMPEROR told me, "and had just the occasion when Lord Cornwallis* came to sign the peace at Amiens. I rushed Nitot to get it into my sword. I told him just put it in the guard, it did not have to be perfect. These jewelers fuss around forever. 'In the sword?' Nitot said, and I knew he did not approve. 'I won my power with a sword,' I told him.

"I thought I might rename the stone, call it 'the Napoleon,' but really, what was the need? Cornwallis could not remove his eyes! I drew his attention, stroking my sword so he might see what we owned. I think he knew it was Governor Pitt's diamond that England had once let escape, and he must have known of the Arabic belief that the general with the largest diamond wins. So I teased him—after all, a newborn government must dazzle and astonish. I had just the tool to show we were not the beggars they expected. I gave them all lots of diamonds when they signed Amiens and Luneville."

Waiting for Cornwallis in the Hall of Ambassadors that July 1801 were the three consuls—Napoleon, of course, was first consul—all the diplomatic corps, adorned and fringed and overhung with braid, the military court in full uniform and decorations. Napoleon was the only one wearing a

---

*Cornwallis, then the English ambassador, signed the peace that ended the war between Britain and France for thirteen months.

simple chasseur's uniform, now with the sword. All the colors and light collapsed into the diamond and surged forth, pricking the walls of the room.

Napoleon was already making a new France from the disorder of the Revolution. In a fury of activity he created the Bank of France, and what became the Civil Code. He made legal reforms, signed a concordat with the church restoring worship to the people, began building bridges and quays, roads, canals. He created our lycées and ended the ten-day week.

" 'Your Monsieur Pitt called me all that was dangerous in the Revolution,' I told Cornwallis later," he said. "He did not know how to respond. Still we made peace, for, as a soldier, he respected me. He was the very first Englishman I liked and he gave me a good opinion of his country."

The emperor told me how Cornwallis had kept his word. When, after much delay, he was to sign the Amiens treaty, he could not sign at a certain time. Then that evening, a courier came from England to challenge certain articles. Cornwallis told the courier he had signed already, for he had given Napoleon his word.

We talked about how Pitt, already ill, resigned over Catholic emancipation in Ireland before the peace of Amiens.

"Their king told people he had rid himself of a man who had been kicking at him for twenty years," I said.

"I know the feeling," said the emperor, and I guessed he was speaking of Talleyrand as well as Pitt.

At about this time, the emperor went to Notre Dame for a Te Deum to celebrate the peace and the concordat. He believed we needed religion to help the poor accept their lot, knowing that the next world would sort things out. The freethinkers and the generals like Bernadotte, who had married the emperor's old fiancée Désirée Clary, sat and scowled.

It was Easter Sunday and Paris was filled with the bells of Notre Dame. Napoleon wore a green court dress with gold embroideries and the Régent in his sword.

"At that time it was my favorite prop," he said. "I brought things back—émigrés, the old calendar, and the diamond. Maybe with the Régent, I brought back too much . . ."

His consular sword evolved through several designs. For the final sword of 1803, the emperor had the Régent set in the center of the hilt, guarded by two winged dragons, for dragons always guard a treasure and are the symbols of power. He planned it all as he planned Josephine's jewels and the way the country would run, in every orderly detail.

There is an etching here of this sword. The dragons rest their throats against the sides of the diamond. Their demon tails, ending in arrowheads, curl underneath the Régent, while their unfurled wings encircle two other immense round brilliants, plundered from those families who fled. The diamonds move in threes up the hilt and curved handle; the throat is of green jasper. The emperor has told me that one of the stones was a button of Marie-Antoinette while others were from Louis XIV and Louis XV, stones from Tavernier, stones that had been stolen in the robbery of the Garde Meuble, and some taken from the émigrés. None were less than 10 carats.

The first consul pardoned the émigrés who had not fought against him and brought back his exiles as he brought back the exiled stone. I had fought against him, but was able to cross the border under an assumed name as the tutor to Lady Clavering's children. At the border, an innkeeper admired how well I spoke French! I was amnestied in April and arrived in Paris in May. I had some money from my *Atlas* then to help my family and buy a small library for the apartment I rented at 6 Rue Saint-Florentin, on the street where the Régent was stolen ten years before. I was thirty-six years old in this strange new France in which it meant nothing but danger to be a chevalier of the Order of Saint-Louis or to have been presented at a court that no longer existed. Only love beyond sanity could have lured me back to my native country, where they now acted *The Play of the Guillotine*. A light sliding fire screen would fall on the actor's neck as the audience called out, *"Il n'était que cela! Rien que cela!"* (It was only that! Nothing but that!) I settled in to do the French version of my *Atlas*.

One of my old friends, Admiral Decrès, who had been in Egypt with the emperor, now was minister of the navy, and soon enough he and others began urging me to join the government. That summer, I went to Versailles, where Lady Clavering had rented rooms in the Petit Trianon, now an inn. It felt very strange to have our dinners in the queen's bedroom. In town the people begged money for food and many still had no shoes and wore rags, living in the abandoned wreckage of the monarchy.

The next year, I went out a bit into the salons, where I saw how Paris had changed. All distinctions were gone, people made much too free. Strangers touched me who should not have and spoke much too loud. Merchants came into the drawing rooms and sat down and made conversation. I heard Russian and English everywhere. Every month there were banquets in the Gallery of Diana, at which the first consul appeared in his crimson-and-gold coat with the Régent in his sword and Josephine at his side. By then Lady

Clavering was trapped and could not return to England, so she placed her daughters in Madame Campan's school. I stopped going to the salons and went only to her.

Few knew I was Le Sage of the *Atlas*. I heard people call my book a whole library in itself, for indeed it included history, geography, chronology, and politics. Then I would cross to the other side of the room to hear guessing—always wrong—as to the identity of this Le Sage. This interest put napoleons in my pocket—fortunate, since I had been forced to renounce my patrimony. Briefly I was rich.

None of the success let me forget my failure. After years of utmost obscurity I did not have to have to face fame full on. The fame was for Le Sage, not Las Cases, and thus, as in England, I could observe it from a remove and savor it doubly for myself and this other self. And then, the years of poring over genealogical tables and maps with a glass so the reader might understand something like England's War of the Roses seemed worth it. Or almost.

The emperor once said if he had known me at this time he would have helped me put out an edition that was less costly and make it part of the universal curriculum in schools. What better praise could there be? My *Atlas* was all I had when I left everything in haste and took my final gamble to follow the emperor here.

The consular sword was part of Napoleon now and painted into many portraits that I have seen. The size of the diamond suited him and our times with their colossal wars, times that saw whole nations being born and the formation of monumental works like the arches of Paris. Gigantic paintings of him—some thirty feet long—could barely express his scope. Baron Gros, who remembered his last session with Napoleon bouncing on Josephine's knees, now, in 1802, painted him as first consul at Liège wearing the consular sword with the Régent, and pointing to a sheaf of treaties.

By 1802, when Napoleon was thirty-three, he had made himself consul for life. He insisted that the people approve the decision in a referendum, and there was a vote of almost 3 million. He crossed out the numbers and changed them himself, making the final vote 3,400,000.

He immediately added the sword with the Régent to the symbols with which he surrounded himself. There were stars and the *N* above a snake biting its tail, the gold eagle holding a thunderbolt or two, laurel for the glory that was Greece and Rome. From republican Rome too came the eagles, along with arches and roads. His golden bees—the symbol of industry—connected him to the medieval age. Metal bees (some said live ones) had covered the corpse of Childeric, father of Clovis, king of the Franks. They were found at Tournai in the time of Louis XIV. He banished the Bourbon lilies and the Bourbon blue; his color for uniforms was green. Symbols of Egypt inspired by his campaign crawled all over the furniture by Jacob and Oeben and Desmalter. This furniture had straighter lines than before, a hard seat, and was rich with palm leaves and dolphins, the random sphinx. Josephine's furniture swam with hard gold swans. All these symbols came together for his coronation as emperor.

Jewelers trotted through the palaces with rolls of drawings and trays of gems. His orders rivaled those of Louis XIV. Jewels were part of his desire to adorn public moments, to change not only Europe but the style of his court. As he combined new nobles with old, he combined new jewels with those of the fallen crown. He had his own ornaments altered—he pointed and sketched—and set up people and regulations to care for what were soon to be the imperial jewels.

In February of 1804, I saw Napoleon for the first time as he galloped past me on his way from his country house, Malmaison. This was at the time of a plot against him, when security was very tight. I was almost arrested because I had not bothered to have my card visaed in two years and I carried English coins in my pocket. The mud from his carriage dotted my coat as if to say, "I claim you," but he was still the usurper to me, even as my old friends were drifting into his court.

The lives of leaders often are marked by one mistake that changes all that follows. In the case of the emperor many would suggest his Spanish or Russian campaigns, the shocking haste of the execution of the Bourbon duc d'Enghien, or his second marriage. Others, including Napoleon's mother and the composer Beethoven, felt he should not have made himself emperor. In the summer and fall of 1803, Beethoven wrote his Third Symphony, and wanted to call it *Bonaparte,* for he saw Napoleon as the hero of his times. When the great German heard that Bonaparte had crowned himself with much misplaced fanciness, he tore off the title page of his work and called it a generic *Eroica.*

Many times I heard Constant, who was the emperor's valet then, tell how the emperor swore and chafed as he was laced into his coronation regalia. He joked about the bills he would receive as he put on the ruffles and laces, the white silk stockings embroidered in gold, the white velvet booties and breeches. He was gartered, buckled, and buttoned with diamonds. Then came the crimson velvet coat and cloak, caught with a diamond clasp. The coronation robe strewn with gold bees weighed half as much as the emperor, who sagged when he put it on; his crown was a diadem of golden oak and laurel leaves.

Then he sent for Josephine's notary, Ragideau—the same man who had told Josephine not to marry a young man "with nothing but his cloak and sword."

"I stood before him in my robes with the Régent in my sword," he said, "and asked if now I did not have more to recommend me than my cloak and sword."

The emperor had planned the coronation with the artist Isabey, moving little model figures around as he moved his soldiers in campaigns. Madame de Montesson, who was considered the widow of the duc d'Orléans, taught his court the old etiquette.

I was not there. Nor did I witness the procession as he rode from the Tuileries to Notre Dame and then back. I missed the bay horses with white plumes, the magnificent coaches, the obelisk illuminated in the Place de la Révolution, the lights between the columns of the Garde Meuble. Here on Saint Helena the emperor has found me out and twisted my ear a bit harder than his usual jest.

"You saw the cortège at least?" he asked.

"I had a ticket, but my patron, Lady Clavering, had a terrible cold at that time and I stayed home."

"You were the evil aristocrat then!" He was still holding tight to my ear.

"Yes, and here am I next to you now."

Letting go, he smiled with much suppressed within. I know he still thinks of me as belonging to the Saint-Germain set, those who were always the "other" to him. Even when they served him as emperor, he felt himself wrong with those people. He did too much or too little for them, it was never right, he said. So he made his own counts and barons—creating hereditary titles based on service to the state, fortune, and influence. Still I knew there were counts and "counts" and the differences in those born that way. His chamberlains were from those the Revolution had elevated as well as from families like mine it had stripped. It amused the emperor that Madame de Montmorency hurried to tie Josephine's shoes whereas the new ladies were afraid to be taken for a maid.

How can and why should I tell him that I did not like him then? We had fought on opposing sides, and back in my own country, I felt I was in a different land. Far from wishing to celebrate his triumph, I had hoped that something might go wrong that day—not to the extent of the infernal machine or the English plots, but nonetheless a flaw, a misstep that might give us a moment's amusement.

I had lived ten years hating him and the movement that had raised him. I had known the myth long before I knew the man. I was not yet persuaded, found the pageantry abhorrent, was uncomfortable with the idea of empire, the fêtes and fireworks, this hybrid Caesarian creature. Even the coronation balloon that was to be blown across the Alps repelled me. I hid at the spectacle of Paris, its windows hung with banners and tapestries and decorated bedsheets in the windows of the poor. It was astonishing to me how he had brought it all back—the procession, the monarchical regalia, all to be painted as large as possible by the painter of the Revolution, Jacques-Louis David. The costumes and crowns, this mockery of the aristocracy, offended me, for I knew friends who had been executed because their paintings hung in our salons or because of the "de" in their names, a crest, the nobility ring, a bit of lace.

I had been at Notre Dame and seen the pope, who had come for the ceremony, at just the moment when Thérésia Tallien, in one of her transparent dresses, was prostrating herself before him. I heard the pope bid her, "Rise and sin no more," and had to laugh into my sleeve.

Then too I could not understand a warrior wearing embroidered gloves and purple velvet Spanish dress, this Corsican of the small nobility, who insisted on crowning his wife, the lovely but shady Josephine, now hung with diamonds. What audacity, when one remembers that none of the queens for centuries, none since Marie de Medici, and not Marie-Antoinette most recently, had been so graced!

I dared not tell him I considered the coronation a sham despite the presence of the pope, because Napoleon was not legitimate. He had not come, as the kings had, from God. To be an emperor was no more legitimate than to be a fake king. The whole thing—the orb of emperors, the hand of justice of the Bourbons, this patched-together monarch with his quarreling family (for the sister princesses had refused to carry Josephine's train)—was steeped in craziness. At the time I could not admit that since the first kings were the best soldiers, it was right for Napoleon to found the fourth dynasty of France. Such a choice had been made by Rome when it turned to Julius Caesar.

So I lied that day on the island and, when he smiled, felt my mouth freeze into a smile that failed to convince even me. It shamed me that he was in such a position that he had to content himself with that grimace. Longwood, our house, was silent at most hours. The kitchen being distant, sometimes the random heated winds were the only sounds as they blew through the rooms.

At that moment of lying, I waited for the shrub trees to stir, shake off their moisture, and creak to deliver me from my face locked in ghastly falsity.

A great confusion of regalia was applied to Napoleon's person that coronation day. They could not get Charlemagne's regalia from Nuremburg, and Louis XVI's crown had been destroyed. Napoleon had a new crown made and ordered Charlemagne's sword sent from Aix. The historical sword, the Joyeuse, was found in a secondhand shop. Since the hilt had the forbidden fleur-de-lys, the jewelers gave it another knob and sheathed it in green velvet covered with bees. By that time the emperor was disgusted and decided to have his own regalia made.

Which sword would he wear? The saber he had worn at Lodi and the Pyramids was meant for a uniform and was too plain. With his Spanish dress he wanted a broadsword. He had the consular sword with the Régent in its pommel. He decided to remove the stones and have them decorate a broadsword for the consecration. Then he changed his mind and kept the consular sword.

His valet, Constant, who said that the Régent was on a black velvet toque, was wrong. The Régent was still in his consular sword, now decreed the imperial sword and suspended from a white velvet baldric that went round the back of his neck and hung across his chest. It was painted into all the portraits of the day.

In his first plan and sketches of the coronation painting, David had shown Napoleon crowning himself with his right hand while his left held the sword with the Régent and pressed it to his heart. In the final painting, responding to a suggestion from his pupil Gérard, he painted the emperor crowning Josephine.

That day she glowed with a cosmetically applied youth. Isabey, the miniaturist, had come in with his palette and tiny brushes and painted her face as a miniature canvas. At forty, with her will and his skill, she looked four and twenty. By the time of his coronation Napoleon had already loaded

Josephine with jewels (the accounts are here). Then he had Nitot make diadems and crowns and five very important sets—necklace, bracelet, belt, diadem, earrings, comb, pins. She had a parure of the choicest giant pearls, two diamond parures. She had a parure of emeralds and one of fabulous rubies. Her pearls were the size of kumquats. She had hundreds, then thousands of jewels and loose stones. He kept buying and she kept buying. She had at her disposal, too, the crown jewels. But not the Régent—that was always his. Alas, she also had opals, ever the harbinger of bad luck. One such opal was called the Burning of Troy.

David's painting was, of course, a big lie. He painted in Napoleon's mother, who had stayed in Rome because of his treatment of his brother Lucien. David painted the Régent into the sword at the very top under his arm, mounted on the *pommeau*. I remember remarking it when I went to see the work. The diamond was above a golden eagle with its wings spread. What a clever fellow this painter David was, for he had been the painter to Louis XVI in the past, then voted for his death. Then he went to see and paint the body of Marat, assassinated in his bath (where Marat sat to relieve a skin disease contracted when he hid in the sewers). Now David was reborn into the empire. He was surely the Talleyrand of painters.

I met David once, remember looking way up at him, unable to keep myself from staring at the wart on his upper lip—a huge lump on the left side that pulled down his mouth—before being commanded upward to his dark blue eyes, just the color of his frock coat, eyes already studying me.*

"A good little face," he said, and he seemed to be wondering if I would ever do anything important enough for him to remember it.

Gérard painted the emperor in his imperial dress with the Régent back in the pommel of his old consular sword. The diamond was but a small part in the day, though all that was upon his person then surely are relics by now. The stone did not migrate. Constant saw it in the hat, Gérard saw it in the consular sword, David in the imperial sword.

The pope blessed the regalia and orb (emperors have orbs) and poured on the mystic oil. In blessing the sword, the pope had blessed the Régent, perhaps removing any curse.

"At last I can get my breath," the emperor told Constant later as he took off his costume and began scratching hard, feverish, and shaking with relief.

---

*Abraham's footnote: David would sculpt a medallion of Count Las Cases.

A Brief Digression on Enemies

AND WHERE ARE YOU JUST NOW IN YOUR CHRONICLE?" SAID the emperor as we returned from our walk. The trees were lace in the sky and the small flying things of the night hit us as we walked into the light, the moth wings at our face at once soft and terrifying.

"I have come again to the time of your enemy, Monsieur Pitt, when he opposed you and the army at Boulogne from across the channel in the summer of 1805. You were so close and yet you never met."

"What has he to do with the diamond except that his ancestor brought it forth? I hope you have not gone too far afield into my life, Las Cases. This is not your *Memorial*."

"Perhaps the fact that we never paid him in full for the diamond was the source of William Pitt's great opposition to France?"

"How fanciful is that!" said the emperor, smashing a handful of fresh almonds with his sword. "True, I did not like Pitt. As to enemies, however, I was opposed not by men but by the elements. In the south, the sea made me lose, and it was the fires of Moscow, the ice of winter that lost me the north. Thus water, air, and fire—nothing but nature. And time, that is the enemy I must now defeat," he said. Then he went inside to continue his dictation to Marshal Bertrand, who had stayed late this one evening.

I once saw Poussin's painting *A Dance to the Music of Time*, in which three maidens and Bacchus dance back to back in a circle as the god of time plays the lyre. I think the dance was supposed to mean that poverty led to labor, which led to riches and pleasure, and finally ruin, as the dance continues. Then, too, I had seen Cressent's bronze clock *Love Triumphing over Time*, in which Cupid steals the hourglass and scythe from Time. In these two objects time was confronted and two views of life expressed; I knew which view the emperor would embrace.

It was then, in the wit achieved on the staircase, that I thought of a response to the emperor's question. He and Pitt were forever bound by the diamond and all the bad magic it produced, though I do not think that either man knew or cared back then. To Pitt, the Régent must have been something left behind long ago, a disreputable part of the past, a detail of his ancestor's portrait, an amusing story. He had gone far beyond his great-grandfather, the merchant governor with the stone. He floated far above some hat trinket. But how can I know? Perhaps the grudge of the past lingered.

If the emperor had a distant and mighty enemy, it was (whatever he says now) William Pitt; and if Pitt had one* it was the emperor. Each alone was big enough for the other to consider. In their speeches, they described each other with the special hatred that is almost love, for who understands you better than your foe, his antenna quivering for your every move? Who anticipates you better, pays such attention, or better knows your tricks? He scans the day's journals for your deeds before his own. He is always sniffing and subtly inquiring without condescending to show too much interest. Since both were men who bewitched their countries, men died, nations and alliances were forged, shifted, or broken as a consequence.

As perverse as the old Madame in my tastes, I have always preferred such an enemy to an indifferent friend to go with me through the years. When devoted enemies compete, each looking over his shoulder at the other's advances with pain, or his stumbles with joy, both achieve more than they would if left on their own. The enemy is a glorious prod. (And here I have many such. Just today one of the generals—I suspect de Montholon— tied my stockings together. Also I think pages of my work are missing. I did not mention this to the emperor, who has always said, "Never interrupt your enemies while they are making mistakes.")

To the English, until Wellington, William Pitt was the only one with the

---

*Pitt might say if any opposed him it was Charles James Fox, who believed in the Revolution. Or he was thwarted by his own constitution or by the madness of King George, which came and went from 1788 on and found this king conversing with an oak tree.

dimension to oppose the emperor's genius. At times, the wars were seen as not between two nations, but between these two immense personages. The great English cartoonists regaled their readers with the stringy Pitt and a plump emperor in tugs-of-war, at table carving up the world in the time of George III.

Later that night, after Marshal Bertrand had returned to his family, I spoke again to the emperor of that time when they stood with their armies directly across the channel from each other.

Pitt, briefly out of power then, as Warden of the Cinque Ports was training his volunteers to resist the emperor should his fleet land in England. Pitt had returned to power in 1804, but as in the case of his father, his spirit and health had been broken. Napoleon had gone to Boulogne to inspect the force of ships and the 120,000 men he had assembled to invade England.

The emperor asked me what those in London thought at the time of his planned invasion. I told him I could not say, for I was already back in France—and captured by Josephine, if not by him. (The empress had written and I had gone to her. She was, as always, wrapped in a shawl. I sat on one of her chairs, resting my arms uncomfortably on gold swans for, perversely, she had chosen this symbol of purity as her emblem.)

"In the salons of Paris, sire, I regret to say they laughed at your invasion, even the English who were there. They called your fleet nutshells floating in a bowl."

"You could laugh in Paris, but Pitt was not laughing in London," said the emperor, whose face had become an alarming color. "He measured the danger and forged a coalition the moment I raised my hand to strike. Never did the English oligarch face such peril. I had the best army I ever had . . . the army of Austerlitz. I could have been in London in four days to free them all." He paused. "I changed my mind."

"In that very year their artist William Blake painted *The Spiritual Form of Pitt Guiding Behemoth*. I saw it years later in London."

"*Behemoth?* I do not understand that *Engleeesh*," he said, very annoyed now and beginning to pace.

"It means a monster. Blake made Pitt an angel with a golden halo and glowing robes riding a whirlwind directing the storms of war," I said, already regretting having brought this up. Pitt was seen to have held off the emperor through force of will.

"I was the one riding the whirlwind and he was no angel, rather the very devil himself."

To prove that the emperor and Pitt disliked each other, I could draw from what the emperor has told me for the *Memorial* and what I have read of Pitt's speeches. The emperor has called Pitt a "scourge" and "a genius of evil" in my presence.

When the emperor first planned his flotilla in 1803, Pitt had increased the war budgets. He was near the end of his life; the nation was his only lover; his line (at least in terms of glory) ended with him.* Napoleon was poised to become emperor of the French, wear the iron crown of the king of Italy, and start his dynasty. It was the year he made his brother king of Holland and ended the Holy Roman Empire. In the spring, while Pitt was forming his cabinet, Napoleon became emperor wearing Pitt's great-grandfather's diamond.

They were alike in their incredibly quick minds, their ability to manipulate sleep. Both had gained ascendancy over older brothers and risen to power young (emperor at thirty-five; prime minister at twenty-four), though Pitt had a head start, being ten years older. His talents, his family's fame positioned him for an earlier rise; his father bred him to his destiny, whereas the emperor rose to meet his.

Both had genius in administration and were reformers, able to look at a whole country and see what must be done for its future. Both created hereditary peers, thus elevating the middle class; both had a policy of repression and stomach problems. Both names were feared and blamed for all the ills in the opposing countries.

And yet in certain ways they were not the same at all. The emperor's genius was for war; Pitt had a poor army, and mostly failed in war after 1793. Pitt was the greatest parliamentary leader of his day; the emperor, despite Talleyrand and Cambacérès and the generals, acted alone. One might lean his elbow on the other's head and was all bones, while Napoleon is plumper with the years and their cares. Pitt, who had been given port wine for his health as a boy, drank wine to excess, while the emperor drinks little. The Pitt I had seen was awkward; the emperor is all grace in his every gesture.

---

*The head of the family, Baron Camelford, who inherited the Pitt craziness, died in a duel having left no children. Previously he shot his lieutenant in another duel and was thrown from the navy. He kept entering France with a special repeating gun to assassinate Napoleon when he was first consul. His cousin Lord Stanhope, also eccentric beyond bounds, so loved our Revolution that he gave up his title and crests, called himself Citizen Stanhope, and lived thus in Chevening, the governor's old house.

Through the diamond and the marriages it enabled, Pitt had become the very model of the aristocrat; the emperor always reminds me that he is risen from the people. Pitt was ever in financial difficulty, his households filled with shocking waste so that he had to sell his own diamonds. The emperor saved on the civil list and lived with magnificence though not neglecting the administration of his palaces. And of course, one served a throne, while the other was the throne. Still there was ever this connection between them.

After the emperor's victory at Austerlitz in December of 1805, Pitt declined rapidly. He felt he had lost and had "the Austerlitz look." William Pitt, age forty-six, died early in 1806, on the twenty-fifth anniversary of his entry into the House of Commons. In this mystical way, the man who wore the diamond killed the man whose family had risen on the stone.

It was Austerlitz that brought me in soul and spirit to the emperor and his empire. It was then, for his victories, that I loved Napoleon as I had always loved France, and I began to live for him. This meant I would break forever from my friends, royalists to whom he was still the Corsican ogre. Pitt had been all my hope once and now his enemy defined my life. Like the diamond, I went from one to the other.

One day on this island we had talked, in the way that prisoners will, of returning to our native land. "You will return," the emperor had said.

"Not without you," we all said at once, knowing this was not quite true in every case. The emperor knew any return for him would have to be decided by England. By then Pitt was long dead, yet the emperor blamed only Pitt for the way England thought of him still.

"Pitt told them I have a whole invasion in my head. They will fear me forever," he said and seemed almost proud. "Yet there is nothing to fear," he continued, looking around as if the English themselves might hear him. "Nothing."

Though down in Jamestown harbor each ship's captain supports him, we knew escape from a second island was an impossible illusion. I imagined him scrambling over the rocks in some futile disguise. He said he felt too old for war and all ambition had burned out. At this we exchanged glances.

And thus we have remained wasting on this poisoned isle. So it can be said that Pitt and his legacy will kill the emperor. Or is it the diamond? Had the stone not raised the family, Pitt in power might never have existed. The Régent might not have come to the emperor. Pitt would not have formed his last coalition in 1805, that, when revived, proved fatal to the emperor.

And so, in time, they will have killed each other.

Four Small Shoes

NAPOLEON, WHO HAD BECOME AS A KING, NOW THOUGHT of his own dynasty, for the point of the empire was to assure a continuous political life. It was his misfortune that he had crowned Josephine, an empress unable to bear him a child. Was it the fall from the balcony that she sustained when he sailed to Egypt, or was it her age? No one quite knew or dared ask why.

The emperor's brother Louis, the king of Holland, married Josephine's daughter, Hortense, and their eldest son was Napoleon.* The emperor considered him his heir until he died suddenly at age five. Josephine tried every means and remedy and trickery to have a child. Then the emperor began to think of divorce.

He had his mistresses, of course, but he still loved the empress. The emperor's secretary Baron Méneval told me how one night at Malmaison they played at the game of Prisoner's Base. The emperor fell while trying to catch Josephine and take her prisoner. They raced all over the grounds, with the panting footmen in their green uniforms following them with torches. The emperor, as usual, played his own way and returned to base without shouting, *"Barre!"* He broke his bounds and was free at last. He raced to Josephine, who had played so hard the silver wheat leaves had fallen from

*Abraham's footnote: Not to be confused with Louis-Napoleon, their third son.

her hair to the lawn. He picked her up and carried her off and that was the end of the happy game.

Then had come the blond Polish countess Marie Walewska that summer at Schonbrun Castle (the castle of the emperor's second wife). She refused him for a while before succumbing for the sake of her country. The countess had his son, proving to him that he could sire a child and that the fault was with Josephine. Later, she would journey to Elba bringing him all her jewels and money. (He claims now he took such loves lightly and mocks me for my sentiments from novels, yet the allies found her miniature in his carriage at Waterloo.) Before he returned from Austria he ordered the door connecting his apartments with Josephine's to be walled up.

Constant once spoke to me of how harsh he was to Josephine in October 1809 when she arrived at Fontainebleau. That first night, she went to dress and emerged in a white satin polonaise edged with swansdown, with the silver wheat ears and blue flowers twined in her hair. The silence of foreknowledge filled the rooms when they were together. One night, a month later, she lay on the floor.

"You will not do it! You will not kill me!" the empress had screamed. Then she fainted and the emperor carried her feet and Monsieur de B——— supported her under her arms and they went down a back staircase and summoned Hortense.

The next month, at the time of the celebrations of the victory over Germany and the anniversary of the coronation, Josephine appeared in the salon of the Tuileries. She wore a simple white dress and no ornaments, a terrible reminder of how she had been at her first reception. All the crowned Bonapartes in ceremonial costume were seated before her. She stood with Hortense sobbing at her side, tears cutting through the necessary rouge on her cheeks. Her son, Prince Eugène, who had resigned as viceroy of Italy because of what was about to happen, stood by the emperor's side shaking so hard he had to hold on to the table as Monsieur Regnault de Saint-Jean d'Angely read the act of separation to the silent room. Because they had both lied about their ages and because one witness had been too young, the marriage was dissolved. Josephine cried so hard she could not continue reading her assent to the divorce. Later, she came to the emperor and they sobbed together and Constant says the emperor pressed her to his heart.

When Josephine left the Tuileries for Malmaison she was heavily veiled. She did not look back and they drew the blinds in her carriage.

In 1810, the emperor held a tiny rose satin shoe that had been made for the archduchess of Austria. He whacked Constant in the cheek with the shoe.

"See, Constant, that shoe is a good omen," he said. "Have you ever seen a foot like that?" (The size of the foot is supposed to correspond to another part of the female anatomy.)

The emperor was marrying a daughter of the Caesars. Marie-Louise was the daughter of the last emperor of the Holy Roman Empire, the empire Napoleon himself had ended when he forced her father, Kaiser Franz, to give up his thousand-year-old title and become Francis I of Austria. Marie-Louise was the great-niece of Marie-Antoinette, and the descendant of Madame, who had made the same journey to marry a stranger at almost the same age. She was a big blond virgin of eighteen and a conquered bride.

The clothes the emperor ordered made for Marie-Louise now covered every surface of his rooms at the Tuileries as he inspected each piece of her dowry. Every day, the couturiers and the drapers came with boxes of white silk (the emperor prefers to see his women in white). He ordered her dozens of dresses, hundreds of undergarments and shoes, court dresses and ball dresses trimmed with the Napoleonic violets and raspberries, tulle evening dresses, hunting costumes in white satin and velvet and gold, nightcaps and blond veils and hundreds of gloves and jeweled fans. He was in a dream, making a new white Josephine, untouched and without flaws, as though such a thing could be.

I was by then living a public life in the emperor's service as a chamberlain and councillor of state. In 1808 I had been made a baron of the empire. The next year I served in the army at Antwerp till the beginning of 1810. I had been appointed chamberlain in December 1809. Though I had issued a new edition of my *Atlas,* I was still hard pressed for money to live among ministers and kings, the crowd of German princes who filled the Tuileries since Tilsit. It cost me the fortune I lacked to join this strut of the uniforms.

Sometimes then I felt the emperor's eye upon me as if he expected me to speak and was puzzled that I didn't. Or perhaps this was my imagination. I did not know how to put myself forward before him. From my usual distance, I was astounded to see the frenzy that seized the emperor before his bride's arrival in France.

Nitot, still his jeweler, walked the halls almost daily carrying trays as he prepared jewels for Marie-Louise. Footmen followed carrying the flat leather cases stamped with eagles.

"More!" Nitot said as he passed me, his heels clickety-clacking, and every day his smile grew. "*Encore plus!*"

One day he took the diamond belt that Josephine had worn at the coronation to make it over for Marie-Louise.

"Too tight—I cannot sit. *Merde!*" I heard the emperor shout at that time, and the Italian tailor sent by his brother-in-law the king of Naples left in tears with all the new clothes he had made for the emperor.

They worked into the nights making white rooms of Josephine's apartments. The emperor ordered bed furniture in the finest point d'Alençon lace with the arms of the empire surrounded by his bees. They carried out Josephine's chairs with swans.

One day, the emperor looked up at the walls. That day in all the palaces footmen removed all the paintings of his victories over Austria. Such was his organization and the way he heeded details.

No one dared look askance as he planned to surround Marie-Louise with Josephine's attendants and Josephine's own daughter, Queen Hortense, as handmaiden in her court. Marie-Louise also had some members of the nobility whose ancient names she might know.

I heard music and, peeking into one of the salons, saw the emperor practicing his waltz with Hortense—all this so he might dance with her mother's replacement. Around and around they went, dipping and gliding, the emperor dizzy. He was holding her close and humming, and I saw in Hortense a vision of her mother young. Suddenly she flinched, for he had trod upon her slipper. Almost immediately, the emperor caught sight of me and I curled myself back around the door and ran.

I was among those who considered the Austrian bride to be ever our misfortune. Marie-Louise seemed to dislike me on sight. She looked once at me with those slanty eyes of hers and I thought of the way a cat licks itself and looks up with both indifference and challenge. I stood somewhere right below her fat Hapsburg lower lip, and like the emperor, the new fair empress, rosy and plump to bursting, never looked down. Her hair, like his, was light chestnut and she had a small version of the Bourbon beak.

She perfectly combined the peculiar innocence with the particular hauteur of a German princess. She had been raised away from court as a country girl. The books she had read arrived with passages blackened or words cut out with scissors. She had been given only female pets. (Under all this lay a sensual hunger equal to that of Josephine.)

In Vienna Marie-Louise married Napoleon by proxy, with her brother the archduke Charles representing the emperor. As she set out from Strasbourg to Braunau in a slow cortege of eighty-three carriages, assorted ghosts and memories followed her. She might have thought of her brothers' toy soldiers and how they had stabbed the ugliest soldier with pins. This was the ogre Napoleon, who had made her family flee to Hungary and her father give up his title. The young archduke had burned his doll saying he was roasting Napoleon.

Now this man, her husband, sent couriers with letters every day. As her answers grew friendlier, he grew more impatient. They were supposed to meet in tents between Soissons and Compiègne but he set out in an un-marked carriage with Murat, his brother-in-law. He waited for her in a church doorway in the rain and stopped the carriage. Her equerry told Marie-Louise the emperor was outside in the rain.

"Could you not see I made signs to you to be silent?" he scolded the equerry.

Then he rushed into her carriage breathless, with the rain spotting his gray overcoat. She was holding his miniature.

"The artist did not flatter you," she said. He took one look and they skipped Soissons, bypassing the elaborate dinner, and he stayed with her that night in her chamber at the palace of Compiègne.

"Do it again," she said, as everyone at court soon knew.

"Marry a German," he told Méneval. "She fulfills the promise of her shoe and is fresh as a rose. She kept the candles burning all night and says that ever since her childhood she has been scared of ghosts and me. The poor child was instructed to obey me and had memorized a pretty speech."

The emperor now permitted himself a romance, for she was the reverse of Josephine, who had come to him from prison and men and an island with leaves the size of trays and sweet foreign winds. Josephine had known the world; now he was the one who knew the world, and ruled it too.

The civil marriage took place at Saint-Cloud. The cortege moved through the Bois de Boulogne, entered Paris by the Rond-Point de l'Étoile, under the unfinished Arc de Triomphe covered with a painted cardboard maquette.

Their religious marriage ceremony was in the Apollo Gallery, the Grand Galerie of the Louvre, where eight thousand awaited. All the nude statues from the Salon Carrée to the Grand Galerie had been covered, and a chapel had been installed. That day it was my duty to bring the emperor's crown and coat back to Notre Dame after the ceremony. The rich heavy coat was placed over my arms and the crown in its tooled red leather case, fitted exactly to the contours of what was within, rested on top. In the carriage I confess that I snuck open the case and gazed at my splendid burden. I did not try it on and merely stroked the coat he had worn.

For the wedding, the Régent had been taken from the consular sword and mounted on the handle of a new white enamel sword, the part the emperor's hand would touch when he brought it forth.

When I handed him the coat and crown he said, *"Merci,"* but did not look at me.

Madame Durand, who served Marie-Louise, has written that Napoleon wore the Régent on a black velvet toque with eight rows of diamonds and three white plumes. The hat was so heavy he put it on and took it off several times.

What if, for this fatal alliance, he had removed the diamond from the sword where it belonged and, like a king, put it in his hat? Was he not then letting down his warrior's guard to say, "I am but a man," and thus, in order to make a dynasty, forgetting that which had made it in the first instance? By transferring the diamond was he then misplacing his greatness?

"Oh, what foolishness!" says the emperor to this. "It was in my sword and no place but. I had another big diamond in my hat. You must not be afraid to ask me when you don't know, and no more of this silly conjecture."

"Soon enough, my fears came to fruition at the Austrian ambassador's ball," I said with some trepidation.

He made no response but seemed to be remembering that dreadful night of Prince de Schwartzenberg's ball. The ambassador had turned his house into a fairyland forest with a tent lined in gauze and thousands of candles burning in lamps. For a while we danced and then a wind came up and drove the gauze billows into the flames. Courtiers caught fire and ran screaming with flames crawling up their silver sleeves. They knocked the ladies aside, stepping on them, slashing at the burning draperies with their diamond swords even as they fell in walls of fire. The smell of burnt flesh mixed with that of black flowers and satin. The emperor, always calm in disaster, had led the new empress from the fire as the princess de Schwartzenberg went back for her children and perished. I, too, was overcome as I led

Henriette out, and my lungs ached for days with every intake of breath. The salons of Paris were quick to remember Louis XVI's Austrian bride and the misfortunes she had brought, and of course, Prince de Schwartzenberg blamed the emperor all his days.

"Sire, did you not tell me for the *Memorial* that love was the business of the idle man, the recreation of the warrior, and the ruin of the sovereign?" I had asked him once as we were playing checkers.

"Maybe so," he said. "It sounds like me."

I had never been any of the three and so felt free to love two women. It was at this time, in June 1810, that Lord Thomas and Lady Clavering were allowed to return home to England. She had forbidden me to go with her to Dunkirk but I disobeyed and jumped into their carriage, where Lord Thomas stared at the floor as we clattered along. That June I stood on the jetty sobbing as their ship sailed away. I saw Claire's mauve glove waving and the feather from her hat pluming like smoke in the wind. My life was torn up yet again.

As I was remembering this now, I found I had to excuse myself from the game for a moment. When I returned, the emperor had replaced one of his captured pieces on the board. I said nothing. None of us did when we played any game with him and each had come to this conclusion on his own.

After Claire left, I lost money through gaming and badly needed a paid situation, so I asked to be appointed master of requests at the Council of State in June 1810. My request was granted. It was then the emperor's brother Louis suddenly abdicated as king of Holland. The emperor sent me to examine the state of the Dutch navy, its arms and buildings, and I set forth that July. He had found a purpose for me and I was ready to serve him and get away. He made me a count of the empire two months later.

Later in 1810, when the emperor visited Amsterdam on his marriage trip, the same people who had marveled over the Régent in its case at Vanlenberghem's could see the stone in his sword. The population was very against the emperor at first but he won their hearts by going about the city with only an honor guard and plunging right into the crowds. He liked Holland because it was orderly.

"France did not conquer you, it adopted you," he told the Dutch. "You share all the favors of the family." He spoke of England, the common enemy, the tyrant of the seas, the vampire of their commerce.

In Amsterdam, he had taken a bust of Peter the Great from Marie-Louise's apartments and carried it off. No one knew why. He went to Zaandam to see the thatched cottage where the czar had stayed when he traveled incognito as Peter Mikhailov to study shipbuilding. The emperor had stayed there half an hour and called it the finest monument in Holland, which, to him, it was.

It is a habit of the emperor's to study his brother rulers who also were known as "the Great" within their own time. There was no one like him living in his times, except perhaps Pitt, so he was left with those who had dominated past ages. I have seen him rereading his worn copy of Plutarch's *Lives of Illustrious Men,* which he treated almost as a training manual. After he defeated Prussia, he went to the castle of Sans Souci to see how Frederick the Great had lived. After the battle of Jena, when the court fled in haste, he found Frederick's sword and alarm clock. The latter is with us now on this island. He had busts of Scipio and Hannibal on his mantle, not as others have such objects, out of distant admiration, but as one who knows himself their equal.

History and its sister, destiny, are ever on his mind; no one was ever so aware or so in service to them. When he planned his invasion of England, it was from the spot where Caesar was said to have embarked. Others sensed this interest of his. He told me the Spanish had brought him the sword of François I. The Turks and Persians had given him arms that supposedly belonged to Gengis Khan, Tamerlain, and Shah Nadir. I told him I was astonished he had not tried to keep Frederick's sword.

"But I had *mine,*" he said in his sweet smiling voice, for he knew exactly who he was, and always had.

In Utrecht, the emperor went off to review his troops in the rain. His generals were all wrapped in their mantles and the emperor made it a point to stand close to a waterspout to teach them what a soldier can endure. At Medemblik, he saw the dikes with sails on the top that protected against the Zuyder Zee.

I remember the emperor in Amsterdam from that time when I was in charge of collecting objects relating to the navy. The emperor's brother, who was then still king of Holland, had joined them, and it was then that the emperor's baby son, the King of Rome, got his first tooth—but curse me, for I have wandered yet again far from the stone.

The emperor has told me that, along with the victories of Wagram and Tilsit, the marriage was one of the best times of his life. Then, too, he has

said it ruined him, because he believed in the kaiser's honor and was deceived when the kaiser joined with his enemies. He felt he had deserved his
few hours of happiness with this girl; but he had carried too plebian a heart
into this alliance—a statesman's heart should be only in his head.

The emperor has often spoken of how different his wives were.
Josephine was all artifice and deception; she had learned to lie in order to
live. Marie-Louise, though sensual in nature, had an unchallenged royal innocence. Josephine, who had suffered, knew how to create graceful worlds
about her and was greedy for things and people and life. She was suffused
with art and mystery; the other was all pride and simple nature, but both
had their price. Josephine passed close by the truth, whereas Marie-Louise
did not know dissimulation or detours. And yet both would betray him.
Josephine borrowed and owed everywhere; Marie-Louise paid promptly.
Josephine marveled at the Régent and coveted it for her person. Marie-
Louise scarcely noticed it.

Alas, both the emperor's wives were wounded creatures. Josephine, a
child who hid in the wind houses of Martinique, was betrayed and abandoned from the start of her first marriage. Marie-Louise, who had fled with
her family again and again, had seen the death of her mother and lived a
childhood of wars.

The emperor gave jewels to both. If there was a ruby set there must be an
emerald one, and a sapphire and amethysts and turquoise, all of them loaded
with diamonds. He used to place the jewels himself, trying out different
parures. When the King of Rome was born, he gave Marie-Louise a magnificent necklace of huge pear-shaped diamonds. And I remember a pearl
the size of a pigeon's egg.

At her Château de Navarre in Normandy, Josephine would pull out her
jewels and fill tables with them, astonishing the young ladies of her fallen
court. Though she was at Navarre and out of power, all around her were still
always in embroidered dress, the sword, the hat with feathers, the servants
in full uniform not frock coat, as Napoleon had insisted and does still for us
stranded here. The uniforms, the ceremonies, the small courtesies and honors are all we have left, as he has said many times.

The next year (1811) the emperor broke up the consular sword again and
moved the Régent into a two-edged sword, a glaive. The diamond went
from the pommel of the old sword right into his hand, for it formed a little

ball on the very end of his handle. The grip was knobby with diamonds as was the sheath. The *baudrier* around his neck and across his chest was rich with large stones and covered with roses from Josephine's belt from the coronation. He went through his whole second marriage with this two-edged sword.

Étienne Nitot furnished new diamonds for them until there were over sixty-five thousand diamonds in the crown jewels and three jewelers in charge. One would get the new stones, another mounted them, and a third kept track of the crown jewels. Bernard Marguerite had the honorary title of crown jeweler. All appeared carrying green velvet boxes and chests in rare tropical woods strewn with bees, sometimes staggering with their weight.

When we wore the emperor's colors in foreign courts, we were considered to be princes. Jewels were the emperor's silent ambassadors and a guarantee for our economy. They magnified the splendors of his court, where seven kings at once might be waiting in his salons. He gave them to his Corsican brothers and sisters, who, wearing crowns and diadems, nodded from thrones in their brand-new courts.

There was one other sword that was very small and that was for the emperor's son, the infant King of Rome. Even before the wedding, sure that he would have a son, he had commanded tiny uniforms and miniature cannon and weapons. When the King of Rome was born, many believed him dead, for after the difficult birth, he lay without breath or heat in his limbs, still as a stone. They gave him eau-de-vie and he coughed himself alive.

By the time he was two, he was a handsome and very smart little blond prince parading about with his own diamonds, his hat with a 14-carat stone, his jeweled epaulettes and plaque, and the star of the Legion of Honor. He lived in a nursery of silver gilt furniture with thousands of books and his own Sèvres plates. The emperor had padded all his walls when he was first learning to walk.

I would see him galloping down the halls on his little hobbyhorse. Once, rehearsing, he commanded me to kneel and I did. That made him laugh and laugh. I never told the emperor this. Often now, I see him look at my son, Emmanuel, as though he were thinking what the King of Rome might grow to be.

In November 1811, I went to Illyria on a commission to liquidate the Illyrian debt. I stayed in Paris for the baptism of the King of Rome, then brought my brother and son, Emmanuel, with me on the journey. I worked with my usual stubbornness and, in little more than four months, liquidated a debt of 80 millions by March. I now took a long working vacation, visiting the forests of Croatia, Carlstadt, Porto Re. General Bertrand was then governor general of the Illyrian provinces and I sent my reports through him to the emperor. I returned and the emperor told me he had seen my wife, Henriette, at court, then commanded me off on an inspection trip of the depots of mendicity throughout the empire. But first I had to attend the baptism of my second son, Barthélemy. We had made Josephine the godmother and she held the ceremony at Malmaison.

That April of 1812 I visited sixty-five cities to inspect the houses of detention and the beggars in the depots of mendicity. The emperor had created these to see if he could suppress the vice of begging and make the beggars so fear the depots that they would try to get out and find work. Wherever I went I saw all that I could; it was like living my *Atlas*, for I studied the archaeology, the geography, I learned the local history, inspected the terrain, the schools, the industry, and navies, and wrote tomes of notes. I found the begging depots did not work, for the men there ate white bread and were in no hurry to leave. The depots cost three times more than the hospices and ten times more than the poorhouse and resulted in a pure loss of 30 millions. I compared hospitals and prisons and workhouses, wrote my reports, and found huge dissatisfaction all over the center of the country the farther I went from Paris. I tried to get some poor prisoners released to correct the worst injustices.

I was there among the wretched of this earth when the emperor went to invade Russia. He never read my reports. All my work was again for nothing until just now on this island when he thumbed through them and agreed there might be an end to the scourge of begging.

After 1812, the emperor no longer ordered new jewels and the Régent stayed where it was, on the handle of his ceremonial sword. He mobilized his biggest army to fight the coalitions even as he began to lose the confidence of our nation. Along with the victories were defeats and many deaths—all of which is known and has been told and retold, lied about, imagined, turned to poetry, glorified, and misunderstood. The diamond no longer had anything to do with any of the battles—nor the dreadful time that followed, a time of hideous *rigolade* when Parisians danced at Wooden Leg Balls with stumps clamped over their legs to mock those who tramped through the Russian snow.

Night Flights of the Régents

O N THE SAME NIGHT BOTH MY WIVES RAN AWAY AND BOTH remembered to take all their jewels," the emperor told me. "You may imagine the rest." He was, of course, referring to that night of March 28, 1814, the time of his defeat. The allies—Prussia, Russia, and Austria—were advancing then on Paris. The emperor was racing to get there even as Marie-Louise, in a state of terrible confusion, was abandoning the city.

Just outside Paris, Josephine was leaving Malmaison for her château in the Navarre. Her ladies took her jewels from the chest by Jacob and she sewed them into the heavily padded gown she would wear. Even as she tried to show strength, her tears fell alike on the diamonds and colored stones that stored so many of her memories. When they dressed the empress, she could barely move. The floors were piled with empty leather boxes stamped with gold bees and crests of the vanished empire.

The late afternoon was heavy with an unseasonal warmth. The early forced roses had been wheeled out into the garden for the painter Pierre-Joseph Redouté, who had been in Egypt with the emperor. He was concentrating so hard he did not notice a bee had drowned in the sweat on his upper lip. He had taken off his hat so that he might lean ever closer to the bloom.

The black swans cruised over the lake and dipped their heads as he bent to the flower. Around him in past summers Josephine's phlox and dahlias, cactus, mimosa, myrtle, and hydrangeas had vied for his attention with the two hundred varieties of roses. Now it was only the one dark pink rose, *gallica regalis,* that claimed him.

"They have sent her plants from Arabia, Egypt, and even England, for they know how she loves them," he said to one of her ladies. "Now who will care for them?"

The empress Josephine walked by, very slowly over the white gravel to her carriages. She was shivering inside her thin red shawl.

Upstairs in the Tuileries in Paris, the emperor's secretary Baron Méneval was separating the emperor's papers and reluctantly burning thick rolls of documents. In the basement the "red ladies" in their amaranth-colored dresses and the "white ladies" were packing up the imperial jewels. They tossed the crowns and scepters, orbs, and sets of emeralds, sapphires, rubies, and diamonds in their green leather cases embossed with eagles and the imperial *N* into trunks. They packed court clothing strewn with jewels that would never be worn again. It took them the whole long night of running room to room and much crying.

Baron La Bouillerie, treasurer of the imperial civil list, supervised the packing of what remained of the imperial treasure. They took the leftover gifts the emperor would give out in his days of glory—rings and jeweled snuffboxes with his portrait with the empress and their child, his plate and gilt. They took the King of Rome's massive silver cradle. They folded Napoleon's clothes and handkerchiefs into the chests. There was something final about this packing, suggesting there would be no return.

That day, the empress had presided over her Council of State. Marie-Louise had wanted to stay; then King Joseph, the emperor's older brother, showed her Napoleon's letter. It said if Paris seemed lost, to send his wife and son with the ministers, dignitaries, and treasure in the direction of the Loire. He wanted no one there (like Talleyrand) who could negotiate with the enemy. He would rather know that his son was at the bottom of the Seine than in the hands of his enemies. He mentioned the fate of Astyanax.

"Who is that?" said the empress, whose education had been selective.

No one dared tell her of Hector's son taken prisoner by the Greeks and flung from the walls of Troy so that none of Hector's blood be left alive. All the new European kings remembered the fate of Louis XVII, another boy king neglected to madness and death in his prison. That the King of Rome had dangerous blood was felt all over Europe.

Marie-Louise wanted to stay—she loved the emperor by that time as he loved her—but there were other voices, panic, rushing about, and collapses, almost comedy mixed with sobs. She had put on a brown cloth riding habit.

During the four years of her marriage, the emperor had ruled and commanded Marie-Louise as if she were one of his troops. His last letter, dated March 16, to Joseph, urged her to flee rather than fall into the hands of the allies, who now incredibly included her father. She was between two emperors then, father and husband. She had Napoleon's brothers around her, too, all of the dethroned kings bickering and staring at her and swanning about, having nervous fits in a way she thought of as histrionic and very Corsican. Her court itself was divided in opinion. There were too many voices and not the one she needed to hear instructing her as he had throughout her regency, when he was at war and she functioned as prime minister. The emperor's own power acted against him then. None dared disobey, no one dared act or even think on his own, for the emperor was the word and the force that bent everything before him. (It is like that still for us here at Longwood.)

She was leaving but the emperor was only 130 miles away, in his fast cabriolet with the horses galloping. He had fought his way home with his "Marie-Louises," the young troops called up under her regency. He had won four out of the last six battles and peace seemed possible if he would give up Belgium. He refused.

I was then in the palace trying to help, being ordered here and there by the emperor's mother, Madame Mère. Her black marble eyes would fall on an object. She would point and wherever she pointed I hoisted the object and wrapped it in raffia shrouds.

"Vite! Vite!" she said, making the word a threat. Her small darkish face was pursed and pleated with the age and fury that had overcome her beauty. Her sharp chin rested on her high tight collar like a rejected gift. After an hour, I longed to join my regiment up on the barricades of Montmartre.

"Don't forget my husband's sword with the big diamond," Marie-Louise told Baron Méneval. "He shall want it. And is it not my duty to keep it safe?" And so Méneval took the heavy sword.

The Régent, a small part of this tragic day, was in fact the ultimate *en-cas*—the object one grabs in times of desperation *in case*. Diamonds have ever been the things to carry off and redeem for funds to live on when all seems lost. The requirements of the empress of France were somewhat different, so she took the whole Imperial treasure.

She was acting on the emperor's instructions; still, it was a bit like a theft.

In his time, Napoleon had sent 2 thousand million into France. Once there had been 400 million worth of his own gold in the cellars; much of this he had spent at the time of the disasters, saving his troops.

"Am I feverish? Feel my pulse," the empress asked her *dame d'honneur,* the duchess de Montebello. She was coughing.

The King of Rome, who was three years old, clung to the furniture and curtains and even the railings of the stairs. He wept and begged not to go.

"I won't go away. Papa's not here, so I'm in charge," he said.

"It is more than I can bear. I have so much to do," said Marie-Louise. "I am pulled in every direction."

"Monsieur! Monsieur!" the boy called out to me. They were dragging him then.

"It will not be so bad," I told him. I was powerless to stop them and had to head for my post defending the city, and yet I lingered as one always does at a disaster.

"Vite!" said Madame Mère.

The equerry and Madame de Montesquiou pried the boy's little fingers loose and carried him screaming out of the palace. They too were no match for this old woman who once had whipped an emperor.

"Where is the bitch?" said Madame Mère of the empress (all the Bonapartes hated Marie-Louise since her father, Emperor Francis, had joined the enemies).

"I hope the fat sow rots," said her daughter Caroline, queen of Naples (then Spain, now nothing) as she brushed by her sister the princess Pauline Borghese, who had posed naked for Canova and was the second beauty of the family.

Princess Pauline was trying to run with a large Sèvres vessel in the Chinese style almost entirely encased in rocailles of rococo gilt bronze.

I saw Queen Caroline stick out her foot.

Princess Pauline fell with a thud. The vase was so encrusted with its gilt sheath that it had merely cracked. She tossed it aside as I gave her my hand. Queen Caroline had skipped away. Princess Pauline tugged on the sleeve of my uniform as I made my excuses about having to go to my post at Montmartre. To refuse aid to a woman this beautiful was very difficult.

"Enough!" said Madame Mère, stamping her little black boot, and the princess and the queen slunk off like small kicked creatures.

At dawn ten heavy green berlines with the imperial coats of arms, dozens of carriages and vans loaded with plate and furniture, archives, and papers lined up, clanking and jangling, the horses snorting and sidestepping at the Pavilion de Flore. Twelve hundred men of the Old Guard were specially chosen to ride alongside the convoy—grenadiers and chasseurs and dragoons, the lancers of the Imperial Guard and the *gendarmes d'élite*. They were leaving in the rain that was moving in thin gray lines over the city and out to Malmaison.

The emperor has told me that if his wife could have made decisions, he would have given a contrary order. He knew the intrigues would start once any decision was given to her. This happened later at Orléans. In the empress, youth combined fatally with weakness as she faced the professional wiliness of Prince Talleyrand, who stayed to betray us, and Prince Metternich, acting for her father. Also she faced Madame Mère.

Here on Saint Helena, we live on the island of second sight. "What might have been" is with us always and "If only . . ." In this lost realm, as it turned out, Napoleon's son was right. If only Marie-Louise had stayed in Paris, all might have been different. The emperor was coming closer and closer. By March 30, the emperor was fourteen miles outside Paris, but she was gone and the czar was living in Talleyrand's house, deciding his fate, agreeing to bring back the Bourbons. The emperor rode on to Fontainebleau.

I told the emperor of the bad effect the empress's flight had on the troops, for I was then chief of the first battalion of the tenth legion of the national guard, charged with defending Paris. We were too few and arms were so scarce that some were reduced to pikes, and her retreat injured us further. On March 31, Paris surrendered and the allies entered.

It was then I first saw that France no longer believed in the emperor. Those of the Saint-Germain set, the émigrés he pardoned, were first to turn and tuck their diamonds into bodices and flee to the country lands the emperor had given back to them. Others buried their napoleons and refused to fight. Already I had sent Henriette and the children out of Paris to Évreux. At the beginning of this dreadful year my first daughter, Emma, had died at age six, and our suffering went on still. I was divided in my duty; as a chamberlain, I should have followed the empress; as a member of the council, I had to be with the emperor or the army.

Marie-Louise was only twenty-two years old, both empress and regent of France, when hectic and crying and trying not to seem frightened, she left Paris, taking the diamond. During his last battles and the Russian campaign, the emperor of course had not worn the Régent. The diamond was for victory, not for bending over soldiers lying frozen into stained foreign snow.

Marie-Louise left in a caravan of failure carrying the residue of imperial pretensions and this group of dethroned bickering kings and queens. It was as if the head of the family had just died and the squabbling already begun.

For the empress it was the reverse of the journey she had made into France on the occasion of her marriage, four years before. Then her Austrian companions had been forced away. Now her French retinue would desert her, and again, all would be taken from her. At five she and her sisters had fled Vienna in a similar caravan of archives, jewels, and nervous nobles. Later had come another flight, caused by the man she married.

Sometimes—no, often, as I have learned—the wrong person is born into these positions. A person so weak, so hysterical, so unfit that one wonders at the royal accidents of life. To be fair, the empress was up against the press of actions and monarchs meeting, troops moving about, and daily defections as her court left in major and minor betrayals. And there was the delay of letters crossing one another in transit, a tragedy of missed chances and misunderstood messages. That first afternoon of the flight, the Cossacks attacked and they all went the last three miles on foot. The melancholy treasure train stopped at Rambouillet, a prison during the Revolution, and now a prison again.

That night, the emperor, on learning that Paris had fallen and the empress flown, went with his troops to Fontainebleau. When my command seemed hopeless I tried but failed to get to him there. We had been told that in April, the councillors of state were to resume their duties and Minister Talleyrand asked me to stay in the Council of State. I refused. I was then separated from my family, my emperor, and all I loved. Perhaps it is my flaw that I have always caved in to the legitimate power. I have always done my duty, and been too obedient. Only twice did I listen to my heart and defy all reason, and the last time brought me here to this rock.

Marie-Louise moved on to Chartres, fifty-five miles from Paris, where we heard she stayed in the prefecture. The ministers were there and Archchancellor Cambacérès and the president of the Senate, the emperor's brothers and their nervous queens. From here Hortense and her brother, Eugène de Beauharnais, left to join Josephine.

The emperor's brother King Joseph came upon King Jérôme and King

Murat, stalled in a doorway by Holbein's portrait of Erasmus; each was refusing to give the other precedence. Then along came Madame Mère and swept them all aside.

"She is worse than the Creole whore," said Madame Mère, again meaning the empress.

The kings and queens were all in bad moods mixed with a certain frenzy. Pauline halted in front of every mirror to powder away tears as Madame Mère sat down to large meals.

"Where is the cheese?" she would say as the servants tiptoed past her in their cloaks.

The ex-kings were rushing about or clustered in hallways whispering in Italian and plotting. But all these Bonapartes combined could not get this young girl to go to her husband then, when she still might have and he was nearby at Fontainebleau. There is nothing more disorganized than failure.

All this while, the ancient diamond accompanied her on this chaotic flight from palace to palace—this journey to what we here on this isle, less kind perhaps than Baron Méneval, see as a travesty, a sad mistake. Lost time combined with confusion as the emperor sent word she should go to the palace of Blois. Still obeying him, she did.

During this week at Blois, from April 2 to 8, she went up and down the great exterior staircase weeping and knotting her fingers on her dress. The staircase was open to the air, filled with the usual gargoyles and medallions, the stone salamanders of François I, and there, her light hair awry, mad around the eyes, she was heard talking to herself as she made her choices. She showed the panic of one who thinks she has finally settled into an indulged life and then sees it disrupted yet again.

Things were so uncertain that the ministers came to her each morning dressed to travel. Everywhere they had stopped, others fell away. People stood up from the table and were never seen again. At each château in the caravanserai more bad news arrived. Her old country was pulling her back in this slow process. She wrote to the emperor that kings Joseph and Jérôme tried to get her to surrender to Austria, but she resisted.

Even the red ladies were in conflict then. Countess de Montesquiou, the baby's nurse, told her to go to the emperor. The duchess de Montebello told her to go to her father for, after all, the allies had won.

It was an unequal fight, for the pretty young duchess de Montebello, widow of Marshal Lannes, was her most intimate friend. At the Tuileries, the empress and her retinue would visit the duchess's apartments every morning. When the emperor was away on one of his campaigns, Marie-Louise hung the duchess de Montebello's portrait in her rooms.

(The emperor has written the word *canaille*—"vile creature"—in the margin here.)

The countess de Montesquiou, wife of the great chamberlain, was fifty then, more than twice the empress's age, and did all for the King of Rome. His "Mama Quiou" was always catching him up, removing him when he was about to disgrace himself with a fit. It was she who, despite the jealousy of Marie-Louise, had smuggled the boy to meet Josephine. The countess was a plump woman of good character, strong virtue, and elegant, simple manners. Always, however, there is that rivalry between the mother and the one who cares for the child. She had this boy's heart and thus Marie-Louise was jealous and doubted her. The countess had carried him to the emperor at lunch every day and best understood his character. The child was, as she told me long ago, proud and sensitive. Once, Napoleon had tried to trick him by offering food, then twice taking it from his mouth. The third time, the child refused the fork.

From Fontainebleau the emperor sent his wife letters every day signed "Nap" and they too were a melancholy reversal of the happy impatient letters he sent as she had journeyed into France. The fatal delays and her failure of will came together. The Cossacks were approaching. She asked the emperor what to do but he did not respond. He knew he had fallen and that she was still young and royal and might rule Tuscany, so he let her decide. Kings Joseph and Jérôme tried to get her to flee.

"I cannot," she said.

The next morning the Bonapartes came to get her. She had not slept and the sight of all of them with their black hair and varying traces of the emperor on their faces was too much for her. She called for her guard and the members of her household to surround her. Enough of the Bonapartes! Now she just sat down and refused to go to the emperor.

This was the time to remember she had married her enemy. She had walked with him evenings arm in arm on the boulevards, incognito among the crowds. Together they had watched the illuminations and seen their own images in the light of the magic lanterns. He had shown her the waterworks at Cherbourg and all the wonders he created. But Napoleon's loyalty, all his jewels and kind affections could not draw her to him in the end. She had the

Hapsburg weakness of will along with the Hapsburg lower lip and tiny royal hands and feet. Metternich told her she could have her own life as duchess of Parma and she should return to Austria.

Three hours later the Cossacks were there to take her to Orléans, and all was over.

I have now found out that early on the morning of April 9, before Marie-Louise left Blois for Orléans, she sent for the jewels. If she was going to travel with the thieving Cossacks, she wanted to wear as many jewels on her person as was possible. She knew they would not dare to search her, an empress and daughter of their ally Emperor Francis. It is hard for us to think of this young empress who barely spoke to anyone, who had lived within an etiquette more binding than that of ancient Versailles, acting like Josephine: tucking the jewels into her clothes, forced to smuggle what she had once seen as her own.

The emperor's double-faced glaive with the Régent on its handle was, of course, too big to hide. In her apartment at Blois she told Baron Méneval to break off the blade. He went over to the fireplace and, putting it under one of the firedogs, snapped the hilt from the blade so he might carry it hidden in his coat.

Méneval obeyed as he always did, for Méneval was me then, and, like me, he had been broken by a force. People like the emperor are so intense, blessed as they are with abnormal powers of concentration and energy, that they wear out those around them till they are but husks spun in a whirlwind. Here on this island I am now the one who gets up with the emperor when he wakes in the night. The Mameluke Ali stands at my bed to summon me to him. Often I rub my eyes and look twice at Ali, this apparition from the shadows, to see that he is not a dream. For many years it was Méneval whom the emperor would have awakened, for he had been Napoleon's most valuable secretary. He alone could bring to his papers the order the emperor required. The emperor would sit on the arm of the baron's chair or perch on his desk as he dictated. Sometimes, in a playful mood, he would sit on his lap. Méneval worked himself ill. When his health failed and he was crippled, he was passed on to the empress as her secretary.

The fallen kings left Orléans, as did Napoleon's mother. Marie-Louise asked Madame Mère to remember her with kindness.

"How I think of you depends on your actions now," said Madame

Mère. Then she looked to her own children and shrugged in a way that showed all her contempt. She was like one of those ancient sibyls of the islands who always know the outcome beforehand.

Marie-Louise kissed her withered spotted hand. Then all the shields were gone and the empress regent surrendered and was brought with her son to her father, who was then in Rambouillet.

Outside her carriage she saw the high black sheepskins bobbing, the lances and bows of four thousand Cossacks galloping on all sides. Their saddles were such that they stood up as they rode. *"Houra! Houra!"* they called out. During the trip from Blois to Orléans the Cossacks plundered one of her wagons, but they did not get the jewels.

Marie-Louise could never get to the emperor now.

The emperor, too, was in a crisis of nerves. This was the week he was forced to give up his throne. He was surrounded, for all his enemies were in Paris—the czar at Talleyrand's house, King Frederick William of Prussia, and Prince Schwarzenberg of Austria, whose wife had burned in the fire at their ball for the emperor, all were there to arrange his future. On April 2, the emperor heard that the Senate had deposed him.

"Talleyrand is like a cat; he can always manage to fall on his feet," the emperor said. He decided to fight and told the troops they would march to Paris, but his marshals talked him out of the plan. Marshal Marmont had deserted to Austria with his other troops.

The emperor abdicated twice, first in favor of his son, and when the allies did not accept this, he gave up everything without conditions. Then he changed his mind and tried to get General Coulaincourt to bring back the document, but it was too late. The final loss of everything he had gained for his son seemed to destroy his will; the Bourbons were coming back to France.

I have heard he was one way, then another during the long days at Fontainebleau. He was in a brooding stupor, agitated, then in a bleak staring depression. When the empress wrote that she wished to console him in his downfall he was humming "La Monaco." He was convulsive, sunk. He did not speak and tore at his own flesh. When the Polish countess Walewska came to him then, he kept her waiting all night and would not see her. He had not enough time to get his wife or child or nation back.

At just this time, Lord Byron turned his back upon his former hero and

wrote his vile poem, which was included in the volume dear Lady ————
later sent us here, for there are friends who believe one must know the worst
even when one is at one's lowest. The poem begins:

> *'Tis done; but yesterday a King*
> *And armed with kings to strive,*
> *And now thou are a nameless thing*
> *So abject—yet alive.*

Lord Byron wondered whether "proud Austria's mournful flower" still
clung to the emperor's side. Of course I did not show this to him.

On April 12, the emperor learned Marie-Louise would not get to rule
Tuscany as he had hoped, but only the duchy of Parma. That day he found
out that the allies wanted to separate him from her and give him the small island of Elba to rule. He wrote to Méneval saying the empress was to return
the imperial jewels to Baron La Bouillerie for the provisional government.
Méneval told him he had returned all the jewels, including the sword with
the Régent.

At Orléans, Marie-Louise stayed in the bishop's palace. Monsieur
Dudon, out of favor with the emperor since he deserted his post in Spain,
had come to claim the jewels for the French provisional government. Talleyrand, still and ever dual (someone said if you hit him hard on the back,
his face would show nothing), had entrusted him with this task.

We recently heard the story of how Dudon deliberately came upon the empress when she was with many people in her salon. He ordered her lady to
claim the long pearl necklace she was wearing.

"Give it back to him and don't say anything," the empress whispered to
this woman as she casually removed the necklace.

Dudon claimed all her personal jewels as well. Of course there were two
sets of jewels fused into each other by the finest craftsmen of Paris. It would
take weeks with inventories in hand to separate the jewels of the kings from
those of the emperor, the émigrés, or the king of Sardinia. No one was then
in a mood to grant any boon to the emperor, so Dudon took the necklace
of gigantic diamonds Napoleon had given her at the King of Rome's birth
and all he had bought upon their marriage in the time of happiness and
splendor.

As I look back over my history of the Régent, it seems that in France the debts are never settled. No matter what the claims, it was the emperor who redeemed the Régent when it was pawned as he said; it was the emperor who, with his savings on the civil list, added to the jewels. Until 1811, he had bought jewels with his savings from the civil list. Then he used 6 million in state funds to cover what he had already bought for 6.6 millions. The state owed him 600,000 napoleons when the empire fell.

The emperor's men protested then, for they believed the imperial treasure was his. Still, Dudon drove the wagons away from Orléans with their 10 million in gold and silver coins and plate, taking even the emperor's clothes and handkerchiefs with the *N*, every fork and knife belonging to the empress, all the tokens and gifts, and the Régent as well.

Another story I have found recently says that Dudon did not get the sword handle, that he had seized all the jewels but the Régent. It was said that the empress kept it always about her person, tucked into her workbasket, and only after he inquired did she put her little hand in among the embroidery to come up with the handle of the imperial glaive. This story shows a spirit worthy of the woman the emperor had loved, but I doubt its truth.

April 12 was the day the emperor lost his wife and child and treasure, a day after he had lost his empire. Heartbreak never comes unattended; each large tragedy comes draped with little versions of itself.

The emperor wanted Marie-Louise and his son back. Finally, he sent troops to get her, but by then she had left Orléans. Prince Metternich had sent her back to Rambouillet and her father. This was the second time he missed her by hours or days. She wrote, "Be on your guard, my darling, we are being duped . . . but I shall take a firm line with my father" (a letter the emperor has shown me).

Now powerless, at three that morning the emperor took poison. Everyone here has talked about April 12–13. The emperor was sitting in his green velvet bed embroidered with roses, with the ostrich plumes and eagles on top. He had emptied the small black silk and leather sack he had been wearing around his neck since the Spanish campaign into a glass of water. Inside was a mixture of opium, belladonna, and white hellebore in a dosage enough to kill two men. Instead he started to vomit. Constant heard him groaning and summoned General Caulaincourt. The emperor was shivering, then ripping at his bedclothes from the heat. He told the general they were taking his wife and son from him. Caulaincourt wanted to get the doctor but the emperor seized his hand with his great mad strength. Finally he had a spasm and the general escaped and rushed for Dr. Yvan. Fortunately, the poison was too old to work.

"Give me another poison," the emperor said.

Caulaincourt accused Dr. Yvan of giving him the poison and so scared the doctor that he rode off the next day on the first horse he found in the courtyard. One of the emperor's Mamelukes deserted as well. In our country at this time, enemies became sudden friends and friends became enemies sometimes overnight. Generals, to whom the emperor gave large houses and fortunes, rode off in the night, never to return.

Yet another tale that I recently learned has Marie-Louise carrying the Régent into Austria, where her father returned it to Prince Talleyrand. I do not believe either story, for they show a sentimentality and loyalty to this last relic of the emperor that subsequent events belied. Rather, in her weakness, the empress bent to her father, the kaiser, and never returned to France.

La Bouillerie became treasurer for Louis XVIII and the treasure moved to the Tuileries. The emperor has told me his actions were a betrayal for he should have carried the treasure to Fontainebleau instead of to the king's brother in Paris. This was but a preview of the mournful defections that were to come, for defeat has few friends and the whole country had turned on the emperor.

The emperor was alone at Fontainebleau in the gardens sitting by the statue of Diana when one day he kicked a hole in the gravel a foot deep. All the Old Guard wanted to go with him to Elba. He was permitted four hundred but it became six hundred, then a thousand men ready to leave all to be with him on an island eighteen by twelve miles. He bid farewell to the Old Guard in the courtyard of Fontainebleau. The black bearskins lined up in the cold in a scene that was painted by many artists.

"Good-bye, my children, I should like to press you all to my heart," the emperor said. "At least I shall kiss your flag!" And they gave him the flag that said, *Marengo, Austerlitz, Eyelau, Friedland, Wagram, Vienna, Berk, Madrid, Moscow,* and he kissed it for a long time as all, even the enemy commissioners, wept. "I will write about the great things we have done together . . . Adieu!" He walked to his carriage and the soldier who was driving touched his whip to the horses. Then all the heads as one turned to stare into his dust.

In the middle of August, on the island of Elba the emperor received the last letter he would ever receive from the empress. This one he has never shown me.

As the emperor made his way to the ship that would take him to Elba, he traveled through the south. There, where all French fevers and pestilence begin, he saw the white flags and heard, *"Vive le Roi!"* and then, "Down with the Corsican!" As Chateaubriand later wrote, "Contagion is a marvelous thing in France."

The emperor had become a foreigner once again, as his false country spit him out. Since his face remained on the gold napoleons and 5-franc pieces, he wore his valet's blue cloak and round hat, rode ahead of his carriage, and ducked his head for the first time in his life.

If the diamond had been his luck, it left him now as did his wife and son, his ministers, almost all those he had chosen and enriched. It was a time of other betrayals, for Josephine was dancing herself to death with the infamous foreign princes. During this time nothing bad surprised the emperor. He sailed to Elba on the English frigate the H.M.S. *Undaunted*.

Marie-Louise no longer wrote to him. Still he had his saddler on Elba make pale blue silk reins for her horse. And he told me he had been decorating her rooms at his villa, Il Molino. He told the artist to paint the ceiling with the symbol of marital fidelity—two doves tied together, the knot tightening as they fly farther apart.

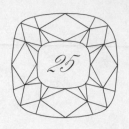

Removing the N's and Bees

THE THEATER WAS WHITE WITH BOURBON LILIES AND THICK with their lugubrious smell. Little dots of white came up from the dark. At first, I had not been able to make out the chant in the Comédie Française. Those in the orchestra were looking up at us for they had caught sight of the imperial eagle on the boxes.

"Down with the goose!" they chanted. "Down with the goose!" Henriette was panicked, and I told her to drape her white veil over the eagle (their goose) as quickly as she could. Then, at last, the crowd stopped, the play began, and I gave my gentle wife a handkerchief for her tears. Young men from the neighboring box then came in with a little hammer and the audience that had applauded Czar Alexander and the king of Prussia when they appeared now cheered as they shattered the emperor's eagle. Things were like that in the warm spring of 1814 after Marie-Louise had fled and Louis XVIII entered Paris. Again, the white Bourbon flag flew over the Tuileries and a fat king lived inside. Cossacks were camped on the Champs Élysées.

On the day the emperor arrived at Elba, the new king rode in to Paris wearing the old wig and pigtail, the satin breeches and stockings. The white cockade, the plumes, the incomprehension of the way things had become rode in with him. Louis XVIII was with his niece Marié Thérèse, who was now the duchess d'Angoulême. Daughter of Louis XVI and Marie-Antoinette, once imprisoned in the Temple, Marie Thérèse had been freed and later married her first cousin the duc d'Angoulême. Now they rode over the same route her mother had traveled to the scaffold on paving stones cracked by heavy tumbrils carrying bodies, passing the scowls of Napoleon's Old Guard grenadiers forced to line up for them. It was said that the duchess fainted as she entered the Tuileries but I do not believe this for she was much too stilted and cold.

I stood under the windows hung with white sheets, among the women with their white lilies, and felt as the grenadiers did. I saw the people cheer the new king and in their cheers was little emotion but their awful hatred of the emperor. Paris then was a shrouded city with covered bumps in the squares where statues of Napoleon had stood. The empire was a kingdom again and those who thought that France began in 1789 (and even those, like me, late to the empire) were deceived. I felt myself turning inward.

On April 12, upon the abdication of the emperor, I had sworn allegiance to the new king. I had made only two such vows in my life. My allegiance to the king's brother had cost me twelve years in exile and my patrimony; I had defended my vow to the emperor with my life. I had been a councillor for the provisional government, but now I lived in a quieter, smaller way, bent to my charts. I worked on revising my *Atlas* with three secretaries. Only in name, I served the pale-eyed king, for I would never disown the emperor.

In Ménière's workrooms in the Louvre, jewelers then were chiseling curved diamond *N*'s from the gold snuffboxes the emperor had designed as gifts. Others were trying to cover or replace the enameled portraits of the imperial family on the pieces. Marie-Louise, the King of Rome, the sister queens and brother kings were pried off and the boxes were given to the enemy generals who still occupied the city. Imperial eagles, stars, and *palmiers* were also removed—all the externals that were never externals to those who ruled, for they confirmed them and all around them in their awesome might.

I do not know if Louis XVIII ever wore the Régent then. He was too old and sick for a coronation though he had the Régent put into his crown. I had vowed to serve him but twice was rejected as councillor of state. I had met him as "Monsieur" when I was presented to Louis XVI in 1790, but had ruined myself with the Bourbons by going to the emperor. Still, I was to be presented once again.

Weavers and seamstresses were on their knees applying the fleur-de-lis over the gold bees as I walked over the carpets of the Tuileries. The king was trying to bring back all that he knew from his youth as the *bel esprit* of Versailles. Back came the levée with the basin, the holy water, and such.

Courtiers again held the looking glass and proffered his coat. They brought forth his sword, the jeweled order of Saint-Esprit, and other decorations on golden trays. Back had come the pomp and etiquette as though it still might sustain a king.

I saw the same old families at court, my former friends returned as though they had never left. They looked at me as if to say, "You, too," and nodded uncertainly as I passed.

"*Bonjour,*" Louis XVIII said and looked as if he might know me. Then he seemed to remember and wonder why I was there (as I wondered myself). He inquired after my *Atlas* then inclined his head, which meant the audience was over. I thought he looked as Louis XVI would if he had been allowed to live to sixty. The look in his eyes, pouched in flesh, was mild and learned, somewhat hesitant, but also pleased to be back.

The king, like me, had years of England on him, for he had been there since 1807. He had spent his years at Hartwell in his court of exiles, after his wife died, always with a male favorite. He read philosophy and the ancients, wrote madrigals and opera scenarios and poems. He read Montesquieu and Voltaire, the epicurean Horace, whom he quoted all the time, and Tacitus, who said, "Voluntary slaves make more tyrants than tyrants make slaves." He thought this applied to the emperor.

At his side, propping up the king, was the favorite, Comte de Blacas d'Aulps, who looked exactly like an ostrich and controlled all access to the king. The king could hardly stand from his weight and his painful legs. He was carried and wheeled everywhere, and when he rose, he leaned on his attendants on both sides.

Louis XVIII lumbered forward in the immense high red velvet boots he had invented for his gout. Under him on one side Blacas d'Aulps staggered on legs that appeared too short for his long body, his flaxen wig as yellow as his face. Blacas as usual was immaculate in his dress. Even in the early morning when he came down from his little entresol above the king's apartments to part the curtains of the king's iron bed and kiss him, Blacas was ever the dandy. Blacas was well known as a collector of porcelain, engraved gems, antique medals. Like all the émigrés, he was attached to the small valuable things they might have to grab if ever again forced to flee.

The king loomed above him, his pale blue eyes filmed with pain, large (the English prince had compared his knee to a young man's waist) as an immense wounded beast. What I was seeing was the past trying to return, a king with a charter, a stranger king who had returned from his incognito wanderings. Before he settled in England he had slept at a grocer's, in a washhouse, and in a tavern, and he had been unable even to wear his royal decorations. Sometimes in those days, he would look down at the empty left side of his chest where they had hung.

His niece Marie Thérèse, the princess of France, then had to sell her diamonds to feed the wrecked monarch. Louis XVIII thought of himself as a writer and a king misplaced in time. He had the learning, the good memory, and the indecision of all the latter Bourbons.

His younger brother Comte d'Artois entered then and, though he had given me the Order of Saint-Louis, pretended not to see me. His lips reversed into the stern expression that, in a Bourbon, is a fearsome thing. The king looked at his brother with the special jealousy the fat have for the slender and the ungainly for beauty. At the same time, he had every reason to feel superior, for his mind was better and he was, and always would be while he lived, the king.

Louis XVIII sat down at his table and immediately began to sweat. Blacas dabbed at the beads on his forehead. Out came platters of fluted, tweaked, carved, and decorated food. Before him was a plate of lamb chops in stacks of three—the king removed the top and bottom chop and ate only the middle one that had retained the juices and fats of the first two. He ate twenty-six of these middle lamb chops.

After luncheon, he tried and failed to get up on his horse, and the fortunate beast was led away, never to reappear, so I was told.

By then, of course, the Régent had been pried from the hilt of the emperor's broken sword. Ménière, who had been Louis XVI's last jeweler, was preparing it for Louis XVIII's crown. The king, however, was unsure about having a coronation, since he believed he was in the nineteenth year of his reign. He felt himself the only legitimate king of France since the boy Louis XVII died in prison in 1795.*

Louis XVIII was caught in what he considered a massive injustice—his

---

*Josephine told the czar that she and Barras, with the help of a native of Martinique who had been in charge of Louis XVII after Thermidor, had helped the boy to escape. She said they had substituted another child, and Hortense confirmed her story. Louis XVIII always believed that the second dauphin was Marie-Antoinette's son with Count Fersen. I believe the boy, whoever his father was, died horribly in prison and so does the emperor. For Josephine, truth was often an unwelcome stranger.

brother, his sister, his sister-in-law, and nephew killed, he forced to run. He had to put things back together by first breaking them apart, so first he broke up the imperial jewels, symbols of the upstart empire that had kept him away.

In England he had collected those crown jewels that found their way there after the robbery of 1792. Somehow he got back the dragon spinel Côte de Bretagne in 1796 and one of the Mazarin diamonds. He was then a king in waiting, trying to reclaim his kingdom and ancestors piece by piece, even as the ancient kings themselves were torn from Saint-Denis and their organs (which had been preserved for centuries in jars) defiled. When he read in the *Moniteur* of the emperor's marriage to the royal Marie-Louise, he had given up all hope of reigning as king of France. He had no children for he loved men in the way of Louis XIV's brother, Monsieur.

Two months after he returned, he had Ménière create new jewels for the duchess d'Angoulême and the duchess de Berri, who had married his brother's (the count d'Artois') other son. Like vultures picking morsels off the corpse and flying off only to return, the Bourbons all dipped into the jewels. I have seen such birds hovering over this island, resting on the wind or waiting in the scrub trees for the small deaths that sustain them.

All this time, the Régent lay neglected in the neglected crown, too grand a stone for the cautious old man propped up by the allies who filled the city.

A month or two after the restoration, which I found unbearable, I went to England to sell a new edition of the *Atlas,* then returned to Paris, Henriette, and my hermit's life.

Like the old kings, Louis XVIII liked to travel from one palace to another—Saint-Cloud, Trianon, Rambouillet, Compiègne, Fontainebleau, Versailles, all of which bore the furniture, the deep prints of Napoleon and his empire. He found rooms draped like military tents, chairs with Egyptian heads and staring sphinxes, Josephine's swans, N's on all the thrones, his crested red books in the shelves. The lyre, the thyrsus, honeysuckle, Greek key frets, helmets and shields, oak and laurel crowns, the emperor's green and stars and omnipresent bees haunted Louis XVIII everywhere he went.

At Fontainebleau, his brother's bedroom had become the emperor's throne room with its crimson velvet and golden bees, its gilt grisailles, laurel crowns, and Roman insignia. Wherever Louis XVIII walked, he walked on bees and looked up to see eagles, and, I must admit, I enjoyed thinking of this.

Some found Louis XVIII charming. Everyone said he told a good story, was deeply learned, and filled with apt quotations drawn from years of reading instead of ruling. They said he meant well, which is never enough in France.

One day, he had himself carried into Versailles, still somewhat empty and ruined. Leaning on his courtiers, he hobbled up the stairs to his old rooms. He had his old furniture brought from the storerooms of the Garde Meuble, dismissed his courtiers, and sat alone among his things in his red velvet chair with its solid gold nails. Then he went down the road to the Grand Trianon, where the emperor had lived, and the marks of Bonapartes were all over these rooms where once Madame de Maintenon and the marquise de Pompadour had presided. He found Princess Pauline's imprint all over the Petit Trianon.

"The bees sting me everywhere I go," he said to Blacas d'Aulps, "and the eagles shit on me."

I was not alone in my allegiance to Louis XVIII, for Talleyrand, by guaranteeing Josephine's annuity, had enlisted her as a liaison between all the old orders (nobles like her first husband, de Beauharnais; Barras and the Revolution; Bonaparte) and the new. As a survivor, she was ever drawn to the victor. She used what she had learned in the prisons and in court to roll on. With her it was always *Roulez! Roulez!* (Roll on!), smile her tight smile, and drift on to the next man, even the czar of Russia.

Sometime after Egypt she had grown into love that was almost worship with the man who had made her an empress. After the divorce (for we tend to love what is lost), she had kept Napoleon's rooms at Malmaison as he had left them—the abandoned clothing draped on the furniture, the history book open on his bureau with the page marked, his pen, his unfurled map—all his relics. It was as though he had just stepped out to walk among the black swans and bursting roses.

Nonetheless, Josephine now received the czar and all Napoleon's enemies. She returned from Navarre, where she had lived with her court, her collections, and her jewels from looted towns, herself once as discarded as the jewels. This was her social renaissance at age fifty. The carriages came back to Malmaison. There was laughter again at her table. She ordered new white muslin dresses and walked with Czar Alexander in her gardens. She sold him her Canovas. She opened her salon and exhausted herself for the emperor's enemies, like Madame de Staël (who once said, "Politeness is the art of selecting among one's real thoughts") and King Frederick of Prussia. A court was forming of foreign enemy princes who might wander through her rooms and finger Napoleon's things. Perhaps mixed in with the glory of being rediscovered was a late revenge for having been abandoned.

I should have been shocked but I had seen too much. Three weeks after he landed on Elba, I heard Josephine was sick with a fever, then quickly died. Some said that my old friend died of diphtheria or grief for the emperor. Be that as it may, she caught cold driving with the czar.

"Poor Josephine! She is happy now," the emperor then said to Fanny Bertrand, who had been on Elba and told this to me. He then did not leave his villa for two days.

Recently, when the emperor asked me what I did after his first abdication, I told him how each night Henriette and I would read Hume's *Philosophy and English History*. By the time we got to James II, the emperor had returned from Elba and Louis XVIII had fled.

For ten months, the Régent had waited for Louis XVIII to be crowned. Instead he became unpopular. He was too old when he got what he wanted, as is often the way. And then the violets started to appear. The ladies wore violets in their bonnets and violet dresses, and men wore their watches on violet chains. Little sketches went about where the intervals between the leaves of the violet formed the emperor's silhouette. "The violet will return in the spring," people said. They were yearning for "Corporal Violet"—Napoleon—*Lui* (Him)—the Forbidden. Is any country more fickle?

After eleven months, the emperor left Elba at the end of February 1815, sailing back on the *Inconstant,* which had been disguised to fool his captors. "I heard you calling me in my exile," he wrote in a proclamation. "The man of genius gets back on his feet," he supposedly said.

He landed at Fréjus with a thousand imperial guards, met the king's troops at the village of Cap, and walked alone in his gray overcoat and black bicorne toward seven hundred guns. His men were singing the "Marseillaise."

"It's him. Fire!" the captain called out.

The emperor opened his great coat and bared his breast. "If there is a man among you who wants to kill his general, his emperor—here I am."

The soldiers dropped their guns, then their white cockades, to the ground. It was a snowstorm! Out came the tricolor cockades from the rucksacks where they had hidden them.

A week before the king fled, on learning of Napoleon's approach, Louis XVIII had ordered his treasurer of the civil list to give the crown jewels and all the diamonds of the exterior domains to his first valet, Baron Hue. We have here his note:

> LOUIS, by the grace of God, king of France and Navarre.
> On the report of the minister and Secretary of State of our house,
> We have ordered and are ordering what follows:
>   Art.1: The intendant of the treasury of our civil list will immediately give back to the general cashier such treasure, to Monsieur Hue, treasurer of our military household, and one of our first valets de chambre, and on his receipt, all the diamonds, jewels, pearls and stones belonging to our Crown and foreign domain.

And so forth . . . until, "Given in our palace of the Tuileries, 13 March 1815, LOUIS." It was cosigned Blacas d'Aulps. When the king learned that Napoleon had returned, he fled, taking the crown jewels, the Régent, and his boyfriend.

The emperor, walking on his soft shoes, was standing above me as I wrote this last. Often, I would feel him in the room, an immense presence filling the space. I would turn, lifting my quill, and the room would be vacant, hot, and damp. It would have been the wind. This time, however, he *was* there and I saw the vein throbbing in his large forehead.

"No, Monsieur le Comte, not at all," says the emperor. "People believe the king fled to Ghent with the crown jewels, but they were long gone. Baron de Vitrolles persuaded the king to send them with Hue to London. I had my spies too!" (On Elba the emperor was plagued by the king's spies, who slunk around making up lies.)

"He took not only the Régent but my personal diamonds and those of the empress as well, and they were never returned, even after I spared his nephew the duc d'Angoulême. You might write a pretty piece on that and how I never could recover them during what they call my 'Hundred

Days'—wrong again, for I ruled a hundred and thirty-six days that time before my defeat."

"Sire, I knew Eugène de Vitrolles for we were émigrés together. He was from the south and younger than I was. It was he who traveled back to France with the king's brother d'Artois at the rear of the allied armies, when they threw white cloths over the statues of you."

"*Mon cher,* it was he who gave them a Bourbon so Talleyrand might push him forward. Otherwise, they would have kept Louise as regent and my son might have ruled. The czar would have supported a regency."

"Eugène was most strange to look at with his large bald head," I said. "He alarmed one a bit on first sight and yet was considered a handsome man. His voice was most persuasive."

"In that way, he compelled the king," the emperor said. "Like the favourite, *non*? They wanted Louis XVIII to ride out to meet me, to scare me off with his magnificence. Ha!"

"The king trusted de Vitrolles, though he was of the reactionary faction around Artois, those who believed the Revolution had never happened. He was more in love with the monarchy and all its trappings than can be imagined. For him, the diamonds belonged only to the Bourbons. Vitrolles wanted to see the Régent on d'Artois."

"Anyway, the king sent off the jewels," said the emperor. "And we know how he left—like a thief who hides from the sun. It is always raining when a king flees, you know. At midnight, they carried him to the Pavilion de Flore. He walked over the paving stones wrapped up like one of the dead—Blacas on one side, some duc on the other, with the guards flinging themselves at his big fat feet. He drove out in shame, the grenadiers in advance, the black musketeers in the rear, and they closed the gates behind him."

"And then next morning you came in," I said. "I was not with the others, but standing with the crowds when I heard the thunder of your approach and the voices crying around me. It was wet and very dark. All your chamberlains were waiting inside the Tuileries. The *dames du palais* in their court robes, all hung with jewels, were crouched on the rugs of the throne room, scissors in hand . . ."

"What are you saying?"

"Yes, they were cutting off the fleurs-de-lis that had been hurriedly applied over your bees, sire." At this the emperor smiled. "And the store windows already displayed your images. Shouts of the greatest jubilation burst around the carriages and a hundred cavaliers carried torches to the gates. The next morning, wearing my uniform, I made my way across the court-yard, now a bivouac for your troops, to the chamberlains' salon for your levée. The door opened and when you walked in, I confess my heart jerked in my breast, and my tears . . ."

"Do not continue," said the emperor.

I had known then the days of my small life had ended, and I would live fully again in his wake. Those who had been his enemies were the first to re-turn for, as the *Nain Jaune* (Yellow Dwarf), a journal devoted to the em-peror, had written: "It is those in power that have visitors. Although the latter do not go to the same address, they always knock at the same door." When the emperor saw side by side letters from the same men, vilifying him, then Louis XVIII, he had shrugged and said, "Such are men."

"The king left in such a hurry that all his papers were on his writing table," the emperor said. "They say I burnt them, but of course I read them first—those of the king that were strange and metaphysical and the atro-cious letters of Blacas, full of unspeakable things, archives of lowness, lying, and villainy."

After his return from Elba, the emperor named me among the new councillors of state and confirmed my title as chamberlain. Then, not yet knowing what he later learned from his spies, the emperor tried to get the Régent and the other jewels back. At the treasury they found the receipt from Baron Hue in place of the diamonds and only 600,000 francs' worth remaining from a treasure of 14,441,645 francs. The Régent, then valued at 6 millions, was gone.

"I could have held the duc d'Angoulême then. We had caught him, but I treated them as they have not treated me, for they never paid me what the treaty had promised," said the emperor. "I let them all leave France. I told them to have the prince give back the funds taken from the public coffers and to guarantee the return of the crown diamonds. The diamonds were never returned to me, nor what they owed me from long ago. They were shameless thieves."

The king had proceeded to Lille. His luggage had been stolen and they had to search all Lille for slippers big enough for his feet. He went on to Dunkirk, finally Ghent. And the diamond stayed in England, back in the land where it had been formed.

Montholon is at the door, waiting for his dictation.

"The ox has been harnessed; now it must plow," the emperor said.

"Sire, did you say, 'The man of genius always gets back on his feet?'" I asked him before he left.

"It cannot always be accomplished, but we try," he answered.

The emperor's brief second reign took place without the Régent and with the allies massing against him. He worked through the days and nights waiting for his wife to return, but she was already in the thrall of the Austrian count Adam Neipperg, the one-eyed devious chamberlain who followed instructions and became her lover. Like the king, the emperor was to learn what he feared most—that history was against the comeback.

At his ceremony for the new liberal empire on the Champs de Mars, where fifty thousand soldiers passed in review before a crowd of hundreds of thousands, he climbed to a throne on the pyramid raised in the center of the field. He moved slowly up the stairs past his marshals and courtiers and ministers, five hundred electors, members of the institute. Boats and barges filled the Seine. He wore the long white tunic of antiquity and the officers waved the flags of his regiments.

"Sire, the French people had conferred upon you the crown, and you have laid it down without their consent," said one of the electors. "They now impose upon you the duty of resuming it."

"Emperor, consul, soldier, I owe everything to the people," the emperor said and threw off his mantle with the bees and seated himself on the throne.

Most of the Bonaparte brothers were there, members of the electoral college and the institute, the old marshals, the peers. His wife and son were missing, as was the diamond in his sword that had brought him luck in both its forms.

He had driven in the coronation coach with his Polish Red Lancers and the imperial guard, wearing his coronation costume, with all the seams released and resewn. This anticoronation was one I saw. My ears were still vibrating from the hundreds of cannons that had gone off at eleven. He was forty-five then and round and the robes were too heavy. I know some who hoped he might turn down the crown and others who wanted him only as a general, not emperor. After all, who can ever go back?

"Let us march on the enemy," he said. "Victory will follow our eagles." And then the cheer was such that I could not hear for the rest of the day.

Seventeen days later the duke of Wellington and Field Marshal Blücher caught him in a field of rye and clover at Waterloo in Belgium. Blücher, whom the Russians nicknamed *Vorwarts* (Forward), had escaped capture by the French two days before Waterloo so he could join Wellington and defeat the emperor.

Out of forty chamberlains named during Napoleon's final reign only three of us came back to rejoin him at the Élysée Palace after he returned from Waterloo. Two of us are with him still on this island—General de Montholon and I. Neither of us will forget the terrible lassitude that took him at this time.

On the day of my forty-ninth birthday, my great, sad adventure began.

I returned to Malmaison with him and vowed to follow wherever he might go. He was astonished for he barely knew me. Until this time, I confess I had not spoken to him outside one attempt when, in trying to report on my mission to Holland, I had become hopelessly tangled in my words. He had moved on to the next man in this gantlet of uniforms.

But I had always been there watching. He knew the work I had done for him, my written reports; he says he knew my *Atlas* then. I am not quite sure. I know that he knows my book now.

"Do you realize where I may lead you?" he asked me. Then the emperor agreed that I might follow him.

When I arrived with my son, Emmanuel, last June 23, I think he then saw how far I would go for him. Two days before, I had begun the notes for my *Memorial*.

After Louis XVIII's second return, he brought the crown jewels back, either from Ghent or from London. He could not wait to reward with the diamonds of France the allies who had defeated Napoleon and killed hundreds of thousands of Frenchmen. He gave the duke of Wellington the Order of Saint-Esprit filled with the diamonds of his ancestors and those from Napoleon's sword. He gave diamonds to Blücher, too.

The other part of restoring was more removing. Off came any remaining bees and eagles. On went Louis XVIII's symbol—ears of corn. He gave his friend the English prince regent the emperor's marble Table of the Great

Commanders showing Alexander the Great surrounded by other famed generals. We have heard the prince regent had begun collecting things of the emperor (and still does).

"I know Blücher and Wellington both have statues of me. I become a cult even as I disappear," says the emperor. "No wonder you picked up my hairs."

Louis XVIII had the allegory *The Clemency of the Bourbons* painted on the ceiling of the emperor's study at Fontainebleau. The duke of Wellington got up on a ladder to take down the foreign pictures from the walls of the Louvre and other museums, to claim some and return others.

The night I wrote this chapter we sat on the garden bench and the emperor asked if I thought there was life up there in the stars.

Before I could answer, he looked up and said, "My little Josephine." I have no idea what he meant by that.

The Emperor Breaks My Code

I HAD TAKEN EMMANUEL INTO JAMESTOWN TO CONSULT THE
Balcombe family doctor for the pains in his heart. While I was away, I
am convinced that the emperor entered our room, found all my papers
for this chronicle, and broke my code.

When I returned he had the overcast look and those little half smiles that
always meant trouble for me and the generals.

The code, based on a simple numerical formula that de Volude and I developed while we were in England, would have given a man with the strate-
gical and numerical genius of the emperor little trouble were he ever alone
with my pages. Until now I had contrived always to lock the compromising
ones safely away.

I had never seen Montholon and Gourgaud look quite so happy since we
landed on this island. They were walking through the wood of gum trees
behind the house and looked almost as though they might link arms.

I went to my room and saw the slight telling disarrangement of things
that showed someone had been there. Traces of the emperor's cologne still
quivered in the baked air. He said nothing as I went in for our dictation.

"Emmanuel is not well," I informed him. "The doctor says he must rest
for the next few days."

"That will give you more time for your little diversion. I wonder what
you intend to do with it."

He flung himself on a chaise and studied his boots; his finger idled through the dust on the floor making ominous swirls that looked rather like battle plans.

"It occupies my time and is a kind of journal, an aide-mémoire, and, Your Majesty, it takes me away in place and time . . ."

I could see that he was struggling with the forbidden knowledge that he had. Finally, he sighed and looked at me with a sad expression. That is all he ever did or said on the subject, yet from that day forth, he was never quite the same with me. I realized I had made another mistake and that he was a man who never forgives twice.

I raced back later to reread all the pages I had written in code—and in truth, saw much he might object to. I did not know what to do, for to make any changes or even any reference to the work was to show him I knew the awful truth of what he had done. Reading my history was one thing, breaking my code was another. Why had I written in code? Why had I needed to get everything down? I felt sorry and I even thought of destroying some of the work, but I didn't.

Five Oranges

ONE AFTERNOON ABOUT A YEAR AFTER I STARTED THIS chronicle, the emperor sat in front of our house. He was sharing the five oranges Lady Malcolm had sent us. Perfect spirals of peel fell at his feet and his lips were faintly orange. Peel tissues had fallen on the painting of Rambouillet on the gold-rimmed plate, covering it like a film.

Then a group of soldiers led by Hudson Lowe came over the ridge. One of our servants came to tell me a British colonel was waiting in my room.

"Tell him I cannot leave without the emperor's permission," I said. My heart was jumping because I knew I had been caught.

"Go see what the animal wants," the emperor said, handing me a section of the fruit. "And above all, return promptly!"

This last was the only command of his I did not obey.

The emperor waited a bit, then went inside. His shutters were closed but I saw the glint of his opera glass through the cracks as the British troops led me away. I looked back and saw the shutters move. It might have been the wind.

After I was taken away, the emperor did not leave his room for fifteen days.

In fact, I had been trapped. When young James Scott, my servant from the Briars, reappeared at Longwood offering to take a letter to England, I accepted his offer. Prince Lucien, the emperor's brother, had written asking for news. This seemed the only way I might answer him since we were obliged to send and receive our letters only through the governor, who opened them all.

I had Emmanuel write in miniature, on a piece of white satin (sewn into Scott's waistcoat), a letter that protested the emperor's treatment. Scott told his parents, who told Hudson Lowe, who used this as an excuse to entrap me for clandestine correspondence. In circumstances I have described at length elsewhere, I never returned to Longwood.

I was now more than half blind; my son, who joined me, had an infection in his heart. Lowe put us in a shack in sight of Longwood and came there to search. This man, always quivering over some offense, now looked more than ever, as the emperor had described him, like a hyena caught in a trap. For me, he was my childhood devil incarnate with his ginger hair, bursting red face, and wild sprouted gray brows. He intended to inventory all my papers and read them. He read even the most intimate.

"This I do not understand at all," he said when he came upon the chronicle of the great diamond. "Is it some sort of code or cipher?"

He seized all the papers including my journal, which he later returned to the emperor. I was kept in this detention for over a month and thought not at all of the diamond. I saw our house on the hill morning and night and could not reach it or know the mind of the one who lived within. My son was very sick and would lose consciousness for half an hour at a time.

I was a prisoner, but according to English law, I might be free if I requested to go back to Europe. And so I did.

The emperor wrote a letter to me that seemed to go one way, then another. He said the "ferocious joy" of the soldiers leading me away was like seeing the inhabitants of the South Seas dancing around a prisoner they were about to devour. He saw no fault in my letters to England, my conduct was "honorable and without reproach." He said I might stay or leave. "Your society is necessary to me," he said, because I alone spoke English. He remembered how many nights I had stayed with him during his sickness.

"If one day you see my wife and son, kiss them for me. For two years I have had no news," he wrote. He said he did not have long to live because of the torments here, the devouring climate, the lack of all that sustains life. He ended this letter, "Be happy! Your *devote*, Napoleon."

"Devote," in English, a final mistake, and one very dear to me.

When he wrote he already knew I had signed the document expressing my wish to leave this island. Through Grand Marshal Bertrand I sent him word that I never would be happy except in his presence and that, far from him, he would know my zeal.

This alarmed Hudson Lowe, who feared I might stir sympathy for the emperor back in Europe. Lowe then said I might go back to Longwood and that, if I didn't, he would deport me to the Cape of Good Hope. The doctor came to say how sad the emperor was, how unwell. I had been a month in captivity. The emperor let it be known that he would let me stay or go with pleasure.

In short the emperor behaved with me exactly as he had with Marie-Louise—he left the final decision to me. He, who lived to command, would never command those he loved. Like her, I lacked what he called "the two o'clock in the morning courage." I fled and never said good-bye.

I asked Hudson Lowe if I could put my seal on the papers he had taken from me and he agreed that I might.

And so ended my seventeen months with the emperor. So ended my thirteen months and nine days on this island of black rocks long ago burnt. So ended my time in this false family built around an emperor father and the memory of what had been. So ended the joy of those first days at the Briars, when I lived almost alone with the emperor in the open-air dance pavilion—those days like a tête-à-tête in the desert, when we spoke without constraint and a real friendship began. We were men who had been at the same school and now found ourselves across the world. We stayed two months in that Gothic tea house that was much like the one of Governor Pitt a century ago in Madras.

At the Briars Marchand had slept rolled in his coat at the emperor's door, where Dimanche kept vigil. Pierron brought food to us that we ate without napkins or cloths like a picnic. The emperor had never, even in his campaigns, been in such cramped quarters. He talked, I wrote, Emmanuel copied. The others were living in town. The emperor then gave me his spurs and the campaign *nécessaire* he used on the morning of the battle of Austerlitz. I was the envy of all.

I have said we were a family, and as such, we had discord and problems. The emperor has said that a little intrigue is indispensable to sovereigns. It was, however, poisonous to me. I knew that both generals Montholon and Gourgaud, who still hated each other, finally had called me "the cockroach."

On this island we were all misplaced as the furniture of other days, the jewels around the miniatures, the emperor's silver washbasin. What were these fine snuffboxes, the imperial china painted with the events of the emperor's life, doing in this dreadful place? What were the generals doing there in uniforms of armies that no longer existed with braid and cordons that tarnished daily in the wet air? None of it belonged in this peculiar isolation. Sèvres china with ibis birds of the Nile, a silver bowl with Josephine's swans, his silk stockings with the crown on the corners, the little roses on his gold-buckled shoes, the servants in livery with gold lace—all were peculiar there, a perpetual affront.

None of us—Grand Marshal Bertrand and Fanny, Montholon and his Albine, General Gourgaud, Cipriani, the valets, Marchand and Ali the Mameluke—would be together were it not for him. We followed him, he was the common purpose. We spied upon one another and put our hands to our brows against the unrelenting sun to study the sea, as boats circled watching us every hour of the day and night. Despite snits and piques, postures and poses, there was something noble in the love that took us all across the ocean and left us here in this, our own green hell with turtledoves.

Where, at first, the emperor felt he was at a masked ball, he had come to feel he was living in a tomb, conducting a dialogue of the dead.

The others said I had come to, and left, this island to serve my ambition. Had not the emperor himself ever been accused of the same? I say now I did not engineer my retreat. I left because they took me away and also because it was time. It is our trade to live in other lives and serve our stories, and every writer knows when the story is done.

As Emmanuel and I sailed away to the Cape of Good Hope on our way to an unknown destination, I felt how I had aged and knew any success I might have would be part of this failure.

I never said good-bye to the emperor. I could not return to Longwood, for to return was never to leave.

I write this now having abandoned my labors midway when I left Saint Helena. I then began a life of wandering, being shunned, a citizen bereft of a country. I was much like the diamond, an object to be passed along, lent to a time and place. I was half a prisoner in that I was a prisoner of the choices I had made. My vision had darkened even further, shapes blurred and dissolved into a permanent mist. My son's heart was still infected.

Having been away from my chronicle of the diamond for so long, I see now that perhaps I was drawn to the stone because it, like me, was a kind of witness. Like the diamond, I was mute, unable to speak in public at the council, quiet with the emperor unless I had something to say. I was not a chatterer, except out of desperation when I saw him low. Yet there were times, sitting by his bath for hours, when I told him my life—the voyage to Illyria, the inspection of the depots of mendicity and the prisons, my days as the master of appeals—and I found my voice. I told of myself among the princes and kings, the generals with their gold-braided uniforms. Then, too, like the stone itself with its scintillations and glimmerings, I kept my secrets.

By leaving I had abandoned my attempt to distract the emperor, to be his Scheherazade in so far as I was able. After a day of his telling his glorious life, when he was tired or low, I would reverse our roles and tell him mine. It fell to me to raise the mood of this great man, to push away the chimeras and prod the dragons. I would bring hot towels when his teeth or his head ached. I would try to make him forget for the moment some part of all he had lost. I was unworthy of the task, yet I was there with those military brutes, skilled in war and helpless in peace. I had come from another time, another world, when things, however false and tricky, were gentle and discreet. The emperor called me his polished diamond.

I had not been with him as one of his generals nor had I distinguished myself on any campaign. I had felt it from the first on board the warship *Bellerophon* going to Plymouth,* all of them spurred and booted in their grand uniforms; Emmanuel and I in frock coat and slippers.

Rereading my old notes, I felt my chronicle of the diamond tilting to the emperor as all things did when I was on the island. It was as though the very house and garden, the gum trees themselves bent toward him by a force unknown to the captive. By his existence, the force he was, he consumed all.

I knew he wanted me at Longwood and yet, away from him, I was his one hope for escape and redemption. I might do what his whole family could or would not, for I was relentless and he knew it.

After eight months trapped on the Cape of Good Hope, separated from the emperor I loved, I returned to Europe. Forbidden to go back to France, I lived for a time in the duchy of Baden-Baden, in Bavaria, by the Black Forest. I wrote to all the heads of Europe to tell of the emperor's plight. I wrote to Madame Mère and her dethroned sons and daughters, but all seemed powerless to help him. My heritage was such that begging was abhorrent to

---

*Where we were transferred to the *Northumberland*.

me, yet I did beg in his name and abased myself many times over. All I had to give him were my words and 100,000 francs. They both did no good.

The Régent's story went on without Napoleon. In my wanderings, in response to inquiries, I received some information on the great jewel. However, it was little wonder that at this time I was unwilling to continue my chronicle of the diamond. It seemed so distant to me then.

The diamond now belonged to the Bourbons, who opposed us, for this second restoration was the time of the White Terror in France. The memory was still fresh of how, in the south near Marseilles, they had hunted down every last Mameluke, slaughtered them, and finally disbanded the imperial guard. They murdered Marshal Brune, then tore him from his coffin, dragged him by his legs over the pavement, and flung him from a bridge, firing at the body. There were massacres at Nîmes.

I found out that Louis XVIII finally did wear the Régent, in June of 1818. Talleyrand, the grand chamberlain and traitor, himself the curse of all enterprises, drew on the king's lily-covered boots and was driven into the forests of Fontainebleau. The king wore a royal blue velvet suit strewn with seed pearls and had the Régent in the front of his cap. He had come to meet Marie-Caroline de Bourbon, who had been married by proxy to his nephew the duc de Berri, son of count d'Artois. The duc de Berri was known for his wild outbursts of temper and rough manner. Blacas d'Aulps had gone to Naples to negotiate the alliance.

They waited at the same crossroads where the emperor had met the pope twelve years before, in the forests where he had hunted; the fleshy old king was in his armchair, the princess kneeling. It was mid-June and the sweat trickled from the hat with the diamond. In front of Marie-Caroline, the king grew redder and redder. Was the Régent, witness to the meeting in the forest of Fontainebleau, the cause of the unhappy end of that marriage? I cannot say, but yet again, an enterprise begun in its presence ended badly.

A year later, on the evening of Dimanche Gras in February 1820, the duc and duchess de Berri went to the Paris Opéra. At the interval, the duchess, who was pregnant, wanted to leave. As the duc was helping the duchess into their carriage at the Entrance of Princes, a saddler in the king's stables named Louvel rushed forward.

"I am stabbed!" said the duc almost calmly as the duchess shrieked without stop. The dagger was sticking from his chest.

"I am assassinated! This man has killed me," said the duc, and he himself pulled out the dagger. "I am dead! I have the dagger!" He looked at the long weapon, now red.

His attendants carried him to the manager's office, where the duchess ripped open his shirt and swabbed at the wound and cloth after cloth dropped to the floor like red leaves. His brother came and kissed his wound. And then, even as the opera continued, began a procession of visitors for the long slow death. Chateaubriand appeared and Minister Richelieu. The duc's men sent for his father, the count d'Artois, and were about to send for the king. D'Artois said if the king came, the etiquette involved would hamper the doctors. That he would not consider forgoing the etiquette shows just how he would be as Charles X. He was soon in tears at the foot of his son's bed.

The duc de Berri asked to see his two daughters (born to his mistress, Mrs. Amy Brown). At five in the morning of this long dying, the king did come and the duc asked that he not execute his murderer. And like the duc de Berri from the days of Louis XIV (who also excelled at death and had hidden bowls of his blood under his furniture so as not to disturb the others), an hour later, this duc turned on his side to die.

"Good God! His hand is cold! Ah, Charles is no more!" said the duchess, who threw herself on the body crying that she wanted to die.

The duc's retinue "saw" only those of the court and not the crowd. In the court, everyone seemed distinct and worthy of notice; the crowd was a blur of inconsequence. Ever since I had lived as Felix in England, I always made myself see the faces of the people. Every once in a while, one of the crowd would separate out and hurl itself at a king or the emperor. That one stood for many others who were either crazy or abused beyond tolerance. Louvel, who came at the duc de Berri to kill him, was but a symbol of unhappiness in the land.

The Bourbons went on for a time but they were finished. Because these restored Bourbons owed their crowns to foreign intervention, few Frenchmen ever loved them. People suspected they had traded territory hard won in war to bring themselves back. Of course, the Bourbons could never like the Revolution, but they could have pretended to understand it. They failed at this.

Seven months after her husband's assassination, the duchess de Berri gave birth to a son who, though known as the "Miracle Child," would never reign as king. Some doubted that the father of this child was the duc de Berri, for that is the way Paris is.

My vision had gone almost completely, and as I looked for a reader, I prepared my volume of *Letters from the Cape of Good Hope* and a history of my life. I had become the pivot of information for the emperor's family, who still somehow bought palaces and country houses while the emperor lived among termites and flies. I wrote to the czar and Prince Metternich, Marie-Louise and the emperor of Austria. I petitioned Lord Castlereagh and the English Parliament. When I asked his stepson, Eugène de Beauharnais, who now was rich and married to a king's daughter, for money for the emperor, he sent 5,000 francs.

At this time, Marie-Louise was degrading herself with Count Neipperg, with whom she lived in scandal and eventually had three children. The King of Rome, nine years old, was now the duke of Reichstadt, kept in Vienna by his grandfather, abandoned by his mother, ever in search of the dream of his father.

During my exile in Germany I thought only of the emperor. I lost myself in this other. I sent him books and wrote in his favor to the Congress of Aix-la-Chapelle. I banished myself from my country and almost destroyed my small fortune. I lived as a Trappist in retreat until I could no longer go on. I had spent the winter of 1819 at Liège, Belgium, the spring of 1820 at Chaudfontaine. I was a wanderer on the face of the continent and wherever I moved, I hauled the same inexorable baggage.

One evening I sank into a kind of half sleep. It was the time when the emperor used to take a last walk in the garden in his dressing gown, though nothing much was to be seen. He would walk by himself, hands clasped behind his back, his red slippers disappearing into the blue steam of the evenings. Now, in a dream, he came back in a strange disheveled version of himself, his pants stained with ink where he had wiped his pen on them, dirt on his thin little slippers. I saw him try to speak, his brow rotating as it does when he is excited. In one hand he held his hat of beaver and silk, all scarred. The trimming was hanging off his right sleeve where he had twisted and pulled at it. And worst of all, his poor sword—all the jewels had been pried off and there was now a big hole where the diamond had been. And this decomposed vision of him, this jerking and twitching version of himself that was not quite a dream, shook me more than I could imagine. I was rooted to my chair as it stood and looked at me and saw straight into my bruised heart.

The next spring on May 5, as I was walking in Malines, the spa near Anvers where I had gone to take a cure, I was met by a sudden fierce storm. Lightning cracked the black sky apart and I heard cannons in the thunder. I knew then, though I had heard no news of the emperor for months, that Napoleon Bonaparte, the captain of my last ship, the general of my soul, had died. I found this out a week later in a letter from Eugène, who told me I had been named the treasurer of his will.

At this, all my failure came upon me. At fifty-five, I turned my back on the world. I saw no one, for all men had become odious to me. I was one of the *isolés* by choice. I had not after all made the emperor's life better, nor had I told his story in a book all might read. Henriette urged me then to return to France, where perhaps I might give new life to his memory. I realized now this was my final mission and got permission to return. I found a small house with a sad little garden in Rue de la Pompe in Passy, at the doors of Paris, and entered my retreat.

It was but half an hour to walk to the still incompleted Arc de Triomphe, but how could I go to Paris, where the white flag of the Bourbons flew? Instead, I went to Malmaison to walk the paths he had and sit under the last tree that had shaded my immortal friend. (Could not this pretty "evil house" have brought as much bad luck as the diamond?) I remembered the day on the island when we had talked of returning, and now, as he had predicted, I had done so.

As a favor, Lord Holland had tried to get back my papers and finally they were returned, including much of this chronicle. But first, I had to put together my life's chief work, the *Memorial of Saint Helena*, which appeared in eight volumes a year later, in 1823. I did nothing else during this time. I no longer heard the voice, felt the magnificent interruption of his presence as I transcribed his words. There was no painful tug on my ear, no figure but a memory sitting on the arm of my chair or my lap. No one came to lean over me and press my head hard to his chest, to correct my mistakes, or to chide me for wandering off on one of my tangents.

Never again would I hear, "Mr. Jailer, Mr. Robber, Mr. Paladin, unroll your old parchments."

Eventually I learned how sick the emperor had been in his last year. There were days that he resembled no one so much as Lord Chatham, for he too stayed in a shuttered room. His men remained with him in the dark silence and the marshals and generals took turns sleeping with Dimanche on a carpet at the foot of his bed. He had Marchand read to him and did not dress and would quote Voltaire: *"Mais à revoir Paris je ne dois plus prétendre."* (But I must no longer pretend that I will see Paris again.)

In this last year he rode a seesaw in the reception room to keep up his strength. At first he rode with de Montholon, then they weighted the opposite end with lead.

He began to give out pieces of himself. He gave Monsieur Balcombe, who owned our summerhouse at the Briars, one of his boxes with a lock of his hair, still such a dark brown, and a small sample of his handwriting, still very bad. And finally he willed that his heart be sent to his wife, who would refuse it.

There was a storm on the night he died and he too must have heard cannons in the thunder, for his last words were, *"Tête d'armée"* (head of the army). Dimanche began to howl then as dogs are supposed to do and she continued all the night until no noise came from her throat, and still she tilted up her black head to bay without sound.

Then the English raised the blue flag that meant, "General Bonaparte is missing," for he was missing for them, for us, and all the world.

Gradually I saw, when my life had no excitement except in the reliving, that my days on the island had been my best time. It was as if I had lived in a large empty house with a panther. I never knew when I turned a corner what would be waiting or creeping there—the excitement was almost unbearable. I had lived long in that heightened state. Now I saw too I had misunderstood my own life.

For the second time in my literary life, I had an immense success—this time with the *Memorial of Saint Helena*. I have been astounded that the reaction has never ceased. People sent me reviews, odes, and ballads from all over. I was read in the streets and what was left of the salons. The liberals rediscovered their democratic themes in the emperor's words and believed in him and what they had lost.

I was but the scribe, the Sully of Saint Helena as he liked to call me, recalling the devoted minister who had written the memoirs of Henri IV. It was the emperor's brain, his charm, the romance of his misfortune that ruled my book. I was but the messenger, and I felt that the small plump ghost who was always with me was finally pleased.

It would have pleased him too that my son, Emmanuel, challenged Hudson Lowe to a duel in London and had been expelled from England.

A year after the emperor died, Pitt's successor, Lord Castlereagh, walked into his dressing room to cut his jugular vein and bleed to death.

Louis XVIII still thought of a coronation and decided to make a new crown. The Bapsts were now the crown jewelers and used the Régent and the biggest diamonds, which they repolished, slightly diminishing them in size. They did not polish the Régent. Evard Bapst designed the crown and Frederic Bapst made it for Louis XVIII's enormous head. He was much too sick to wear it, though.

At the end, this leaning king sloped so far forward his head was almost to his knees and his forehead developed a dent from crashing so often to the bronze rim of his writing table. He was cut and bruised, but he would not permit himself a cushion.

"The King of France might die, but must never be ill," he said. He sat bowed over double and would be carried out, deep in sleep on his throne. And so it might be said, he slid off the throne of France. Soon enough the dukes and princes were throwing their flags and coat of arms down the stairs into his tomb. They threw his crown and scepter and the hand of justice, his spurs, helmet, and breastplate, sword, shield, and gauntlets, and as each struck and clattered down the stairs of the vault, they kept calling out, "The king is dead!"

Count d'Artois, who succeeded his brother and reigned as Charles X, decided on a coronation in 1824, to be held exactly the way the old kings had them at Rheims. In the evening of the ceremony, Evard Bapst, who was in charge of the crown jewels, arrived with the crown he had just made smaller to fit the new king's head.

The crown had eight delicate branches set with eight fleur-de-lis in diamonds and sapphires to represent the Bourbon blue, and again it cannibalized the past. It had the emperor's stolen hat diamond, diamonds found with the people during the Revolution, those taken from the emperor, from the king of Sardinia, and émigrés long dead. At the very top on the surmounting double fleur-de-lis was the Régent.

Charles X studied the crown. His long fingers in thin white kid gloves reached to seize it by one of the very delicate branches. The king wore big glittering rings over his gloves. Bapst, filled with terror that it might break, was at first unable to speak.

"Sire, it is very delicate," he finally squeaked.

"I don't give a shit," said Charles X, who nonetheless put it down.

The crown united all the regimes of France that Charles X could not, for he was given to hunting and religion and the ways of the past, when he had been the *vrai chevalier*. Instead of keeping great vellum books of his jewels, he kept the records of his hunts. Henriette has described to me Baron Gérard's portrait of him, the ermine cape, the features made gross with age—those big lips!—the crown topped by the Régent beside him on a cushion.

His devotion to the church became obvious from the time of his coronation at Rheims, when he kneeled to be crowned by a priest. And then everyone remembered the emperor, how he had taken his crown from the pope and crowned himself, and the people felt pulled back even further into the old Bourbon mess. For it was all back—the ermine, the knee breeches, and the mysterious, hard pride. The royalists even claimed to have found drops from the holy oil vial broken in the Revolution and applied them to his head. Sticking their hands through holes in his robe, they anointed him between his shoulders and on his arms. Then the doves flew through the cathedral into noise of the trumpets and the guns.

Charles X refused to buy back the Great Sancy when Bapst, who had retrieved it, offered it to him. Bapst tried again and said the pope was interested, and that except for the Régent, it was the best jewel of the crown.

"Well, then, I already have the best," said Charles X, with a shrug.

Five years later, in 1829, I attended the sale at Malmaison of the emperor and Josephine's furniture. The auctions went on from the end of May to the end of July. My daughter Ofresie led me along the gravel path and told me of the neglect that had come to the gardens. I bent to feel the withered stems of the plants Josephine had brought to France. Some of the emperor's men came back to buy pieces of him, for somehow we all must have believed that a person can live in an object—that his presence could enter a chair and invest it with a remnant, some particle of all that he was.

The day that I went they were selling artifacts from the red-and-black council room that had been built as a military tent with pike staffs and war trophies and the busts of celebrated soldiers. There had been twenty-eight seats in the room and I was determined to own one of them. First six chairs were auctioned as a group to a Monsieur Fabien for 107 francs. Then stools, those *tabourets en X* made by Jacob Frères, were auctioned in pairs. The first pair went for 36 francs and I was about to bid on the next when they fetched 94 francs.

"Who is bidding?" I asked Ofresie, who described a man whom I knew to be Gourgaud.

Then came the emperor's red-and-black armchairs with their palmettes and acanthus scrolls, their seats of napped wool. I remembered at my son's christening how Josephine had pointed out the one chair whose armrests Napoleon had scored with his penknife in one of his restless moods. This was the one I wanted. I had Ofresie inspect each one previously so she might tell me when this particular one came up. The chairs began to sell— for 70, then 100 francs.

"I think the general has captured them all," Ofresie said. "Now comes yours."

Just then the auctioneer announced that the final chair had been withdrawn, that the family was keeping it and it was going to the duke of Leuchtenberg, Eugène de Beauharnais' son. (Eugène had married the daughter of the king of Bavaria, and had died five years previously.)

Montholon sat down beside me and talked to me in that loud voice people reserve for those who can't see. As he was talking two *lits de repos* (sofas) were hammered down for 200 and 212 francs. Gourgaud bought them as well. It was like being back on the island.

I bought nothing that day, but before we left, I stroked the arm of the chair the emperor had gored, and broke off a little splinter of wood.

I Say Adieu

B Y 1830, CHARLES X WORE A GENERAL'S UNIFORM TO OPEN the Assembly. He refused to dismiss ministers the people hated, for he knew where any concession had led his brother. An absolutist to the end, he said, "No compromise, no surrender." He published the ordinances of July 26 that repealed the electoral law, dissolved the chamber, and ended press freedom. Then he withdrew them, but—in the Bourbon pattern—it was too late. The proclamations had gone up that morning:

CHARLES X CANNOT REENTER PARIS.
HE HAS SHED THE BLOOD OF THE PEOPLE.
THE DUC D'ORLÉANS [LOUIS-PHILIPPE] IS A PRINCE
DEVOTED TO THE CAUSE OF THE REVOLUTION.

The Régent had crowned another king whose reign ended in revolution and flight. Like his brother Louis XVI, Charles X was hunting when it happened. He was shooting rabbits at Saint-Cloud as the crowds gathered in the Rue de Rivoli and axed up the cobblestones for barricades.

It all seemed so horribly familiar. The Swiss guard fleeing the Tuileries were running down the muddy Champs Élysées. Versailles and Notre Dame flew the tricolor. And so began *Les Trois Glorieuses,* our three-day July Revolution, when every house was a fort and everyone was armed. Despite my poor vision, I was then commander in chief of the national guard of Passy and heard the forbidden "Marseillaise" sung again.

Charles X is supposed to have said, "I see no middle way between the throne and the scaffold," to which Talleyrand, still nudging the elbow of power, replied, "Your Majesty forgets the post chaise."

The king and court left for Trianon in the middle of the night as Louis-Philippe, the duc d'Orléans, was proclaimed "King of the French." That was the second end of the divine right of kings.

Louis-Philippe embraced General Lafayette and rode into Paris, as Charles X had done, on a white horse. We crave kings even as we behead them or drive them off. Even as we laugh, we bow.

At Trianon, the widowed young duchess de Berri strapped on two pistols, dressed herself as a man, and then fled for Rambouillet. Charles X took the Régent and the other crown jewels with him.

What did he think he was taking with the diamond? Money, of course, and thus power and the freedom that comes from power. In this piece of the old life he was capturing the possibility of a new life. The diamond would always announce, *This is who I once was.* The Régent was a piece of the glory that was gone and also a way to be safe. Baron La Bouillerie, who was so quick to turn over the emperor's treasure, now was guarding the jewels for Charles X.

When Charles X abdicated, his son became Louis XIX, and immediately renounced his rights. Then Charles X abdicated again, this time in favor of the son of the duchess de Berri, the Miracle Child, who was nine years old then and known as the comte de Chambord.

Fourteen thousand people marched from Paris to scare away the last Bourbon. They went in omnibuses and fiacres, people falling over the sides. When the mob arrived at Rambouillet they found that Louis-Philippe had already negotiated the return of the jewels and that they were locked into a special fitted carriage. Surrounded by singing rioters, they marched the jewels back to Paris. And the last king of France gave up the Régent to the new "King of the French."

I think Louis-Philippe, the great-great-grandson of the regent, will be the last to wear the diamond in my time. In fact, he has not yet been brave enough to wear it. To become King of the French, he signed a document wearing his general's uniform, seated on a throne surrounded by tricolor flags in the Chamber of Deputies. Four marshals handed him the symbols of the king—the scepter, the sword, the hand of justice, and that same confection of diamonds and sapphires with the Régent on top that Charles X had worn. He barely touched it and did not put on the crown for he was trying hard to imitate ordinariness. There have been seven attempts to kill him so far; one was another infernal machine—twenty-five muskets strapped together and misfiring into the crowd.

Louis-Philippe is a different sort of king—one seemingly without arrogance, with a big appealing family, his sons in public schools, and a private life none can reproach. He prefers the Gallic cock to the Bourbon lily as his symbol, for he is a bourgeois royal, a king in a time of universal revolution, tiptoeing between citizen and monarch, holding his green umbrella. As the son of the regicide Philippe Égalité, he does not share his ancestor Monsieur's love of jewels (through the generations, all traces of Monsieur's flamboyance have leaked away). Louis-Philippe was not about to take on a diamond that announced so many kings. Still, in this strange way, the diamond bought by Madame's son has been returned to her distant grandson.

Half a Bourbon, half an Orléans, yet the first thing Louis-Philippe did was to finish the emperor's Arc de Triomphe. He opened a Napoleonic museum, a Museum of National Glories at Versailles. He allowed actors to play the emperor. He carved his battles into the Arc de Triomphe, restored his statue to Place Vendôme. It was brave of him in this age of *romantisme* to revive the dream of toppled glory.

Now I, too, like the old duc de Richelieu and Madame du Barry, had lived into another era, one beyond my imaginings. And though I rarely went out at night, when I did, I could almost see, as the streetlamps are lit by little flickers of flaming gas. Great iron trains take people from Paris to Saint-Germain, and with them and the new hissing lamplights, better times may have arrived. At my door were many stiff brown cards bearing daguerrotypes of those who had come to call. Alas, they all looked alike to me for I could see only their shapes, and I did not admit visitors anyway.

At that time, I received a letter from a young writer who had spent the July Revolution correcting his novel *The Red and the Black* and reading my *Memorial*. Henri Beyle had been a dragoon in the Italian campaign and crossed the Alps with the emperor, had been with him at Moscow in 1812, and as a writer had taken the name Stendahl—a name that we have since come to know. He knew I would agree that the emperor was the greatest man since Caesar and that his "superiority lay entirely in his way of finding new ideas with incredible speed, of judging them with complete rationality, and of carrying them out with a willpower that never had an equal."

In the time of Louis-Philippe, the ban was lifted and we were once again permitted to write of the emperor. Not only Stendahl, but Victor Hugo and Alexandre Dumas and Honoré de Balzac wrote of him then, and Ofresie has read me their works, her voice a mellifluous drone until she comes to sections involving the emperor, when she becomes quite dramatic. She has counted fourteen plays about the emperor in the theaters of Paris, none of which I will see.

The Régent and all the crown jewels then were locked in a great vault in Evard Bapst's house at 30 Quai de l'École. A guard stood out front day and night for two years until the jewels were removed in 1832, inventoried, and placed in the vaults of the civil list in a wing of the Tuileries. Everyone knew there was a secret stair in that building and that Monsieur de Verbois, the treasurer, who had one of the three keys, lived on the first floor. Verbois kept the private jewels and the money of the king's family as well.

That was the year of the riots, of the dreadful curse of cholera from the filth of the city when carts with corpses slogged through the narrow putrid streets, when people stood up at the opera, clutched themselves, and fell over dead. I was glad for the distance of Passy, where I could not smell the chlorine or see the churches that stayed wrapped in black.

One evening Henriette and I ventured into Paris to the duc de ———. Even on the Faubourg Saint-Germain, I found that the distinctions— whether the hostess would greet one at the door or at the foot of the stairs, in the middle of the room or at the landing—had disappeared. (But what can one expect, for the king himself is too familiar. He hugs and kisses people and even talks to journalists.) As everyone knew, the duc kept a skeleton in his closet. That night he showed it to a young composer named Frédéric Chopin, who placed the skeleton next to him on the piano bench and played the saddest music I have ever heard, a music of loss that made the bone man rattle and caused me to think of the emperor.

The Régent remained hidden in a wall. Constant Bapst, Evard's heir, then had one of the three keys. No one—not Louis-Philippe, his queen, or his sister—has dared wear any of the crown jewels in public.

At this time when the tricolor flew, the king was mocked, and the statue of the emperor was back on the column in Place Vendôme, I slowly emerged from my house and returned to public life. It was a time of industry, a rich time, and I often wondered what the emperor would have made of this new Paris. At sixty-five, I became a commander, lieutenant colonel of the national guard. I was elected representative from Saint-Denis, sat on the left of the chamber, and finally received the Legion of Honor. Then, as though I had been wrong to poke my head outside, the bad things began to happen.

One morning, I put my hand on Henriette's shoulder as I had done for so many of her sixty-two years and, for the first time, found it hard and cold.

On her tomb I incised, *"I await here for the one whose happiness I made and I am sure he is longing to arrive."* I felt then that the ghosts of my life were collecting, whispering in my parlor as they waited for me—the headless ones, the torn soldiers, my lost daughter Emma, Henriette, and my friend de Volude—the last long dead battling the one I had come to live for.

Then I was ruined by a bad land deal. I had to sell the jewels that Josephine had given Henriette when the empress became godmother of my second son, Barthélemy. Finally, I had another loss of vision and had to resign as representative from Saint-Denis.

At this time, a young Jewish man who had just finished his studies appeared on my doorstep. He had heard of my recent inquiries about selling my jewels and about the Régent. He felt he might aid me in any of my endeavors for he felt indebted to the emperor. After all, Napoleon had made his people citizens of the nation-states he created in Italy and Austria and Germany. When Napoleon conquered Italy, it had meant an end to the Inquisition and the dismantling of the ghettos in Rome and Venice, also Mainz and Frankfurt. It was the Jew, who has chosen to remain anonymous here, who later helped me fill in some gaps in the history of the stone that involved his people. He also helped me sell Henriette's jewels to one of his people. I shall call him "Abraham."

I could scarcely make out his features, but I knew from the way his shape loomed above me, the outline of his shadow, that he was a tall man and, by the prominence of the bones on his young hand, that he was thin.

"Very skinny, Papa," Ofresie told me, "and such disappointed eyes. His hair is not much for he is all forehead and his clothes . . . well, you have held his sleeve. I have mended it now. He carries his Hebrew books about with him and whenever he has an instant, he studies them."

I do not know his past, and if I did, respecting his wishes, I would never tell.

Abraham is a young man of these times—a bit too angry, and too full of the *romantisme* that drew him here. He speaks of Berlioz's *Symphonie Fantas-tique*—its opium eaters and witches' sabbath—almost as his religion. He came home from the café with the long program. I can guess why the theme of hopeless infatuation so appealed to him.

He was in the balconies for Victor Hugo's *Hernani* when the whole audi-ence whistled and stamped because they had never heard acting like that be-fore. He came here laughing and excited to tell Ofresie how the balcony cast lines with fishhooks to catch the wigs of the bourgeois. He too has his Saint-Simon, the socialist, a far different one, though distantly related. He is now my eyes, describing dances where men and women hold each other close and twirl around. When I danced, whole ballrooms pranced together in pre-scribed steps, barely touching, glove to glove. And he tells too of the men's high polished hats and stiff collars propping the chin. They wear beards now and some have a strap that goes under the foot of their pants to stretch them tight and show the legs as our breeches did. Light cabriolets are whipped through the streets spraying arcs of mud, and all is in flux and somewhat incomprehensible.

One day Abraham told me he had seen the king, a round little man wear-ing a toupee, walking on the Rue de Rivoli. He was carrying his famous green umbrella.

"Hello, my friend," Louis-Philippe said pleasantly enough to Abraham and shook his hand with the "dirty glove" he reserves for members of the lower orders. Abraham was unmoved and reminded me of how Louis-Philippe had locked Daumier in jail for drawing him as a pear (a pear means one easily fooled).

Abraham read to me how Napoleon's son, the King of Rome, the little boy I knew born a king, died of consumption in Vienna. He had become the duc de Reichstadt and a prisoner of Austrian palaces. He who had coughed himself into life coughed himself out of it at twenty-one. At this sad news I took to my bed for the rest of the day.

Ofresie, who was then twenty-two, kept house and read to me when Abraham could not. She rose at five and worked all day researching, copy-ing and recopying, cooking and cleaning, too, for we were poor again be-cause of my bad land deal. And thus I pushed forward, writing of the Régent in this time when it was so completely hidden from sight.

When I had been an émigré and seen how some among us looked down on the others and made them suffer, when I had lived as "Felix" and gone out at night with my one rewashed shirt and ancient title, I lost interest in all but the necessities of life. I had never before worked for money. I never again wanted to go slip-sliding over the waxed parquet of palace floors. After my land deal, I counted up that I had lost 894,600 francs in my life and been the victim of fifty-two thefts. This painful list included in it my gambling losses, which always took place in the best homes—at the de Luynes', the Luxembourgs', the Montmorencys'.

I had lost a fortune yet I became fascinated anew over the grandeur and doom of the diamond and how it matched the emperor—now especially when I see what has followed him. (As Abraham often reminds me, with the Laws of September we live again with press censorship and only two hundred thousand out of 35 million who can vote.)

Once the emperor scolded me for writing of a lifeless thing. Then I had no response, but now I see what I only guessed then, that things *are* the people who own them, and beyond them, because the tomb outlasts the man, though maybe not his ideas.

And then I was rescued again. One of the chiefs of the liberal party convinced me to stand and I was elected to the Assembly.

My son Emmanuel, who had become a lawyer, had gone to London in 1835 and seen the duke of Wellington studying his own image at Madame Tussaud's waxworks on Baker Street. The wax duke had been placed alongside the wax emperor. Nearby were Napoleon's coach, his hairs, his toothbrush, and—gruesome to contemplate—the camp bed on which he died. My son had watched the duke studying himself and the emperor, and though he was bursting to say much, had managed to say nothing.

It was Louis-Philippe who had the emperor's body brought back to France and the tomb in Les Invalides. This was right after one of our small revolutions.

Emmanuel, then a deputy and councillor of state in the Assembly with me, returned to Saint Helena, for I was seventy-four and too infirm for the journey. With him were the grand marshal Bertrand and General Gourgaud. It had been twenty-four years since my son went there as a boy of fifteen and climbed the black rocks and copied out the emperor's words.

He told me how the emperor's tomb under a weeping willow in the Valley of Geranium on Saint Helena had been marked by a black slab with nothing written on it but *"Cy git"* (Here lies). Hudson Lowe wanted to write "Bonaparte" and my countrymen wanted to write "Napoleon" upon it. The war had continued even then. This black slab as much as the diamond was Napoleon's stone.

Emmanuel was scandalized at how neglected and looted he found Longwood. He was there in my place for the funeral cortege, when they opened the four coffins and brought the emperor home, the people kneeling by the banks of the Seine. He was there for the ceremony at Cherbourg.

I could not see the procession through Paris to the Invalides, when my fickle race spared Napoleon's remains no honors. I was shut in my gray world, but I heard the horses' hooves on the sand, the snap of the flags of his victories, and the clanking of the ceremonial weapons. I felt the brute cold of the December day for it was well below zero when Emmanuel fetched me some bourbon from a vendor. In the stands in front of Les Invalides, Gourgaud and Bertrand greeted me, and Victor Hugo took off his hat to me as he passed. I saw only the shadow of a big man. I heard people stamping their feet and felt the caress of women in furs sidling by me like a movable forest of creatures. I heard the cannon, smelled the incense from the urns, and felt the sun break out at the time when the catafalque approached. Everyone gasped and I heard, *"Vive l'empereur!"* as the single white stallion followed. His saddle was empty.

Emmanuel described for me the big sad circus, the hollow love that, with my *Memorial,* I helped inspire. He told of the statue of the emperor in his coronation robes on top of the Arc de Triomphe and how there were plaster eagles and pyramids and random victory goddesses all around. Sixteen horses were caparisoned in gold, crouching plaster nymphs held orbs. Eight shrouded goddesses held up the coffin covered by swags of purple velvet and the flags of those he had conquered and then been conquered by. Everything was draped and shrouded. A huge moving tower, like a circus wagon, the emperor would have said, laughing. I felt bitter and closed in my heart as I stood bowed in the cold sun. I was a piece of ocean foam sliding across a beach, blowing itself to nothing.

I had lived through more than one time when the statues came down and the street names were changed, when houses were pocked to the touch and inside smelled of smoke, when titles were given or taken away, and France spread itself all over Europe. I felt as though an enormous volume, its pages fragile and shedding, had been turned to its back cover.

I knew Marshal Bertrand had given the emperor's arms—his swords from Austerlitz and from Champ de Mai 1815, a dagger, a saber, and a box with pistols—to the citizen king. They were put into the same armoire with the crown jewels and thus, along with the other weapons, the emperor's swords have joined themselves to the Régent once again.

I live with this among many other regrets. In the days when I was master of requests, the crowd of courtiers and my own timidity held me back from the emperor. The rapport that was so quickly established at the Briars might have come to me sooner had I not been so hampered by awe at the Tuileries. I could have had more time with him.

It was the cursed island that changed us and, in imprisoning him, in a strange way, freed me. It gave me courage and a chance to speak without the others. It gave me time, and in this he became my captive.

Now when I return to this island in my mind, the time is always twilight, when we walked out and the sky was a streaky lavender and red dome and an evening damp had settled droplets on the bent plants and all the guards were sleepy and anxious to be replaced. We walked over the island ruins, quiet in our ruined hopes. Those evenings and the time in the summerhouse were all I lived on. I felt selected from all the universe, and the rim of the island became the border of my being. I was taken, engrossed forever. I was reliving the emperor's life and the lives borrowed for this chronicle. That was what was real, and the fact that I was losing all sight, the squabbles, and racing rats then meant nothing at all. There was only the emperor, my son whose heart hurt in his chest, and the unsteady but enticing flicker of the distant diamond.

I am sorry too that I did not go back when the emperor sent for me on Saint Helena. I confess now it would not have been to bid adieu, for I would have stayed. I have not lived one day since that I did not hear his voice, his last command.

"Et surtout, revenez promptement!" (And above all, return promptly!)

And here I end the story of the Régent in my time. Perhaps the diamond swallowed all my light. Or was it an illumination upon all that happened, a searchlight in that demanding dark that is time? Therein all see it from the shadows of their own skewed perceptions. What was the Régent to me? A way in, a piece of carbon crushed by forces, a bright toy. Are we not always children crawling toward a bright toy?

Did it steal the light of its wearers? What did it give, versus what it took?

Had my years of contemplating it and its brilliant owner taken my sight from me? These thoughts weighed on me. Did the diamond enhance what was inherent and always there?

Once the emperor told me, "The truth is that everything about us is a wonder. Everything in nature is a phenomenon."

I was happy never to have seen the diamond except in the emperor's sword, where it belonged. I leave another—I hope it will be Abraham—to end this chronicle. I am blind now and could not see the great stone if it were to be placed into my hand. Though I might see some light around it and feel its shape, I would miss its true owner too much.

I am almost indifferent as to whether or not the diamond is worn again in a republic, kingdom, or empire. I think I have seen the end of kings and emperors. For me there was only one who deserved to wear this accident of the mines of Golconda. It was an exception, as was he. And now, I shall obey his last command and return. I am late, but I expect to embrace him soon.

PART IV

Abraham's Epilogue

I, "ABRAHAM," HAVE TAKEN UP THIS STORY TO CONTINUE THE work of the noble Count Las Cases and tell of the diamond in my time. Even though I regret that the count gave so much of himself to the history of this trinket, how can I let it go? All the rest of his work is finished—the additions to the *Memorial*, his *Memorandum* and *Atlas*—all but this. And so, as we dismantled his house and I sought other work, I obeyed Ofresie's precious request and kept my eye on the diamond.

Little does the count tell in his chronicle of his last days what his service to the great emperor cost him. He was broken, his nights troubled by tropical sweats and fever dreams from which he would awake into the midnight of his vision.

On the special ruled paper Ofresie prepared for him he had written: "Now I find myself waiting without fear, even with some sort of satisfaction, for the time when it pleases the dispenser of all things to call me to him. . . . There I will find again with delights those I have loved." What Napoleon called the "negative moment" (when life ceases) was upon him. He died in his sleep on May 14, 1842, at the long age of seventy-six.

I saw in Count Las Cases a man of the most distinguished nature, honorable and true in all his dealings. Then, too, this small very masculine man possessed a sweetness and the ancient manners that made all love him. It is not hard to see what had drawn the emperor so close. I hoped to serve him as he had served his Napoleon.

As a Jew, of course, I could not go where he had gone as a senator and chamberlain in his quest for the diamond. I could supply and fill in, however, some of the story of the Jews of long ago, and this I have done, albeit without his skill. From the first, my people surrounded the stone, hovering nearby, never quite possessing it. They had pieces of it but never the whole. They were there on the side, rolling and pushing it along its road. It was, after all, the Jew Cope who cut it and Abraham Nathan who sold the pieces cut off. We were needed by that world, but never quite of it.

For six years after the count died I was the reader for various friends of his. His sons helped me find work so that I did not have to plant liberty poplars for our national workshops and might stay close to my books and papers.

King Louis-Philippe abdicated and fled in such a hurry that he had no time to grab his toupee and had to tie a kerchief on his head. Wearing goggles and disguised as Mr. and Mrs. William Smith, the king and queen of the French fled the Tuileries in a cab.

We are ever attempting to combine two ingredients—monarchy and revolution—that cannot help but curdle. Those who favored what they considered the real Bourbons and the Bonapartists who believed in the emperor's nephew Louis Napoleon had both opposed this Orléanist king.

By chance I was acquainted with the porter at the Tuileries who protected the Régent in the February Revolution of 1848, which gave us the Second Republic and Louis Napoleon.

Alain Nô, his name from the lake in the Sudan where his ancestors were captured, was a large man of Nubian blood who worked in the cellars of the Tuileries rinsing things and carting things away. He dusted the bottles and turned them, carried off the slops, beat the sheets and rugs, threw buckets of water on the stone floors and got to his knees to scrub. He read many books and had written a most affecting letter to the count about his *Memorial* and *Letters from the Cape of Good Hope*. We had met Nô, and the count, ever generous, had helped him a bit and given him some of his own volumes.

Nô told me (for I was then ill with fever) of the uprising when the troops around the Tuileries retreated inside, locked the gates, and fled. In the cellars he heard echoes of the booms, random shots from the barricades, thuds and cracks as the mob tore the stones up from the streets. They burned the park seats and looted the gunsmiths. Nô smelled smoke and blood, saw men in blue smocks running, then stopped in indecision, head scarves flying, top hats shot clean through. The mob threw sofas and chairs from the palace windows and Voltaire's bust sailed by him to smash upon the stones. As the people ran past, wearing priceless tapestries as blankets, Honoré de Balzac, who was like a god to Nô and most of Paris, stood off to the side, leaning on a windowsill, writing notes.

The mob invaded the Tuileries apartments and then the cellar under the vaults where the Régent was locked. Since there were no guards, they shot at the heavy door, and as it fell, they cheered. There stood Nô with his sleeves rolled up and a hatchet. At the door to the treasure and the Régent, Nô steered them off to the cellars of the commander of the national guard, where they drank themselves into a stupor and some even drowned in the rivers of wine. Through his underground window Nô then saw the gold legs of the throne of France pass by and was shocked to see Balzac carrying off its draperies and trimmings.

The next day Nô was drafted to help take the king's valuables to the treasury on a hospital stretcher. The jeweler Constant Bapst came to get the Régent and the other jewels. As the vaults were opened, there was madness as dozens of national guards began grabbing the cases and stuffing them in their rucksacks and vests. Bapst was racing here and there, watching everyone at once, hitting himself in the chest, refusing to pick up a single jewel.

"Nothing in the pockets!" he kept shouting. "You could not have designed a better way to steal these jewels! If I knew you were doing things like this I would have thrown my key into the Seine."

Nô and the others, their coats swollen with priceless padding, began a procession through the underground passage, crunching over the broken wine bottles, everyone following a general carrying the large case with the crown bearing the Régent. They put the boxes down in an office and threw a tablecloth over them.

The new minister of finance opened the red case with the crown.

"What is that monster worth?" he said, pointing to the Régent.

"Twelve millions," said Bapst.

"We must sell it to the emperor of Russia," said the minister, who had decided to sell all the jewels. Bapst and the experts stalled as long as they could waiting for another king, a museum, or an emperor to save them.

The emperor's nephew Louis Napoleon, that complicated man with the frozen face, brownish teeth, and little billy goat beard, stopped the sale and saved the Régent. Ten months after the Revolution, with our new universal vote, we made him president of France. The idea of a Napoleonic return was there long before he was, planted first with the count's *Memorial;* then, twenty years after Waterloo, Louis-Philippe had made Louis Napoleon possible.

Napoleon, both real and mythic, was in Louis Napoleon's blood. His grandmother Josephine and his mother Hortense had never let him forget. As a boy he had known the emperor and seen the crowds roar and weep for him. In exile he had written *Les Idées Napolienne*. Revering all that belonged to Napoleon, knowing all might someday be his, he kept the Régent, his uncle's diamond, safe and became Napoleon III, our emperor during the Second Empire.

My friend Nô went back to the cellars.

By the time of the Second Empire, I had become the reader for Betty, Baroness Rothschild. I left the small house in Passy and now found myself in a court. I lived in splendor in rooms crowded with treasures such as to make a thief weep with confusion. The Rothschilds—Betty and Baron James—had bought Hortense's mansion on Rue Laffitte and crowded it with their collections. They amassed painted porcelain, crouching blackamoors, and the furniture of a few Bourbons ago. Whenever I sat down to write I would have to clear the surface of a great mass of noseless antiquities with archaic smiles. Such constant beauty was at first a shock but I quickly became used to it, ready to meet the baroness with a book when she came in from a carriage ride through the Bois, fell on a gilt chaise, and waved me over to read. We sat under Giorgione's *La Tempesta* or sometimes the portrait Ingres painted of her.

"About me the goblins danced, / In narrowing circles then advanced," I read from her favorite, Heine.

"And seized me, held me prisoner there . . . While mocking laughs rang everywhere," Baroness Betty would continue from memory.

In those days there were thirty for lunch, sixty for dinner. The chef was Antoine Carême whom Baron James had stolen from the czar and the English prince regent. Carême made no concession to the dietary laws and delighted in presenting the baron with a whole piglet blanketed in oysters and stuck with brochettes of forbidden pork, on the tops of which pastry cherubs trumpeted his victory. Very few Jews were invited anyway.

Baron James, who like his father came from Jew Street in the Frankfurt ghetto, ran Rothschild Frères. He learned to have his clothes made in London, join the Jockey Club early on, and buy the best of men in each discipline. He studied what was prized and, quickly as he could, made it his own.

Baroness Betty had married her uncle. For a time all came to her salon, where the words flew fast, splattered as heavy raindrops, and were repeated all around Paris. Heine had always been there, posing against walls where masterpiece crowded masterpiece, slapping his gloves against his thigh, watching Betty to see his effect, while eyeing Balzac as he read aloud.

We fed those whom I read—de Musset, Alexandre Dumas, and George Sand, who usually arrived with Frédéric Chopin, who taught the piano to Betty and her daughter. Balzac hung around drinking the baron's coffee and hoping to get "advice" on his money. Lizst played duets with Paganini, and when there was an occasion to celebrate, Rossini wrote the music. Once Baudelaire left a pink glove that I kept.

Even living in that world I never thought I would see the Régent, for my position was such that it seemed impossible. And then, by a strange circumstance, I did see the diamond, and very close at that, and more than once.

The baroness brought me to the Exhibition of 1855 in the new Palace of Industry in the center of the newly paved Champs Élysées. And there, in a gang of Rothschilds, I first saw the diamond that had so obsessed Count Las Cases. It was not in a glass case.

Baron James, wearing his new decorations, walked heavily and very slowly because of his gout. My own feet throbbed, for here was all the industry and materialism of my age collected and flaunted one summer evening during the Crimean War.

Suddenly, as officers pushed aside the crowds, a swarm of overdressed people approached and we stepped aside for Emperor Napoleon III and Empress Eugénie, who were with Victoria, the queen of England; her husband, Prince Albert; and their young daughter Vicky, the Princess Royal. All I could see was the empress, who was wearing the Régent on top of a diadem. Flames of diamond licked at and curled around the stone to which Las Cases had devoted so much study. Everyone collapsed into bows.

Her beauty was a shock. The diadem perched on coils of hair, trapped between gold and red, the color of the horses they call roan. Her sapphire eyes slanted downward and her skin was the palest pink velvet. One eye slightly above the other gave her the particular allure of imperfection.

"*Passez,*" said Eugénie in a hoarse voice gruffer than one would imagine. She had a Spanish accent.

"*Passez donc,*" (you pass), said the queen of England.

Eugénie looked over and winked at Betty, who, when others snubbed her, had taken in the young Spanish countess, Eugénie de Montijo. I watched the empress retreat, the soft swollen slope of her shoulders disappearing as the group passed beyond Monsieur Foucault's pendulum. She was Andalusian, like Count Las Cases way back, but English in her beauty and rather tall. I had never seen anyone walk like that—a floor-skimming glide next to the little British queen, who stomped along without pause like a tiny determined pachyderm.

The emperor was staring over the miniature queen at one of the showy women of the times. Heavy lids half closed his eyes, and under a chestnut mustache waxed up and twisted out past his cheeks, puffy lips suggested his sensual nature. He shuffled along, distracted from the exhibits, his waist girdled tight, tilting as though he might walk forever in a circle.

"Don't be too impressed," the baroness said in our fiacre. "He may be more than a copy, but he is less than the original." And then she began explaining to her daughter how Eugénie had cultivated the *sentiment de la toilette,* that genius of the closet, and how she rehearsed all her duty dresses right down to the underwear on a wicker mannequin that her maid sent down on an elevator from her closet.

"Now you have seen your diamond," said the baroness. "It has gone from his crown with eight gold eagles to this horror—the Diabolical Diadem as the emperor calls it because the leaves of flame are like hellfire burning up the Régent."

"He does not know which of his heroes he is today," said the baron. "Is he Caesar, or Napoleon?"

"It's hard to be obsessed by not one, but two greater men," said the baroness.

Eugénie too had fallen in love with the contagious glamour of the first Napoleon, the romance of the broken man. Her father had been in Napoleon's army and when she was a girl Stendahl had filled her with his stories of the emperor.

As the four grays clopped along, workmen paused to stare at our fiacre trimmed and monogrammed in gold. Just then the horses stumbled on some rubble from the destruction of Saint-Simon's house. Baron Haussmann was tearing up all the streets to put down macadam, widening all

Paris with his boulevards and making a terrible mess. Everything was coming back bigger and wider and charged with splendor. The women then wore immense crinolines called "cages." Sometimes, as they swept past candles, they caught fire; sometimes, the papers told us, they were blown out to sea like big balloons. Even our universe had expanded, with the discovery of a pale green orb named Neptune.

A few days later, Betty came rushing in to breakfast followed by her maid still adjusting her. It seemed half her day was spent changing clothes for the next part of her day. I dove to catch the Greek kouri her dress had swept from a table.

"Extraordinary!" she gasped. "The two biggest diamonds in the world in one room. Last night at the Hôtel de Ville."

I waited for her to collect herself, for I now saw she had become almost as interested in the Régent as I. She told me that at the ball Queen Victoria had worn a mammoth oval diamond called the Koh-I-Noor in a big heavy tiara, while Napoleon had the Régent in the hilt of his sword.

"The queen kept looking down at his sword," Betty said. "Finally the emperor said, 'Yours looks a bit bigger.' 'Not at all,' she said. 'It once was,' Albert said, and he looked just furious. It was his idea to have the diamond recut and it lost eighty carats. Albert himself put it on the mill at Garrards. The duke of Wellington rode up to see them do it and he also got to put it on the wheel. They say that diamond is cursed unless a woman wears it.

"Soon enough everyone caught on to the two diamonds and they all began walking by, making circles with their fingers and discussing the brilliance. I would say your Régent, even though cut in the old style, is both bigger and more brilliant. The Koh-I-Noor is too flat, too thin. It has no play."

The empress got the Régent back and wore it to a ball for Queen Victoria at Versailles. Napoleon III had decorated the Hall of Mirrors just the way Louis XV had for one of his balls there, at which he wore the same diamond. The women—bare shouldered, their hair *à la bacchante*, with long curls at the back entwined with vine leaves and bunches of grapes—waltzed around the staid little queen.

"How beautiful you are!" the emperor said when he saw Eugénie in her white dress with branches of grass and diamonds around her waist and sage leaves with drops of diamond dew in her hair. She stood at the top of the stairs and let herself occur to the room until there were so many gasps it sounded as if everyone were choking.

"The queen's jewels weren't bad either," said the baron. He was holding Naïade, the newspaper made of rubber for idle young men to read in the bath, which he had just taken from Alphonse, his son.

Soon after the exhibition closed in 1856, Eugénie placed the Régent in the center of a new diadem known as the Greek Diadem because its diamonds were set in a Greek frieze. The ancient world was preoccupying this sham empire, too.

The empress had given birth to the prince imperial, Louis-Eugéne-Napoleon, and he was baptized in June of that year. Hundreds of thousands of visitors hung from windows or stood on bridge railings and roofs to see the procession to Notre Dame. The cathedral, with its banners and red velvet drapes, opened like a gigantic glowing mouth to swallow the women in their jeweled gowns, the heavily uniformed generals and marshals, the papal legate, and the baby prince in his long lace dress.

The fine new sand was spread so thick on the square that the eight matched bays could not draw the heavy state coach. The running lackeys behind the coach then stooped to push it forward by the wheels. Around me I heard the snickers and hoots never far from Parisian throats quickly silenced by Eugénie's beauty. As the lackeys pushed on, through the carriage glass a small frown at the difficulty of splendor rippled the empress's brow, and her thin nostrils flared. Then she came out of the carriage of a previous king into the summer evening wearing a white dress and the silvery streak that was the Greek Diadem with the Régent.

Outside we heard the *Vivat* composed for Napoleon's son, and I remembered the outcome of other events marked by the Régent's perilous glitter.

The Greek Diadem too was dismantled and remade, for we were in an age of perfectibility and frantic festivity without end. Whole ballrooms went whirling by—waltzing, twirling, hoop grazing hoop—the empress among them, diamond fringes bouncing in her deep gold hair. She was strewn with diamond stars and currant bush leaves, dripping with diamond icicles, snowballs, and tassels. Louis-Napoleon, his love ever nudged by guilt, gave her black pearls and a huge yellow diamond.

Among the baroness's set whatever Eugénie did became the thing to do; wherever she went, like Biarritz, became the only place. Some people lived just to copy her, for it was all written about. At Villa Eugénie in Biarritz, the women chased the men over chairs and sofas, kicked balls at lighted candles, and screamed at the bullfights. They watched tables rise into the air as the spiritualist David Home floated out one window and in another. Eugénie was thirty then, copying Marie-Antoinette, who had long obsessed her, and as it had been for that queen, the Régent was part of her young antic days.

She led all the *mondaines* of Paris in a great chase. Working with the English couturier Worth, she tweaked the passementeries, galloons, and fringes on her dresses and drove the ladies mad. At the Mer de Glace, Eugénie wore a green veil to protect her eyes, and the next day everyone wore green veils. The new "department stores" were filled with copies of everything for the middle classes, even the furniture that the baroness called "Almost."

The baroness said that anyone might chart the politics of the Second Empire by the colors the empress wore, which everyone also copied; the *cheveux de la reine*, the Mexican blue, Bismarck brown, then *eau de Nil*.

Eugénie's guests at Compiègne needed professional packers to prepare fourteen trunks for a weekend. Louis Pasteur, who gave scientific demonstrations there, said they were killing him with pleasure.

Still, not all were overwhelmed. Whereas I once would have thought of firebombs, now I merely felt lonely as the operetta danced by. Artifice lurked in the splendor, a distraction from the misery and anger around the corner in the baron's soup kitchen in the Rue de Rivoli.

Soon Betty would take me off to her new palace, twenty miles east of Paris, where the grandeur was intense and choking. At Ferrières, on the old estate of Napoleon's police chief, the baroness had been inspired by the doges of Venice. Footmen raced around heaps on marble busts and ranks of statues, past bronzes and tapestries and silver tarnishing in the necromantic light. Their mistakes crowded their treasures in rooms dense with things. Curtains covered curtains, tapestries covered damask; every goblet and box was encrusted or inlaid with something even more precious. The greedy profusion of Van Dycks overwhelmed the profusion of Rubenses and made all impossible to see. An underground railway brought the food hot to the dining room with its painted leather walls. The baron's hands shook on plates that Louis XV had used.

"Eugénie is remaking the Greek Diadem yet again and this time your diamond will surmount it," said the baroness one afternoon. "She fiddles with her jewels because of her husband's affair with Marguerite Bellanger, a person of no consequence whom he cannot resist. Surely you have read hints in the papers if only you would take your nose out of *L'Univers Israélite* and your radical journals.

"She is one of those *cocodettes, horizontales,* marble girls, call them what you will, that are all over. Eugénie goes out in her carriage and La Bellanger is always passing by, flaunting herself. So what does a neglected woman do? She plays with her houses or her jewels or the country of Mexico. The emperor has appeased Eugénie with that vassal Catholic state and let her meddle fatally.

"Ah, but now the emperor has almost killed himself through the exertion of his amours—he was carried home prostrate. Eugénie went to see that woman, and it is over. Like the baron, she stuck out her hand and it was not empty."

I was in a crisis for Ofresie, who, married at forty to one of her faith, had died suddenly during the typhoid epidemic. I had not seen her for months and, when Emmanuel wrote me, I thought of ending my life. Instead I took long bitter walks and intensified my pursuit of the damned diamond since it was all I might do for her.

I became even more a man of books and read until I required spectacles. The magnificent library at Ferrières was filled with old books with clasps, volumes in vellum and parchment with the pages uncut. Here were books bought in lots from the Revolution, new works by Jules Verne, and old manuscripts, many in German and the Hebrew and Yiddish that the baroness read. I lifted the tissue shields on priceless illustrations, stroked watered-silk covers, and fine-tooled leather bindings smelling of time, neglect, and potential treasure. I dusted Redoute's *Choix des Plus Belles Fleurs* with a chamois cloth and thought of Ofresie in the garden of the house in Passy. I turned fragile pages burnt by time, dotted with red rust and heavily foxed, the words breaking off one by one. I ran my thumb on the hard gold of their page rims and traced the crests of families that no longer existed.

One day I found a collection of the little confession books that the ladies of the times made for one another in which they would ask each other questions and write down the answers. I found one thin notebook bound in blue cloth that Eugénie had done with her lady the countess des Garrets. It had no date. Eugénie's favorite authors were Plutarch and "the two Napoleons."

"What would you have liked to be?" the countess asked her.

"Unknown and happy," Eugénie replied.

I haunted booksellers and felt myself begin to breathe only in the sweet dank rot of old volumes. I went to the back tents of fairs where the mushrooms grew and the lawns sank from moisture.

And it was here at Ferrières that I made a discovery about the diamond that I thought might have pleased my little lost friend. To help my English, I had been reading a very old pamphlet by an anonymous author when I came upon these lines:

> *Asleep and naked as an Indian lay*
> *An honest factor stole a gem away;*
> *He pledged it to the knight; the knight had wit,*
> *So robbed the robber and was rich as Pitt.*

This last line was crossed out by hand and *"So kept the diamond and the rogue was bit"* was written above the crossed-out line. I grew very excited and rushed to the baroness with my find.

"I believe that is Monsieur Alexander Pope," said Betty, "in his own hand. He must be making reference to your diamond. You have made a literary discovery. Let us read further."

And so we went back and read in this "Epistle to Bathurst," the story of Sir Balaam, who in some respects was like the count's Governor Pitt and in other respects was not all the same. Still, I felt it validated the work of Count Las Cases in some further way to think that such as Monsieur Pope had occupied himself with the diamond, even if he repeated a story that was probably untrue.

The baroness insisted on making me a present of this very rare manuscript and I accepted.

It was many years before I again heard anything of the diamond, years in which I lived steeped in borrowed luxury, almost forgetting it was not my own, reading the great works of the writers of my day to the baroness. I read louder now.

There were lines everywhere these days, even at the Louvre, where they waited long to see Napoleon's toothbrush. Outside, the stonemasons hammered, closing the Rue de Rivoli side of the Louvre. In the Place Vendôme the emperor had replaced the statue of Napoleon in his overcoat with a new statue of Napoleon as a Roman emperor, at last combining successfully his two obsessions.

The baroness had just come from being wheeled about the opening of the 1867 Universal Exposition in the Palace of Industry on the Champs de Mars. Someone had compared the immense elliptical glass and iron structure to a black pudding on a plate of parsley.

"We are whom we are obsessed by," she told me. "Eugénie has loaned the exposition all her bits of Marie-Antoinette and she loaned the Régent as well. You will find it there among the plush curtains and the aspidistras."

At this my interest in the diamond revived at once. I had to see it again. There had just been a military review at Longchamps during which ten thousand cuirassiers charged the stands where the emperor sat with Czar Alexander and King Wilhelm of Prussia. As they galloped ever closer the emperor threw his arm up over his head. Eugénie, Chancellor Bismarck, and Czar Alexander did not flinch. On the way back a Pole shot at the czar, hitting his horse and spotting his gloves with blood. The next day I went to the Palace of Industry.

In the heat the galleries formed ring upon ring of shimmering marvels, around which I sensed a collecting unease, a feeling of things dying slowly in the sun. A young Englishman brushed by me that day carrying a small red book, *Das Kapital*. I always notice books and with reason would remember this one.

Three Prussians blocked my view of the diamond and would not move along. The tallest, taller even than I was and twice my girth, wore a white uniform with an eagle on the helmet. A massive saber insured the slight distance around him. One of them I recognized as King Wilhelm said to a general weighed with decorations I later learned was von Moltke:

"*Und* what is that rock?"

"The diamond of Herr Pitt," said the big man, who, I now realized, was Chancellor Bismarck. All over Paris, the ladies were rushing to wear Bismarck brown and its silly variations—Bismarck *malade* (sick), Bismarck *en colère* (angry), Bismarck *glacé* (cool), Bismarck *scintillant* (brilliant), Bismarck *content* (happy).

"Pardon, I would like to see into the case," I said. None of the Germans moved. I saw the beginnings of Bismarck *en colère* flushing the chancellor's neck above his high collar.

"The Jew becomes nervous at the sight of a diamond he cannot have," said the general.

"I am a student of the diamond," I answered. "I have spent many years tracing its history." But I might have been speaking to the deaf, for they formed a human fence around the exhibit and stayed there talking loudly, barking laughter while the gendarmes fidgeted.

"I believe diamonds and Jews go together," said the chancellor. "And one is so ugly."

"And so black," said the king.

Finally it was my turn in front of the Régent and I bent as close as I could. In its case, disconnected from humans, it was but one of many wonders splayed on velvet. And yet I felt a vibration, an energy as if it were a living thing pulling at me. I have heard tell of lost objects finding their way back to their owners. A man drops a ring in the sea and years later cuts open a fish and finds the ring there as though object and owner are imprinted with each other, connected with bands of invisible energy. I felt this tug from the Régent in the case.

As the crowd kept whispering *"Grosse pierre!"* I was reminded of a small painting by Caspar David Friedrich that the Rothschilds had just bought. It showed two men from the back looking at a crescent moon. The moon is filled out to a circle by earthshine, the reflection of the sunlit half of the earth on the dark side of the moon. To me the Régent had its own earthshine, for I had come to believe that all the people who ever wore or held it were reflected within the great gem.

I waited my turn again, stared at the Régent with the smile of special knowledge that others so often resent, and was forced along by the impatient crowd.

Plotters—anarchists, socialists, and crazies—tried to blow up Napoleon III nine times! Once I was in the crowd for a review at the Place du Carrousel when the emperor and his son rode out of the palace. I felt the crowd press all around me until I feared they would squeeze the last breath from my body. They drove me into the grille, so close I saw the steaming velvet nostrils of the little prince's sorrel pony. A horse reared and they all galloped back into the archway of the palace. That was one attempt and it had badly shaken me. And there were those who, whenever bread cost too much, chose to remember that Eugénie was foreign. Again it was a pattern—fall in love with the exotic, copy the exotic, then blame her for making you love her, and turn on her.

The trouble I had felt at the exposition had emerged. When Emperor Maximilian was executed in Mexico, the visiting monarchs melted like specters into the white steam of departing trains. After the exhibition ended in November, the Régent disappeared from view, or at least my view and that of the Rothschilds. Baron James had grown yellow, and then, yellower. The last time I saw him, he ordered me to read the baroness something that would make her happy. After he died, as we tore our sleeves and covered all the gilt mirrors, I knew well there was no such work for her in all literature.

In 1869, Eugénie opened the Suez Canal with her cousin Ferdinand de Lesseps, who had built it. She left from Venice on her yacht *l'Aigle* with her little court and a hundred new dresses. She lived in the palace the khedive built for her, saw Luxor, Thebes, and Karnak, and visited the house near the Red Sea where Napoleon had lived.

"The kings of the West shut him up in an island where he died," a Mussulman told her, "but at night his soul comes and rests on the edge of his saber."

The next spring, 1870, Napoleon III had become a constitutional ruler of the liberal empire, another one of our contradictions in terms. Eugénie then wore the Régent as a pin in her hair and had two copies made. Because things were precarious, she began to wear only these crystal copies. This was the time of three Régents, two of them false.

Betty's son Alphonse, who was now head of the bank and family, had passed the emperor's message to Gladstone in Rothschild code about how France would not accept a German king in Spain. When King Wilhelm refused assurances, France declared war on Prussia, a war Eugénie encouraged.

The emperor, pale and bent with pain because of a stone in his bladder, went off to war by train with his fourteen-year-old son. He sent home a proud telegram about how the prince had picked up a bullet fallen at his feet and soon enough all Paris was laughing at "the child of the bullet."

Now Eugénie had become the empress regent of France. The war went badly and three days after our defeat at Woerth, she removed the jewels from the Tuileries. In a large sealed fir box they were sent to the vaults of the Ministry of Finance, then on to the Bank of France. The governor of the bank put them in a bank box labeled "Special Projectiles" and sent them by cargo train to the arsenal at Brest. If anything went wrong, the ship *Hermione* was to sail with the jewels to Saigon. And thus, in what became the Revolution of 1870, Eugénie saved the Régent as her husband had saved it thirty years before.

The empress regent would not allow the emperor to surrender and forced him into the battle of Sedan by saying that if he retreated there would be a revolution in Paris. Then he did surrender and Eugénie stood on the steps to his rooms, her face red, her hair coming down, her fists clenched.

"Why didn't he get himself killed?" she screamed. "What a name he will leave to his son!" (When historical figures reveal themselves there is always someone to hear and remember.)

Paris was rioting, for the full blame of Sedan fell on the emperor, and as I have learned, France never forgives failure or even mistakes. I was away at Ferrières, for once glad of the abundance of objects wrapped around me; the prettiness of the past in all its bulk and attractive confusion had become my consolation.

Eugénie had learned how not to escape from reading of Marie-Antoinette's failed flight to Chalons—the hesitations, the heavy carriage, the fatal pretensions. On Sunday, September 4, she heard the now familiar cries of *"À bas l'Espagnole!"* (Down with the Spaniard), the "Marseillaise" being sung, and saw the crowd dancing the Carmagnole. Right out of her well-cultivated fears, they were coming up the Tuileries garden paths, tearing the eagles from her gates, lowering her flag as the history she pursued was pursuing her in the same rooms.

Eugénie had to escape through the Louvre, for the rioters were at her doors. She hurried through the Great Gallery, the Salle Carée, where, at *The Raft of Medusa,* she supposedly said, "Look, another shipwreck!" She rushed through the Apollo Pavilion and past the ancient wide regard of the gods and creatures of the pharaohs.

Her friend Prince Metternich, the Austrian ambassador, got her a cab and slammed the carriage door on her and her reader.

That day, the mob broke into the treasury searching for the crown jewels. They found only the models with false stones and the rumor grew that Eugénie had made off with them.

Years later, I found out the rest of the story only because Betty had a toothache. The handsome American dentist Dr. Evans, who had rescued the empress and helped her get to England, was back at his practice in Paris.

He told a long story about how he had posed as the doctor of a mental in-valid leaving the asylum. After many inns and carriages and near escapes, he found an English lord with a yacht to take Eugénie to the Isle of Wight. The empress of France, first forced into disguise as a lunatic, now was turned from an English hotel because of her wet and messy appearance. At last, at Brighton, she was reunited with her son, who had escaped from the war in the ever useful peasant smock. They made their way to Camden Place at Chistlehurst in Kent, where she lives today. Her husband was still in prison in Wilhelmshohe then.

"At the end she gave me her gloves," Dr. Evans said, indicating a glass where the narrowest black gloves were framed within.

"That is how a Spanish woman thanks one who has risked himself for her," he said. "Open wider please, Madame la Baronne."

After Eugénie, the Régent no longer decorated royal bodies. In the vaults of Brest it joined the ingots and the most famous pictures of the Louvre. In this time of vanished kings and emperors, when nations fused, the Régent was either shut away in vaults with three keys (one was never enough) or very much stared at. It has never been worn again.

The count had seen how as the Régent's setting changed, so had the France around it. The diamond went from hat to shoulder to crown of the kings, who shrugged it off as they became less powerful. It moved to an attic in our great Revolution, to war plunder when it was pawned in military times, to the sword of him who won the wars, and back to a diadem and crown in the Second Empire, whose insecure end was marked by the false Régents. The Régent was hidden again during our next three revolutions, all of which I lived through. Once the Régent's shape was set, it proved the constant, the invariable, that matched its times and reflected them as the manners, clothes, houses and châteaux and hovels changed around it. (But now I hear the strict little count cautioning me, "Don't lecture! Don't inter-pret! Don't go on so!")

Of course the commune went searching for the Régent and the crown jewels in the vaults of the Bank of France. The finance minister thought they were on the *Hermione* sailing for Saigon. When, after the second reign of terror, the commune lost, it decided to burn all Paris. During the seven days of civil war in May, the Petroleuses, these madwomen, carted gasoline to the

Tuileries and burned the palace down. They burned Saint-Cloud, the Palais de Justice, the Hôtel de Ville—all the places where the diamond had danced through time.

On May 28, 1871, the Régent and the other jewels were taken from the arsenal at Brest and put in the hold of the ship *Borda*. When the government regained Paris from the commune, the ingots and works from the Louvre returned to Paris, but the jewels—about seventy-eight thousand of them—stayed in the ship's hold until 1872. Then they were returned, still in ill repute, and banished to the cellars of the minister of finance at the Louvre.

And now the Régent was overtaken by events, left behind, out of sight again in the dark, flaring unheeded through the years. I began to wonder then, was it ever really important, or did the count, because of his long-ago mistake, because he picked up the emperor's hairs and had no way to explain, hurl himself at the diamond as a distraction from the conditions of his life? Did he not come to see in it far more than it ever was? No one misses it now. Karl Marx, whose book I had noticed six years ago at the exposition and who I now read privately, understood that things drive men. The Régent, this thing that had driven so many men, was gone then, along with the kings. When it reappears I will write again for I am too tired now to be a detective of the invisible any longer.

Louis-Napoleon, the fallen emperor, was released from prison and landed at Dover in March 1871. He joined Eugénie and the prince imperial at Camden Place, where he lived in the court of illusions, plotting his own "return from Elba" by entering France through Belgium.

Eugénie had written to Betty on her pale blue crested notepaper: "People who fall from a ground floor seldom hurt themselves in the fall; I have fallen from so high that everything has been broken inside me."

The next year Louis-Napoleon died of the chloral administered for two operations for the stone in his bladder. A month later Betty received a catalog from Christie, Manson and Woods Ltd. On June 24, 1872, in their great rooms on King Street, they were selling *A Portion of the Magnificent Jewels, the Property of a Distinguished Personality, Also a few fans and parasols.* The baroness began to read the list and study the pictures with her glass when she cried out, "Eugénie has had to sell her jewels!"

Various jewelers and assorted Indian princes bought some and a Rothschild bought most of the rest. I cannot say who.

Betty accused me of being morbid but I had kept track of the peculiar fates of those who saw the Règent in the exhibition of 1867. Baron James had died, Louis-Napoleon fell from power, the Turk Abdul-Aziz stabbed himself with a scissor in his harem, and Czar Alexander II was assassinated by a bomb in the street. Of course, all these things might have happened anyway.

And then, in 1879, after a brave fight, Eugénie's son, the prince imperial, was murdered by Zulus. They said he was found wearing the old bullet that caused him to be mocked as a coward. On the way to Zululand to see where her son was killed, Eugénie stopped at Saint Helena and was met by an old woman carrying violets. This was Betsey Balcombe, the little girl who gave violets to the emperor and the count when they arrived at the Briars and who found the jeweled box that caused the count to think of the diamond. The hand that draws the circles was completing this one.

The Règent and the crown jewels were again in a vitrine at the Universal Exhibitions of 1878 and 1884 in the State Room at the Louvre. They were in a circular case covered by an octagonal window that lowered into the case at night. The Règent had been mounted as a single stone right under Eugénie's comb. The obsolete crowns, extinct orders, the swords and crosses and useless plaques were impudent triumphs over time and disfavor. This was dangerous in a time when men in suits with square faces and spectacles ruled my country. These bureaucrats were angry at the seditious jewels that had no place in a democracy where luxurious objects were almost immoral.

In 1882, experts had declared certain pieces inviolate and saved them for the Louvre, the Museum of Natural History, and the School of Mines. The Règent, Charles X's coronation sword, a brooch of Eugénie's, and the Côte de Bretagne, the only surviving jewel of François I, were safe then.

At the time of the second of these exhibitions, Betty handed me a letter from an English niece who had been to stay at Swallowfield, the house Governor Pitt bought in 1719 with money from the diamond.

Auntie, I know your reader who collects stories about the Pitt diamond will be interested in what happened to me there. One night when, as is all too usual with me, I could not sleep, I went down to Queen Anne's

gallery to look at the family portraits. I was tiptoeing about in my dress-
ing gown when, at the other end of the hall, I saw a dreadful apparition—
an almost naked Indian man with a great leaking gash on his thigh. I swear
he had no substance and his bare feet floated inches from the floor. He
looked at me with his hollow eyes and I could not move.

He drifted closer and closer until he was almost on top of me. I was in
a state of such terror that I cannot describe. I had halted under Kneller's
portrait of Governor Pitt posed with the great diamond in his hat. And
then, worse horrror—the apparition pointed to the portrait and spoke
growly Indian words that, of course, I did not understand. The servants
found me in the gallery the next morning under the painting.

My hostess, Lady Russell, told me I am not the first to have seen this
revenant. For a century all the owners of Swallowfield have seen him in the
quadrangle, on the parapets, vanishing into the colonnades. He floats
through the stone gateway in the garden and strokes the vines that cover
this house like a wrapping of green fur. Then he is gone! Those who live
here think he is the slave searching for his lost diamond or that he is sent
by some Indian idol to find his stolen eye.

"What do you make of that?" Betty had asked me. "And why do you
smile?"

It was because just then I was seeing the emperor and the smaller man
who loved him as they walked through the craters of Saint Helena with Dimanche scampering ahead, her tail twirling with joy.

"But the diamond was not *ever* the idol's eye," Napoleon is saying.
"Haven't you learned anything?"

Las Cases holds fast to the emperor's arm and touches the captured hairs
in his pocket. "I wonder if . . ."

"Leave it a mystery, *mon cher*," says Napoleon.

"It is a mystery to me," I said to Betty.

Four years later, as I clutched the velvet banisters, pausing at every step on
the stairs to Betty's rooms, I heard her maid shriek as though she had just
seen a mouse. I sat down on the steps, looked around at the walls now
whirling with my fright, and knew what had happened. The baroness, who
was eighty-one, and I have both been waiting for death, making the little
jokes each evening that sustain us as we compare our infirmities, while say-

ing nothing of them to Alphonse and his English wife, Leonora. Now it had happened.

I did not go up to look. My legs were shaking like tent poles in a desert wind and my cane had fallen to the bottom of the great stairs.

I went down very slowly to the drawing room, where Alphonse had hung the Ingres portrait. As the servants rushed about, I pulled over a chair, and stayed there. I saw Betty during the siege of Paris when Bismarck had taken over Ferrières. As our carrier pigeons and balloons circled above, people dropped mail for us, and those who escaped in this dangerous method often paused to doff their hats to the baroness from on high as she sat, large, black-wrapped, and immensely dignified, a kind of Jewish mummy in her chair on the lawn.

Inside the Rothschild palaces, I was often confused in my heart. Then Betty would always come by and tap my shoulder and we would reread *L'Enfant Maudit,* which Balzac had dedicated to her, or *Un Homme d'Affaires,* which he had dedicated to Baron James, and I would be healed. In the portrait, the young elegant baroness bent forward to me with her serious regard.

Betty left me a legacy with which I bought a small house in Passy near Rue de Pompe where I had lived with the count and my secret beloved, Ofresie. Both the count's sons were long dead. Still I continued to make rather desultory inquiries about the Régent.

And then one day in February of this year 1887, Monsieur Dauphin, the finance minister, who knew of my interest, invited me along when they photographed the crown jewels before they were to be sold.

We descended into the black stone vaults of the Ministry of Finance with a bunch of officials and his ten-year-old daughter. Monsieur Dauphin unlocked the vault and began to take out hundreds of oddly shaped red leather boxes that looked like they might contain the instruments of a miniature orchestra.

All the officials, in frock coats, drops of frost hanging from their moustaches, encircled us, huffing and heaving with excitement. I leaned against the stone walls, damp with the crimes of the past, as drafts cut into my bones. Shadows of giant gray men danced across the vaulted ceiling in the misty light of the photographer's electric arc. The first box contained a large comb dripping fringes of diamonds. It still had a red-gold hair clinging to it.

Monsieur Dauphin pointed out to his daughter one of the smallest boxes, in the center of which, in a navy velvet crater, half-swallowed, was the hard glitter of the Régent.

She gave a little yelp of admiration, then clasped her hand over her mouth.

"Go on, pick it up!" said her father. "At least you will be able to say you held the Régent in your hand."

All the men in dark coats, breathing clouds, watched as she put the Régent in her palm and her face grew fiery. She blinked at the photographer's flash, then quickly put the diamond back in its box.

"You have touched a great diamond," Monsieur Dauphin said. "Now you will have luck all your life. That is the belief of the land where this diamond was found, no?" he said, turning to me.

"Perhaps," I said, and when he looked displeased, I added, "Yes, surely."

As they opened more boxes the photographer captured each jewel, his head disappearing under the cloth and bobbing out. Then the jewelers took up little hammers and, with grating sounds, began to smash and pry apart the bigger jewels to get to the salable stones. As I watched, one crushed Napoleon III's crown into a gold ball and took pliers to the pommel of Louis XVIII's sword.

"This is the last time these jewels will be together, for they are all going to be sold," Monsieur Dauphin told his daughter. "But not the diamond you held. That is for the Louvre."

"But why?" she asked, and the men, some of whom did not agree with the sale, especially now, having seen the artistry of each piece, looked at him.

Monsieur Dauphin did not explain that the jewels were dangerous to the uncertain Third Republic, that it was afraid of diamonds and empty crowns. His daughter's flushed face was what the republic never could combat, the normal reaction of a child holding a lump of something beautiful and precious and especially important because it had belonged to five kings and two emperors. Her blush was just what would make the Third Republic auction off the jewels later that month in a series of sales that brought low prices and allowed men like Monsieur Tiffany of New York, America, to carry off our historic diamonds. It was the danger that awe was contagious and might bring back the kings.

None of the men picked up the Régent that day until Monsieur Dauphin looked over at me, and I nodded. As they all watched, I walked over to where the Régent had been set aside. In my unsteady hand the ancient diamond was heavy and cold and sharp as desire.

A few weeks after the sales of the crown jewels, I permitted myself an extravagance and hired a carriage for the day. We passed the steel stump of Monsieur Eiffel's tower being built on the Champs de Mars, where twenty years ago I saw the diamond. I told the driver to stop first at Les Invalides, for I wanted to see Napoleon once more in his tomb. At the entrance to the crypt I walked between bronze statues holding the orb and imperial scepter. I was now an old man with a stick creeping through silent crowds, afraid to fall on the hard floors, afraid of being jostled.

He was there inside his six coffins, enclosed in his red porphyry sarcophagus raised up from the marble star on the floor, with his battles and achievements depicted on the walls and his soldiers, the count's companions, standing stone sentinels around him.

A soldier from the last war stood beside me looking down at the bier.

Perhaps he is not worth your tears, after all, I thought, and must have said the words aloud, for he turned fierce eyes upon me.

Tapping my way up the stairs of the Louvre, I entered the Apollo Gallery, where Napoleon had married Marie-Louise and the red-heeled kings had strutted with the diamond. Their royal leftovers filled the cases along with the last of the historical jewels and the Régent. The diamond was next to a white enamel elephant, recalling the India from which it had been taken long ago. I stood in front of the diamond I had touched, now caught under strong glass, its power forever contained, its glory—once forbidden—now forgiven.

The dangers of Napoleon and the dangers of his diamond were trapped by coffers of marble and glass. It was better they were both gone from the world, that their harm and dangerous brilliance were locked away.

Those who came to stare at them from behind high railings might soon know the connection between the Régent and the man who brought it back to France, for I had finally taken the count's last work to his publisher.

I had seen the diamond first in my middle age, and now, at great age, I saw it, as I saw Napoleon, with the revisions and reconsiderations of time. The rays of this precious thing and the decayed body of this important man were best sealed into their tombs, stared at in stone palaces. At last I was free of both. Let them stay there, let them abide. Let the monsters sleep.

Acknowledgments

Every writer—good or bad—deserves a lucky moment, and mine happened when Michael Korda said, "Of course I want to publish it," and edited my book in the way any writer hopes is possible at least once in a career. I am grateful for the quality of his mind and heart, his constant kindness, historical knowledge, attentiveness, and quick response to any question. I thank him for all the time he gave me.

But first there was Pete Hamill with his red pencil. I never knew a friend to be so generous. And then there was that in-house editor with his Mont-blanc, Edward Kosner, who paid my bills and always stood by me.

There are also the dead, the long dead, the far and forgotten, those who told me of their times, the witnesses, the biographers, novelists, essayists, and historians who looked back long before I did. I needed them all.

Madame was first. I discovered her on my own bookshelves in Volume IX of *The Secret Memoirs of the Courts of Europe*—part of an incomplete set I had bought at a book fair and ignored for twenty years. I then read her letters in *A Woman's Life in the Court of the Sun King*, edited and translated by Elborg Forster, and also in collections edited and translated by Gertrude Scott Stevenson and by Maria Kroll. I entered the French court with *Memoirs: Duc de Saint-Simon*, edited and translated by Lucy Norton, and could not leave until I had read my way through portions of floors seven and two of the New York Society Library. All historical errors are my fault alone.

Only Count Las Cases could tell my story. I discovered him in the remarkable *Mémorial de Sainte-Hélène* with its invaluable Preface, Chronology, and Notes (see below). His great-nephew of the same name told me what I did not know of his life in the 1959 biography *Las Cases: Le Mémorialiste de Napoléon*.

After reading a brief history of the Régent diamond in *Famous Diamonds* by Ian Balfour, I came to Germaine Bapst's *Histoire des Joyaux de la Couronne de France* (1888) and then Bernard Morel's *Les Joyaux de la Couronne de France* (1988), both of which I used extensively, as well as Lord Twining's *A History of the Crown Jewels of Europe*. For expertise on cutting, I thank my dear brother, master jeweler Buzz Baumgold, as well as John Nels Hatleberg and Cary Horowitz.

At my request, Miriam Leonard, a young scholar from Cambridge, found *The History of the Pitt Diamond* by Henry Yule, *Swallowfield and its Owners* by Lady Constance Russell, and *Diamonds and Coral* by Gedalia Yogev, and photocopied many biographies of the Pitts, Zacharias Conrad Von Uffenbach's description of London in 1710, and other bits of diamond lore for me.

I am indebted to many histories, like Simon Schama's *Citizens*, *Seven Ages of Paris* by Alistair Horne, and Olivier Bernier's books and lectures; biographies, like Antonia Fraser's *Marie Antoinette*; compendiums; French children's books, novels, and memoirs such as those of the Countess de Boigne, edited by Anka Muhlstein, and those of the Count de Mercy-Argenteau. I could not have understood anything without the constant aid and pleasure I got from reading Jacques Barzun's *From Dawn to Decadence*.

For the feeling of Saint Helena, I especially liked *The Emperor's Last Island* by Julia Blackburn, *The Black Room at Longwood* by Jean-Paul Kauffman, and *The Exile of St. Helena* by Philippe Gonnard.

Among Napoleon books I should single out Proctor Patterson Jones' *Napoleon* and Vincent Cronin's *Napoleon*, but there is no end to the texts I have used.

I thank my agent Amanda Urban of ICM and Carol Bowie at Simon & Schuster. Leslie Field, old friend and author of *The Queen's Jewels*, sent constant clippings and faxes from Bath. I appreciate her encouragement—and discouragement, at the proper times. Many friends disappeared during the years I lived in the past, but some, like Edward Jay Epstein, reappeared and talked me through dark stretches with intelligence and good humor. Like Napoleon, I forgive their defections and hope for their return.

Thank you, Dali, ever the monarchist, for the regent's "con-fus-ion," which I took from you, and thank you Sunday, the dog who came out of the woods and became Dimanche. I hope you are at play together.

Source Notes

pp. 9–10, italicized portions: Emmanuel de Las Cases, *Mémorial de Sainte-Hélène*, Vol. 2 (Paris: Editions du Seuil, 1968), pp. 1299–1300. Translation of passage by Julie Baumgold.

pp. 47–48, extracts: Henry Yule, *The History of the Pitt Diamond: Being an Excerpt from "Documentary Contributions to a Biography of Thomas Pitt"* (London: Hakluyt Society, 1888).

p. 113, extract: Pierre Gaxotte, *Louis the Fifteenth and His Times*, translated from the French by J. Lewis May (Philadelphia: J.B. Lippincott Company, 1934), pp. 58–59.

p. 123, extract: Emmanuel de Las Cases, *Las Cases: Le Mémorialiste de Napoléon* (Paris: Librarie Arthème Fayard, 1959), p. 250–251.

p. 156, information about the robbery: Germain Bapst, *Histoire des Joyaux de la Couronne de France* (1889), pp. 447–452. The facts about the robbery were unknown until Bapst uncovered them in 1888.

p. 265, italicized portions: Bapst, p. 570, footnote.

Also used as source:
Bernard Morel, *Les Joyaux de la Couronne de France: Le Fonds Mercator de la Banque Parabas* (Anvers: Albin Michel, 1988).

About the Author

JULIE BAUMGOLD is the author of the novel *Creatures of Habit*. She is a former contributing editor of *New York, Esquire,* and *Vogue*. She has been an essayist (*Best American Essays 1996*), poet (Mademoiselle Poetry Prize), and the columnist "Mr. Peepers" for *New York* and *Esquire*. She lives on Amelia Island and in New York.